Prepared To Fall
A Golden Oakes novel

E.J. SHORTALL

This is a work of fiction. Names, characters, places, brands, media, and incidents are either the product of the author's imagination or are used fictitiously.

PREPARED TO FALL

ISBN: 978-0-9932979-4-6

Copyright © 2016 E.J. Shortall

Published by E.J. Shortall
Cover art by E.J. Shortall
Photographer: Eric Battershell
Cover Model: Garrick Murdie
Stock images courtesy of Deposit Photos

The following story contains mature themes, strong language, and sexual situations. It is intended for adult readers

DEDICATION

This one is for you D (formally known as the Child Giant).
You amaze me each and every day with your kindness,
compassion and strength. I love you and am so proud to be
able to call you my son!

ACKNOWLEDGMENTS

I'm going to start off by thanking you, the reader. When I wrote Liv and Nate's story in Prepared To Fight, I had every intention of that being a standalone. Then people started reading and contacting me saying how much they loved not only Liv and Nate but Adam, Cassie and Wesley, too. They wanted more. Who was I to deny those wishes? It took a while for Adam and Cass to be open and honest with me about their story, but once they did, oh boy, how I fell in love with these two characters! For months they have consumed me, filling every waking moment—and many sleeping ones, too. I would never have explored their relationship, and consequently been filled with such powerful emotions, if it wasn't for you. You had faith in my characters even before I did. You trusted they had a story to tell, and you believed in them. So the whole Golden Oakes series is dedicated to you, I hope you enjoy them all.

Rhiannon, I can never send you enough kissy/hugging/heart emoji's to say how thankful to you I am. From the moment you read Prepared To Fight you saw my vision and wanted more. In fact, you wanted so much more that you came up with the titles for Fall and Win for me. So this is also dedicated to you. Thank you!

My ever-faithful beta group: Karen S, Brandi, Alison, Geraldine, Kathy, and Rhiannon. Your encouragement and kind words never ceases to amaze me, and after I get over the nail-biting phase, your words always leave the goofiest of grins on my face.

To the wider author/blogger community: It truly is like having an extended family spanning the entire globe. Just like with any family, there are ups and there are downs, but what I can always trust in is that when I'm having a bad day or a moment of weakness or insecurity, you are always there to pick me up and remind me why I'm doing this.

Lovely ladies of the Indie Erogenous Zone, we have all been on this journey together from the very beginning and I just want to say how proud I am of each of you for your successes and strengths with not only your writing accomplishments but in real life too. You are all legends in my eyes.

Ladies of Shortall's Sexy Sirens—my street team, thank you for all your support, encouragement and tireless pimping. You are the best!

Special mention for Amanda, thank you for regularly entertaining me with your short voice clips. Keep 'em coming.

To Eric Battershell for your amazing photography and for bringing Adam to life through your lens. Although I am going to have to ask you to stop posting so many gorgeous images on Facebook before you make me bankrupt. ;)

Garrick Murdie, thank you for being such a lovely guy and for being my perfect Adam. To Liv and the team at Hot Tree Editing, thank you for pulling out your magic editing cloths and polishing this up into something I hope the readers will love as much as I do.

Emmy, thank you once again for your amazing proofreading eye. I'm so glad someone pointed me in your direction.

Jennifer at More Than Words Promotions: thank you for your ultimate professionalism and hard work in helping with all my book promotions! Your tireless work is very much appreciated.

And finally, to each and every blog, author and individual who has ever posted, shared, promoted, mentioned, liked or helped in any way shape or form. I wouldn't be doing this if it weren't for you. You are ultimately the heart of this amazing community.

CHAPTER ONE

Cassie

"GET THAT CUTE LITTLE ARSE of yours here right now."

I'd known the call was coming. I'd anticipated it as I'd been sprinting through the doors of Golden Oakes. Late. Much later than I should have been. It was bloody typical that the day I needed it least, people couldn't follow a simple set of instructions. In the end, I'd left Colin to deal with the drama of the exploded condom machine in the gents' changing room and hightailed it out of there.

I had more important things to do.

Racing through the streets of London, I'd slowed to the speed limit only for the occasional traffic camera or speed bump—why on earth did London have so many of those bloody things? They were annoying and a pain in the arse, especially when you were running late.

And today of all days I couldn't be late.

But I was—thirty minutes late.

Nate was going to go apeshit.

I puffed out a frustrated breath and continued rifling through shoes at the bottom of my closet with one hand while the other held my mobile phone to my ear.

"I'm still at home. I got held up at the gym."

I breathed a sigh of relief when my fingers brushed across the missing black snakeskin pump. It had been hiding right at the back, under a pile of tennis and running shoes. Dragging it out, I swiped away the thin layer of dust and dropped onto my bum to wrestle the shoe on my foot.

"Well, you better hurry the fuck up and get here. Seriously, if you aren't here on time, the beating Nate gave Sanchez will be nothing compared to the shit storm he'll rain down on *you*." My close friend Wes snickered as I wiggled my toes into the uncomfortable heels.

Nathan Oakes's temper was not something I wanted to get on the wrong side of. Ever. Generally, he was a pretty laid-back guy. However, when his buttons were pushed it was like watching a volcanic eruption—all you could do was stand out of harm's way and wait for the danger to pass. And being late for his wedding rehearsal was a certain call for a blow-up of epic proportions.

"I'm on my way. Barring a sudden alien invasion or nuclear attack, I'll be there in thirty. Tell him to chill out. I mean, God, even Liv isn't this stressed."

Standing, I steadied myself against the dresser,

trying to gain my balance. I didn't understand the pompous need to dress up. All I wanted to do was throw on a pair of shorts, a T-shirt, and my favourite Nikes.

Wes grunted. "It's your funeral if you're late. Just sayin'."

With a resigned sigh, I ended the call promising I would be there as soon as possible and dropped the phone into my small clutch bag. I took one last look in the mirror on the back of my bedroom door and grimaced. I was used to wearing my black spa tunic or comfortable sportswear, and I hardly ever wore make-up. Being this dressed up, I felt awkward. It wasn't me. But the short purple dress I wore was nothing compared to the elegant ensemble I'd be forced into on Saturday.

Shaking my head of all thoughts of the coming weekend, I made a hasty retreat to the door. I had somewhere to be, the prelude to the big event of the year—the nuptials of my close friend and MMA hero, Nathan Oakes, and his lovely fiancée, Olivia Buchanan. I might not have been comfortable dressing up, but I was beyond happy for my friends. They suited and complemented each other completely, and had been madly head over heels in love since they both finally gave in to their stubborn feelings.

Smiling at the memories of how far they'd come as a couple, I stepped out into the balmy evening air. If nothing else, tonight would be interesting... because *he* would be there.

I SAT IN the front row of the church and watched in

bemusement as Liv and Nate smiled their way through their vows and discussed the order of events with the priest. Why they needed a rehearsal was beyond me. Weren't weddings supposed to be simple things? A time for couples to declare their love and commitment for each other. It wasn't like they were staging some hugely extravagant theatrical show. Surely all that was needed was for the bride and groom to show up on the day, and say "I do". But no, traditions stated that anybody of any importance in the show had to rehearse. Because they obviously couldn't be trusted to say a few words to each other without fucking it up.

I rolled my eyes and diverted my attention to the intricate cherub carved into a wooden plinth. I had better things to be doing with my time than watching two lovesick puppies moon over each other. Their love and devotion were sickeningly heart-warming. Okay, it was cute, and I couldn't be happier for them. Not that I would ever admit that out loud to them. I had too much fun giving them shit for their over-the-top displays of affection.

My relationships? That was a whole other story. I hadn't been particularly lucky when it came to love. Over the years I'd had several relationships, some lasting a couple of weeks, others several months. But I'd never found *the one*.

Several months earlier I'd had a brief fling with *him*—*him* being someone I'd grown quite close to while we were in France. I'd been out there supporting Nate's training for his fight with Ramone Sanchez, and Adam had been out there supporting Liv. At the time I'd hoped maybe something could happen between us. He'd been funny, caring and so easy to talk to, and we just seemed to click. Then it all went wrong when we'd ended up in the sack for one explosive encounter. That brief moment in time had meant the world to me, not so much for him.

After, when our heart rates had settled and we'd returned to reality he backed off into his corner, and we went our separate ways. He hotfooted it back to London without giving me a second glance, while I stayed with my friends to see out the rest of their celebrations.

His rejection hurt at the time, the way he just ran out with his head hung low and eyes full of regret. But then I realised what his deal was. He was majorly hung up on someone else, someone who didn't reciprocate his feelings. I was never going to be able to compete with that, so I had no choice but to move on.

And I had moved on. To Jay. It was still early days for us as a couple, but I was in love with him, and those feelings grew stronger every day. Plus, he came with added benefits.

For me, Jay was the ultimate catch. He was charming, friendly and had more than proved himself in the supportive department. Even before we became a couple he'd been there for me for me during a difficult time when others hadn't been. He'd talked to me and held me when I'd needed it, and he'd helped me see nothing about what happened had been my fault. He had been my rock.

After that our friendship and subsequent relationship just seemed to grow. It was easy.

By day Jay was a successful banker and often hinted at a financially secure future for us with a nice home, cars, holidays, the works. By night, he was the principal instructor at my kick-boxing club. He put me through my paces several times a week, pushing me to always do better, work harder. He really was perfect for me.

Despite my love for Jay, I had to admit that I still held a soft spot for Adam. Despite how hard I tried to forget what happened between us in France, I couldn't seem to shake him completely.

At the back of my mind, I'd always wondered how things would have turned out with Adam if we hadn't had sex. Would our friendship have grown into something more? But I hadn't seen him since. And now, here we were, forced into the same room by friends oblivious to our past.

My gaze trailed back to Olivia—who was struggling to contain her giggles while repeating the vows the unimpressed priest was reciting—then over to Adam. As though he could feel me watching, he turned his hypnotic bright blue eyes on me. Liv managed to regain her composure and practice her words of forever with Nate, while my gaze remained captivated by the man I once had hoped things could have been different with.

CHAPTER TWO

Adam

I KNEW THIS DAY WOULD come. It was inevitable, unavoidable. Being a part of Olivia's wedding party, there was no other choice. However, no number of internal pep talks could prepare me for the reality of actually seeing Cassie again.

Several months ago, when we'd spent days together talking and laughing, enjoying each other's bodies, I'd come close to putting my feelings for Liv to the side and trying to date Cassie. Instead, I did the shittiest of shit things and walked away from her.

No, I ran.

With no explanation or apology, I merely packed up my stuff and took off without looking back.

I was a loser, a pathetic idiot pining over someone who was never going to feel the same way. Liv assumed I was over her. She thought I'd come to my senses after my desperate declaration of love to her when she first met Nate. She couldn't have been further from the truth. I'd loved her in a romantic sense since we were fifteen years old, but I'd pretty much been hooked on her since I was six. That kind of love and devotion doesn't just disappear overnight, no matter how hard you try.

Cassie had been a welcome distraction at a particularly painful time. Nate had just confided in me that he planned on proposing to Liv. I knew then that I'd lost the battle nobody else realised I'd been fighting. The fairy-tale ending was over. All hopes of Liv falling into my arms for our happily ever after were gone. She would say yes to him, of course she would; she loved him.

Like the idiot I was, I turned to Cassie when I knew it was game over. Yes, it was wrong. Yes, it was the bastard move. Did I regret it? Of course I did, I'm not *that* guy. But I was hurting and needed something or someone to take away the pain.

After returning from France, I avoided going to Golden Oakes gym. I started running and purchased a few free weights for my home. If Liv invited me to any social gatherings that might have had me bumping into Cassie, I came up with one pathetic excuse after another to decline. I couldn't risk the humiliation and shame of seeing her again. The wedding, however, was not something I could avoid, not unless I wanted to risk losing Liv altogether. She made it quite clear that she would absolve me of best friend status if I didn't agree to be a part of the wedding party. I knew she was just trying to guilt me into being a groomsman, but still, I would never do anything to upset her. No matter the personal hell it would put me through.

My time was up. I needed to man up and face the music that was Cassandra Burton.

ALTHOUGH THE LIGHT in the church was dim, I could easily see Cassie standing at Olivia's side. It was the first time I'd seen her since leaving her looking confused and all sex mussed in a French bed. Liv was laughing her way through her practice vows while Nathan smiled down at her in adoration. I wasn't taking much notice, my attention focussed only on the petite brunette grinning at Liv's behaviour.

Cassie looked amazing in a deep purple dress that hugged her chest and flared out from her slim hips, resting just above the knee. My gaze slowly travelled south to the black shoes on her feet. I stared for a moment thinking how sexy the heels made her shapely legs look. When I realised my thoughts were veering into inappropriate territory, I steered my attention back to her head. Her dark hair gleamed in the golden evening light shining through stained glass windows and cascaded down her back in an ebony waterfall. She had never looked so beautiful. I'd only ever seen her in casual sportswear or jeans before. Tonight she looked amazing.

"You're staring."

My eyes darted briefly over to Wesley, Nathan's younger brother, then returned to Cassie.

"Huh?"

"Cassie; you're staring at her," he murmured in amusement.

"I'm not staring."

He chuckled. "Of course you're not," he muttered under his breath.

I so was staring.

Dragging my scrutiny up from Cassie's perky breasts, I finally made it to her eyes and found her staring right back at me. Her eyebrow rose in an I-caught-you-checking-me-out way. A devilish tilt lifted the corners of her lips and her eyes brightened. I'd been expecting death glares not friendly amusement. My stomach churned with shame remembering her hair spread across the pillow, her cheeks rosy from the heat of our passion as I shut the door behind me when I ran out on her. I didn't deserve her smiles.

I plunged my hands in my pockets and toyed with my keys, returning my attention to the happy couple. The sands of time were rapidly disappearing in my figurative hourglass. There were no more excuses, no more hiding away. It was time to square my shoulders and deal with the issue. Cassie deserved an apology and tonight I would deliver it. Tonight I would beg for her forgiveness if I had to. I needed to make sure the air was clear between us for the sake of Liv and Nathan's wedding, for Cassie, and for my sanity.

WHEN IT CAME to the marital celebrations of Nathan Oakes, no expense was spared. The ceremony was taking place at St. Matthews, a grand old church near Nathan and Olivia's Bayswater home. Kensington's world-famous Rooftop Gardens had been hired out exclusively for the reception. As an aperitif, the rehearsal dinner was being held in a swanky London hotel. It all seemed way too over the top and extravagant. When Liv shared their plans with me, I couldn't have been more shocked. My Liv, the girl I'd grown up with, wasn't the showy type. At all. She'd always laughed at and mocked pomp and pageantry. She didn't even buy into the hype of royal weddings or the other main processions. It was one of the things I loved about her: she wasn't afraid to shun convention and follow her own rules. A bit like Cassie.

Shoving those useless thoughts to the back of my mind, I squared my shoulders and entered the private dining room. I couldn't wait for the evening to be over for so many reasons. Immediately my gaze latched on to Cassie talking to Liv, Nathan, and Wesley in front of a large, ornate window. She was smiling, laughing and joking, enjoying a private moment with her closest friends. I envied their natural camaraderie. And the fact that they had so quickly sucked Liv into their welcoming arms. Away from me.

Now's the not the time for a pity party, idiot!

Stepping further into the room, I debated grabbing a stiff drink first or going over to do the best friend thing with Liv. I decided on alcohol, knowing some Dutch courage was going to be needed to face Liv and Nathan… and Cassie. Taking a step toward the bar, I noticed Wesley wrap an arm around Cassie's shoulder. He pulled her against his chest and placed a kiss on the top of her head. Instinctively—and without justification—my eyes narrowed and my hackles rose. I froze in place and watched as she turned adoring eyes toward his and laughed. I knew it meant nothing. They were friends, close friends. That knowledge didn't stop the unwelcome and unfamiliar pang of jealousy from tightening across my chest.

What the hell? What do I have to be jealous of?

Time. I needed time and space to gather my thoughts and pull on my mask. Liv would be expecting her happy, accepting best friend, and Cassie would be expecting....

What would she be expecting?

I knew I had to speak to her, to explain my lack of judgement and inexcusable actions in France. I needed to apologise for being a world-class dick. First, I needed that drink.

Turning my back, I'd taken only two steps toward the bar when Liv spotted me and called out my name. Sucking in a deep breath, I walked by Liv's parents, greeting them with a smile and a polite hello as I passed and made my way over to the happy group of four.

"There he is." Liv beamed when I stopped beside her. "We thought you'd got lost."

After nodding greetings to Nathan and Wesley, my eyes focussed on Cassie's. She was watching me with a smirk tugging on her naturally dusky pink lips. I stared at them for a moment, thinking how she didn't need thick layers of brightly coloured lipstick or gloss to make her mouth irresistible.

"Cassie," I greeted awkwardly, dragging my eyes up to meet hers.

"Adam."

"Where did you get to? We were worried you were going to miss the meal," Liv said, pulling out of Nathan's embrace to give me a quick, friendly hug.

"I had trouble parking," I lied, hugging her back.

"Well, I'm glad you're finally here." She linked her arm through mine and started leading us toward the large oval table in the centre of the room. "And so is Cassie."

Her tone was teasing so I tilted my head to meet her amused grin. Before I could respond, she was pointing to a seat. "You're here, Ad. And Cassie, you're here." I didn't fail to notice that as Cassie stepped up to the indicated seat beside mine, everyone else sat where they wanted. I threw a frustrated glare in Liv's direction; she laughed and wrapped her arms around Nathan's waist as they made their way around the table. She winked, lowering herself onto the chair that Nathan pulled out for her. I had a feeling it was going to be a long, tortuous night.

I SAT AWKWARDLY through the starter, listening to the conversations taking place around me. I wondered how soon I'd be able to sneak off without seeming rude.

"You can talk to me, you know."

Cassie's whisper startled me, pulling me from my thoughts.

"Sorry?"

"I don't bite, Adam. You can talk to me."

I puffed out a resigned sigh. "I know."

"Do you? Because the way I see it, you would rather be anywhere but sitting here with me right now."

I mumbled, "You aren't wrong," under my breath and took a large swig of wine. The cool liquid soothed my parched mouth.

"If this stranger danger thing you've got going on is about what happened in France, you don't—"

Fuck. She was going there, straight in for the kill. No forced pleasantries. No small talk pretending we were anything other than mere acquaintances. I cut her off before she could say anything else. "About that. Cassie, I'm sorry. It wasn't—"

"It wasn't me, it was you, yada, yada, yada." Resting back in her chair, she crossed her arms and rolled her eyes.

I frowned, feeling like a total prick. "Well yeah. Something like that."

"Adam it's—"

"Cassie, I'm sorry—" We both spoke in unison just as a waiter appeared with our main meals. Using the brief reprieve to regain my composure, I shifted my chair, putting some much-needed distance between us. The past was the past; I couldn't change what had happened even if I wanted to. Cassie was a great girl, and before I'd fucked up, she'd been a lot of fun to be around. Sitting there, I felt no animosity or regret from her, just acceptance. I decided to make one final, heartfelt apology to hopefully put the whole incident behind us.

Looking at the steaming plate of food in front of me, I picked up my cutlery and said, "I truly am sorry, Cassie. The way I treated you, running out on you, I shouldn't have done that. I was an arse."

A gentle hand rested on my arm. "Stop apologising. I know what that night was all about. Believe me, I understand." She leant in closer, her warm breath caressing my ear as she spoke. "I get it. You love her and you were hurting in France. You're a great guy and were a lot of fun to be around. No hard feelings." She smiled her warm, charming smile, instantly settling my nerves.

The guilt that had been suffocating me for months suddenly vanished. I felt lighter, freer. The band of worry that had been persistently tightening around my chest disappeared. I could finally breathe. In those few words, Cassie eased much of my guilt.

"What are you two whispering about over there?" Liv asked too brightly from across the table.

"Wouldn't you like to know," Cassie batted back and with a smirk she began cutting into her food.

For the rest of the meal we talked, we laughed, and we joked with Wesley. Everything I'd been feeling from before—the shame, the guilt, it all faded into the past, right where it belonged.

"Why haven't I seen you at the gym recently?" Cassie asked later as we were getting ready to leave.

"Too ashamed. Didn't want to bump into you," I admitted, watching Liv say goodbye to her parents.

Laughing, she poked me in the gut playfully. The muscles tensed and squirmed under her touch. "Yeah, well, that needs to change. We can't have that sexy body getting all podgy now, can we?" My startled grunt had her laughing harder before she backed away. "I better see you there tomorrow evening, Adam. No excuses."

I stared at her with a grin on my face. "I'll be there."

I AWOKE WITH a groan Friday morning, grimacing at the persistent high-pitched beep-beep-beep assaulting my eardrums. It was far too early. I wasn't ready to face the day. I'd barely managed to get three hours of sleep having tossed and turned throughout the night. My mind had been racing a million miles an hour trying to process a range of conflicted feelings and emotions.

Reaching for the alarm, I slapped at the snooze button and pulled the duvet over my head. I just needed another ten minutes.

Last night had been good, a much-needed opportunity to make things better with Cassie. And I was so glad I had. I'd enjoyed her company immensely. But, despite the relief I felt at knowing Cassie held no ill feelings, it had still been a bittersweet night because of Liv.

When the alarm blared at me again, I fell out of bed, my head throbbing like it had been battered with a crowbar. I somehow managed to shower and shave, and pulled on the first suit I tugged out of the closet— black, it was fitting for my mood. I quickly inhaled two cups of coffee before driving into the office.

The bright lighting of the Ashworth-Moore reception dazzled me as I stepped through the heavy glass doors. Pulling my sunglasses back over my eyes, I sucked in a deep breath and rubbed my aching temples. Today was one of those days where I would need to keep my head, focus on work, and pray I'd make it through the day unnoticed. If I could just lock myself in my office with another gallon—or three—of coffee, a box of Ibuprofen and no interruptions, maybe I'd be able to toss out the jackhammer that had taken up residence under my skull. One could only hope.

My head was down, and I was only a few feet from relative safety when….

"Adam! Get that handsome face of yours over here."

"Fuck," I hissed under my breath, turning to face Trish, our over-friendly receptionist. Sat behind the ostentatious white marble desk, she grinned widely with what looked like a nail file in her hand. She wasn't your clichéd ditzy blonde receptionist, no, not at all. I rolled my eyes at my own sarcastic dig and reluctantly headed toward her.

The mammoth reception desk—and Trish—were my father's attempts at trying to show superiority in London's architectural cattle market. It was ridiculous. He wanted to show class, elegance, and sophistication. What he got was a foyer more suited to a five-star London hotel, and an opinionated, loud-mouthed, receptionist. The whole scene didn't really mesh and was kind of ironic when you considered our business. Thank God he was at least savvy when it came to hiring the most talented architects. That included Liv, who had, since designing Nathan Oakes's place in France, become highly successful and had doubled turnover with the new European arm of the organisation she was heading up. I was so proud of her, even if she left me looking like a mediocre chump most of the time.

"Morning, Trish," I uttered quietly, pulling the dark glasses from my eyes.

"Whoa, someone had a good night last night. You look like shit."

"Gee, thanks. Make a guy feel good, why don't you." I cradled the back of my sore head and leant against the desk.

"You know me. I tell it as it is." She leant in close

and studied my stinging eyes. "I thought you were just having a meal after the rehearsal? Shouldn't the heavy drinking have been saved for after the wedding?"

She had a fair point, but I'd hardly touched any alcohol the night before. My pounding head and bloodshot eyes came from my restless night and lack of sleep. When I'd returned home, I'd collapsed onto my sofa and thought about the evening. It had been hard seeing Liv and Nathan so happy and excited about starting their new life together. I'd tried so hard to not wish it had been me hugging her and whispering sweet nothings in her ear. It had been unbearable to know that would now never be a possibility.

Then my thoughts drifted to Cassie. Her easy forgiveness and acceptance of my fucked-up head had knocked me sideways. We'd effortlessly fallen back into chatting like old friends, distracting me from my melancholy. In fact, for much of the evening, it had felt like it was only Cassie and me in the room. Everyone else around us had seemed to fade away.

"I didn't sleep that well," I replied dismissively and pushed away from the counter. Telltale Trish didn't need to know what was going on in my head.

"You met a hot chick, huh?" Her wide grin had me shaking my head.

"Nope. No women."

Her perfectly drawn-in eyebrows furrowed in confusion. "But… you always find a hot chick."

I couldn't deny that. Trish had overheard too many of my conversations with the guys about my latest distraction.

"Don't forget Liv's get-together this afternoon," she shouted as I walked away. "You need to get her into the conference room at four. And remember, it's a surprise. She has no idea about it."

Groaning, I made my way up to my office thinking it wouldn't remain a surprise if Trish kept shouting. Taking a seat behind my desk, I powered up my computer, not looking forward to the little event Trish had arranged for Liv's last day as a single lady. She'd been organising the wedding shower—whatever that was—for weeks. She'd been excited at the opportunity to plan something for a female colleague for a change.

JUST BEFORE FOUR, I switched off my computer and made my way along the corridor to Liv's office. She was busy studying something on her screen, her fingers frantically dancing across her keyboard. With her oblivious to my presence, I settled against the doorjamb and watched her. My princess. My childhood love. Except she wasn't mine and tomorrow, she would be committing the rest of her life and love to someone else.

I chuckled when Liv suddenly cursed, her elbows dropping heavily onto the desk as her hands wove into her long chestnut waves. Her eyes left her screen and zeroed in on me.

"Problem, Liv?"

"No," she snapped, dragging her fingers through the length of her hair.

I stepped into the room and lowered myself into a seat at her desk. "No? So you always growl like a pissed-off tiger then?"

Her eyes narrowed in warning. "Fuck off, Adam."

My grin widened. The easy way I could wind her up

when she was pissed off was one thing I'd always loved about her. We would throw playful insults back and forth until she calmed down, then we'd laugh off whatever had irritated her in the first place.

"Does Nate know he's marrying a premenstrual wildcat?"

"Hardy-har-har. Your comedy skills kill me." Her head shook in exasperation.

"I know. They're a roaring success."

"You are such an idiot, Adam." My arm flew up just in time to shield me from the pencil she hurled in my direction.

"Ouch! That hurt." I rubbed my left arm, pretending to be in pain. "I see all that training Nathan has been giving you is finally paying off, huh? That's some right arm you've got going on there, princess."

Her hands planted on the desk as she leant forward glaring at me.

"Stop calling me that," she seethed through gritted teeth.

I chuckled. "Whatever you say... princess."

I'd called her *princess* for as long as I could remember and had no plans of ever stopping. It had started off as a jibe at her princess ways when we were little—in reality, she had been nothing like a princess, far from it. She had been more of a boy than I was. Later, as we got older and my feelings toward her began to change, I used it as a term of endearment. She was my princess, my fair maiden to look out for. Only it was a different knight in shining armour who rode in on his gallant steed to save her.

"Gah, I give up!" Her hands flew into the air in surrender as she fell back in her chair. "You're never going to give up that name are you?"

Never.

"Nope."

Shaking her head, she sighed. "So… why have I never had a hugely inappropriate or embarrassing nickname for you?"

I shrugged. "Because I'm just too amazing for one?"

She snorted and rifled through some papers. "What can I do for you, Adam? I've got to get finished up here. I want plenty of snuggle time with my future husband before I kick him out at midnight. I absolutely refuse to play around with superstitions."

The lusty glaze over her eyes told me there would be no snuggling taking place that night in their home. And didn't that thought hurt like a bitch?

"You're done."

"What—" She squealed like a strangled cat when I reached over and hit the button to switch off her computer.

"Adam! What the heck? I wasn't finished with that yet!" she yelled.

"Yes, you were. It will all still be there for you in three weeks." I didn't want to think about her semi-naked body sunbathing in the Maldives… with Nathan. "You have something more pressing to attend to right now."

"I do?" She looked down at her desk diary in confusion. "I don't have anything scheduled."

"Last minute addition," I said, rounding her desk and pulling her chair out.

"But, but…."

"Just trust me on this." She gave a wary nod and

held on to the elbow I extended toward her.

"This better be legit, Adam, or so help me God, you will suffer. Remember I have a strong, handsome, sexy as fuck MMA hero training me these days. I will kick your arse."

My chuckles echoed off the walls of the corridor as I led her to the conference room.

"NO OFFENCE TO Trish, but this sucks," Liv whined a while later. She'd had the shock of her life when I'd led her into the decorated conference room to a round of applause and an exuberant hug from Trish.

Liv's pout and bored expression had me choking on the cheap lukewarm fizz I'd just sipped. Wine spewed from my lips, spraying the ridiculous human-sized bride and groom balloons anchored down by a ball and chain—Trish's attempt at humour.

"No need to be like that." I chuckled, grabbing a napkin to wipe my mouth. "Trish has been planning this for weeks."

Liv grimaced and then faked a smile as two guys from Finance offered their congratulations as they passed. "She should have saved her time and money. Since when am I a "bridal shower" kind of girl? This isn't some freaking romance novel."

I shrugged and looked around at the other people in the room. Trish was the only person looking remotely happy. Everybody else looked bored, checking their phones or watches, or huddled together in small groups for whispered conversations. They all loved Liv, but I was sure they were only there for the free food and drink.

"Don't rain on her parade. You know she loves

you. Maybe if you'd invited her to the rehearsal meal last night she wouldn't have felt the need for this." I gestured around the room with arms out wide. Liv followed my lead, looking around, but her reaction was the same as when we'd first walked in. Embarrassment. When she'd seen the corny decorations and colleagues politely clapping, she'd attempted to turn on her heel and walk back out. I'd had to clasp my hand on her shoulder and steer her into the room. It wasn't that she was ungrateful; she just wasn't comfortable in those kinds of situations. It was ironic when she would be centre stage in less than twenty-four hours.

Yanking my arms down, she pulled me into a quiet corner.

"Speaking of last night.... What was going on between you and my little fitness freak friend?"

"Who?" I asked.

"Cassie, you dumbass. I saw you two whispering sweet nothings to each other all night long."

"We were?" I blinked, feigning innocence.

"Yes, you were. It was kind of cute. So spill, what's the deal?"

"We were just talking." She huffed and levelled me with a don't-fucking-fuck-with-me glare. "What's that look for? We were just catching up."

She lifted her glass to her lips and muttered over the rim. "Uh-huh. I'm sure that's all it was."

I fought a laugh as she took a sip and grimaced at the foul tasting liquid. "What exactly are you trying to say, Liv?"

"Oh, I don't know, maybe you don't *catch up* with women."

"Meaning?"

With a look of disgust, she placed her glass on the window ledge and then levelled me with her be-serious glare. "Come on, Adam. You have to admit it's not in you to just *chat* with a woman. That is unless you are trying to talk your way into her knickers."

And there it was, direct hit to the heart number one. According to Liv, I was a player extraordinaire, happily whoring my way around the female population of London. Yes, I'd had my fair share of women. Yes, I enjoyed sex. What she didn't know, though, was that I'd only been using them in an attempt to forget. To try and get over my feelings for her. It was easier to let her believe that I was an uncaring, arrogant bastard rather than for her to see the pathetic puppy dog waiting in the kennels, hoping he would be picked next to be loved by her.

"You know," she continued, oblivious to my internal reflections. "Cassie is a great girl. You two actually have a lot in common. And you got on well in France." Her lips pulled up into a calculated smirk, her eyes suddenly sparkling with mischief. "You should spend time with her, really get to know her. You might find there is more to a woman than a willing vagina."

I shook my head. "So crude, Liv. Always so crude."

AS SOON AS I could get away with it, I escaped the conference room and sloped back to my office. Dropping into my chair, I cradled the back of my head and stared at the floor between my knees. The situation was stupid. Pathetic. I needed to get over Liv. I knew I did. However, I wasn't sure how to, or if I would even be able to.

I gave myself a mental scolding for being such a pussy and pushed away from my desk. I had to pull myself out of this funk. And I only knew one sure-fire way of doing that. The gym. I'd run, row, and weight lift my frustrations away. A good workout always got the positive endorphins flowing. Besides, I'd told Cassie I would be there.

CHAPTER THREE

Cassie

JAY STOOD TO MY SIDE, covering his hands with blue protective hand wraps. While he continued regaling me with the latest news from the kick-boxing world, my eyes kept darting toward the front entrance. I should have been listening; after all, these were potential opponents for the big fight he was talking about. Instead, my focus was on the sliding glass entry doors every time they opened. I glanced at the huge clock on the wall, noting the digital display showing it was already seven fifteen. Adam should be there any minute. He always arrived around seven.

How do I even know that? Why do I know that?

After clearing the air between us the night before, I'd been eagerly anticipating Adam's visit. Before the-incident-that-will-no-longer-be-spoken-of in France, we'd got along well. Training had never been more enjoyable than when I was working out with Adam or we were running through the vineyards and gorges near Nate's property together. We'd had a good partnership, full of encouragement and motivation. I wanted that easy friendship and joviality back.

"You waiting for someone?" Jay asked.

I looked at him. "What?"

He pointed a wrapped hand toward the main entrance. "You keep looking at the doors as if you're expecting someone specific to walk through."

"Oh." I hadn't realised my actions had been that noticeable.

"So who is it?"

I shrugged. "Just a friend. He promised he'd be here tonight for a workout. I said I'd join him."

"Him?" His stormy grey eyes narrowed.

"He's a friend of Liv's. He hasn't trained here for a while."

"He's going to be disappointed then," Jay said, wrapping his muscular arms around my waist and pulling me against his chest.

"Why do you say that?" Perplexed, I tilted my head back and looked up into his eyes.

"Because Bianca's coming."

"And?"

"So you won't be able to see him. You need to come and train with Bianca." He stared down at me like I was a clueless idiot.

"What are you talking about?" Frowning, I pushed against his chest. I had work to do. "I can't train with you tonight. Colin's out so I need to stay out here and watch the front desk because Wes and Nate aren't here either."

Jay rented studio space from Golden Oakes for his kick-boxing club. It worked well for me with training and preparing for fights. It didn't work quite so well with Jay being so close and expecting me to be in there with him training every night.

"Cassie, your fight is only a couple of months away. To be victorious, you have to think like a winner, you have to fight like a winner, and you have to train like a winner. You have to live, breathe, and sleep this. You have to train hard every day." His face creased in annoyance.

Pulling out of his grasp, I stepped back and crossed my arms over my chest. "I do train every day. You know as well as I do that it's not just about what happens in the studio. I need to work just as hard in the gym for endurance and strength as well as the technical stuff."

"Bianca is our strongest female fighter beside you. We're lucky she's joined us. You should be grateful, Cassie, not whining about a bit of extra training."

I spluttered, lost for words. Was he serious?

"When she's here, you need to spar with her. You need to prepare. She can't always get here at the moment due to her work commitments, so when she is here, you need to be too. You will be there, Cassie," he said with finality.

I hated it when he was like this. I understood his passion for me to do well. He was a champion in the sport himself, regularly winning the fights and competitions he entered. He wanted that same level of success for each of his students. And he was willing to do whatever was needed for us to achieve it. Bianca had joined the club a few weeks earlier, having recently moved into the area, and had quickly impressed Jay with her impeccable skills. Jay couldn't believe his luck; she came with fight experience and, along with me, was ready to enter the biggest fights. Unfortunately, her working hours meant that she couldn't commit to a regular training schedule and therefore, couldn't agree to fight in any competitions, much to Jay's irritation. That left the burden of success well and truly on my shoulders, and therefore his full focus was on me.

We were in an awkward stare-off when I felt a tingle of awareness shoot up my spine as someone stood beside me.

"Hi, Cassie."

Jay's unwavering gaze remained trained on me while I looked at our companion.

"Adam," I greeted with a smile, my sour mood suddenly lifting. "I'm so glad you made it."

"Is everything okay?" Adam flicked his eyes between Jay and me.

"Yep. Just a slight misunderstanding," I said. Jay's eyes narrowed. "Nothing to worry about. Adam, this is Jay. Jay, this is Adam, Olivia's best friend."

"Nice to meet you, man." Adam thrust out a hand in greeting. Jay ignored him, keeping his hard gaze on me. He was making me feel uncomfortable, not to mention embarrassed. What was his problem?

Asking Adam for a moment alone with Jay, he said he needed to get changed and strolled off toward the locker rooms with his sports bag.

When Adam was out of earshot, I turned on Jay.

"What the fuck was that?" I seethed.

"He was interrupting our discussion," he said dismissively, checking his wraps were secure.

"You were rude, Jay."

"He'll get over it." He shrugged and then his head jerked up in realisation. "Is that who you were waiting for earlier? Your *friend*?"

I hated the way he said *friend*, like it was a ridiculous notion that I could possibly have friends beyond him. For some reason he was pissed off and fishing for an argument. I had no plans of giving him the satisfaction of biting.

"Yes," I replied calmly, even though I felt anything but calm.

"Then you're definitely coming with me." He reached out for my hand. I yanked it away and stepped back.

"You're not my keeper, Jay." Tears of frustration pricked the backs of my eyes, and I desperately tried to blink them away. No way was I going to show him he was getting to me.

"You're right; I'm not. But I am your trainer and your boyfriend. What's so wrong with me wanting to push you to be the best?"

"Nothing," I said, deflating slightly.

"Cass, if I have to stop you from getting distracted by your friends so you focus, then I will." He reached up to sweep a strand of hair behind my ear. "So, I'll see you in the studio soon, yes?"

I sighed. "I can't. I have to work."

"So come in when you can."

I pinched the bridge of my nose feeling the beginnings of a headache. We were going to continue talking each other in circles.

"You know I'm closing tonight, with Nate and Wes out preparing for the wedding. I won't have time to train with you. I have to be available out here."

"You need to be available for... no, you know what?" he barked, throwing his hands in the air, earning a few curious side glances from those nearby. "Just do what you fucking want. I'll see you tomorrow. Maybe." With that he strode away, his long legs carrying him away quickly.

I stared at his retreating back for a moment wondering what the hell just happened. He'd never spoken to me like that before.

A few minutes later, Adam reappeared, and my unease melted away. I was at least happy to see him.

AFTER CHECKING MY treatment room, I shut off the lights and locked up the spa for the night. I ambled back into the main workout area, wondering if Adam was still around. After a quick chat, I'd left him alone to check on things. I hadn't been gone long, but I didn't know his full training schedule. As I'd hoped, he was still there pushing weights in the free weight section.

I couldn't help but admire his sexy physique as I moved closer. I'd worshipped his body in France; of course I had. It was difficult not to look—and touch—when he'd been moving intimately against and in me. But he was leaner now, more defined. Sculpted. Sexy. It was evident he'd continued working out during his absence from Golden Oakes. His black T-shirt pulled taut across his back and shoulders, showcasing each rippling muscle as he pushed an impressive amount of weight. My eyes skimmed along his arms, trailing the thick veins that popped out in resistance to his strength. The addition of the tribal tattoo framing his left shoulder and bicep was a pleasant surprise. A hot, sexy surprise. It made me wonder if he had any more, and if he did where they were.

"You gonna stand there and stare at me all day?" My eyes snapped to the mirror, finding Adam smirking back at me.

I felt my cheeks heat, no doubt stained crimson with embarrassment.

"Perk of the job," I replied nonchalantly, hoping to move on. Fast.

"You always check out the guys training?" His teasing grin was a mile wide.

"Not all, only the tall, blond, fit, hot ones with gorgeous blue eyes."

What. The. Hell, Cassandra! Where the fuck did that come from? Back off. Back OFF!

Biting my lip, I looked away quickly.

"Just those guys, huh?" He placed the weights down, chuckling.

I couldn't help but sneak a surreptitious look at his torso when he lifted his shirt to wipe sweat from his face. Good grief. If I thought he looked good clothed, the sight of his bared flesh—all ripped, slightly tanned and delicious—had me positively swooning, and generally I wasn't a swooner. Working with Nate and Wes, I'd just kind of become immune to being surrounded by good-looking muscular men all the time. But Adam seemed different somehow.

I swallowed hard and directed my gaze elsewhere. I shouldn't be lusting over someone I now considered a friend, especially when I was in a relationship with someone else.

Bad, Cassie—very, very bad.

"So…." I cleared my throat. "I should maybe…."

"Cassie?"

"Yeah?

"I was only messing with you. No need to get weird on me."

I closed my eyes briefly, appreciating his sincere tone. When I opened them, Adam's shirt was back in place, and his friendly smile replaced the teasing smirk.

"What time do you get to escape?" he asked, reaching for the weights to put away.

Easy, everyday, friendly conversation—this was good. This I could do.

"Not till late tonight. I have to close up."

His eyes widened. "On your own?"

"A few trainers will still be here."

"Where's Wesley?"

"He's doing something with Nate for the wedding. He did offer to come back for closing, but I told him I'd be okay." I felt I needed to explain.

We started walking back toward the locker rooms. I was a little disappointed that I'd not had much of a chance to speak to him, or train with him—although, if I was going to act like a leering perv around him then maybe it was a blessing in disguise.

"Do you want me to stay and help you?"

What a gentleman.

I shook my head. "No, you're good. Thanks, though."

When we reached the hallway that led to the locker rooms and swimming pool, I stopped and offered him a smile. He didn't seem happy. His usually bright eyes were dull, expressing his concern.

"You shouldn't have to do that by yourself, Cass."

Cass? That was the first time he'd called me that. It sounded good coming from his lips.

"I won't be by myself, the rest of the staff will leave at the same time," I reassured.

"I still don't think that responsibility should fall on you."

"Look, if it makes you feel better, I'll go and ask Jay to stay," I said.

He looked around, eyes intently studying everyone. "He's still here?"

"Next door in the kick-boxing studio."

"You do that here?" He looked genuinely interested.

"Yeah. You want to see the place?"

He smiled. "Sure. As long as you don't try to kick my arse when we're in there."

I snickered. "Not today. I can't mess up that pretty-boy face for the photos tomorrow, can I?" I patted his cheek and walked toward the door at the end of the hall that led to the private entrance at the back of the studio.

"Please," he said, following behind me. "You'd never get me."

I turned to face him, my brow lifting in amusement. "Is that a challenge, Mr Ashworth?"

He shrugged. "Maybe."

"Just you wait."

His grin widened. "Bring it on."

Oh, I would. I couldn't wait.

THE STUDIO WAS empty when we walked in. The only indication that Jay was still around was the hip-hop music blaring through the sound system. When classes and training sessions were in progress, Jay was ever the professional and the music would be off. As soon as he was out of official trainer duties, the music came on. It was the same in his car, his flat; he'd even hijacked my stereo at home with his playlists. I wasn't a fan. I much preferred top forty pop with a generous helping of alternative rock.

"This is my domain," I said to Adam, opening my arms wide and spinning in a full circle.

He looked around, his eyes taking in the wall covered by punching bags and other training pads. I laughed when he startled at the sight of the three punch dummies in the far corner. I had to admit they were very realistic and had scared the shit out of me when Jay first had them installed. Now I just used them to kick the crap out of. It was very therapeutic after a stressful day.

"I didn't think you were coming." Jay walked out of the door that led to the studio's own changing and restroom facilities.

"I'm just showing Adam the place quickly."

Ignoring Adam, he stepped toward me, his face hard and disapproving. "You know it's members only in here, Cassie."

"Maybe he wants to join," I said petulantly. He obviously hadn't gotten over his earlier pissy mood. His eyes blazed a fiery, scathing look my way. We were, after all, in his domain and what he said went. "Anyway, where is everyone else? I thought Bianca was coming."

Just then the door Jay had just come through opened. Bianca strolled out, dragging her fingers through her shoulder-length auburn hair.

"As you can see, she did come. We trained. Now she's going."

"Hi, Cass," Bianca said with a smile, stopping at Jay's side. "It's a shame you couldn't make it for training. You know, you really need to start wearing him out more. He nearly killed me tonight." She winked and then left, shouting her goodbyes on her way out.

"Did you want something?" Jay asked, sounding impatient.

Jay wasn't particularly known for his impeccable social skills or patience, but he had always been polite and friendly. His actions tonight were disconcerting. I wanted to call him out on his crappy attitude but feared I'd just be poking the bear. I decided to leave it and pretend I wasn't about ready to strangle him.

"Adam's worried about me being here by myself to close up. Can you stick around?"

He pulled a set of keys from his pocket, twirling them around a finger. "Sorry, I can't. I'm going out."

Oh? Where? He hadn't said anything. No, I wasn't going to go all mistrusting girlfriend on him. But I couldn't help feel the sting of hurt that he didn't want to stick around, though.

"Thanks for nothing," I mumbled under my breath.

I plastered a fake smile on my face and told him it was okay, that I'd see him tomorrow for the wedding. Adam then followed as I left, slamming the door behind us.

"I'll stay with you," Adam said adamantly when

we'd made our way back into the main gym area.

I sighed. "You don't need to do that, Adam. Honestly, I'll be okay. I've closed up several times before."

"I don't care. I'm not leaving here until you are safely on your way home, so you might as well just accept it."

Rolling my eyes yet feeling a tingle of gratitude for his caring act, I pointed toward the offices behind reception. "In that case, we might as well go and get comfortable."

We spent the next hour chatting about everything and nothing. At one point he asked me about Jay. I admitted we could be quite fiery together, but that he was a good guy and only wanted the best for me. Jay hadn't been himself tonight, and I felt the need to make excuses for his behaviour. I didn't want Adam thinking poorly of my boyfriend based on a couple of short interactions.

When it came time to close up, Adam patiently waited while we went through closing procedures and I set the alarm system and locked up. We said goodbye to the other staff and walked toward the parking lot.

"Thank you for staying," I said when we stopped beside my car.

"No problem. I don't like the thought of you having to come out here alone in the dark. Anything could happen."

He was such a gentleman.

"I appreciate your concern," I replied. I meant it. It was such a thoughtful, selfless thing to do.

"So, I'll see you tomorrow?"

"Yep, I'll be the one in blue falling over in her

heels."

Laughing, he opened my car door for me when I hit the key fob.

"Have a good night, Cass." His head dropped forward and my breath caught. Was he going to kiss me? Then, when he seemed to realise what he was doing, his head jerked up and he stepped back, burying his hands in his pockets.

"You too, Adam."

I got in the car and buckled up, my hands trembling slightly. I put the car in gear and reversed out of my spot. As I drove away, I kept an eye on my rear-view mirror. Adam was still there, his expression thoughtful as he watched me leave. I smiled to myself. I was happy he was back in my life… as a friend, of course.

CHAPTER FOUR

Cassie

WARM AUGUST AIR HIT US as the wedding party and guests slowly exited through the oak doors of St. Matthew's. The ceremony had been lovely, and I was thrilled that two of my closest friends were now happily married. But I needed air.

The old church had been too humid, the stagnant air oppressive. Dust particles and the faint perfume of incense floated in the air, a suffocating, cloying scent that had me desperate for fresh air. In the heat, the bodice of my silk dress seemed to tighten and constrict by the minute. I had no idea how Olivia was coping in her stunning designer gown. I could admit it was beautiful in a Kate Middleton way with all its silk and lace. But it was just a dress, a lot of material and totally unnecessary for one day. I'd told Liv many times over that *if* I ever got married—and it was a big *if*—I would be demanding a small beach or registry office wedding. Somewhere I could wear whatever I'd be comfortable in. She'd just laughed and said, "You'll see. *When* you get married, you'll end up with the big wedding, wearing an elegant dress." Did she know nothing about me? That was never going to happen.

While their many guests congratulated Liv and Nate, I hobbled into the shade where Wes and Adam stood talking. I laughed at Adam, who seemed to be as uncomfortable in his formal wear as I was in mine. He was tugging restlessly at the collar of his crisp white shirt and the midnight blue tie that matched my dress perfectly. Stopping at his side, I held on to his muscular arm with one hand for balance while I bent to yank off the shoes that were killing my feet. It was funny, but after the short amount of time we'd spent together the night before, I felt comfortable with him, like he was already one of the gang and we'd been close for years. It was nice.

"What are you doing?" he asked with a chuckle, looking down at me.

Straightening, I held the offending shoes out in front of me. "These shoes are bloody killing me."

He shook his head, his warm blue eyes shining in amusement. "Let me guess; you'd rather be in your Nikes?"

"Damn right I would. Who the hell thought it was a smart idea for women to wedge their feet into unnaturally shaped footwear? I bet it was some sadist idiot that wanted to watch his poor wife suffer. I nearly face planted into Great Uncle Benson's lap walking down the aisle." I shook my head in dismay.

Wes looped an arm around my shoulder and gave an affectionate squeeze. "It's a good thing you didn't. I don't think you mimicking a BJ on Liv's geriatric relatives was in Horrible Helga's schedule." He jerked his chin in the direction of the impatient wedding coordinator.

My nose wrinkled in disgust. "You're disgusting, Wesley Oakes! And, I swear to God, I thought I knew those two. What the fuck were they thinking hiring her for this shindig?"

Wes snorted. "She came as a highly recommended celebrity wedding planner. I don't think Liv was too keen on the idea, but Nate, in his wisdom, wouldn't budge. Apparently even the paparazzi are scared shitless of her and wouldn't dare try to get any unauthorised snaps of the big day."

"Yeah, well she better not try ordering me around—"

"Where are the maid of honour and best man? Is it too much to ask for the wedding party stay close by? We are on a schedule here," the dragon lady bellowed, flailing her clipboard above her head.

Adam chuckled, and Wesley growled several expletives and threats of illegal chokeholds that he'd ignore her tap out for. Similar thoughts swirled around my mind while I roughly shoved my feet back into my painful shoes.

"Have fun," Adam chirped when Wes and I begrudgingly stomped away. Looking over my shoulder, I glared and showed my displeasure with a middle finger salute that just made him laugh that much harder.

"GROOMSMEN! Where are my groomsmen?" I

had to laugh when I looked back to see Adam's face pale, his shoulders dropping in defeat as he followed us.

SOME TIME LATER, after being manhandled into various positions for an absurd amount of photos, my facial muscles screamed for relief from all the forced smiling. Don't get me wrong; I couldn't be happier for Olivia and Nate, they deserved their Happy Ever After. I was just ready to ditch the dress and heels and change into something more... me.

Finally, we heard the magic words, "Okay, that's all we need for now." *Thank God!* "We'll see you all back at the gardens for more."

"What the fuck? How many coffee table books and photo frames do they plan on filling?" I groaned, hopping from one foot to the other trying to ease the burn on my soles.

Beside me Wes, Adam, and Jay tittered. "What's up, babe, missing your trainers?"

Turning into Jay's warm body, I beamed up at him. "You know it." He'd been in a much better mood today. He'd turned up at my house early with a delightful breakfast and a quick apology session beneath the sheets before letting me get ready for the wedding. Then he'd met up with me again outside of the church. He was still indifferent to the others, but I figured it was because he didn't know them that well.

Jay's firm lips pressed against my hair and his arms wrapped around my body, holding me close. Resting my cheek against the calming rise and fall of his chest, I luxuriated in the rare moment of tenderness. Jay wasn't an affectionate man, not really. Our physical relationship usually consisted of him kicking my ass on the mats in the gym or studio. Very rarely would he pull me in for a hug or kiss. Even in the bedroom he was more about his pleasure than mine. It wasn't ideal—or very satisfying—but I sucked it up and got on with it. What he lacked in physical affection, he made up for through his support and caring attitude. Being a romance sceptic, I didn't need the constant reassurance of Jay's touch to help me get through the day.

I stole a glance toward my other friends noticing Adam's usually bright eyes clouded with confusion as he regarded Jay. I knew Jay had given him a poor first impression, and I desperately hoped that Adam would see the good guy underneath the obnoxious arse mask Jay had worn the night before.

I felt myself relax against Jay when Adam looked my way and smiled. I liked to think we'd become good friends and friends were the most important people in my life. With my parents being almost strangers to me, my friends were my family.

My smile grew broader watching Liv and Nate walking toward us. Liv was desperately trying to hitch up the mountain of silk and netting of her dress with one hand while holding Nate's with the other. Despite her battle with the dress, she merrily hollered, "Coming through, make way for Mr and Mrs Oakes."

Everyone laughed and welcomed the beaming bride and groom. I couldn't remember ever seeing Nate so happy and relaxed. Liv had been good for him.

She released her grip on the dress and took her flowers from Nate. I couldn't help the titter that escaped my lips. Seeing the brawny, tattooed MMA star carrying flowers was just too funny. By his side, Liv looked absolutely stunning with her long dark hair expertly styled into loose curls falling around her shoulders, decorated with simple yet elegant diamond pins. Her long veil fluttered behind her in the balmy summer breeze. Her face was painted with more make-up than I'd ever seen her wear before. And with her twisted lips, and brows that were drawn into a frown, she looked just like a pissed-off Disney princess. I struggled to contain my giggles.

Pointing her perfectly arranged bouquet of cream roses, gerbera daisies, and baby's breath at me, Liv huffed, "Why on earth did you let me get a bloody meringue, Cass? And what about these heels? You know I don't do heels." She lifted a foot, the pointed toe of her ivory satin shoe poking out from beneath the hem of her gown. "I should have got that simple Grecian-style dress. Since when do I love meringues?"

Turning in Jay's arms, I tried to hold back an exasperated sigh. I'd gone dress shopping with Liv and her mum, Pam. I'd told Liv over and over that she'd be more comfortable in something simple, but when Pam saw her in the meringue, she'd burst into tears and sobbed something incoherent about her princess. Seeing that much emotion from her mum had softened Liv's usual steely resolve, and she'd caved.

"I seem to recall telling you—over and over—that you should go for that cute A-line dress. And don't even talk to me about heels."

Liv ignored my tone or didn't hear me because Nate was nuzzling her neck. "I love meringue, especially when it has cream, strawberries and... you," he growled against her skin.

Liv's cheeks heated as Wes muttered, "Gag," beside us, acting out a heaving motion with his fingers near his lips. I laughed and lifted my eyes to see Adam's sad expression. Burying his hands into his trouser pockets, he looked away. Adam had come so far in letting go of his infatuation for Liv, but I knew he still struggled at times. Now that we were friends again, I hoped I'd be able to help him get over her and find someone new to love.

And wasn't that just the weirdest thought to have? Because somewhere in the deepest, darkest recesses of my mind, I knew that I didn't want him loving someone else. I wanted him to love me.

"Seriously, you two," Wes continued, waving a hand in the air. "Can you save all that crap for your room later? Don't we have somewhere to be? I need a stiff drink after coping with horrible Helga."

Holding on to his wife, Nate chuckled. Liv playfully elbowed him, but I could see she was trying to hold back a laugh. "That's why we came over. When we get to the gardens, we're having more pictures taken." Wesley and Adam groaned loudly. "Cass, I've told the photographer and *Horrible Helga* I want pictures of you with Wes, one with Adam and one of the three of you." Behind me, Jay's body stiffened, and the fingers that had been holding me softly now dug almost painfully into my hips.

Ignorant of my slight grimace of pain, Liv continued, "Are the three of you going in the other car?" She gestured toward the two fancy Rolls Royce cars parked in front of the church.

The grip on my hips dug deeper, the new pain

barely registering through my rapidly increasing irritation.

Before I had a chance to pull away or stomp on his foot, Jay spoke, a hard tone lacing his otherwise composed voice. "Cassie is coming with me."

Liv looked at me and then Jay, confusion clouding her brown eyes. She knew this wasn't what we'd agreed. I was supposed to be travelling in the second car with Wesley, Adam, and Liv's parents.

Her lips pursed as she prepared to argue Jay's plans but I cut her off quickly, saying it was alright. I should travel to the reception with Jay. She looked a little uneasy but nodded when I gave her a reassuring grin.

"Okay then. I guess we'll see you all there." She looked me over one last time and only when she seemed satisfied did she grab Nate's hand to head toward their car, impatiently hiking up the hem of her dress again as they went.

Wesley and Adam also gave me confused glances before glaring at Jay. At the car, they said they'd meet me at the reception.

"You're not having your photo taken with those two," Jay hissed into my ear when the car pulled away.

Pulling out of his hold, I spun to face him. "Of course I am. Why wouldn't I?"

"I don't want you having your picture taken with other guys."

What the hell?

"Are you being serious right now? You know these guys are like family to me, Jay! Why are you acting like a giant prick about this?" Throwing up my arms in exasperation, I turned to stomp my way toward the parking lot where Jay's car was parked.

I hadn't even taken two steps before strong fingers dug into my arms, holding me back. "It's not happening, Cassandra."

"You are not going to tell me what to do, *Jayden*. If you can't handle the day and everything that goes with it, just go. I'll come and see you at your place tonight." I grimaced in pain as I ripped my arm from his hold and continued walking away from him.

THE DRIVE TO the Kensington Roof Gardens was silent and awkward. Jay's quiet, stiff demeanour had me staring out the window wondering again what the heck had crawled up his arse. If it hadn't been vital for me to get to the venue as quickly as possible, I would have opened the door and escaped at the next set of red lights. Walking the remaining distance—even in uncomfortable heels—was preferable to dealing with Jay in that kind of mood. As it was, I needed the ride. So I focused all my hurt into anger and watched the lively streets of London pass by in a blur.

In the parking lot, Jay eased the car into the first available space and switched off the ignition. We both remained silent and pensive for several moments. Things had never been this awkward between us. His fists clenched and unclenched around the steering wheel over and over as he stared through the windshield.

Suddenly sucking in a deep breath, he exhaled it slowly and turned in his seat to face me. "Cassie, I'm sorry. I overreacted. It's just… I'm… I'm a fucking idiot, I know." His shoulders dropped in defeat and he settled puppy dog eyes on me. It was a look I was never able to resist on him.

"This is a wedding, Jay. I'm having my photo taken with my friends," I murmured.

His jaw clenched and I knew he was still unhappy, but he gave a nod, accepting this was going to happen. I'd never allowed a man to dictate my life before and had no plans on starting now.

A few minutes later, hand in hand we rejoined the rest of the wedding guests in the vibrant, glamorous rooftop gardens one hundred feet above London's Kensington High Street. People happily stood around chatting and laughing while sipping from champagne glasses. Others strolled through the gardens admiring the scenery. A wonderful aroma of lavender, roses, and wildflowers filtered through the distinct scent of city air. It was hard to believe we were in the middle of London.

We grabbed glasses of champagne from a passing waiter and made our way over to a quieter, shaded corner. Wesley and Adam stood talking to a few of Nate's ex-fighting buddies while the happy couple had more photographs taken. Plastering on a broad smile, I stepped into the crowd with Jay right behind me, keeping a possessive hand on my lower back.

Adam and Wes still seemed to be a little wary of Jay, throwing heated looks in his direction. After a few minutes their tension eased off and they all got into a heated debate about what body conditioning techniques were most successful. Wes, Adam, and I were then called over to the arbour for our photos. We each had one taken with the bride and then the bride and groom before they disappeared into the crowd for a much-needed drink. We were several shots in when I chanced a glance at Jay. Immediately my happy, carefree smile disappeared. He was resting against a wall with his arms crossed over his chest and scowl lines furrowed his brow. I tried a reassuring smile, but all it seemed to do was heighten his displeasure.

"What's wrong?" Adam whispered. His fingers, resting on my waist for a deliberately posed shot, flexed as he followed my line of sight.

"Nothing." I stepped away from his hold and turned with a smile to address the photographer. "Are we done here?"

"There are just a few more shots the bride asked for." He indicated for me to step back with Adam and lifted his camera to his eyes.

Suddenly, a hard, calloused hand gripped my wrist, yanking me away from Adam.

"You've got what you need," Jay sneered, glowering at the photographer and then at Adam.

"I'm sorry, sir, but the bride would like a few more shots of her maid of honour," the photographer calmly said, lowering his camera.

Jay ignored him and continued pulling me away from my friends. I didn't want to make a scene and potentially spoil the day, so I obediently followed, my heels clicking loudly on the stone pathway, while internally I was fuming.

"Cassie!" Adam and Wes called out, their voices alarmed and angry.

Looking over my shoulder, I shouted that I was okay and hoped that my eyes told them to leave it. They reluctantly nodded, but I could feel their eyes on us as we walked away.

"What are you doing? For God's sake, Jay, what is

your problem?" I whisper yelled when we were far enough away to not be heard. I stopped walking and tugged on his hand encouraging him to face me.

"My problem is those guys had their hands all over you." I flinched slightly at the dark hardness in his eyes. He was beyond pissed. Well, so was I.

"You're ridiculous. We've already talked about this, and my view hasn't changed. These people are my friends, my best friends. Besides, the photos kind of go with the territory of being maid of honour, don't you think?"

"I saw the way you were looking at him." He looked over his shoulder toward the guys. His lip twisted into a sneer, not liking what he saw and grabbed my arm again, pulling me even further away from the wedding guests. "I saw the way he was looking at you. He wants you."

"Let go of me. You're making a scene." I fought against his firm grip but it was no use, he was so much stronger than me. His fingers dug into my flesh as he ushered me further toward the wall overlooking the busy streets of London below.

Suddenly, Nate, Wes, and Adam were at my side, each of them glaring at Jay with menacing darkness. They demanded to know what was going on.

"Nothing's going on," Jay said calmly, dropping my arm. "I just wanted to spend a bit of time alone with my girlfriend. Didn't I, Cass?"

No.

With a forced smile, I nodded, hoping to diffuse the suddenly hostile atmosphere. I didn't want to be the cause of any tension on Nate's wedding day.

"Everything's fine; we just wanted a quiet minute

away from everyone."

I knew from their expressions that they didn't believe a word, but they would let it go... for now. Wes's blazing eyes made it clear he'd expect answers from me later. I, therefore, made a mental note to avoid him for the rest of the night.

The Master of Ceremonies announcing it was time to sit down for the wedding meal broke the silent tension surrounding us.

Wes's tight jaw eased into a mischievous grin. "Speech time. Get ready for your humiliation, big bro." Slapping Nate on the shoulder, he laughed as he walked toward the dining room. Nate followed, grumbling about Wes keeping his speech clean. Yeah, that was never going to happen.

"You sure you're okay?" Adam asked quietly.

I nodded with what I hoped was a reassuring smile. "Everything's fine. Come on, let's go eat."

A waiter passed nearby with a half-full tray of champagne glasses. Needing something to calm my jittery nerves, I ducked between Adam and Jay and grabbed a glass, drinking it down quickly as I followed Nate and Wes.

The men caught up to me quickly, Jay possessively placing a hand on my lower back. His gentlemanly act didn't fool me, though. I could sense his tension through his stiff posture and the pressure of his fingertips pressing against my body. That tension only amplified when, upon checking the seating plan, we discovered I would be at the head table with the bride and groom and Jay was seated several tables back with some of Nate and Wes's training pals. Adam sat at the table nearest to me. I could have pelted him with food during the meal if the desire to do so had been there.

Throughout the meal, I kept watch over at Jay. His posture remained stiff and unwelcoming. It was evident his tablemates were trying to encourage him into their conversations, but his responses seemed to be a series of sharp head nods or shakes. I felt a bit guilty that he knew nobody else at the wedding and had been forced to sit away from me. Then I remembered telling him it would have been better for him to just come to the evening reception. He had been resolute; nothing was going to stop him from accompanying me. He had brought this on himself.

Wes didn't disappoint with his speech. Spilling all the dirt on his brother, he had everyone in the room laughing. Then, Nate and Ed, Liv's dad, had everyone shedding a tear or two with their praise and love for Liv in their speeches. After that, it was time to retreat to the terrace for drinks.

I'd been talking to Ed and Pam for a short while when Jay approached. Placing a hand at my elbow, he gestured for me to walk with him. I looked him over briefly and could tell straight away he'd been drinking more than the wine served with the meal. His cheeks were flushed, eyes half-lidded and glazed over, and his hair in disarray as though he'd been raking his fingers through it. He'd loosened his red tie, and his shirt was half-untucked.

He led us across the terrace to a seating area surrounded by tall, manicured conifers. As I lowered myself into a dark rattan chair, Jay dropped to his haunches in front of me and took hold of my hand.

His speech was slurred when he spoke. "I'm sorry about before, baby. I was an idiot. Forgive me." From behind his back, he produced a single long-stemmed white rose. "Your favourite." He smiled, a cocksure tilt of his lips. He seemed so proud of himself for giving me my favourite flower. Except it wasn't. White lilies were.

"Jay, where did you get the flower?" I took it from him and laid it gently on the glass table.

"From the table centrepiece."

I gasped. "Jay, you can't go stealing flowers from the displays."

He rolled his eyes and pulled a chair in front of mine, caging me in with his knees on either side of mine. "It's not like they're going to miss one flower." Grabbing the rose from the table, Jay slapped the bloom against my chest, crushing the delicate petals. "Just take the flower and be grateful. I was trying to be romantic."

I placed the battered flower back on the table. "I am grateful. It was a sweet gesture... it just feels wrong."

"Cassie, are you okay?"

I looked over Jay's shoulder. Adam stood beside a tree clipped into a spiral. With the early evening sunlight behind him bathing him in a golden glow, he looked imposing, like a gallant hero.

Under his breath, Jay grumbled something about interfering pricks and pushed his chair back hard. It scraped loudly along the stone paving and toppled over. Before he could turn to face Adam, I grabbed his hand. "Let's go to the bar for a drink." The last thing he needed was more alcohol, but I had to get him away from Adam before his belligerence erupted into something that would no doubt ruin the wedding for everyone.

As we walked hand-in-hand past Adam, I offered him my usual self-assured grin. I needed him to know everything was okay. Jay was just not feeling himself at the moment. Everything would soon be back to normal.

CHAPTER FIVE

Adam

I DIDN'T LIKE HIM. I'D only met him that one time before but it was evident to me that Jay was a major dickhead. Things about him rubbed me the wrong way, like the way he looked through Cassie as though she were nothing. Or the way he put his hands on her like she was his possession to do with as he pleased. Yet she seemed to stand by and allow him to dominate her. That wasn't the Cassie I knew. My Cassie was strong-willed, boisterous and opinionated. She was blunt, honest, and held nothing back verbally, physically, or emotionally. At least that's what I thought.

I watched the two of them walk away, torn between wanting to chase after them and leaving them alone like her pleading eyes had asked. Getting into an argument on Liv's wedding day was probably not the wisest decision to make so I went in the opposite direction toward a second bar.

Several glasses of single malt and a conversation with Wesley later, I was back at the bar. It had been a wonderful day, and Liv's happiness made me happy, but I was ready to get out of there. I felt antsy and desperately wanted to shed the suit and tie in favour of a pair of shorts and bare feet. I stole a glance around the terrace, watching the people dotted around in small groups chatting and laughing. Some I knew, others I didn't. I wasn't in the mood to discuss the state of the economy, or the latest trend in civil engineering. I couldn't even muster any enthusiasm to engage in any of the many sports related discussions taking place. Fuck, I was a bore.

I gestured to the barman for another drink and while he poured the whisky, I checked my watch, sighing that it was only nine thirty. I needed to get out of there.

"Not having a good time?"

I accepted my drink and looked to my side to the source of the sweet feminine voice.

"It's been a long day. I'm just tired now."

The tall blonde nodded toward my tie that was now loosened, my top button undone. "Were you in the wedding?"

"For my sins, yes."

She laughed, her wide green eyes sparkling under the white light of the bar's spotlights. "Forced into it, huh?"

"Something like that."

Over the rim of my glass, I looked her over. I

searched my memory bank—which was now fuzzy from the alcohol—trying to determine if I knew her. I came up blank. Surely I would have remembered those big eyes, the cute button nose, shoulder-length platinum blonde bob, and plump ruby-red lips.

"Do I know you?"

Shaking her head, she replied, "No, I don't think so. I'm Justine."

Justine? Justine? No, I definitely didn't know a Justine.

"It's nice to meet you, Justine. I'm Adam."

She took my outstretched hand and shook it gently. I noticed how her palm was slightly damp and trembled at our touch. That reaction from a female was unusual. More often than not, by the time I touched a woman, we'd have already been flirting and would be about ready to dive beneath the sheets. Justine's subtle quivering seemed kind of endearing, cute.

"Are you nervous?" I asked.

She sucked down the contents of her champagne glass and then gestured to the bartender for a refill. Shooting me a nervous look, she asked, "Am I that obvious?"

"Not really, but your shaky hand is kind of a giveaway."

She laughed awkwardly and clasped her hands together. "Sorry. I'm not great with big social gatherings. It's worse when I hardly know anyone."

A few guys I recognised as training buddies of Nathan and Wesley crowded around us, forcing me to take a step closer to Justine. She was tall for a girl, much taller than Cassie. She must have been around five ten, just a few inches shorter than my six-foot frame, so I found myself gazing easily into her eyes.

"Is it the bride or groom you know?" I asked.

Breaking eye contact, she replied, "Both. Sort of. Although I'm really here because of—"

"Oh good, you're both here." Cassie joined us at that moment, throwing an arm around Justine and grinning widely. I didn't see Jay. "Adam, this is my best friend and roommate, Justine. Juss, this is Liv's best friend, Adam."

"*The* Adam?" Justine asked, eyes wide.

The Adam? What had Cassie been telling her?

"Yep."

"I guess the gorgeous blond hair, sparkling blue eyes, and cute dimple should have been my clue, huh?" Justine said and then immediately looked away, her cheeks flushing bright red.

Gorgeous blond hair? Sparkling blue eyes? Cute dimple? Shit, they made me sound like some idiot from a romance novel. Scowling, yet feeling strangely elated, I gaped at the two of them, vowing to grill Cassie later about what she'd been saying about me.

"Where have you been?" I asked Cassie, changing the subject.

"Dancing, drinking, laughing... you know, having a good time." She shrugged, swaying to the music played by some up-and-coming local rock band. They were actually pretty good, in a top-forty pop-rock kind of way. Not my typical music of choice.

"Where's the boyfriend?" I asked Cassie, looking around for Jay. He definitely wasn't my typical person of choice. I was a laid-back kind of guy, liked to think of myself as friendly and welcoming. I didn't prejudge and took people at face value until they proved themselves either way. But Jay? I'd taken an instant dislike to him and couldn't hide that fact when I sneered the word *boyfriend*. I hadn't meant to, but the idiot didn't appear to be worthy of Cassie's love.

Her eyes blazed at me fleetingly, apparently not liking my tone. I didn't give a shit.

I'm just looking out for you, Cassie.

"He went to the little guys' room. He'll be back in a minute."

Good, that gave me time to address what I'd witnessed earlier.

"Cass, about earlier. Was he—"

She shot me a warning glare. "Don't, Adam. Just leave it, please."

"But—"

"I said, leave it!"

Justine rapidly flicked confused eyes between the two of us.

"Anyway," Cassie continued, inhaling deeply to regain her jovial composure. "There's my man so I'm off to dance again."

She offered a little wave as she scurried over to where Jay stood like a bouncer on the edge of the dance floor. What was with the guy? Could he not lighten up for just a minute? Did he not want his girlfriend to have a good time? I watched her sidle up next to him and say something close to his ear. His icy gaze remained locked on me, though. I lifted a challenging brow and his face contorted into a sneer. Yeah, we were never gonna be best buds.

"Well, that was awkward," Justine said.

"Yeah." Although *awkward* didn't really describe

how I felt. Angry, frustrated, protective—*what the hell?* Those were better adjectives to describe my feelings at that moment in time. "Shall we take our drinks out onto the terrace?" Now that the alcohol was flowing freely through my veins, I felt a little light-headed and needed air. I also needed to get away from Cassie and Jay before I did something I would regret.

"Sure."

We grabbed fresh drinks and went outside to sit in a quiet corner of the terrace—the corner Cassie had been sitting in with Jay earlier.

Maybe we should sit somewhere else?

Taking a gentle hold of Justine's elbow, I steered us toward the wall surrounding the terrace instead.

"What was that back there?" Justine asked, leaning against the wall, watching the party going on around us.

Ignoring her question, I asked, "How well do you know Jay?"

"Jay? I'm not close to him or anything. Why?"

"I'm worried about Cassie being with him. From what I've seen, the guy is a dick."

She choked on a mouthful of champagne. Laughing, she said, "He's all bark and no bite."

He'd been biting earlier. I scowled at the memory of his fingers digging into Cassie's skin as he led her away.

"It's the fighter pro in him," she continued. "He's a bit of a control freak. He's harmless, though."

I laughed silently, humourlessly. I'd seen the small grimace on her face when his hand was wrapped around her arm. Watched the surge of fear flash in her eyes.

"Are you sure about that?"

She offered a reassuring smile and went on to explain how Cassie had encouraged her to take up kick-boxing with her a year earlier. That was where she first met Jay before he and Cassie became a couple. According to Justine, Jay was a passionate man, dedicated to his training and getting the best out of others. He was fiercely protective of Cassie and would do anything for her. She also admitted that Cassie and Jay's relationship could be a little fiery, but Cassie was no shrinking violet and wouldn't stand for any bullshit from any guy she dated. That sounded like the Cassie I knew, but not the Cassie I'd seen today.

Somewhat appeased by her words, and confused by my own intense need to protect Cassie, I decided to let it go. Cassie already had a group of close friends surrounding her if she did ever need help.

By the time Liv and Nathan were ready to leave to consummate their marriage—I was shocked to realise that it no longer hurt to think of it—Justine and I had spent a couple hours talking and laughing. She told me many hilarious stories of Cassie's antics when they were growing up—apparently they had known each other since the second year of high school—and I hung on every word, soaking it all in. I reciprocated with stories of Liv and me. We didn't discuss Cassie and Jay anymore, but I did keep one eye on them. Things seemed to settle down, and she spent a lot of time with a gentle hand on his chest looking up at him. When they disappeared early, I guessed they were ready for some alone time.

Conversation between Justine and me was easy. We discovered we had a lot in common and were reluctant to separate when the evening came to a close. I was smiling wide when I helped her into the back of a black London taxi. Not because of the hint of thigh I caught as her legs swept inside the vehicle, but because I'd asked for her number with the hope we could meet up for a drink sometime. She'd eagerly agreed.

A day I'd been dreading for months actually turned out okay, in some ways better than okay. And for the first time since I was fifteen, my heart didn't appear to be stubbornly hung up on my feisty best friend.

"JESUS, CASS. GIVE a guy a break will you."

Cassie laughed as I fought to catch my breath on the treadmill several days later. We had what was now considered our ritual battle of will, or rather what my pride didn't want to accept—Cassie beating my arse at whatever we challenged each other to do.

"Come on, big guy, faster, you can do it. No pain, no gain."

I watched aghast as she increased the MPH on her machine and adjusted to the new speed with ease and grace.

"Fuck," I growled, hitting the screen on my treadmill to match her pace. She knew I wouldn't give up the challenge easily.

For such a little thing, Cassie was a machine. I considered myself fit and strong, usually acing any fitness tests the personal trainers occasionally threw my way. Next to her, though, I looked like a bumbling fawn. Where I wheezed and sweated profusely, Cassie barely panted from exertion. A slight sheen of perspiration coating her warm beige skin was the only sure sign the running was more than a gentle stroll.

"Two more minutes," she yelled over the hum of machines around us.

I stole a glance at her from the corner of my eye. Her attention was on a television screen hanging from the ceiling playing a raunchy music video. I nearly missed a step when the corner of her lip twitched into a mischievous smirk. I knew that look. It was the you-better-watch-your-arse look.

I looked down at my screen—one minute thirty. I had this. She was not going to beat me today. I'd wipe that smirk off her face. So, with a smirk of my own, I bravely hit the speed increase button again and went all out. It felt great. My lungs were burning, but I felt alive and victorious.

Until she stole that victory right from under me.

With a strangled yelp, I lost my footing and went flying off the back of the treadmill, nearly ploughing into a mountain of a guy walking behind me.

"Sorry," I apologised through laboured breaths. He wasn't impressed.

With hands on my hips, bent over trying to catch my breath, I looked at Cassie standing by my side. She had her teeth clamped on her bottom lip, trying not to laugh.

"Whoops. I seem to have accidentally hit *your* stop button."

My eyes narrowed. "You *accidentally* hit it?" I wheezed.

She nodded quickly, fluttering her eyelashes in a way that had me wanting to scold her for the dangerous stunt, and hug her for her comedic timing.

"Admit it, it was funny," she said, grinning. "Your

face. It was hysterical."

"Yeah, hilarious."

"Oh come on, grumpy. Time to hit the weights." Her warm hand wrapped around my bicep and urged me to follow her through to the main weight room.

"Maybe I don't want to do weights today," I groused like a whiny child.

"And not continue defining your mighty six-pack?" I grunted when a hand slapped against my abdomen. "I think not."

"I don't know why I bothered coming back to this place. All you do is abuse me," I said as we walked toward the free weights.

"You know you love it." Her bright toothy smile lit up the room.

She wasn't wrong. In all the time I'd been going to Golden Oakes I'd always felt like working out was a chore—well, apart from the occasional meaningless hookup I got out of it. They were always just a way of letting off steam in a different way to punishing myself with cardio or weight routines. They helped me forget for a short while that I felt numb... dead inside.

Since I'd returned and had been working out with Cassie, things felt different. I felt alive, inspired, and eager to please her. It was a strange thing, but our growing friendship meant a lot to me. I wanted to work hard to prove myself to her. I wanted to be worthy of her friendship.

We collected our dumbbell selections—hers lighter, mine much heavier—and found our spot in front of the mirror. With a synchronicity that usually came from training with someone for a long time and not a matter of days, we began our reps, occasionally meeting gazes in the mirror with encouraging smiles and nods.

My biceps, triceps, and lats were burning, fatigued. I'd started my cool down stretches when Cassie moved in front of me. She was picking at the dark nail polish on her tips of her fingers. She looked a little worried.

"Adam, can I ask you something?"

Pulling my arm across my chest for a delightfully painful stretch, I nodded. "Of course."

"I was talking to Justine, and she said you two were hoping to go out. I wanted to ask…."

"Yes?"

She exhaled quickly. "Do you like her? Like—*like* her?"

I dropped my arm and repeated the stretch with the other, watching Cassie in the mirror.

"She seems like a great girl. Why?"

"Are you planning to fuck and fly on her?"

My arm dropped along with my jaw.

"No! Why would you think that?"

"She's sweet and innocent, Adam. She deserves more than that. No woman deserves that level of disrespect."

I sighed, wondering if she recognised her own situation in that statement. "Cass, my intentions towards your friend are nothing but honourable. I promise. I'm just taking her out for a drink. Do you not want me to?"

"No, it's not that." Her arms folded over her chest as she looked at the floor. "I want you to, I really do."

"But you don't trust me?" The truth stung.

Her eyes shot to mine. "No! God no…." Sighing, she softened her posture, offering a warm smile. "I'm not explaining myself very well. I'd be happy to see you with Justine. You are both great people who deserve a whole heap of happiness. It's just that I worry about Juss being too trusting. She's already had her heart broken too many times."

"I'm not planning on breaking any hearts, Cass."

"I know." Her small hand came to rest on my forearm. "Can I be honest with you?" I nodded. "I really like you, Adam. I hope we become great friends. I've not felt this comfortable with anyone—other than the guys, Liv, and Justine—for a long time. Because of that, and knowing what you've been through, I want you to be happy. You deserve the love of a good woman. Someone like Justine."

Any tension that had begun building left me on a deep exhale. Wrapping my arms around Cassie, I pulled her into a hug.

"Thanks, Cass. I'll be good to Justine, I swear. We'll take it one day at a time and see what happens. And I'd like to think we are already great friends." I smiled down on her and brushed a loose strand of hair behind her ear, my fingers remaining in place for a moment too long as our gazes locked. Cassie's lips parted, her sweet breath tickling my chin as I stepped closer.

The clunk of weight hitting the floor nearby broke the moment and we quickly pulled apart, returning our weights to their stands. After a few minutes of completing our cool down stretches in silence, pretending nothing had just transpired between us we grabbed our water bottles and towels and walked toward the locker rooms.

Something had been playing on my mind since the wedding, and I needed to talk to her about it.

I stopped her outside the ladies' locker room with a hand on her shoulder.

"Cass, is everything okay, with you and Jay I mean?"

She stiffened under my touch and refused to meet my eyes. *Strange.*

"Cass?"

"Yeah, everything's fine. We're great. He's great. Nothing to worry about." Her too quick reply was a bright red flag to my already concerned conscience.

"I'm not blind, Cass, I see how he treats you," I said softly.

When I slipped my hand down her arm and rested it over where Jay had been grabbing her, she flinched.

"Does he... is he treating you well?" I sucked in a deep breath; afraid her answer would confirm my suspicions.

She pulled away and took a step back. "Of course he does, he's a great guy."

"But does he treat you how you deserve to be treated? He was a prick towards you at the wedding, Cass." I felt my temper boiling and knew I had no right to judge their relationship. But I couldn't stand by and watch a friend getting hurt, especially when I was beginning to care a great deal for her. I needed the truth. I needed her to open her eyes and see how he was mistreating her.

"You know nothing about him or us! He cares about me," A finger poked into my chest. "Don't you stand there acting all high and mighty. He is good for me and I love him."

I stood tall, not reacting to her obvious evasion. "But you're not really happy are you, Cass?" She didn't seem like the type of person who would willingly be walked over by a guy. I'd seen her get into arguments in the gym just because someone didn't wipe their bench down after them.

All colour in her face drained away and she back away to the locker room door.

"Cass?"

"I'll see you tomorrow," she whispered.

As the door closed behind her, the last visual I had of her was of dull, lifeless eyes. The playful sparkle in them that had first drawn my attention to her in France all those months ago, it was gone.

CHAPTER SIX

Cassie

JUSTINE HELD THICK RED PADS while I threw a series of lightning-fast jabs, hitting the leather with such power she stumbled back a step. I stepped in again, repeating the sequence and adding a right hook, followed by a knee strike and then returned to the jab.

"Jeez, Cass. What's with the killer vibe tonight?" she asked, flexing her arms, holding the pads tighter.

"I don't know what you're talking about." I blew a stray lock of hair out of my eye then stepped in again.

One-two.

One-two.

One-two.

I repeated the hard-hitting punches, following up with a turning kick. Immediately regaining my balance, I hopped forward to repeat the sequence.

I felt great, on fire.

I was also trying to forget. Forget Adam's pleading eyes as he asked me about Jay. Forget the recent anger in Jay's. Forget everything other than kicking arse. Adam was wrong, there was no problem between Jay and me. We were fine.

Justine's face pinched in pain when a particularly brutal kick sent her tumbling onto her arse.

"You know exactly what I'm talking about," she grumbled, standing and rubbing her sore backside. "I'm not Nathan Oakes you know. You need to take it easy on poor little me."

"Taking it easy is for losers," I bantered with a smirk. Bouncing on my feet to keep warm and energised, I kept my arms up in a defensive pose, always prepared for an attack.

Justine repositioned the pads and focused pleading eyes on me. I felt a momentary pang of guilt for possibly hurting my friend. She only came along to support me and for exercise. She wasn't dedicated and passionate about kick-boxing like me. Justine had no intentions of ever competing; she just wanted to train and have fun along the way. Me? Aside from my friends, kick-boxing was my life. I lived it, breathed it. I wanted to be the very best at it.

"Yeah, well I'm more than happy to be a loser. We're not all about to hit the big time with professional fights."

I barked a hard laugh. "I think you have this fight confused with something else."

It was true that if I won my next match, I'd be shot into contention for bigger global fights. For that to be a possibility, I would have to fight the best of the best in the UK. It was a tough ask, but I was prepared to give absolutely everything to realise that dream of fighting in huge arenas.

Launching into another sequence of punches and kicks, I misjudged a landing and stumbled, but quickly regained my stance. Jay's angry voice bellowed across the room, and I fumbled the next kick. I landed heavily and gasped at the sudden pain in my foot.

"Cassie, what the fuck was that?"

Jay weaved through the other students continuing their drills, their attention now on us. Scowling, he stopped in front of me with his arms crossed. It was a pose meant to intimidate and show his authority.

I ignored my smarting ankle and stood tall, defiant. "What did I do?" My stance and power had been perfect. Apart from that last minor mishap, I'd delivered the punches and kicks accurately, and I'd kept my guard up at all times.

"How many times do I have to tell you to watch your left leg?"

"My stance was perfect," I countered, feeling the eyes of everyone in the room on us.

"No, it wasn't. You looked like shit. If you go into your fight like that, you'll be on your arse before you know it."

Jay was known for being tough. He pulled people up on their errors regularly and had no remorse when telling them their techniques needed work. He'd never been rude or nasty about it, though. His feedback was usually constructive and never left me feeling like an imbecile.

"What is your problem?" I seethed under my breath, my voice trembling slightly. His tension and

71

dark, sharp eyes were chipping away at my usual steel resolve.

"My problem is that my big fight potential is sparring like a fucking amateur. For what it's worth, Justine might as well enter." He nodded in her direction. Her eyes widened, you could tell she was uncomfortable being drawn into our argument.

His words were like an icy blast to my ego, freezing my confidence. Jay had always been my cheerleader. He was always praising and offering rewards for things done well, and when things needed improvement, he would calmly go through it with me until I'd perfected it. Recently, though, I'd noticed he'd been picking on the smallest of errors. He'd begun chastising me in front of a room full of people, making me feel small and useless.

"Well, if that's how you feel... fuck the fight. And fuck you." Tugging off my gloves, I threw them at him and turned away quickly, wincing at the pain in my foot. Tears began to burn the backs of my eyes, but I'd be damned if I'd let him see how much he had upset me.

Keeping my head held high, I ignored the shocked faces of my peers and rushed across the room. I needed to get out of there.

I shoved the door open and steamed through it.

"Whoa! Where's the fire?"

I barrelled into a firm chest, and looked up into a pair of bright blue eyes and a comforting wide smile. "Adam!" I breathed in a rush of air,

His strong hands gently gripped my shoulders, steadying me. An immediate calm settled over me.

"What's the rush?"

"Nothing, I just—"

His eyes searched mine, and his smile faded. "Cass, what's wrong?"

Looking over my shoulder, he peered through the small glass window in the door. Even without being able to see what he did, I knew who he was watching. The same frown he'd worn at the wedding when Jay was a dick wrinkled his forehead.

"I just... I need to get out of here."

"Cass—"

"I'm alright, Adam, honestly." I pulled out of his hold and stepped away, plastering on a fake smile.

"What did he do?" Adam asked, his voice gruff.

I edged away. "Nothing."

"Cass—"

"Nothing's wrong, Adam. I hurt my ankle, that's all. I just need to ice it. I'll see you later."

Before I even managed a few steps, he reached out for my hand. I stopped walking. "As long as you're alright." He stepped in front of me, frowning, he looked down at my feet. "Make sure you get your ankle looked at. I hate the thought of you being in pain."

I softened at his sweet words. "That's sweet of you, but I'm alright, no significant injury. You know me, clumsy arse. I fall over fresh air."

He chuckled, but the crease above his brows remained. I could tell he wasn't convinced; he was concerned. It was wasted emotion because everything was fine. Yes, maybe Jay should tone down his public admonitions. But I also needed to stop being so sensitive to his criticism and be more understanding of his need to push for perfection.

"Will you be here tomorrow?" I asked.

He nodded. "Yeah, I'll be here. But I wanted to ask, are you closing tonight? That's why I came by, to see if you needed me to stay."

A strange warmth cloaked me, melting away the last of my anger and frustration. He was always so caring and thoughtful.

"No, thank you, but it's fine. Wes is here."

He briefly looked disappointed but then released my hands and stepped away. "Okay. Have a good night, Cass."

"You, too, Adam. And thanks."

As I turned to walk toward the staff room to grab my things, I stole a quick look over my shoulder. Adam rested a shoulder against the wall, watching me. I couldn't help but compare him to Jay. After all, what girl wouldn't notice and compare a sweet, handsome, and compassionate guy to a dude who was easy to look at but blew hot and cold? If things worked out for them, Justine was going to be a very lucky girl.

So why did that thought piss me off so much?

A couple hours later, my anger at Jay had subsided and I was indulging in a *Notting Hill*, chocolate, and wine binge while icing my aching foot. Jay wouldn't approve of the wasted calories but stuff him. I didn't care. I was my own person, and if I wanted a little stress relief in the form of comfort food and alcohol, then I would damn well have it. He didn't control me.

A strange scraping noise coming from the hallway abruptly pulled me from my slightly fuzzy, somewhat sugared-out daze. The sound grew louder and was followed by a loud bang and a muttered curse. My heart began to pound erratically in my chest. I'd always thought that if some idiot were stupid enough to try and break in, I would unleash the Cassie-hound on them. However, when faced with that very possibility, my limbs froze.

I briefly considered that Justine had returned home drunk and was fumbling around. That thought instantly vanished when I remembered the text I'd received from her earlier saying she'd been called in to cover a shift at the hospital where she worked as a nurse. She wouldn't be home until the morning.

The only other person with a key was my mother. But if it were her, she would have walked in calling my name, announcing her arrival. She had once walked in on me with an ex, and it hadn't been pretty. We'd been in a compromising position on the couch, still fully dressed, thankfully, but things had been close to turning x-rated. It had been such a shock to Mum's prissy self that she was now always cautious when letting herself into my home. At the time—and at any opportunity since—she'd given me the third degree and lectured me about sex before marriage and not choosing my partners wisely. According to my mother, ladies should remain celibate until they were in a long-term, committed relationship. Waiting until my wedding night would have been preferable. It was always the same with her: she wanted me to live the same stuffy high-society life she'd slithered her way into. The thing was, my mother was full of double standards.

The creaking of floorboards and heavy tap-tap of footsteps told me my visitor definitely wasn't my elegant, petite mother. That meant only one thing: I had an intruder.

With shaking hands, I grabbed my phone from the end of the couch. My finger was poised to hit 999 when a silhouetted figure appeared in the living room doorway. My body trembled against the dark eyes that shone almost demonically in the low glow of the television. They stared straight at me.

"You need to get that fucking door looked at, Cassie. Any idiot could easily force their way in."

My phone fell from my hands. The fear I'd been feeling instantly dissolved into a strange concoction of relief and anger.

Jumping up, I placed a hand over my pounding heart and glared at my boyfriend. "Jesus Christ, Jay, you scared the fucking shit out of me. And how the hell did you get in?"

He sauntered further into the room and placed a bag on the coffee table. He then turned to hand me a large bunch of white roses.

"Like I said, you need to get that door looked at. It wasn't latched properly. It easily opened when I pushed."

"Why were you pushing? You didn't even knock."

He shrugged. "I did knock." He did? I hadn't heard anything. "Anyway, if you'd just let me have a key, I could just let myself in with no problems."

"Or you could've knocked again or maybe phoned," I muttered under my breath.

Ignoring me, he shoved the flowers toward me again, his lips pulling into a grim line of agitation. "Just take the damn flowers, Cassie."

Still pissed off, I took the blooms and offered a weak, "Thanks for these. I'll put them in a vase," while adding, *Call the locksmith... again,* to my mental to-do list.

In the kitchen, I took out a tall glass vase and filled it with water. My mind raced with conflicted thoughts. I was glad to see Jay. After the way I'd stormed out on him earlier, I knew we needed to talk and clear the air. But the stab of hurt was still there, still too fresh. I needed a little time and space to regroup and compartmentalise his cruel words.

Jay's thick arms that were covered in sleeves of colourful artwork slipped around my waist, pulling me back against his warm, solid chest.

"Are you mad at me?" he asked, kissing along my exposed neck.

I stiffened under his touch. I wasn't going to forgive him that easily. "You upset me, Jay."

"I know." He hooked a finger under the spaghetti strap of my vest top and slowly eased it over my shoulders and down my arm. "I'm sorry."

"Am I really doing things that badly? Am I really that crappy?" I hated that my shaky voice betrayed the insecurity he'd awakened in me.

He threaded his fingers through mine, easing the death grip I had on the edge of the counter.

"There's always room for improvement, no matter what level you're at."

"Did you really need to humiliate in front of everyone, though?"

He shifted me around to face him, our hands still entwined between us.

"Cass, you need to stop being so sensitive. That wasn't humiliation. I was simply pointing out your errors to help you improve. If I don't push, you'll have no hope of winning your fight."

I sighed and dropped my head forward, not wanting to meet his gaze. I couldn't agree with him, not on this. There were ways of telling someone they were shit and needed to improve, and yelling at them in front of a room full of people was not it. Plus he was my boyfriend. He was supposed to care about and encourage me.

I thought back to recent weeks when he'd been anything but caring and encouraging. If anything he had been harsh and angry. I had to believe that his behaviour was all part of his plans for preparing me for the fight.

"I hope you're hungry. I brought food with me." He eased his hands beneath the hem of my top and caressed the skin of my lower back with his thumbs.

"I could eat something," I breathed as I shivered. He knew the exact spot to stroke to get a reaction. All I'd eaten since lunch was a few squares of chocolate, my appetite having disappeared after our argument at the studio.

We ended up sitting cross-legged facing each other on the floor eating Thai food from the coffee table.

Throughout the meal, we exchanged small talk about the club and my training schedule. Despite our seemingly *ordinary* interactions, I was still on edge. Something sat heavily at the back of my mind, preventing me from relaxing with him completely.

During a break in conversation, I noticed him studying me over the rim of his glass. His eyes were dark, assessing, and his head tipped to the side.

"What?" I asked, fidgeting under his scrutiny.

"You know, you really are a very attractive woman."

I cleared my throat, surprised by his out-of-the-blue compliment "Thank you."

"I'm a lucky guy."

Smiling weakly, I reached for his empty plate. "And I'm a lucky girl."

He placed his glass on the table and leant back onto his hands. Looking up, his eyes tore straight through me in a look that said he wasn't aiming for sweetness and light. "And don't you ever forget that. You're mine, Cassie."

A dark feeling of foreboding seeped into my being. I'd known Jay for a few years and never in our interactions outside of the studio had he been so domineering. Jay was the kind of guy who took his art seriously and demanded absolute focus and dedication from his students. Away from all things kick-boxing, he was someone I could easily talk to without fear of judgement or any form of derision or ridicule.

Or he had been. This new side to him confounded me.

"You know I am."

"All mine."

Frowning, I studied his eyes, hoping to see into his soul for an idea of where this was all coming from. "What's this about, Jay?"

"I just wanted to be sure you knew who you belonged to."

"Excuse me?"

"You heard."

I bristled. Who did he think he was? The only person I belonged to was me.

"I'm not an object or possession, Jay."

"To me you are. You're my possession."

His words halted me from retreating out of the room. I turned back abruptly.

"What are you trying to say?"

He stood, moving like a tiger about to corner its prey "I'm saying you seem to be spending a lot of time with that Adam guy. I don't want him getting any ideas. Or you."

"It's not like that between us. Adam's just a friend."

"Does he know that?"

"Of course, he does," I snapped. "He's going on a date with Justine, for God's sake."

He crouched so we were eye to eye. "That means nothing. He's a guy. Guys dick around. It's a well-known fact."

I swallowed, hitting the wall as I took a step away from his menacing stare. "You?"

"What do you think?"

"I like to believe you wouldn't do that to me."

He nodded but didn't reply.

We continued staring at each other for many seconds. My nerves tightened and twisted with increasing apprehension at the darkness in his eyes. Eventually, he stepped back, taking a seat on the couch.

"Do the dishes then come and join me," he said casually, patting the cushion beside him.

In the kitchen, I rinsed the plates and stacked them in the dishwasher. My hands shook under the towel I dried my hands on. Jay's behaviour was becoming more and more unpredictable. One minute he was the friendly guy I'd met through the club. That guy I respected, cared for. The Jay that seemed to be slowly emerging was arrogant, self-centred, and somebody I didn't recognise.

Leaning against the wall, I rested my head back and stared up at the ceiling. Adam seemed sure Jay had issues. He'd challenged me on it a few times, but I refused to admit anything was wrong. As strong and independent as I liked to believe myself to be, I needed Jay. I loved him and had to believe this strange new side was merely him projecting unknown stresses onto me. There was something deeper going on with him that he wasn't telling me.

"What are you doing in there, Cass? Bring me in a drink, would you," he shouted from the living room.

My head dropped forward as I let out a silent groan of frustration. Whatever was going on with Jay, I still needed to be me. I couldn't allow his moods to change who I was.

"Coming," I called out, reaching into the fridge for a beer for him and a bottle of water for me.

In the living room, Jay had switched over from the movie channel to a UFC fight rerun. I tried to ignore the stab of irritation at his inconsiderate actions.

"You took your time," he said, taking the bottle from me without looking away from the TV.

I dropped onto the opposite end of the brown leather couch and curled my legs beneath me. Absently playing with the silver lily pendant on the chain around my neck, I snuggled into the corner and stared at the TV. For the first time ever, I felt no thrill of excitement from watching the guys on screen performing their art to perfection. In fact, I barely noticed the programme at all. All my thoughts were on Jay and why he seemed to have suddenly changed.

"Cat got your tongue?"

Looking at him out of the corner of my eye, I considered questioning him about his recent attitude. Then I remembered the cold darkness in his eyes earlier and thought better of it. I wasn't in the mood for another argument.

"I'm just tired."

"Then let's go to bed."

"What? You're staying?"

Jay switched off the TV and stood, reaching for my hand. "Of course, I'm staying."

Taking his hand, I let him pull me up. "But... I'm..."

He swept hair from my shoulder, grazing my bared flesh with his fingertips. "Come on, Cass, I've had a busy, stressful day, I need to bury myself in you and forget everything else for a while."

He led me through the living room and up the stairs to my bedroom. Inside, he closed the door behind us and kicked his shoes off. I stood awkwardly by the side of the bed. Sex with him at that moment didn't feel right. Tensions were running too high, and I had unresolved questions I needed answers to.

"As cute as that little outfit is"—he jerked his head in the direction of my grey jersey sleep shorts and white camisole top—"I'd prefer you out of them. Strip for me, Cass, and then get on the bed," he said as he began stripping his own clothes off.

I frowned. Unlike our previous times together, Jay offered no gentle caresses, no sweet-talking or seductive removal of each others' clothing. He watched, waiting for me to comply.

"I'm sorry, Jay, but I'm not in the mood for this. Tonight has been one almighty shit storm of emotions."

Ignoring me, dark eyes glared into mine. "Your clothes, Cassie, take them off. Now."

Wrapping my arms around myself, I snapped. "What the hell has got into you? You're being an arse." Finally, my inner confidence spoke up.

"There's no need to yell," he growled. "What's so wrong with me wanting to see my girlfriend naked in her bed?" He walked over to where I'd moved to lean against the wall—as far away from Jay as I could get without jumping from the window. His hands gripped my hips, tugging me forward so our bodies were pressed close together.

"I want you," he whispered in my ear, taking my hand and pressing it against his growing erection. His hand trailed around to my buttocks and squeezed. "I need to be inside you, Cassie. I need to feel you squeezing me, calling out my name...."

With each lust-filled word, my resistance faded away. He was so close I could feel every breath tickling my now sensitive skin. The masculine scents of his soap and cologne wafted around us. His fingertips eased beneath the hem of my shorts and teased the elastic edge of my underwear. I shuddered and squirmed with need as he deliberately kept his touch a hairsbreadth away from my core that begged for attention.

"Just say the word, Cass, and it's all yours." He moved my hand and pressed his rock-hard dick against my tummy.

"Jay," I breathed, arching my back, my body's desire to be pleasured betraying my mind's need to remain defiant and in control.

"Do you want me, babe? Do you want me to take it all away and make you feel good?"

I didn't want to want him; I was too annoyed and confused. However, when he started hitching up my top with one hand, the other pulling down the waistband of my shorts in search of my centre, I couldn't deny the uncontrollable gasp or the quickening of my pulse.

"Yes." My one-word response came out desperate, a husky whisper. Now free of my clothing, Jay's fingers lightly skimmed back and forth over my exposed breasts, cupping and squeezing them to drive me wild with desire. "You're mine, Cassie... These are mine." His voice was low, husky and seductive as he pinched a nipple, rolling it between his thumb and forefinger. "And this is mine." I gasped, not completely prepared for the sudden invasion of the two fingers that pushed inside me.

"You are mine, Cassandra. Completely. Utterly. Unquestionably."

I felt dizzy from the swirl of sensations and emotions. Mostly, I felt frozen, pulled under Jay's spell. Thoughts of anger vanished. All I could concentrate on was his voice in my ear, his fingers doing delicious things to me and the voice in my head saying, *Now, Jay, please, take me now.*

"Tell me you're mine. That I can have you right now." The warmth of his lips left a blazing trail along my throat.

Cocooned in his cleverly woven web of seduction, I melted into his touch. "I'm yours, Jay."

"Good girl."

Suddenly his hands were gone, leaving me bereft

and needing more. He lifted me from the floor, and with my legs wrapped around his hips, he carried me to the bed. My body writhed against his, begging as he kissed and licked his way up my body. I was on fire. Needed more.

My voice sounded alien, moaning a garbled version of "Please, I want you."

He quickly shed the last of his clothing and crawled along the bed until he was braced over me. Gazing into my eyes, he sank himself deep inside me in one hard, deliberate thrust.

I gasped at the sudden fullness and tiny bite of discomfort from not being completely ready for him and then relaxed into the feeling.

His dark, stormy eyes remained locked on mine demanding my total focus while he continued pounding his pleasure into me. I gripped his biceps and lifted my hips desperately seeking the peak of sensation I hoped was only a breath away. Then, with a deep guttural groan, Jay pushed hard one final time burying himself deep as he pulsed and tensed, emptying himself into my body. Marking me as his.

Several silent minutes later, Jay finally lifted his muscular body from mine and dropped onto his back, his breaths slowing from exertion.

With the intensity of the moment gone, I realised that he'd expertly played the role of master manipulator. He'd seduced me into giving him what he wanted without any care for my needs. He'd taken me to bed knowing there would only ever be one of us reaching ultimate pleasure. It left me feeling used and dirty.

Disgusted with myself for falling for his games, I

scrambled from the bed and ran to the bathroom. Jay didn't so much as lift his arm from its resting place over his eyes.

Shutting and locking the door behind me, I slid down the wall and rested my head against my knees. Tears of anger and another unfamiliar emotion welled in my eyes. I sat there for a long time with unwanted thoughts and memories tumbling around inside my head.

Eventually, I pulled myself up and walked to the shower, setting the temperature to max. I turned and stared at my reflection in the mirror while the water heated. The girl looking back at me wasn't the same girl who would never have let a guy use her like Jay had. This girl had a new sadness clouding her once bright eyes.

After a scalding hot shower, I dried off and wrapped myself in my fluffy robe. I needed the comfort of its softness and warmth. In the bedroom, Jay had fallen asleep, his naked body tangled in the covers as he gently snored. At that moment, I couldn't stand to be near him, so I grabbed a blanket and pillow from the closet and headed downstairs, careful not to wake him.

Lying on the couch, I felt a bone deep cold despite the humid summer night air. I wrapped the blanket around me and curled into a ball, hoping sleep would quickly find me.

Several hours later I was still wide awake staring into the unlit fireplace. All I could think about were the recent changes I'd noticed in Jay. And then I thought about Adam again and how different he was. I wondered if maybe at another time, in different circumstances, we could have been together. He was certainly the type of guy any woman would dream of being involved with.

My phone vibrated on the coffee table, startling me. I glanced at the screen and saw a text message notification from Adam.

With my wayward and confused thoughts about him, I knew I shouldn't have opened the message. It was late, and he probably wouldn't be expecting an immediate reply. Whatever he wanted could no doubt wait until the morning. Couldn't it? Then I thought about Jay. He'd made it perfectly clear that he didn't approve of my friendship with Adam.

My eyes darted to the stairs, checking for signs of life on the first floor. Before I knew what I was doing, I'd grabbed the phone and pressed my thumb on the sensor to unlock it. I pulled up his message.

Adam: Just wanted to make sure u r ok. Hope I didn't upset u earlier

Falling back against the cushions, I wrapped the blanket around me and replied.

Cassie: I'm good. Don't worry. You didn't upset me

Adam: Thank God! I was so worried. U r up late

Cassie: So are you ;)

Adam: Couldn't sleep

Cassie: Me neither

Adam: Want to talk about it?

Cassie: Nothing to talk about

Adam: That's not good. I need u to bore me to death with your usual chatter so I can get to sleep

I chuckled and tapped out a quick reply.

Cassie: Oi! Cheeky bastard. What is that supposed to mean?
Adam: Lol! Nothing
Cassie: Adam!
Adam: Cassie

We continued firing friendly banter back and forth for nearly an hour. By the time we'd said goodnight, my eyes were drooping, and I had a smile on my face. I finally fell asleep with my phone cradled against my chest and images of Adam laughing in my mind.

"WAKEY, WAKEY, SLEEPING beauty."

I groaned, burying my throbbing head into the pillows. "Get out, Juss, it's too early."

Snickering, she moved around my room. "It's nearly ten, Cass."

My eyes flew open. I immediately regretted the impulsive action when bright sunlight shone through the large bay window.

"Shit! Jesus Christ, Juss! Are you trying to blind me?"

"Nope. Just bringing you into the land of the living." She paused a moment and then dropped onto the end of the couch, pushing my legs out of her way. "Why are you sleeping down here? Did you have an accident in the bed or something?"

Or something.

Sitting up, I stretched my arms over my head, moaning at the delightful pull on my aching muscles.

"I didn't want to sleep in my bed last night."

"Why?"

What did I tell her? That Jay hurt me the night

before, so much so that I couldn't bear to sleep next to him. That Adam's concerns about Jay's behaviour were starting to have an impact. That I didn't want to believe Jay was becoming anything other than the caring guy I'd always known. That the text conversation with Adam brought the first genuine smile to my face in several days. Or that I fell asleep thinking about him.

I shrugged and untangled myself from the blankets.

"Jay was snoring." That at least was the truth.

She nodded as if she could well believe it and stood. "Can I get you a coffee?"

I smiled. "That would be great."

While Justine worked in the kitchen, I folded the blanket. I thought about going up to my room to see if Jay was still there but I didn't know what I'd say to him if he were.

"So," Justine said, placing a steaming mug of coffee in my hand. "What did you guys get up to last night? Should I be grateful I was working so I didn't have to listen to the endless sounds of hot and heavy make-up sex?"

If only.

Noticing my lack of response, the smile on her face disappeared. "Cass, what's wrong?"

I cradled the mug in both hands and lifted it toward my lips. "Nothing."

"Don't do that. Don't freeze me out."

My mouth opened to protest, but she held up a hand, halting my words.

"You forget I know you better than anyone. We've been friends most of our lives, Cass. I can tell when something's troubling you."

I sipped on my coffee and stared at the blank TV screen. "I'm fine, honestly."

"Does this have anything to do with Jay?" She curled into the armchair, staring at me expectantly.

"Why do you ask that?"

She shrugged. "I dunno, it's just... there's something different about him recently."

"Different?"

"The sudden possessiveness and disparaging comments. And what's with the flirting with Bianca?"

That got my attention. My eyes shot to hers. "What flirting?"

"Oh come on. Don't tell me you haven't seen the little looks between them, the flirty touches."

"No. He's training her like me. Of course, he's going to have to touch her."

She rolled her eyes. "Don't be so naïve, Cassie. Those aren't innocent touches. He flirts with her all the time. There's something going on with those two, I'm sure of it."

"You're wrong. He cares about me; he wouldn't cheat," I insisted, but my words were void of any conviction.

"Maybe in his own way he does care. But, Cassie, you need to open your eyes and see how he's changing. And, most importantly how you're changing because of him."

"What the hell is that supposed to mean? I'm still me. I haven't changed."

She sighed. "You're in denial. You're holding on to the ideal guy you respect for his kick-boxing achievements, and not the everyday guy who is happy to manipulate and abuse you."

I stood and walked toward the door, seething. "You're wrong. And I'm not talking about this anymore."

Her words were a bitter blow. Deep down I knew there was some truth to them, but I refused to acknowledge it.

"Cass, wait! Please. I'm sorry. Don't go. Let's talk about something else."

I paused in the doorway, and my head fell forward. I nodded. "Okay. What do you want to talk about?"

"It's on."

"What is?"

Her smile was broad and excited when I turned around.

"My date with Adam. We're meeting for drinks on Friday."

"That's great, Juss... I should go and see if Jay's still in bed."

Walking upstairs, I felt guilty for not joining in my friend's excitement, but at that moment, a strange numbness consumed me. Justine had opened a Pandora's box for me to deal with and I didn't know where to begin. Maybe it would be easier to just close the lid and ignore the nastiness floating around me.

I grabbed the door handle, unsure what I wanted to find on the other side. Part of me wanted Jay to be there in my bed, still snoring gently. He'd smile when he woke and saw me and show me that these growing fears about him were unwarranted. The other part of me wanted him gone so I could be alone.

As the door swung open, I breathed a sigh of relief... Jay wasn't there.

CHAPTER SEVEN

Adam

I HATED TUESDAYS. THEY WERE a bit like being sucked into a vortex that held you in a constant state of limbo for twenty-four hours. On Monday mornings, I knew it was only the beginning. I would mentally stand taller, my stance hard and ready to battle on with the week ahead. On Friday mornings, I knew I'd be escaping in a matter of hours. I'd push on through the day while thinking about the evening and weekend ahead. I had something to look forward to. Even Wednesdays could boast the title of the halfway mark. Tuesdays offered nothing more than a dull afternoon meeting with the senior execs. If I could skip Tuesdays, I would.

This particular Tuesday was no different, and I didn't even have Liv around to pull funny faces at during the meeting.

My father was going around the table checking the status of the projects of our biggest clients, and then droning on about profits, competitors, new clients... the usual crap. When Harry and his monotone voice pulled out a ream of paper to give the low-down on the Haversham contract, I completely switched off.

Turning my attention to the window, I forgot about Harry and allowed my thoughts to drift to the women in my life. Olivia would be back from her honeymoon soon, and I felt a little apprehensive about that. She was a married lady now, and I wasn't ashamed to admit that I feared how that would affect our friendship. No matter what path life took us along, I knew that I needed her. She had no problem calling me out on my crap, believed in me, and always lifted me when my spirits were floating around sewer level.

Above all, Liv always knew the right thing to do. I wondered what she'd do or say when she discovered that Jay wasn't the gentleman to Cassie they all believed him to be. I could see it, the darkness in him. But I didn't know how to talk to Cassie without pushing her away. It was evident she didn't see it—or refused to see it. My biggest fear was what he could be capable of. He was a strong guy, and Cassie was tiny. For all her smart mouth and sass, she was still petite. In many ways she was vulnerable. She liked to appear cocky and self-assured, but there was a sadness hidden in the depths of her brown eyes. I hoped one day she would trust me enough to open up and spill her secrets.

I wondered if I should see if Justine could help me work out what was going on. She'd been working a lot recently and was finally getting a day off. That meant we were going out for a meal Friday evening, and I planned to talk to her about Cassie and Jay.

"Adam! Get you head out of your arse and concentrate." Chuckles echoed around the room at my father's impatient outburst.

I cleared my throat and met his gaze. "Sorry."

"You know, if you can't cut it in your position, I could always put you in the mail room."

There were more titters and even a few blatant laughs as I glared at the old man. I'd never wanted to hit my father until that moment. It took every effort to stop myself from rushing at him with my fists flying.

"What did you want?" I asked, shortly.

"I *want* you to listen and concentrate. I *want* you to tell me you are finished with the Tresdell building contract. I *want* you to do the bloody job I pay you for."

I clenched my fists into tight balls beneath the table as my anger reached boiling point.

"The Tresdell plans *are* finished, we'll be signing them off tomorrow. I'm ahead with the Brightmann project, and Mrs Harvey is pleased with what I've come up with so far. I think it's safe to say I'm doing my *bloody job*."

I pushed my chair back with force and stood. I couldn't sit there for another minute staring at the face of the man I loathed. If he pushed, I was likely to fall over the edge yelling things no son should ever say to their father.

"Sit back down, Adam."

"You've got what you needed from me," I said, yanking the door open. "Now I'm getting back to do the job you pay me for."

In my office, I sank into my chair with my head in my hands. Why did he always make me feel like the naughty little boy caught stealing sweets from the jar? This career had always been his dream for me, not mine. Growing up, all we ever heard was how his sons would follow in his footsteps and one day take over the business. I'd had other dreams. I'd wanted to work outside, maybe owning an outdoor activities centre. That was what I loved, being a part of nature, physical activities; there was nothing better. Liv often joked I'd been born in the wrong place. She thought my blond hair, blue eyes, and lean body gave me the perfect surfer boy look and therefore I should have been in California or Bondi Beach.

Instead of following my dreams, I'd played the dutiful son and studied architecture at Cambridge. Just as he'd wanted. I'd been working my nuts off since to try to impress him. All I wanted to do was make him proud. I think I finally understood that was never going to happen. Why would he feel proud when it was what he expected?

I looked up when my door flew open.

"What was that in there, Adam?" My father demanded, marching into the room.

"I could you ask the same thing."

"How dare you disrespect me in front of those people? You may be my son, but you are also an employee, Adam. I expect respect, manners, and professionalism at all times."

Slamming my palms flat on the desk, I shot to my feet glaring at him. "And what about giving me respect, manners, and professionalism?"

"You have to earn it," he replied matter-of-factly.

"I have to earn it? What the hell, Dad? I have done nothing but work hard for your respect since I was little. You can't do it, though, can you? You can't acknowledge what I've given up to be the person you want me to be, to follow your dream."

He barked a sharp laugh. "What you've given up? Where would you be if it weren't for me? Living in a cold, dark cabin surrounded by kids sent to you because their parents and schools want a break from them? That's your dream? For God's sake, Adam, when will you see this career is stable, respected, and gives you life's luxuries? It's a *career*, not a bloody hobby."

I met his glare. "If it meant I was happy, I'd gladly give it all up!"

"Why don't you then?"

This was when he knew he had me. No matter how frustrated I became with my life, he was aware that my family loyalties would always come first. My grandfather founded the company in the 1970s and worked hard to build it into a highly respected business. His hopes had also been for my older brother, Caleb, and me to join the family business one day. The difference between my grandfather and father was in their expectations and hopes. My dad expected it, my grandfather hoped for it. I'd promised my grandfather on his deathbed that I would one day join the company and work my way to the top. I'd only been fourteen at the time and had no idea what I wanted to do with my life. But I'd always held on to that promise made to a man I loved and respected.

"You know I won't," I said.

Defeated, I retook my seat.

A triumphant smirk pulled at his lips. "That's what I thought. Anyway, the main reason I'm here is that you mother is complaining that she hasn't seen you. Give her a call." And with that, he turned and strode out.

Slamming my eyes shut, I leant back, scraping my hands through my hair. Gripping a handful, I inhaled a few deep breaths, exhaling them slowly, purposely.

Fuck him.

Fuck him and his high-handed, obnoxious attitude.

Fuck overbearing parents who think they can control your life.

My temper had somewhat subsided when my phone started ringing.

"What?" I barked.

"You always answer like that, little bro?" Caleb laughed down the line.

"Of course I do, it's so professional," I replied wryly. "What do you want, Caleb? I'm trying to work here."

"No, you're not."

"Yes, I am."

"Not."

"Am."

"See, you're not. You're arguing with me. You're not even doing a very good job of it."

As much as I wanted to hold on to my father-induced anger, Caleb could always ground me with a few witty phrases or a well-timed gag.

My head shook in amusement. "What can I help you with, Caleb?"

"I'm bored."

"And?"

"And I want you to come out and play."

"What, are we six again?"

"You're the one whining like a six-year-old. And what's wrong with being six again anyway? They were the best years of my life. If I remember right, I got to kiss Abigail Smith in her Wendy house when I was six."

I chuckled. "Once a player, always a player."

"Hey, I'm a happily married man now."

"So you say."

"Listen, I would love to stick around and chat about the delights of having a great woman— something you wouldn't know about—but we're losing vital drinking time. Why are you still there?"

I twisted my chair round and looked out of the window at the bustling London street below. "Um, I believe I told you I'm working."

"And I said you're not. I bet you don't even have your computer on." I looked over at my screen, and as he'd predicted it was black. "You're finishing for the day and coming out with me. I'll see you down at the Fox in thirty."

That was my brother; he could never take no for an answer. I was sure that was the only reason his wife Rachael finally agreed to marry his sorry arse. She probably eventually grew sick of his whining and said yes just to shut him up.

Checking my calendar for appointments, the first thing I noticed was the highlighted event showing Liv's return date the next week. I missed her. The place had been quiet without her around. And right then, I needed her to vent my frustrations on. Instead,

I made the decision to stick the middle finger up to my father and join my brother for a few beers.

I SPOTTED CALEB the moment I stepped into the pub. It wasn't quite five o'clock yet so the place was still reasonably empty. Even if it had been packed, it would have been near on impossible to not notice my brother standing at the bar. Caleb was different to me in so many ways. He had an imposing presence that was hard to ignore. Where I stood at a decent six foot with a lean, athletic physique, Caleb's six-five, muscular frame towered over people. His jet-black hair was in stark contrast to the golden blond I'd inherited from our mother. Even our eye colours differed—mine were a dark sapphire blue, his were honey brown. The only similarities between the two of us were the trademark Ashworth strong jawline and the way we both liked to keep our hair just slightly too long with that just-got-out-of-bed appearance. In Caleb's teenage years his style usually was because he was just falling out of bed and had no time for grooming. Times hadn't changed much.

"Yo! Little bro, you made it," Caleb bellowed, spotting me in the doorway.

"What's the emergency?" I asked, taking the beer he held out as I approached.

"Rach is out of town. She's taken the rug rats to see her parents for a few days. I thought I'd take the opportunity to catch up with my little brother." He gestured toward a nearby table with the neck of his bottle. "Shall we sit?"

"So what you're saying is, you have no one to cook

for you and you're too much of a pussy to stay home alone."

"Fuck you, little man."

I laughed pulling out a chair. "How are Rach and the kids?"

His face broke out into a beaming smile. For all his faults, Caleb was a fantastic father and husband. He loved his wife and kids more than anything. I sometimes envied what he had. He'd stood up to our father and refused to have anything to do with the family business. He followed his dreams and trained as a firefighter and was slowly making his way up the ranks. Despite being regularly told that he was being cut from any future inheritance, Caleb continued to profess he'd done the right thing. If only I had been as strong. The nerves and fear for his safety were always there, but I totally respected and admired him. He put his life at risk on a daily basis trying to protect society and their possessions. I designed their fancy new home after the first had been destroyed. There was no comparison. I was no hero. I didn't run into burning buildings to save people.

"They're great. Bobby won a drawing competition at the nursery last week, and Izzy is now running around keeping Rach and me on our toes." He shook his head, laughing at his seventeen-month-old daughter's antics.

"So Bob's inherited the Ashworth creative gene, huh?" I joked.

"Don't let it go to your head." He playfully punched my arm. "He'll follow in his old man's footsteps, mark my words."

"That's not always a good thing," I grumbled.

The smile melted from Caleb's face. "Is Dad still acting like an arse?"

I took a swig of my beer and stared across the room for a moment. "It feels like no matter what I do or say, it's never good enough," I admitted. "He uses every opportunity to cut me down in front of the others."

"So get out. Screw him, Adam. You don't owe him anything."

Shaking my head, I said, "I owe him."

Caleb's bottle crashed loudly against the table. "Jesus, Adam. You really believe that?" I shrugged. "That man has one agenda: money and power. He doesn't care about whom he hurts or manipulates, as long as they're following his plan."

I couldn't deny it. My father had always been focused and career driven, and I'd seen his ruthless nature more than once.

"He put me through university, Cal. Do you have any idea how much a Cambridge education costs?"

"But at what cost to you?"

"Can we not talk about this anymore?" I said, standing abruptly. The conversation was digging into my already fragile soul. "Do you want another drink?"

His expression softened as he placed a hand on my arm. "I just want to see you happy, Ad."

"Who says I'm not?"

When I returned to the table with refills, Cal had my phone in his hand.

"Who's Cassie?" he asked with a wide grin. "She sent you a text. Is she hot?"

I snatched the phone from him. "She's a friend."

"Uh-huh." He snatched the phone back, swiping

his finger across the screen. "And you're supposed to be seeing her tonight?"

"I see her most nights," I said stretching for the phone, but he held it just out of reach as he gawped at the screen.

'Looking forward to kicking your butt tonight. Be prepared," he mimicked in a singsong voice, reading Cassie's text out loud. "She sounds like a right catch." He laughed.

Giving up on retrieving the phone, I slunk back on my chair with my beer. "She's a friend of Liv's. She works at the gym so we've been training together recently."

"Speaking of Liv…." Slowly his brow furrowed into a frown, his eyes lifting to meet mine. "Please tell me you're not still hung up on her." He turned the phone around to show me the photo gallery. I didn't need to see it, though; I knew there were a lot of pictures of Liv on there. As friends, we had a lot of memories catalogued on the small device.

"Adam, she's married," he murmured.

"You don't think I know that?" My hand shot out for the phone and this time he let it go.

"Man, you have to let her go."

"I never had her to let go of." I tucked the phone into my pocket.

"But you've always loved her." It wasn't a question. "You were never going to be anything more than friends. You have to know that. She was always so strong-willed and feisty. You're too sensitive. You're like chalk and cheese."

"You make me sound like a goddamned pansy."

He shook his head. "No, you just need to find the

right woman to compliment and complete you."

"Now you sound like the pansy."

I ducked away from the flying beer mat he hurled at me. "When did you last risk your heart to go on a date that didn't involve getting horizontal and exchanging bodily fluids?"

"I have one this Friday actually," I said, rolling my eyes.

"Really?" His eyes lit up. "Tell me more."

"Jesus, Cal. You sure you're not growing a vagina? You sound like a girl."

"Fuck off!" He growled a deliberately deep and gritty sound.

I paused a moment, thinking about Justine.

"She's a friend of Cassie's, we met at Liv's wedding...."

We spent the next couple of hours catching up and ridiculing each other's football teams. I told him what I knew about Justine, and about Cassie; how athletic and smart she was, how good she was at kick-boxing, and how easy it was to talk to her. I briefly explained how we'd first met in France and that we'd enjoyed each other's company even then. I didn't tell him just how much we'd ended up enjoying each other that one night.

"Are you sure you're going out with the right girl on Friday?" Cal asked, pushing his fifth empty bottle aside.

"What do you mean?" I sank the last dregs of my beer and placed my empty next to his.

"I've listened to you drone on about two women tonight. Only one of them makes you light up when you talk about her, and it isn't your Friday date."

"Are you talking about Cassie? She's just a friend."

"Right." His eyes lit in amusement as he drawled out the word.

"It's not like that between us. Yes, I like her... a lot. We get on well, but she's in a relationship—one I'm a little concerned about." I grimaced at the memories of the way I'd seen Jay treating Cassie. "I might have my faults, Cal, but cheating or causing someone to cheat isn't one of them. Even if the guy is a huge prick."

He put his hands up, laughing. "Okay, I get it. It just seems to me that you have deeper feelings for this girl than you care to admit."

Shaking my head, I stood. "You're delusional. We're just friends, remember that."

I used the restroom and headed back to the bar for refills. I was already feeling a small buzz from five beers and no food. There was no doubt I'd be suffering at work the next day, but it was good to just chill out and catch up with Cal. I hadn't realised how much I'd needed this time with him.

I was paying Tony, the bartender, for the beers when my phone began to vibrate in my pocket. I half expected it to be my father calling to yell at me again. I was pleasantly surprised to see Cassie's name flashing on the screen.

"Cass," I greeted happily, holding the phone to my ear with one hand and grabbing the necks of both bottles with the other. I nodded my thanks to Tony and turned back toward our table.

"Where are you?" she asked, sounding a little disappointed.

"Having a couple of drinks. Why?"

"I thought you were coming in tonight."

"I am… Oh shit. What time is it?" My eyes darted around the room looking for a clock.

"It's nearly eight. Are you not coming?"

My heart plummeted at her hurt tone. I placed the bottles on the table, trying to avoid Cal's inquisitive gaze.

"I'm sorry, Cass. I totally lost track of time. I've had a few drinks so I doubt I'm going to be fit for anything tonight."

"Oh… okay. I guess I'll see you tomorrow then."

Finally, I met Cal's interested gaze. Where I'd been expecting to see teasing and mocking, I found him watching me with the kind of support and interest only a caring sibling could offer.

"Sorry," I repeated, feeling like a ginormous arse.

"I guess I could… come and join you. If you don't mind, that is. I'd hate to interrupt your evening. No, actually it's fine, I'll just—"

Chuckling, I cut off her babbling. "Cass?"

"Yeah?"

"It's fine. Why don't you come and join us?" I raised an eyebrow at Caleb checking he was okay with us being gatecrashed. He nodded his approval.

"Are you sure?"

"I'm sure. Get your arse here pronto; I want to introduce you to Caleb."

"Who's Caleb?"

"My brother."

"Wow, there's two of you?" She laughed and it was music to my ears. "If you're sure it's okay, I'd love to join you. Where are you?"

The new brightness in her tone made me smile. "We're at the Fox on Old Station Road."

"I'll get changed and make my way over. I'll be there soon."

"Just friends, huh?" Caleb smirked when we'd said goodbye and ended the call.

I settled into my chair. "Just friends," I confirmed, lifting the bottle to my lips.

Forty-five minutes later when the door opened, I smiled watching Cassie stroll in. She looked lovely in a pair of blue jeans, a white Golden Oakes T-shirt that fitted her petite frame perfectly, and her ever-present Nikes. She'd left her dark hair loose, hanging around her shoulders. Under the lights of the bar, it shone as though still wet from a recent shower. Looking at her right then, I began to realise there was nothing sexier than a woman who felt secure with her looks, who didn't feel the need to dress up and plaster make-up over her face. Or maybe it was just Cassie. She looked beautiful.

My smile slipped when a guy followed in immediately behind Cassie and spoke into her ear. When she said she'd join us, I hadn't even considered she might bring Jay along with her. I wasn't sure I'd be able to stop myself from wanting to introduce him to my fist if he was a prick to her again. I heaved a deep sigh of relief when the guy straightened and stepped away, and I registered that it was Wesley.

When Wesley walked to the bar, Cassie turned around and our gazes met. Her lips tilted up in the cute I'm-trying-to-remain-cool way she had. As she made her way over, I looked over my shoulder at Caleb and immediately regretted doing so. He was watching me with a broad grin that spoke of devilment to come. Maybe inviting her along wasn't such a great idea after all. I shot him a warning glare.

"Hi," Cassie said cheerfully when she stopped beside me. "We missed you tonight."

"We?"

"Okay, me. I missed you." She shrugged, unabashedly staring into my eyes. "I had no one there to compete against."

"You must constantly be looking for the easy win then if you're competing against Fatam here." The low rumble of Caleb's laughter came from behind me.

Cassie peered around me and smiled. "Fatam?"

Closing my eyes, I shook my head in disbelief. I hadn't heard that particular nickname from my brother since I was a slightly overweight fifteen-year-old. Caleb had been an obnoxious eighteen-year-old who thought it hilarious to persistently rib me about my slightly protruding belly, thick neck, and flabby arms. He'd called me Fatam for almost a year before I finally had a growth spurt and shot up in height. Suddenly, the fat was almost gone, and a new me was emerging. I started running and then going to the local gym. That was the time I discovered my love for outdoor activities. I'd been on an outdoor pursuits adventure weekend with the school and found I couldn't get enough of the zip lines, mountain biking, canoeing, and all the other things we were able to try out.

That was also the time when my father reminded me of my pledge to my grandfather after I'd returned home and proudly stated I knew what I wanted to do with my future. He'd shot me down immediately and told me I *would* be studying architecture. There had been no reasoning with him after that. With one son breaking free, he'd reinforced his reins and went in heavy with the guilt trip until I just accepted my fate.

"Let's ignore he said that," I said, opening my eyes again. "He has this condition that makes him spew all sorts of idiotic crap from that big mouth of his."

"That's right, it's called bigbroitis," Caleb joked, and stood, extending his hand out to Cassie. "Seeing as weasel here has no manners... Hi, I'm Caleb, Adam's older, bigger, and much more handsome brother. You must be Cassie. He has told me so much about you." I shot him a murderous glare. *Leave it alone, Caleb*, I warned with my eyes.

She shook his hand, grinning. "It's nice to meet you, Caleb. Sadly Adam hasn't returned the favour."

"He hasn't? Wow! That hurts. I thought I meant everything to you, little bro." He slapped a hand over his heart, pouting.

"Please, ignore him," I said to Cassie, pulling out a chair for her. "Like I said, most of what comes out of his mouth is bullshit."

Caleb grinned and then excused himself to the toilets, leaving Cassie and me alone.

I took the seat next to hers, shifting it in a little closer.

"I'm glad you're here," I said genuinely.

"Thanks for agreeing to us coming. I wasn't feeling it there tonight anyway."

"Why? What happened?" My immediate thoughts were of Jay doing or saying something to upset her.

"Nothing particular, it was just a busy day. I needed a night off, I guess... I hadn't realised until you didn't show that working out tonight didn't seem so appealing. It feels like I'm there twenty-four-seven at the moment."

Wesley appeared at the table with drinks for us all. "The bartender told me what you were drinking," he said, reading my questioning expression.

"Cheers." I lifted my bottle in thanks. "Aren't you supposed to be closing up tonight?"

Cassie choked on a mouthful of beer, her eyes shining with humour.

Wesley shrugged. "We did already. There was an unfortunate incident, and we had to close early. Damn shame if you ask me. But what could I do?" He shook his head in remorse.

Cassie continued grinning as I looked at them, confused.

"I'm not sure Mrs Berkley will ever want to shower and change there again. I don't think she'll want to take the risk of indecent exposure again," Cassie said.

Caleb rejoined us, and I introduced him to Wesley.

"So what happened?" I asked, trying to work out what the joke was.

"Fire alarm," Wesley said seriously. "We had to evacuate. It was mayhem."

"There was a fire?" From the edge of my vision, I saw Caleb sit straighter, always ready to be the fire-fighting hero.

"Not exactly."

I didn't understand what was funny about the situation, and why Wesley was so blasé about the incident. It seemed pretty serious to me. "So it was a false alarm?"

"Yes, each time."

"Each time?"

Wesley nodded his head. "Yes. The alarm kept going off. Some short circuit in the system somewhere." Cassie snorted.

My eyes danced between the two of them. "Did you get it fixed?"

Unable to contain it any longer, tears spilt from Cassie's eyes as she burst out laughing. "You should have seen it, Adam. The place was mayhem. Semi-naked people were running about everywhere thinking there really was a fire."

Finally, the penny dropped. "You faked it?"

Wiping her eyes, Cassie nodded.

"But why?"

Wesley shrugged. "Why not? I needed a night off and to do that I needed to clear the place. It was the quickest way of getting that to happen. Why should Nate have all the fun while the rest of us work our nuts off?"

"But..." I honestly didn't know whether to be appalled at the idiocy or impressed by the ingenuity.

"We needed a fire evacuation practice. We've now had one." Finally, Wesley cracked a smile.

"You do realise my brother here is a firefighter, right? He takes fire safety very seriously," I said. Wesley's face paled, his grin immediately slipping away. He looked at Caleb and visibly shrank into his chair seeing my brother's less-than-impressed face.

I looked at Cassie and winked. She grinned. It was nice to see her acting so happy and carefree. There had been a change in her from the time we'd spent together in France. Then, she'd been so relaxed and bubbly. She hadn't taken shit from anyone, and would have frozen anyone in place with her ice tongue. But she had definitely become more reserved and defensive, her previously fiery personality more subdued. The differences weren't major and were only noticeable if you took the time to actually look. I wondered how much of the change in her was down to Jay's influence.

Watching her be the Cassie I remembered, I couldn't help but laugh along with her.

As the night wore on, Caleb eventually made his excuses and left, telling Cassie he hoped to see her again soon. I wasn't so sure he was as eager to see Wesley again. Shortly after, Wesley got chatting to a girl at the bar and disappeared, leaving Cass and me alone.

When she yawned, I realised how late it was getting and offered to see her home. After calling for a cab, we made our way outside to wait.

The evening had turned chilly, so when Cassie started shivering, I offered her my jacket. She took it gratefully, wrapping it tightly around her slim body.

We settled into the back of the cab, and Cassie gave the driver her address.

"Come here," I said, pulling her across the seat when she was still shivering. I wrapped an arm around her and gently rubbed it along the sleeve of my jacket, trying to warm her.

"Thank you," she whispered. I felt a sudden surge of contentedness when she snuggled in close, resting her head against my shoulder with a deep sigh.

I should have moved her aside. It felt too intimate. Wrong. We shouldn't have been that close. But when she nuzzled into my neck, yawning deeply, I could smell the fruity scent of her shampoo and felt the silkiness of her hair against my skin. At that moment, what was surely so wrong, felt so right.

"Where was Jay tonight?" I asked, needing the distraction of conversation.

"I don't know. I only saw him briefly during the evacuation," she replied with another yawn.

"He didn't stick around to make sure you were okay?"

She shook her head. "No. I guess he knew Wesley would have everything under control."

"So he was okay with you coming out tonight?"

She turned her eyes up to mine for a brief moment before resuming her position buried in the crook of my arm. "He doesn't own me, Adam. I don't need his permission."

A moment later, I felt her body relax against me further. Her soft breaths slowed and feathered over my neck and I realised she'd fallen asleep.

I pulled her closer and buried my nose in her hair, inhaling her scent. "Thanks for tonight, Cass," I whispered, and watched the bright lights of London passing by outside the window. I felt so comfortable holding her and hoped the taxi driver took his time. I was in no rush for the journey to be over.

CHAPTER EIGHT

Cassie

"CASS, WE'RE HERE."

Yawning, I slowly blinked my eyes open but felt reluctant to pull myself from the warm body I was snuggled against.

"Come on, I'll see you in."

With great effort, I sat up and looked out the window, rubbing my tired eyes. We were outside my house. My dark, lonely house. I'd had such a great evening with Adam, Wes, and Caleb. I couldn't remember the last time I'd felt so at ease around another group of people—apart from Nate and Liv, that was.

Adam opened the car door and helped me out. While I fished through my bag for my keys, he popped his head back in and asked the driver to wait a minute.

"You're shattered, aren't you," Adam murmured,

his voice soft and soothing. He took the keys from me as I yawned again. Leading me to the front door, he placed a comforting hand on the small of my back. His warmth seeped through the material of his suit jacket, making me want to curl up in his arms again. He'd been like my very own comfort blanket in the cab, and I'd effortlessly drifted into a peaceful sleep.

"Do you want to come in?" I asked.

"I would love to," he said, pushing the key into the lock. "But the cab driver is waiting for me." He frowned, looking at the door. "Cass, I think there's a problem with your door." The door then creaked open with the light pressure of Adam's touch.

I sighed and reached for the keys. "I know. I need to get it looked at."

Adam looked horrified.

"You know it's like this?" I nodded, feeling a little embarrassed.

"It's not safe, Cass."

I pushed the door wide open and stepped inside, turning to face him on the step. "I know. I'll get it looked at, I promise."

There was an awkward silence for a moment, and I wondered what he was thinking.

The honking of a car horn finally grabbed his attention. He looked over his shoulder and indicated one minute to the driver.

He looked torn when he turned back to face me. "I've got to go. Are you going to be okay by yourself?"

"I'll be okay. I'll put the inside bolt on. Don't worry about me."

"Of course, I'll worry. You're a young woman living in London. It's not safe."

His concern reached deep into me, warming me through. Without thinking, I touched his cheek, enjoying the feel of his light stubble under my fingertips. "I'll get someone out to look at it soon, I promise."

"I don't like it, Cass. I hate the thought of you being here alone. Maybe you should—"

Placing a finger over his lips, I whispered, "I'll be fine."

"Promise me you'll lock yourself in, and keep your phone close, just in case."

I smiled. "I will."

Stepping closer, he searched my eyes, a multitude of unspoken questions playing out across his features. The smile fell from my face, and I swallowed hard. I bit my lip and tried not to lose myself in his ocean eyes.

"I had a good time tonight… with you," he said, his voice deeper than usual.

"I did too." My reply was nothing but a breathy whisper.

"I'll see you tomorrow night?" I nodded.

"Goodnight, Cassie."

A noise that sounded remarkably like a whimper escaped my lips when he leant in and placed a warm kiss on my forehead. He lingered there for a minute before turning to walk away.

My heart raced as the stupid organ slid south to settle in my stomach with a crazy flip. I wanted his lips back on me, his arms wrapped around me in a warm embrace.

"Adam, wait! Your jacket." I ran the few steps along the path and handed him the coat. "Thank you for tonight. For caring about me." Standing on tiptoes, I placed a quick kiss on his cheek and ran back into the house.

With the door closed and bolted, I leant against it and heaved a deep breath. What was I doing? When had things between Adam and me changed? Where had these feelings come from? I was in a relationship, and he was about to date my friend. I shouldn't be feeling anything for him. He was a friend. Nothing more.

I shook my head and played it down as tiredness. Everything would look different after a good night's sleep.

I made my way up to my room and screamed when I opened the door. Hidden in the shadows of the darkened room, someone was lying on my bed.

"Where the fuck have you been all night?"

"Jay, Christ, you scared me. How long have you been here?" Placing a hand over my pounding chest, I stepped further into the room, trying to squint through the darkness to scrutinise his mood.

"Long enough to know you haven't been home since you left the gym." He stood and stalked toward me, his eyes bright steel in the weak light of the street lamp outside the window. "I've been calling you. Why didn't you answer? Were you avoiding me?"

"No. My phone must be on silent."

"How convenient." He moved in close, forcing me to step backwards until my back hit the wall. "Did I hear a male voice with you downstairs?"

I gulped, my mouth going suddenly dry. Did I lie or tell him the truth? I'd never lied to him before; I'd never needed to. But with his recent volatile ways, I feared what he would do if I told him about Adam.

Deciding to ignore the question altogether, I put on a fake smile and tried for a distraction, something that was guaranteed to get him thinking of something else. "How was training tonight?" I dropped my hands to the hem of my T-shirt and slowly began lifting it over my chest. "Did Cameron finally pull off a turning kick without falling over?"

His eyes remained hard on mine, and I feared my little strip distraction wasn't going to work.

"I forgot to tell you," I said, dropping the shirt to the floor and starting on the buttons of my jeans. "Justine said a couple of the nurses from the hospital might be interested in joining. She's been telling them all about you and the club."

Finally, as I kicked the jeans off my feet, his eyes left mine and skimmed down my body, hovering over my white lace bra and the nipples underneath that had hardened.

I flinched when he moved his cold hands to my neck and then stroked them along my shoulders and down my arms. "Tell me, Cassandra. Was there a guy downstairs just now?"

Tightening his fists around my wrists, he pressed me against the unforgiving hard wall. My body stiffened, every muscle responding to the icy coolness of his voice.

"Tell me!" he bellowed when I didn't reply.

"Y-yes," I stuttered. "It-it was Adam."

"Adam?"

My whole body trembled as I tried to cower away from his demonic glare. "Yes. We shared a cab home."

"What the fuck? You think you can cheat on me?" I

screamed when an arm lifted, his hand stretched ready to strike.

"No, Jay, don't. It wasn't like that, I promise. He just wanted to make sure I got home safely. I was with Wesley and Adam's older brother, too." My words tumbled out in a desperate rush.

"And that's supposed to make me feel better?"

"Yes… no…." I sucked in a deep breath, trying to calm my racing nerves. I needed to try to soothe and reason with him before things turned ugly. "There was nothing to it, I promise. I'm with you, you know that."

"Do I? You show me you're mine by fucking around with other guys?" His voice was still deep with anger, but his hand relaxed to his side.

"I swear there are no other guys, not in that way. I… I love you."

"Good. Don't forget that." His mouth crashed over mine, taking me by surprise. He lifted a hand to my cheek, tilting my head in a way that allowed him to force his tongue through my lips. It was then I realised he'd also been drinking; he tasted of hard liquor and a bitter, sour taste I didn't recognise. I whimpered in unease. He mistook the small sound as pleasure and grabbed my thigh, lifting it to rest around his hip.

"I own you, Cassie," he growled against my ear, holding me firm when I tried to squirm away. "You are nothing without me." His firm fingers dug into my thigh, travelling further, lifting my leg higher. "Remember you are where you are because of me." I gasped in pain when I felt a sudden intrusion into my unprepared centre. "You need me. No one else can get you where you want to be."

Slowly, my deceitful body began to conspire against me and softened to his questing fingers. My feelings of unease and apprehension were masked by adrenaline and increasing pleasure.

"You feel this, Cassie? This pleasure? I do this to you, just as you do this to me." He rocked his pelvis forward, rubbing his denim-covered erection against me.

"So I'm going to ask you again, who do you belong to, Cassie? Who makes you feel this good?"

He'd cast his evil black magic over me. My thoughts were incoherent, and I could focus only on the sensations he drew from me.

"You," I whimpered, feeling a second finger enter me. "You do."

"That's right." He smiled triumphantly against my lips. "Now be a good girl and turn around for me."

His fingers withdrew and dug into my hips, forcing me to turn around and brace against the wall. Before I had time to focus on the wrongness of the situation, he'd ripped away my underwear and slammed his rock-hard cock deep inside me. A startled scream left my lips, but he was ruthless in his agenda, pounding harder and faster, telling me over and over that I was his. My cheek burned from the friction of it rubbing against the textured wallpaper, but I dared not move.

By the time a guttural growl rumbled against my ear as he forced his penis deep one final time, I was breathless and gasping for air.

And numb.

I felt nothing. No fear, no anger, no sadness; I was merely there, lost, unsure what had happened.

"Fuck," he finally whispered against my hair. "You

are so unbelievably sexy. You turn me inside out, Cassie."

He pulled out and led us to the bathroom. I watched in silence as he ran a washcloth under the tap and then used it to wipe me clean. He was talking, but I wasn't listening. My focus was locked on the strange woman with glazed-over eyes and pale complexion staring back at me through the mirror.

"Come on, let's get to bed."

Taking me by the hand, Jay led us through the bedroom to the bed. He pulled the covers back and waited for me to settle before climbing in behind me and covering us both.

"You amaze me, Cassie," he said, tightening his arms around me and pressing a kiss to my hair. "I can't stand the thought of you with another guy. You have to know that. I will never give you up."

As he continued kissing my head and shoulder, I stared off into the distance with silent tears leaking from my eyes.

EMERGING INTO THE kitchen the following morning, I flipped the switch on the kettle and pulled out a seat at the small bistro table. My eyes were sore from the mixture of crying and lack of sleep. I'd been restless all night, debating with myself. I wondered if the recent changes in Jay's behaviour were my fault. If maybe I was somehow letting him down, or disappointing him. I could see why he might have thought I was cheating on him; in a way I was by spending so much time with other men.

I pulled my feet up onto the edge of the chair and

rested my cheek on my knees as I looked out of the window. I thought back over the days since Nate's wedding, of the time I'd spent with Adam and Wes, and of the time I'd spent with Jay. I'd been larking about and enjoying my time with the others, but the time I'd spent with my boyfriend—the one I should be having quality time with—had been restricted to training or reluctant evenings together. It was no wonder he was acting out; he was looking for some form of attention from his girlfriend. I'd been so stupid.

Wrapping my arms tighter around my knees, I closed my eyes and thought back to that moment we'd gone to bed before he'd finally fallen asleep. He'd been so affectionate, kissing my head and gently stroking my skin. I'd been so angry at his outburst that I hadn't seen what he was feeling. With my actions, I'd hurt him.

So what did we do about it? Things needed to get better. *I* had to make them better. I couldn't risk our relationship turning sour, because I needed him.

Jay was a very visual person. He appreciated beautiful things and always noticed someone or something's physical attributes before delving to what was underneath. I thought that maybe I was no longer attractive enough for him. If I tried a bit harder with my appearance and stopped living in sportswear, then I would hopefully please him. I believed that was what it all came down to… I was no longer pleasing him, but I wanted to.

I vowed then and there to make an extra effort. I would train harder in the studio to make him proud. I would dress smarter and act more like a lady. I would become the person he needed me to be.

When Jay stepped into the room a short while later dressed only in a pair of tight-fitting black boxer briefs, I jumped from my seat and hurried over.

"I'm sorry, Jay. I'm so sorry," I snivelled, wrapping myself around him.

"You're sorry for what?" he asked, taking my hands and pulling them from him.

"For last night. For going out with my friends and not telling you. For not answering my phone… for so many things. I know I've not been a great girlfriend recently."

His eyebrows shot up for a moment as if he were shocked by my confession. The look was quickly replaced with impassivity again.

Gently pushing me away, he sat in the seat I'd vacated and stretched, showing off his amazingly sculpted torso. "It's okay. I know you've had a lot going on, but you really shouldn't let it cloud your judgement, Cassie. Either we're in a relationship, or we're not. Going out with other men is hugely inappropriate no matter how innocent it may seem. It makes *you* look like a slut, and makes *me* seem like an idiot."

I rested back against the counter, biting my thumbnail as I considered his words. I hadn't thought about it like that. In my eyes, I'd just been spending time with my friends. I hadn't thought how that would look to his friends or people he knew.

He stood, studying me for a moment. "I need to go and have a shower. Can you make me something to eat and coffee, I need to leave soon."

I offered a bright smile. "Of course."

While Jay was in the shower, I quickly ran upstairs and changed into a short sundress and a pair of white flip-flops with large daisy flowers on them. Back in the kitchen, I got to work on his breakfast of an egg-white omelette with spinach, fruit salad, and coffee. Foods he loved. By the time he re-emerged, I had it all laid out on the table.

"Thanks," he said, taking his seat and diving in immediately.

I sat opposite nursing my own coffee, waiting for him to notice my dress. I needed his approval before he left.

He briefly looked up, meeting my eyes. "Remember I'm out of town for a couple of days… at that conference. I'll see you at the gym Friday night." It wasn't a question; he was demanding I be there.

I nodded. "I'll be there."

He gulped down the last of his coffee and wiped his mouth. "I have to go. Keep your phone on in case I need to speak to you, and no going out with the guys."

He kissed the top of my head and then walked from the room. I heard him shuffling around in the hallway before his footsteps faded and the slamming of the front door announced he'd left.

I sat there staring at the table, a little bewildered. He hadn't even noticed my dress. Perhaps I should have quickly done something nice with my hair and applied a little bit of make-up.

I was still considering what I could have done better when Justine skipped into the room. "Hey girlfriend, what's up?" she chirped, heading straight for the kettle.

When I didn't reply, she turned, holding out a

spoonful of coffee granules. Her bright smile abruptly disappeared. "Cass, what's up?"

"Nothing."

"You're wearing a dress."

"And?"

"You never wear a dress."

"I wanted to today," I reasoned.

"Bullshit. You hate wearing dresses."

"Not today," I snapped, jumping to my feet. I wasn't in the mood to get into another discussion about my relationship with Jay again. She wouldn't understand. She already thought he was a dick. I didn't want to have to admit to my best friend that our problems were all down to me. I knew Justine, she wouldn't believe our issues were because of me; she'd want to lay all the blame on Jay. I loved her for that, but it wouldn't help our situation if she confronted him and made things awkward. It was best that I kept my relationship issues to myself.

"Why?" she asked, trailing behind me out of the room.

"Why what?"

"Why the sudden change? Why the sharp tongue? Why are you so evasive?"

"I'm not. Can't you just leave it… please?" I bent forward to gather the post from the doormat.

I heard a sudden gasp and then Justine was on her knees behind me, lifting the hem of my dress.

"What the fuck, Juss?" I pulled the dress down and stepped away.

"What are those?"

"What are what?"

"Those." She pointed toward my right thigh with a

scowl. I suddenly realised what she was asking about. Memories of Jay's fingers digging into my flesh the night before flashed through my mind.

"The bruises, Cassie. How did you get them?"

I quickly skirted around her, desperate to be away from her questioning.

"Please, Cass, don't run away and ignore this. Talk to me," she begged when my feet hit the first stair. "Did Jay do this to you?"

I froze, my gaze fixing on a small stain on the carpet a few stairs up.

"You can't let him treat you this way, Cass. It's not right."

I whirled around, shaking my head. "What's not right is people getting all up in my business, assuming they know what's going on," I yelled. "You don't know anything about Jay and me, so just stay the fuck out of it."

I ran up the remaining stairs to my bedroom. Slamming the door closed behind me, I fell to my knees and buried my head in my hands. I suddenly felt so alone. My friends didn't understand. Even though he wasn't himself at the moment, Jay was good for me, for my training. I had known him for a few years, and before we became a couple he had supported me through a difficult time in my life that even Wes and Nate were unaware of. All they had ever known of me was what I'd wanted them to see. When I was hurting, I'd hidden it behind a mask of sass and arrogance. Jay had always been able to see through me, though. When he'd introduced me to kick-boxing, he had given me something to live for. I suddenly had to focus and put my trust in another person again. I had someone new to respect and looked up to. To admire.

When my life was turned upside down and everything I'd ever believed of myself was proven to be a lie, I'd clung to someone who wouldn't judge and was there for me. Jay. Our relationship might not have been a storybook romance or even conventional. We fought and were combustible together sometimes, but it worked. It was what made us, us.

I had to keep that faith alive and believe in Jay now.

The vibrating buzz of my phone on the bedside table startled me awake. I'd fallen asleep curled into a ball on the floor. My head throbbed, and my mouth was dry. An acrid taste coated my tongue. I licked my lips and winced at a sharp pain. Pulling my hand to the painfully swollen area, I realised I'd bitten deep into my lip in my sleep.

The phone went silent and immediately started buzzing again. I heaved myself to my feet and stumbled across to the bed.

I answered with a shaky "Hello."

"Cassie? Is that you? You sound strange."

"It's me," I said. "I bit my lip. It's a bit sore."

My mother tsked, and I could imagine her shaking her head in annoyance. She was an elegant lady—well-dressed, perfect make-up and not a hair out of place. She could also be a bitch. She hated that I might look anything but perfect also. Of course, that meant she hated the way I looked constantly. My trainers and sportswear had never made it into her list of approved apparel. She also hated that I hadn't followed in her footsteps as a trophy wife.

"That was careless of you, Cassandra. What must you look like?"

"That was careless of you, Cassandra. What must you look like?" I mimicked under my breath so she couldn't hear. There was no concerned "Oh dear, sweetheart. Are you okay?" I shouldn't have been surprised. She had never cared.

"I look like me," I said. "It's nothing major."

"You really need to be more careful with your looks, Cassie. If you want to keep that young man interested in you, you must always look your best for him." And didn't that just feed into my latest fears about not looking good enough for Jay.

"What did you want, Mum?" I asked needing her to get to the point. I tolerated her now, she was my mother after all, but ever since the truth came out, I didn't know how to act around her. I loved her, but also despised her. Because of her lies I'd lost so much. Still, I'd been brought up to respect my elders so I usually played the dutiful daughter.

"Your father—" I coughed at that, I couldn't help it. "—and I request your presence at dinner this Friday. We are having a small gathering and would like to show a united family front—"

"What? No. Mum, you know I can't stand those things, especially now," I gasped, cutting her off. Our family was anything but united.

She continued, choosing to ignore my outburst. "I'll email you all the details. And, Cassandra, please dress nicely."

When the line went silent, I heaved out a strangled scream and hurled my phone against the wall. It clattered onto the wooden floor with a satisfying thump. My mother, the well-respected wife of a business tycoon in the pharmaceutical world, just didn't get it. She cared more about appearances than her only daughters feelings. A daughter who at that moment needed a caring mother's shoulder to cry on.

CHAPTER NINE

Cassie

"HELLO, BEAUTIFUL." JAY GREETED ME with a smile when I pushed open my front door on Friday evening. He stepped away from the small closet under the stairs, walked over, and wrapping his arms around me, he pulled me close. "I missed you. Where've you been? I expected you to be home an hour ago."

"I had to stick around for a while longer. Colin had to rush off early, some kind of family emergency or something," I replied evenly, trying to hide my confusion at him being there. He'd been at his work conference for the last few days, and other than a couple of simple text messages, I hadn't heard from him. We certainly didn't have any plans to see each other.

"They work you too hard at that place. You should

cut back your hours." He took my hoodie and hung it over the end of the bannister. "Just think how much extra training time you could get in if you weren't working so much."

I followed him down the hallway. "I love my job. Why would I want to cut back?"

He turned and gave me an unapologetic shrug. "Because I want you to."

Studying him for a moment, I waited for the crack of a smile or the crinkle of teasing eyes. It didn't happen.

"I'm not cutting my hours back, Jay. I need the money."

After dropping my bag on the small side table, I brushed past him and made my way into the kitchen for a drink. Jay stood in the doorway gripping the doorframe above his head, watching as I pulled a glass from the cabinet and filled it from the tap.

"You don't need money. I'd look after you."

I spluttered on a gulp of water, shooting him an appalled look. "Excuse me?"

"It's something I've been thinking about. We'll talk later. Right now there is something in the living room for you, and then we need to get ready for dinner at your parents' place." He turned to walk into the other room.

Ignoring the first two parts of his statement for a moment, I focused on the dinner part. "What do you mean *we*? How do you even know about that, I didn't mention it?"

He glanced over his shoulder, giving me a withering look that said he knew everything to do with me.

"How did you know, Jay?" I repeated, following

him through the hallway.

"Your email account was still logged in on my laptop. I saw the message your mother sent." He shrugged as if it were no big deal.

"You read my emails?" I shouted incredulously and swallowed down the ball of frustration threatening to explode in me.

"If you didn't want me looking, you should've made sure you were logged out." That caused me to pause. I couldn't actually remember the last time I'd used his laptop. It certainly hadn't been recently. Before I could ponder it too deeply, he sniped, "Can I show you this so we can get on the road?"

The thought of him being there made me feel physically ill. The evening was going to be tough enough as it was, I didn't need the added stress of having Jay with me, not with the way he'd been acting lately.

"You're really coming?" I swallowed, praying I'd misheard him.

He stepped further into the room, and then turned, narrowing his stormy grey eyes at me. "Of course, I'm coming. I left the conference early to be here... for you."

"Why?"

"Jesus, Cassie," he said severely, throwing frustrated arms in the air. "Why do you always fucking second-guess everything? I wanted to, okay? I need to make sure you're alright. I know you don't like it there. Now come in here so I can give you your surprise."

Knowing better than to continue an argument, I took his extended hand and followed him into the living room. Standing just inside the doorway, I took in the large bouquet of white roses sitting on the coffee table.

I stared at the flowers with my mouth agape. It was such a sweet and kind gesture, and usually, I would have jumped into his arms to offer a thank-you kiss. But the sight of the white blooms just added to my irritation.

"They are beautiful, Jay. I love them, I really do," I said, my voice sounded flat and lacking any real gratitude.

"But? You don't exactly seem enthralled by my gift." He lifted one of the blooms from the water and held it out to me. "I thought you'd like them. At the very least be grateful."

As I took the rose from his hand, my finger skimmed along the stem, catching on a thorn. A small ball of blood formed on the wound, staining a delicate petal as I lifted the injured finger to mouth. I drew in a deep breath as I sucked the blood, using the delay to consider my next words.

"Please don't take this the wrong way, but I have to ask; why do you insist on always buying me white roses? I don't mean for that to sound ungrateful, because I'm not. It's just...." How could I explain it without coming across as raging bitch?

"Because they are beautiful, elegant flowers, Cassie."

"And they are. But white lilies are my favourite flowers."

He nodded. "I know. You have pictures of them everywhere. *I* don't like them, though. They represent death." His face wrinkled in disgust.

A bitter taste of hurt and anguish clogged my

throat, threatening to choke me. I quickly turned away from him. He knew why I loved white lilies. He was aware they were the favourite flower of the only woman I'd ever known as a grandmother, for whom I had tremendous respect and adoration.

Growing up, Nana's house always had a large bunch of lilies in a crystal vase on the mantelpiece whenever I went to visit. Jay knew that, despite everything that went down, she—and the scent of those flowers—felt like home to me. I'd been so touched when she passed away and left the house to me, and I vowed to keep her memory alive by filling her home with pictures and ornaments of the white flowers. To hear Jay dismissing my deepest feelings, and therefore my memories of the happiest time of my life, hurt like hell.

Feeling overwhelmed with everything, I wiped a stray tear from my eye and brushed past him. "I should get ready."

"Wear something nice." I looked over my shoulder at him as I ascended the stairs. He'd pulled out his phone and was tapping away on the screen. What did he care what I wore? Obviously, my feelings and desires meant nothing to him.

THE DRIVE TO my mother's place was made in silence. Jay concentrated on the road, occasionally fiddling with the sound system, killing my hearing with hip-hop music. I spent the time staring out of the window. Internally I fumed at the high-handed way he'd ended up dictating what I wore. It was ironic that he'd been blind to my clothing choice before when I'd tried to dress nicely for him. Today I'd first dressed in a pair of tight jeans and a black silky camisole top—I'd even opted for knee-high boots instead of my Nikes. It hadn't been good enough, though. Jay demanded I change because my outfit showed too much skin.

"You'll have all those old men ogling your tits," he'd said. "You think your mother will appreciate you turning up looking like a hooker?" My eyebrows had shot into my hairline, and I'd tried to argue that a cardigan would solve the problem, but he'd merely glared. His look told me I needed to suck up my angry retort and change my clothes. I hated it. I hated that he felt he could dictate these things to me. However, brooding was far preferable to the attitude I would no doubt have suffered otherwise.

My mother lived out of town in a big house in a highly respected area of Hertfordshire. Just like her, the house was all about the show. With its large rooms decorated in rich jewel tones and accessorised with furniture and ornaments from her native Thailand, the place looked more like an expensive boutique hotel than a home. There was never a thing out of place, and God help you if you left a crumb or coffee stain anywhere.

Out of place was exactly how I felt walking through the teak and glass double door front entrance. When she'd said "small gathering," I'd expected maybe another couple or two, or some of Phillip's work colleagues. I certainly hadn't expected the twenty or so other people standing around chatting and nursing crystal glasses filled with champagne. They were money people, all dressed in their finest suits and dresses, and wearing ridiculously expensive jewellery. I looked down at the conservative navy blue dress and nude ballet flats that Jay had eventually approved of. Then I looked at him in his tailored charcoal-grey suit with matching tie. We were dressed to fit into an upper class world, a world I didn't feel part of or comfortable in.

Why am I here? This isn't me.

"Cassandra, you made it."

My mother flounced into the room pulling me from my thoughts. Wearing a traditional Thai dress in red and gold silk with a gold wrap, I had to admit she looked stunning. Her dark hair had been set into a low side bun and adorned with a large gold silk flower. Everyone's eyes were on her as she floated across the room.

"Mother," I greeted formally, kissing each cheek she presented. "You remember Jay, right?"

"Of course." She smiled and extended her hand. "It's lovely to see you again, Jay. I'm so glad you could join us."

"I wouldn't miss it for anything, Mrs Burton. Thank you for inviting me." He took her hand and gently lifted it to his lips, kissing the back.

Confused, I looked between the two. "You invited him? I thought you got the details from my email," I directed to Jay.

"Of course, I did. He is your boyfriend," Mum said.

"Yes, but...." I had no other words. It concerned me that my mother was somehow in contact with Jay. Knowing how interfering she could be, I'd always tried to keep my personal life away from her.

"Come, let me introduce you to everyone. Jay, I'm sure you'll fit in very well. Many of the men here tonight work in finance, too. In fact, I'm sure Larry Hopkins works at your company. Perhaps you know him?"

As she walked off, I stared at Jay. How did she know so much about him? They had only briefly met once before, and the only thing I'd told her about him was that he was my kick-boxing coach. I'd hoped that would keep her away from him, seeing as she hated the fact I did something *so brutal*. Apparently, that didn't matter to her; she'd dug anyway. And now she knew about his real position as an investment banker, she would no doubt start putting on the pressure to take our relationship to the next level. Everything was about status and money with her.

"She's quite a force," Jay murmured, taking my hand and walking us further into the lion's den. "We better get mingling."

We spent the next few hours talking to my mother's guests and sitting down to a catered meal of Thai traditional food. It was awkward and deathly dull. Jay kept me by his side the entire time but very rarely included me in his conversations. If I did try and get involved, he would laugh off my comments or make a point of correcting me in front of everyone. That left me feeling hurt and irritated, and I wanted more than anything to disappear.

After another joke at my expense about my *simple massage therapist job*, I excused myself to the bathroom. I needed distance before I exploded. Jay knew my position at the gym was much more than a simple massage therapist job. He was aware that my role went beyond massages; it served to help our clients recover from injury, restoring their strength and often self-esteem.

I used the facilities, washed and dried my hands, and then stood staring at my reflection. There she was again, the stranger in the mirror. There was a time when I would have stood up to Jay and my mother. I would have proudly explained my love of helping people overcome life-altering injuries, or giving them the confidence to make massive lifestyle changes for the sake of their health. When had things changed? When had I become so insecure and unsure of myself?

Leaving the bathroom, I went in the direction of the kitchen. I grabbed a drink from the counter and slipped through the door onto the large decked terrace. A couple of guests were in the garden chatting and smoking, but it was mostly quiet. I quickly made my way along the pathway that snaked its way to the rear of the grounds. There was an enormous old oak tree at the end of the garden that I'd often hid behind when I was younger when I'd needed to be alone. I needed that same privacy now.

I stepped around the thick trunk and came face to face with a tall, lithe man, his features momentarily illuminated orange by the end of a cigar as he took a drag.

"Sorry. I'll leave you alone," I said, backing away.

"What, you don't want to spend time with your old man?" Phillip asked, blowing smoke in my direction.

"I'm sorry I disturbed you, Phillip. I'll just…" I looked back towards the house. "I should get back to the party."

"You're just like her, you know," he said, stepping from the shadow of the tree and into the ray of yellow moonlight.

"I'm sorry?"

He nodded, as though just realising something. "A whore, just like your mother."

Stunned into silence, I watched as the man I'd grown up believing was my father dropped his cigar to the ground and stamped it out under his foot.

Stepping closer, his face was mere inches from mine when he said, "Tell me, Cassandra, how many other men are you screwing behind that poor fool's back? Does he know you're only after his money? I guess the apple doesn't fall far from the tree."

Gasping, I backed away. "Phillip, don't do this."

"Why? You are your mother's daughter. It's only the truth." He briefly looked me up and down. "Although, dressed like that I'm sure even she wants to deny parenthood. You're not quite living up to her high standards."

"You're a bastard, you know that?" I spat.

"Better than being the bastard child." He laughed, a low, dark rumble.

Unable to hold back the stress of the evening, tears burned my eyes and slowly fell drop by drop down my cheeks. I furiously brushed them away, not wanting to appear so weak in front of this man turned monster.

"Oh come on now, Cassandra. There's no need to cry like a child," he sneered, tracking me as I backed away.

"What happened to you?" I whispered. "You used to be such a great guy, a wonderful dad. I loved you. If this is how you treat people, I'm glad you're not my father." Turning on my heels, I ran back along the path and around the side of the house. Phillip called out, his deep voice echoing around the garden. I ignored him. I couldn't stay in that place around those people a minute longer.

As soon as I hit the grass verge at the front of the property, my legs buckled under me. I fell to my knees, cradling my head in my hands as silent tears continued to stream down my face.

Blinding white light suddenly illuminated the inky black night sky, followed quickly by a deafening crack of thunder. Heavy raindrops began falling slowly, the occasional droplet hitting the earth around me. Another flash of lightning cut through the darkness. As the rain grew heavier, I closed my eyes, tilted my face skyward, and let the refreshing water flow over me, washing away my torment. I had always loved summer storms—the intensity of the thunder and lightning, the unpredictability, being totally at Mother Nature's mercy. It all added to an exhilarating experience. Tonight, as the rain soaked into my hair and clothes, I wished I were that little girl with a loving father who would chase her around the garden in the rain pretending to be the big scary storm monster. I wanted to be the innocent little girl who was oblivious to her mother's selfishness and lies. The woman who didn't have to worry about how she was acting around her possessive and controlling boyfriend.

I wanted to be loved.

"What the fuck are you doing?" Another flash highlighted Jay jogging down the driveway with his suit jacket raised over his head.

I ran my hands through my wet hair and tilted my head to the side, watching him approach. He was angry. At that moment, I couldn't find it in me to care. I felt numb, dead inside, and just wanted to be alone.

Pulling myself to my feet, I began walking away. I had no idea where I was going or how I would get there, but I wasn't going to stick around.

"Where are you going?" I'd only managed a few steps when Jay's hand tightened around my wrist and pulled me back. My foot slipped on the wet grass, my ankle turning under me. I yelped at the pain coming from both my foot and the wrist Jay still held tightly.

"I asked you where the fuck you think you're going." He placed a finger under my chin, tilting it harshly until I looked at his face. "You think you can just walk out on me? I had to fucking make excuses for you in there, Cassie. I looked like a fucking prick not knowing where my girlfriend was when she was supposed to be by my side. I was talking to your mother and the director of an ad agency. I probably just lost business because I had to come find you."

I tried jerking out of his hold, but he just gripped tighter.

"I had to get out of there," I said, hoping he'd understand the pain in my voice. I began shivering, my teeth chattering as the chill of the rain finally registered.

"No, what you had to do was stay by my side."

"You don't understand. Phillip... he was in the garden... he said some vile things." I looked at him with pleading eyes. He knew the history; how my mother had seduced Phillip into marriage so she could live a luxurious wealthy life in the UK. How, despite their marriage, she continued sleeping her way around the male wealth of London. How, two years previous, we'd discovered that Phillip wasn't my blood father. It disgusted me to think of how she'd behaved. How she'd hurt Phillip, a man who had always been nothing but a gentleman. Despite the years of adultery, he wouldn't divorce her. He refused to hand over half of his life's worth to *a heinous whore*—his words. So they both continued to make my life miserable while pretending to society that they still had the perfect marriage.

Tugging me towards his car, Jay shot me a murderous glare. "When are you going to get over it? Family shit happens all the time."

He might as well have slapped me, his words stung just as hard. He'd always seemed so supportive and understanding of my situation. He'd talk to me after training sessions, often until the early hours of the morning, letting me purge every ill thought, every bad memory until eventually I'd fall asleep.

"Get in the fucking car, Cassie." His Audi beeped to life as we approached and he yanked the passenger door open for me. I slipped inside and curled myself into a ball in the seat. He slammed the door shut and then stalked around to his side. He started the engine and drove off, the wheels squealing and aquaplaning from the sudden too-fast acceleration on the wet road.

We both remained silent on the way home. Jay was still furious. He drove too fast and held the steering wheel in a white-knuckled grip. Ignoring him, I stared out of the window, shivering. I thought about Adam and how kind and considerate he'd been with me just a few days before. I remembered the warmth of his hand on my cheek and the compassion in his eyes.

He was out on his first date with Justine, while I was stuck in the car with an unpredictable monster.

CHAPTER TEN

Adam

PULLING UP THE SLEEVE OF my white shirt, I checked my watch again: 8:26 pm. Justine was late. I'd been feeling on edge about this date all week. It wasn't nerves—Justine seemed like a sweet girl, and I was confident we'd get on well. I just felt weird about the whole *dating* thing. Eventually, after many internal debates, I concluded that I was out of practice. After all, I hadn't been on a proper date since my university days. Girls tended to come and go, but they were usually one-time things to take the edge off my sexual frustrations. They didn't involve awkward conversations or feelings, and very rarely would they require an encore. I'd become the living, breathing cliché of a male slut. I wasn't proud of that status, but it had served me well while I waited for my girl to notice me.

But she never did. Now she was taken, and I was moving on.

I thought of Liv and her latest Facebook status showing a picture of a blissfully happy couple standing in the clear, shallow waters of the Indian Ocean. She and Nathan had their arms wrapped tightly around each other, her head resting against his shoulder as they looked at the camera smiling. She looked so happy and content, and my heart twisted. For the first time, though, I realised it wasn't twisting out of jealousy or sadness; it was twisting with pride and happiness for my best friend.

A waiter approached, asking if I wanted to order. I checked my watch again: 8:32 pm. Where was she?

Resigned to the fact I'd been stood up, I downed the last of my beer and asked for the bill, explaining my date hadn't shown.

I used the bathroom and walked back out to the main area, checking my phone for messages. Justine hadn't seemed the type to stand someone up.

"Adam! God, I'm so sorry I'm late." I looked up to see a flustered Justine hurrying through the restaurant. She stopped in front of me. With a contrite expression, she sucked down a deep, calming breath. "I'm sorry. An emergency came in at work, I couldn't get out."

Feeling an immense flood of relief that she hadn't been rejecting me, I smiled down at her. "You're here now." I rested a hand on the small of her back and gestured to the table I'd been sitting at. "Shall we?"

Acting the gentleman, I helped Justine into her seat then moved round to mine. We ordered drinks when the waiter approached, looking a little confused. Thankfully he remained professional and slipped away without comment.

"So—" we both said in unison while studying our menus.

I put mine down and chuckled. "You go first."

"I feel so bad for being late. Were you waiting long?"

"Not really. It's fine, honestly."

The waiter dropped off our drinks and took our food orders before disappearing again. I sipped on my drink and watched Justine intently as she told me about her day at the hospital and the emergency that had made her late. She was so passionate and animated about her work. It was admirable.

Our food arrived, and while we ate we continued to chat. By the time our desserts were placed in front of us, though, my mind was drifting. Justine was great, and our conversation about her job had been interesting, but something was missing. We had no spark or connection. I had no interest in opening up to her about my life or career, and there was absolutely no desire to want to touch her physically. She felt more like a friend than a possible love match.

I watched her cut into a piece of lemon meringue pie and lift it to her mouth. I tried focussing on her lips, watching as they opened around her fork and pulled the dessert into her mouth. She licked them, stroking away crumbs and a dab of cream. It could have seemed like a somewhat erotic act, and I waited for my dick to stir to attention, but it didn't happen. There really was absolutely nothing there.

Justine was attractive. With shoulder length blonde

hair styled into a simple bob, big, expressive emerald-green eyes, a perky little nose dusted with freckles across the bridge and delicate ivory skin tone, she was the type I would usually be attracted to. However, as I watched her eat her dessert, I imagined it was a petite, dark-haired woman sitting across from me. She had big brown eyes that sparkled with humour and intelligence. More recently, though, they'd held a hint of sadness and detachment.

"How is Cassie?" I asked Justine out of the blue.

For a brief moment she looked surprised, maybe a touch hurt. Her fork hovered in mid-air. "She's okay, I guess."

"I'm worried about her."

Justine placed her fork down and rested her hands in her lap. "Why, what's up?"

"I know you said before that Jay is an okay bloke, but I think he's bad news. Something's going on, but Cassie won't talk to me. She shuts me down whenever I bring it up."

She nodded. A passing look of concern for her friend washed over her face.

"I've noticed a change in her, too. She's been more withdrawn, quiet. It's down to Jay, I know it is."

She ran an uneasy finger along the edge of the table, considering her next words. When she looked up, sharp, determined eyes met mine.

"I think he's hurting her, and I don't know what to do about it."

"What do you mean he's hurting her?"

She bit her lip nervously and paused a moment. "She had bruises on her thighs the other day. I've seen marks on her wrists, too. She completely denies they were because of Jay, but I don't believe her. I'm worried about her, Adam. How can I help her when she doesn't listen to me?" The more she said, the more her words became pleading and desperate.

Grabbing her hand, I squeezed it gently, reassuringly. "I don't know if she won't talk or admit there is a problem, but I promise I'll do what I can to help her."

"Thank you," she whispered sadly.

As we continued to voice our concerns for Cassie, any hints of the evening turning romantic had gone. We became two friends desperate to help another.

"I'M IMPRESSED. YOU know, for a puny surfer boy." Lowering the bar to the safety of its stand, I flicked my eyes up. Wesley stood behind my head, grinning. "I can see why Cassie likes training with you so much now. You make her look good."

Laughing at his teasing, I sat on the edge of the bench wiping sweat from my face with a towel.

"For someone so tiny, that woman's a machine. She's been nagging me to try kick-boxing with her, but I'm too fucking scared to let her anywhere near me. She'd take me out with one of her kicks before I could blink."

He chuckled. "You should give it a try. It might be... fun."

"There is absolutely nothing fun about having your arse handed to you by the Karate Kid in disguise."

"I wouldn't let Cassie hear you call her that. She's very protective of her art. It could end with you on your back." His eyes widened in mock horror.

"Whatever. Where is she, anyway?" I'd been looking for her since I'd walked through the front door. After Justine had revealed her concerns to me on Friday, I'd spent all weekend worrying about Cassie. I sent her several texts that went unanswered, and she hadn't been around when I'd dropped into Golden Oakes hoping to find her. Colin, one of the personal trainers, said she hadn't been in. He'd seemed a little surprised because she was usually a regular fixture. She hadn't been on the roster to work, though, so he hadn't been too concerned.

My worries had kept me agitated and tense. I'd been snippy at work all day, and eventually, everyone got the message it was better to leave me alone.

When Cassie hadn't been in the reception area to greet me that evening, my anxiety levels increased to epic levels. Those I spoke to said she was around, they just weren't sure where. So, while I waited for her to appear, I took out my torment on the gym equipment. The punch bag had already been through a rough pasting that even Nathan Oakes himself would have been proud of. Then I'd moved on to the weights. Piling on more plates than usual, I'd pushed myself to the point of near exhaustion just to try and block out the thoughts of anything being wrong with Cassie.

"She had a late client. They must be running over," Wesley said, grabbing more weight to add to the bar. "Spot me?"

I watched the shiny silver bar rise and fall as Wesley bench-pressed a ridiculous amount of weight, but my mind wasn't focussed on the task. My eyes kept flicking to the front of the room where people came and went. None of them were Cassie.

"I'm down here," Wesley grunted, pushing the bar up.

"Sorry," I said, helping return the bar to the rack. "My mind drifted off for a minute."

"You don't say. I could've been buried…." His words were lost on me because at that moment Cassie walked into the room with a sad-looking young girl.

Stepping away from Wesley, I watched the two make their way through the room quietly talking. I paused beside a pillar, my gaze riveted to Cassie's profile as she placed a hand on the girl's arm. My gut clenched into a painful knot. While Cassie attempted to offer comfort and reassurance, a deep sadness filled her eyes. She looked lost and alone, a woman who was in need of help.

Cassie, sensing my presence, turned, and for the briefest moment her body tensed. Our gazes met. I wanted to run to her and demand answers. I wanted to know why she had been ignoring my texts, why she refused to admit to a problem with Jay. Mostly I wanted to pull her into my arms and hold on until the pain she held disappeared. Even then I wouldn't let her go.

She said something to the girl, and then they slowly made their way toward me through the maze of equipment and people.

"Adam." Her voice held its usual calm and confidence, but I detected the wary undertone. Something was bothering her.

"Hi." I nodded a greeting to Cassie's companion. "Do you mind if I steal her away for a minute?" Without waiting for a reply, I wrapped an arm around Cassie's waist and urged her into a quiet corner.

"Adam, what are you doing? I have a client." She squirmed out of my hold.

"Where were you all weekend?"

"That is none of your business."

"I sent you several texts. Why didn't you reply?"

"I was busy."

"With Jay?"

Her eyes narrowed, turning dangerously dark. "Yes. He is my boyfriend. How was your *date* with Justine?"

Was that a hint of jealousy I detected?

I shrugged. "We had a good time."

Her arms fell back to her sides, her body seeming to sag in resignation. "I'm glad. She deserves a good guy in her life."

"So do you, Cass," I murmured.

She pulled her thumb to her mouth and bit nervously on the nail. "Jay is a good guy," she mumbled.

I took a deep breath, feeling unsure about my next words. "I know, Cass. I know he abuses you."

She gasped. "What? No! That's ridiculous!"

"No, it isn't." I moved, forcing her to step back. There I could brace a hand against the wall, caging her in. I could see it in her eyes; she was getting ready to bolt. "You know I've seen how he treats you, and Justine said she's seen bruises. You can't let him treat you this way."

All colour drained from her face. "You talked about me?"

"We care about you, Cass. We can't stand by and watch what he's doing to you. Something has to change."

I stood so close I could feel her heavy breaths

against my cheek.

She narrowed her eyes dangerously, and with shaking hands, she pushed hard against my chest. Stunned, I stumbled backwards and fought to regain my footing. She stepped forward, stabbing a finger into my chest. "There is no problem. Stay out of my life, Adam. You can tell Justine to go to hell, too."

Fighting the urge to chase after her and plead with her to listen, I watched in dismay as she stormed away.

For several minutes, I stood against the wall watching Cassie patiently and calmly working with her client. Wesley shot me a what-the-fuck-was-that look. I shrugged, not knowing how to answer. I'd seen first-hand what Jay was doing to her, and having Justine back up my theories only strengthened my resolve to help her. I'd thought that with our support she'd acknowledge there was a problem and let us help her. Her complete denial made things more difficult.

Occasionally Cassie would glance over and catch my eye. The murderous scowls she shot me were enough to let me know I'd stepped way over the line. Pushing away from the wall, I headed for the changing rooms, knowing no matter what she said, or how she looked at me, one way or another I would get her to admit Jay was a problem. I would protect her and help get Jay out of her life for good.

I LEFT WORK early on Tuesday figuring I needed to find Cassie to apologise. If I had any hope of trying to reach out to her and have her listen to me, she needed to at least be talking to me.

There was a different energy buzzing around

Golden Oakes that afternoon. I noticed it the moment I stepped through the doors. It was hard to pinpoint exactly what had changed because everything looked the same. The difference was in the effort people were putting into their workouts. Something, or someone, had given the gym goers a new sense of purpose and motivation.

The girl at reception told me Cassie had back-to-back clients so wouldn't be free for at least an hour. I would have preferred to speak to her straight away. I'd hoped we could clear the air so we could get back to our easy friendship. I was already missing her little quirks, her friendly jibes and warm smile. In the short time together since we'd reunited, I had grown fond of her. Her distance worried me.

I decided to wait for her in the small health bar just off the reception area. I'd be able to see her emerge from the spa there.

I grabbed a bottle of water and settled in for the wait, taking a seat in an armchair in the corner. I could watch the news on the TV screen and still look out for Cassie.

I got so caught up in the news of another political scandal that I didn't see Olivia enter the bar.

"Hey, hey, loser. How's it hanging?" My eyes flicked from the screen to my grinning friend as she stopped beside the table. "What, no welcome back for your oldest friend?"

"When did you get back?" I stood and pulled her into a hug with a huge smile on my face.

"We landed this morning. I'm fucking shattered but Nate, being the control freak he is, wanted to come check the business hadn't gone to shit while we were away. I swear he doesn't trust Wes with anything."

"Nathan's here?" I asked, releasing her to sit back down. His presence would explain the newfound energy around the building. Nathan Oakes was a huge local hero. Most people only joined his gym in the hopes of being able to say they'd trained with him.

Liv rolled her eyes. "Yep, the honeymoon is well and truly over."

"So, how was your trip to paradise, *Mrs Oakes?*"

She sighed dreamily, resting back in the chair with a goofy grin on her face. "It was incredible, beautiful, relaxing… exhausting—"

I cut her off when her expression turned horny, and I could only imagine what memories she was recalling.

I choked on my laughter and held up my hands. "Okay, okay, I'm glad you had a great time, but I really don't need all the details."

Her tanned face flushed crimson. "Yeah, sorry about that. Let's just say we had the most incredible time. How about you? What's been happening around here?"

We spoke briefly about work and other mundane details. Eventually, the conversation came around to Cassie. Because I hadn't been around Cassie and the gym after our one night in France, Liv and I had never discussed her. I'd avoided those conversations at all costs. I wasn't sure how much Liv knew about Cassie's relationship with Jay.

"He did what? I want to fucking kill him!" she yelled after I explained what I'd seen at the wedding.

"It's not just that," I continued, placing a calming hand over hers. "I'm sure there's more going on that she's not admitting to. Justine has seen bruises on her, and I saw how vile he can be toward her. I'm worried about her, Liv."

Studying me for a moment, her angry expression softened. "You like her."

"She's a great girl. What's not to like?"

She shook her head. "No, I mean you like her, as in have feelings for her. Strong feelings."

I stared at her, trying to figure out where this shit was coming from. Eventually, I started laughing. "That's crazy, Liv."

"Tell me something, Adam. Why are you so concerned about her? Why does it upset you so much thinking that she's hurting?"

"I'd feel this way about anyone in that position. Nobody deserves to be treated that way."

She shook her head. "I beg to differ. You're a wonderful guy, but I've never seen you act so concerned and protective about a woman before."

"There was one I would have killed for," I mumbled dropping my eyes to the table. Apart from my mum and Caleb's wife, Rachael, Liv was the only other woman I'd ever felt a sense of protectiveness for.

Liv moved into the seat next to mine and took one of my hands in hers. Her voice was soft when she spoke. "Adam, you know I love you. We've been best friends forever. But it could never have been like that between us. You know that, right?"

My head swam with a sudden rush of emotion. I'd tried to block out my feelings for Liv when I realised things between her and Nate were serious. Having her bring it up now of all times felt a little overwhelming.

"I know," I said quickly.

Her head slanted to the side, and she studied me with assessing emerald eyes.

"Will you do something for me, Ad?"

"Of course, anything."

Her lips tilted in a small smile.

"Ask yourself if your concerns over Cassie's well-being are as strong, if not stronger than those you once held for me. Because I think they are."

I let my eyes drift toward the spa entrance. Liv was right. I had moved on and accepted that our relationship was and always would be one of close friends. The usual feelings and reactions I had around her were absent. My heart wasn't pounding with yearning; my hands weren't itching to reach out to pull her into my arms.

Liv stood, placing a warm hand on my shoulder. "Fight for her, Adam. You deserve to be happy, too."

Nate appeared in the doorway as she strolled out. The love for his new wife was so easy to see in the way he stared into her eyes and pulled her into a protective hug. As he held her and she giggled, behind them the door to the spa opened and Cassie stepped out. Across the room, our eyes met and locked. For the first time, I recognised I did have feelings for her. I just wasn't sure how deep they ran and what I was supposed to do with them.

CHAPTER ELEVEN

Cassie

I SMOOTHED DOWN THE MATERIAL of my white T-shirt and retightened the tie on my black tracksuit pants. Being used to wearing short, form-fitting shorts or boxer shorts, the thick material felt foreign against my legs. I worried the new clothing would somehow impede my workout or affect my kicking abilities, but when Jay mentioned how provocative my old garments were and that he didn't appreciate the way other guys looked at me, I conceded to his demand that I wear something different. Anything to make him happy.

I was fussing with the hem of my top as I stepped through the spa entrance and I looked up into Adam's intense gaze. I froze.

After our run-in the night before I'd been anxious

about seeing Adam again. His questioning of my relationship with Jay was becoming too much, far too personal. When my last client of the day phoned to cancel at the last minute, I'd raised my face toward the sky and thanked whatever mighty being was up there for saving me from any awkward encounters. The evening workout sessions with Adam had, until recent days, been my favourite part of the day. Our friendly chats and humorous banter always left me with a smile on my face and a bounce in my step. I'd miss that. However, with his recent interfering ways, I needed distance and an earlier than usual workout would give me that. I'd quickly changed into my new—uncomfortable—threads with every intention of finishing my workout before Adam arrived.

Knowing I couldn't stand like a statue in the doorway all evening, I sucked in a deep breath and stepped further into the lobby. People walked by, coming and going from their own workouts, but I barely noticed them. Despite my pounding heart and urge to flee, I was rooted to the spot, caught in Adam's intense blue stare. He was hunched over a table in the health bar, his arms crossed over his sculpted chest. His expression was unreadable. He looked like he'd been there a while.

My step faltered halfway across the white tiled floor as I debated making a run for it into the gym, or continuing over to Adam. I could pretend everything was okay and hope he didn't mention yesterday.

The decision was made for me by an overly exuberant tanned brunette throwing herself at me.

"Cassie! Oh my God. Girl, I missed you. How are you?"

I froze again, this time to allow for a tight hug from Olivia that nearly squeezed the life out of me.

"Liv. Can't. Breathe," I wheezed.

"Shit. Sorry." She chuckled, relaxing her hold. Stepping back, she kept a hand on my upper arm and looked me up and down. Despite the new cover-up clothing, I felt more exposed than ever under her intense scrutiny. Her fingers drummed rhythmically against her thigh, and I knew she was preparing to ask something, something I wouldn't like.

Hoping to avoid any possible awkward questions, I smiled and stepped out of her hold. "I didn't realise you guys were back already. How was the honeymoon?"

Liv's eyes brightened and momentarily flicked behind me. She shot a quick glance over my shoulder to Adam, who had moved to stand a few feet away.

"It was incredible, such a beautiful place," she gushed. Pausing, a sly smirk formed over her face. She looked at Nate, who had yet to say anything, and then back at me.

"You know," she said, grinning, "you should come round to our place Friday evening. We could show you the wedding and honeymoon photos... maybe not *all* the honeymoon ones." Her newly tanned cheeks flushed red, and I didn't want to imagine what photos we couldn't see.

"Sounds great." I nodded, eager to catch up with my friends and share in their joy. Then my smile faded. "I need to check if Jay has any plans first."

I heard the quiet whisper of a curse from behind me and saw Liv shoot a warning glare at Adam over my shoulder.

"That's okay," she said, threading an arm with mine. "Let me know what he says. Although selfishly I hope you can to make it. I can't wait to catch up with all the gossip. It will be great to have the whole gang together." Her smile was broad and excited as she led us further into the gym.

I felt Adam's eyes on us until we'd disappeared around the corner. I tried to keep up with Liv's chattering but couldn't shift the apprehension of waiting for Adam to find me. By the time I'd finished my workout, I'd realised he wouldn't be joining me. So why, considering I was nervous about seeing him, did my stomach fall in disappointment?

JUSTINE JOINED ME at the gym on Wednesday evening. It was the first time I'd seen her for more than a hello and goodbye since our argument and her date with Adam. I missed my bestie. Due to staff shortages, she was being scheduled for more night shifts than days, and when she worked nights she mostly stayed over at a colleague's place near to the hospital. She loved living with me and financially it made sense because I only asked for help with the bills. However the hospital was on the opposite side of town, so when she was leaving work early in the morning, exhausted, the last thing she wanted to do was jump on the tube to get home. I understood but missed those simple times before busy work and training schedules had taken over.

"So, how was your date with Adam the other night?" I asked her, dodging the punch she threw at me. It only just missed. She was getting better.

She smiled and bounced on her feet, her blonde

hair swishing around her heart shaped face. "It was good. He's a lovely guy, so down to earth."

Inexplicable nausea suddenly shot through me, compromising my defence. Justine capitalised on my momentary weakness and caught me with a kick right in my stomach.

I landed heavy on my backside with a loud "Oof."

"Cassie! Keep that fucking defence up. What have I told you?" My eyes shot across the room to find Jay scowling at me. He shook his head in disgust and turned back to Bianca. She looked my way, shrugged, then returned to punching and kicking the pads Jay held. He seemed to be spending more time one-on-one with her recently.

"Bitch," I muttered under my breath, dragging myself to my feet.

"I hope you're keeping an eye on those two. I don't trust them one bit," Justine said, glaring at the pair.

"Ignore them. Come on, I want to know more about your date. Tell me everything."

She shot another evil glare over my shoulder before resuming her fight stance. "There isn't much to say. We ate, we drank, and we talked."

My knee reflexively lifted to counter her kick, and I followed up with a swift jab to her unguarded chest.

"Ow."

I snickered. "Justine, keep that fucking defence up," I mimicked and she laughed. "So, any making out at the end of the night?" I had no idea why I asked that because I really didn't want to know. The thought of the two of them together like that was like a physical pain.

But you want them to get together, Cassie. You want your

friends to be happy. And you're with Jay.

She looked wistful when she replied. "Sadly, no. After the meal, he drove me home and said he'd see me soon." She frowned. "It was all very... friendly."

I exhaled a relieved breath. "So what did you guys talk about?"

She shrugged. "The usual. Work. Hobbies. You."

"Me?"

"Yeah. It would appear you've made quite the impression on our Mr. Ashworth."

I scoffed, my face heating. "Don't be silly."

Before she could reply, Jay yelled at us again to focus.

"Seriously, Cass," she whispered, shooting a look at Jay. "Adam's really concerned about you."

I brushed it off with a wave of my hand. "That's ridiculous. I'm fine. So... when are you seeing him again? Is he bringing you to Nate's on Friday?" I bit my lip waiting for her answer. I didn't want him to. I didn't want to see them together.

"I don't know. He didn't mention going, and we haven't discussed any firm plans yet. It's so hard to commit to anything at the moment with my hectic schedule."

I wanted to kick myself, annoyed that my discreet attempt at finding out if Adam would be at Liv and Nate's had failed.

FRIDAY CAME TOO quickly, and I soon found myself standing uneasily at Jay's side in an elevator. We were heading to Liv and Nate's fancy penthouse apartment to look through their wedding photos. I'd secretly been hoping Jay wouldn't want to join me. I wanted so desperately to enjoy a carefree evening alone with my friends. Other than the recent night at the bar with Adam and Wes, I hadn't enjoyed time alone with them for months. Since before Jay and I became an official item. When I'd asked him, though, he'd insisted he come with me, and I became resigned to the awkwardness of having him by my side all evening.

The elevator pinged as it stopped on the twentieth floor. I readjusted the bag strap on my shoulder and turned as the doors slid open. Before I could step out, Jay grabbed my elbow, holding me in place as he crowded his firm body against mine from behind.

"Before we go in there, who do you belong to?" he asked, his cheek pressed against mine.

I stiffened, the same cold feeling I'd been experiencing with him recently washing over me. "You, of course," I said, hoping my voice sounded confident.

"Okay. Good. Remember that tonight."

My somewhat merry mood took a nosedive as Jay held my hand and led me along the bright hallway.

Jay didn't say another word until we stood outside Liv and Nate's place. I knocked, and the door swung open. Liv greeted us warmly, wearing a bright smile and even brighter clothes. The cream and aqua of her sleeveless maxi dress highlighted her enviable golden tan. The deep v cut in both the front and back showcased her new leaner physique.

Flipping her long deep chestnut hair over her shoulder, she gestured us inside. Their apartment was the same as I remembered it from over the years, only now it missed the bachelor vibe. Liv had brought life and happiness to Nate, and she'd also added vibrancy to their home that had been missing before. In many ways I envied them. I loved my house and all the memories I had of the place from childhood, but it lacked that same warmth their home had. I knew that came from the unconditional love and respect they had for each other. I could only pray that my house would one day feel the same.

"I'm so glad you made it," Liv gushed, taking my white hoodie from me. I hadn't wanted to wear it, but Jay had been lounging on my bed playing with his phone when I'd been getting dressed. As soon as he saw me in the same tight jeans and camisole top I'd tried to wear to my mother's, he'd scowled and demanded I wear something more casual. So I ended up in a pair of baggy jeans and a loose fitting T-shirt. "It's only your friends," he'd said, dismissing them and the event as being anything of significance.

His unreasonable demands infuriated me, but I followed his wishes of staying covered up to keep the peace. I hadn't been in any mood to argue with him.

"We wouldn't have missed it for anything," I said to Liv, taking a seat on the couch. Jay sat beside me already looking bored. "I can't wait to see the photos. You certainly had enough of them done." I chuckled at the memory of the dragon lady bellowing out orders at the wedding.

Liv flopped down on the seat opposite. "You're telling me. I still have nightmares about that woman now. I would have been happy with the few shots I wanted with friends and family. The rest, the ridiculously dramatic, overly posed ones were a waste of time and energy."

"So come on," I said excitedly, bouncing in my seat. "Where are they?"

Her grin grew wide, but she shook her head. "You're going to have to wait. We're having dinner first."

I sniffed the air, and my stomach growled its appreciation of the wonderful aroma of tomatoes and garlic wafting through from the kitchen. "You cooked?"

"Are you fucking kidding? Do you want to die?" Wes said wryly, walking into the room from the adjacent kitchen, handing me a bottle of beer as he passed.

"Sorry, fella, I didn't realise you were coming. I would have brought one out for you, too," he said to Jay, rounding the couch behind Liv to stand by the open French doors leading onto the balcony. I noticed the hint of a smirk when he lifted his bottle to his lips and took a large swig.

"I'll get him one."

Hearing Adam's deep voice, my hands shook. Resisting the urge to look at him, I quickly placed my bottle on the coffee table and hoped nobody noticed my sudden unease.

I had managed to avoid Adam all week by working out early or between clients and then spending every evening in the studio with Jay. All the extra training was having a positive impact on my technique and power, but a negative on my happiness. I refused to admit it to myself, but I missed Adam. I missed his bright, comforting smile, the deeply seductive baritone of his voice, and even the way he teased me. I missed the way we could so easily lose ourselves in a conversation and then suddenly start laughing when we realised we should have been doing something else.

But for the sake of my sanity and relationship with Jay, I needed to keep my distance from him.

Returning to the room, Adam handed Jay a beer. A silent warning glare passed between the two, heightening my apprehension further.

Liv either hadn't picked up on the sudden tension in the room, or she chose to ignore it. Either way, she startled me when she jumped to her feet and said, "Cassie, can you help me set the table please?"

"Sure." Standing, I looked at Jay. He glowered at Adam's back, burning hatred through his immaculately pressed navy shirt. My eyes darted from Jay to Adam to Liv and back. I didn't know what to do. I didn't want the evening ruined because of an overboil of testosterone.

"Come on." Liv grabbed my hand and pulled. "They'll be okay," she whispered, leading me away from the guys into the formal dining area. Although it was still part of the open plan living area, smoky glass blocks formed a partial divide that provided an element of privacy.

I looked around in confusion, seeing the large glass dining table already set with crockery, cutlery, and glassware for six people. A large crystal bowl sat in the middle housing a huge candle nestled in brightly coloured stones.

"Um, Liv, I think it's already done." I gripped the back of a cream leather seat and continued admiring the table.

"Yes it is. I did it all earlier." She pulled out a chair and nodded toward the one I held. "Sit."

"What's going on?" I pulled out the chair and lowered onto it.

"That's what I wanted to ask you. You come in here looking like someone just shot your puppy. Adam is pissy. Jay is pissy. Wes is being... well, Wes." She shrugged with a grin. "You've been like this since we got back, and I want answers."

"You'll have to ask Adam what's crawled up his arse, but I'm fine. Jay's fine. We're just tired I guess. We've been doing a lot of training this week."

She narrowed her eyes and pursed her lips. "Nope. Sorry but I'm not falling for that crap. You're one of my closest friends, Cass, like a sister. Something's going on, and I want you to tell me."

"I... There...." I exhaled in a rush. "Everything's fine. Nothing's going on." Plastering on my brightest smile, I pushed the chair back and stood. "Seriously. Everyone needs to stop worrying."

"We'll stop worrying when we get our Cassie back."

Nate lounged casually against the glass wall. His arms were crossed over his broad chest, his biceps straining the sleeves of the white Ralph Lauren polo shirt he wore. His face was serious, almost grim as he continued to stare.

The smile slid from my face. "I don't know what you want from me. I'm here. I'm me."

"You may be here in person, Cass, but you aren't here in spirit." He looked at Liv and back at me. For the first time I could remember, the tough fighter looked sad. "I'll bring the food in."

"I'll help you," Liv said, following him from the room.

Alone, I sank back into the chair with an irritated

sigh. These people were supposed to be my friends, like family, so why could they not listen when I said there was no problem?

I spent the duration of the meal brooding over their words. Conversations went on around me, but I barely heard any of it. When we'd all finished, and the table had been cleared, everyone moved into the living room while Liv grabbed her laptop.

"Let me just set it up and then you can scroll through the photos while I make coffee."

She set the machine on the coffee table in front of me and browsed for the image folders. Then she left me alone, telling me to take my time going through them.

I flicked through the first dozen or so quite quickly. They were the standard pre-wedding shots of the bride getting ready, her flowers, shoes… all stuff I wondered if it had really been necessary to capture. I giggled when I came to a candid shot of Liv and I huddled close together. We were all dressed and ready to go, holding glasses of champagne. We'd been whispering, jokingly conspiring against the wedding planner, coming up with gruesome ways of putting an end to our misery.

I looked up to crack a joke about it with Jay, but his attention was once again fixed on his phone. I frowned when it vibrated in his hand, and he moved out onto the balcony to take the call. I stared at him for a minute, hurt that he didn't want to share these happy memories of my friends with me.

Continuing to navigate through the album, there were pictures of the bride and groom during the ceremony and then the posed shots afterwards of them standing outside the church doors. I rubbed my palm over my chest at the sudden overwhelming feeling of pride and happiness for my best friends. My favourite images were the unobtrusive, candid shots. In those pictures, the photographer had managed to capture so much more than just two people standing in front of a camera. Every picture spoke of their absolute love and devotion; it was evident in the way they smiled and gazed into each other's eyes.

I didn't need to look to know Adam stood behind me. I felt rather than saw him move. A tingling awareness shot straight through my veins and added to the already overflowing tenderness in my heart. He perched on the back of the couch and looked over my shoulder while I continued clicking through the photos. The familiar scents of his cologne and shower gel hit me, halting me from doing anything more than staring at the image on the screen in front of me.

"Pretty special huh?" he said, his voice soft and tender.

Sucking in a deep calming breath, I continued clicking through the pictures. "They make a beautiful couple."

He was so close I could feel his body heat through my shirt. It was an oddly scary yet welcome feeling.

I felt his eyes on my face. "I wasn't talking about Liv and Nate."

My breath hitched at the suggestion behind his whispered words.

Worried about his reaction if he saw Adam sitting so close, I checked on Jay out of the corner of my eye. He stood with his back toward us, his elbows leaning against the balcony railing as he looked down on the streets of London below still talking on his phone.

I blew out a deep breath. "What are you doing, Adam?"

He shifted closer, his chest a feather-light touch against my shoulder. "I'm checking out the… photos."

Even though I knew it was wrong of me, my eyes closed as I took a brief moment to indulge in the comfort of Adam's scent and proximity.

Despite trying to stay away because of Jay, Adam had become a source of comfort and torment to me. I found myself longing for his smile, or the briefest of touches. I wanted to hear his laugh, his tender voice, his determination when we'd push each other. But despite his faults, I was with Jay.

When I reopened my eyes, it was with the determination that I could not allow those feelings for Adam to affect me again.

Liv, Nate, and Wes were laughing in the kitchen, and Jay was still outside talking to… I had no idea.

I began clicking through the images, once again losing myself in Liv and Nate's happily ever after. When I got to the pictures of the bride and groom with their wedding party, a lump appeared in my throat. We all looked so happy standing together, our bright smiles masking our frustration with the wedding planner but clearly showing our love for each other as a close group of friends and relatives. It suddenly occurred to me that there hadn't been many happy days since that day.

The next image I clicked on shattered my resolve; so much for not getting emotional. Smiling back at me on the screen was a petite brunette looking happy with her hair styled into a semi-updo with curls framing her face. Her dark blue silk gown skimmed her curves and highlighted her bright cheerful brown eyes—eyes that were more dull these days. Next to her stood a handsome blond man looking sexy in his perfectly tailored suit with white shirt and a tie that matched her dress.

As I slowly clicked through the next few images, my pulse rate sped up. My stomach clenched with a newfound realisation: Adam and I looked perfect together. It was in the way he stared into my eyes as the photographer caught us in an unguarded moment when we were talking. It was how my eyes lit up as we laughed together at some blunder. It was in the way I looked so at ease and happy when he had his arm wrapped around me as we smiled into the camera.

I stared at that last image for several minutes trying to calm my rioting thoughts and racing pulse. I shouldn't have feelings like that for Adam. I *couldn't* have feelings like that for Adam. He was my friend. Right? Someone I could trust even though things had been strained between us in recent days.

Feeling the subtle changes in Adam's posture and breathing, I chanced a quick peek over my shoulder. His blue eyes met mine, and then refocused on the laptop screen. He swallowed carefully, studying the photograph as intensely as I had been. Was it possible he felt the same as me?

Liv and Nate walked into the room with a tray of drinks. Liv placed the tray on the coffee table and sat on the couch opposite while Wes disappeared somewhere else in the apartment.

"So, what do you think?" Liv asked, curling into Nate's side.

I slammed the laptop lid closed and stood abruptly. "They are beautiful. Amazing photos... I... um... Please excuse me for a minute, I'm just going to...." I trailed off, not really knowing what I was doing. My head was dizzy, and I needed a moment alone to rid it of the jumble of confusion.

Walking into the kitchen, I heard whispers but chose to ignore them. I went straight to the fridge and grabbed a bottle of water. Twisting off the cap, I rested back against the counter, allowing my head to fall forward. I had never been so confused in my life. My mind knew I was in a committed relationship with Jay, but my heart and body suddenly yearned for Adam. I longed for the way he'd looked at me in those photos, the way he'd held me close, and the way he always seemed to want to protect me.

When did that happen? When did our comfortable, casual friendship become something more?

What the hell was wrong with me?

Adam was a great guy. If he trusted someone and welcomed him or her as a friend, then he was loyal and protective. That was it. It had to be. There were no feelings there. Right?

I stared at the floor, the water bottle shaking in my hand when he walked in. His steps were slow, apprehensive, echoing off the wooden flooring as he made his way across the room. His black dress shoes appeared in my line of sight, and I swallowed hard. Could I do this? Could I look at him and seem normal when my head and heart were at war? My head told me to walk away, to find Jay and get the hell out of there. My heart screamed that I needed to acknowledge that there were issues with Jay and that Adam was everything I wanted. Everything I needed. I could live in denial and pretend nothing was wrong, but Adam knew. He saw *me*. Underneath my mask, Adam saw the real Cassie.

"Cassie," he murmured. "What's going on?"

I shook my head, the concern in his voice almost shattering me. I had so many things I needed to say, but I didn't know how.

He placed gentle fingers beneath my chin and lifted my face to meet his comforting gaze. His eyes were clouded and troubled looking into mine. "You can't keep avoiding me, sweetheart. Are you ready to talk to me?"

Turning my eyes toward the living room, I nodded. "Yes," I whispered.

Adam seemed to sag in relief and tense in defence at the same time.

"Tell me."

"I... we...." A single tear slid down my cheek as I tried to compose my thoughts and find the right words.

Adam cursed quietly under his breath and pulled me against his body, wrapping me protectively in his arms.

"You don't need to tell me everything now, Cass. Just answer this one question for me... am I right? Is Jay abusing you?"

Those few words hit me like a wrecking ball, blasting me with the shame and absolute realisation of what had been going on, what I'd been denying. I swallowed down the sudden urge to vomit. I had never felt so on the edge of a precipice in my life. I was sure that one wrong move and I would be falling, and there would be no stopping me until I hit rock bottom.

Nodding my head against Adam's chest, I pinched my eyes tightly closed.

"Yes." The single word was nothing but a sad breath on my lips.

Adam's whole body tensed. Fury radiated from him in fiery waves.

Gently gripping my shoulders, he moved me to the side.

"I'm going to fucking kill him."

"Adam, no!" Panicked, I gripped his wrist and held tight. "Please don't. Not here. Not now."

Adam looked at me then out toward the balcony. He swore loudly and ran shaking hands through his hair, gripping it in tight fists.

"Cass—"

"Please, Adam. You can't confront him here," I desperately pleaded. "It will only make things worse. Let me... let me talk to him. I know things can't continue as they are. Just... give me some time to talk to him. Please."

He blew out a deep rush of air and closed his eyes.

Finally, he turned to face me. His eyes were wide and dark with anger. "Cass, you don't know what you are asking of me. How can I fucking let you leave here with him today knowing with absolute certainty what I do? How can you expect me to turn a blind eye and not say anything?"

I closed my eyes, willing the tears back.

"I know I'm asking a lot. I just need time, Adam. Please, just give me time."

Suddenly his arms were around me again, holding me in a tight embrace. He pressed his lips to the crown of my head. "This is going to kill me, Cass. You have to know how much you mean to me, right?"

I choked on a strangled sob and fisted his shirt. Why did he have to be so damn nice? He wasn't just breaking through my defences, he was obliterating them.

Adam sucked in a deep calming breath and ran a soothing hand along my back. "When will you talk to him?" he asked.

"I don't know... this weekend maybe," I said quietly.

He shook his head. "It has to be sooner. You need to talk to him tonight and get him the hell out of your life."

I caught movement out of the corner of my eye and looked away to see Jay walking across the balcony toward the door. "Please, Adam," I said frantically, stumbling out from his arms. "Just let me do this my way. I will speak to him. Just give me time."

"Cassie—"

I took another step back, shaking my head. "I can't do this now, Adam. Please... not now." My eyes were pleading for his understanding when Jay stepped into the kitchen.

"Cass, we need to go." Bile rose in the back of my throat. I couldn't be sure that Jay had seen me standing so close to Adam, or seen Adam touching me. Therefore, I didn't know what he was thinking. Fear and guilt ate at me as I moved to follow Jay out of the room.

As I passed, Adam tenderly held my arm. "Talk to him, Cass. If you don't, then I will."

Nodding weakly, I held his gaze as I backed out of

the room.

Before we left, we gathered in the living room to say our goodbyes. Adam, Wes, and Nate glared at Jay menacingly. Their behaviour startled me. After what I'd just admitted to him, I could understand Adam's reaction, but not Wes or Nate's. What was their problem?

I could see it was taking all of their restraint not to lay into Jay. Liv threw sharp, warning looks to a bristling Adam and practically had to hold Wes back. His face was red with anger, his hands pumping in out of a fist. The air in the room was oppressive, heavy from the weight of three hostile men. I stood close to Jay and prayed we got out of there before someone exploded.

What is going on?

Nate and Jay had a very brief conversation about the studio and kick-boxing, but it was awkward and forced. Nate was stiff and tense, barely containing his fury. I could see his need to lash out at Jay.

I looked around my friends in despair. They knew. They had to know. Why else would they be acting in such a way? I wanted to disappear into the cracks in the floor boards.

I shrank back and hit a hard body. Jay's arms immediately wrapped around me and I caught Adam's glare. He moved to take a step toward us and I quickly shook my head. Pleading with my eyes again to give me time and leave it.

We said goodbye and made our way out to the elevator. Each of my friends had hugged me and whispered words of encouragement and even sorrow for not noticing a problem earlier. That, of course, made me feel worse and had Jay shooting odd looks my way. Even I hadn't wanted to acknowledge what was going on in my own life. How were they supposed to know? Then shame returned knowing that they were aware of what was going on. I didn't want them treating me any different. I didn't want their pity or sadness. I definitely didn't want them to look at me any different.

As we stepped into the elevator, I kept my eyes averted and shrank into the corner. I couldn't read Jay, but he had to have felt the uncomfortable vibes rolling off the others. He had to have sensed their animosity. If he did, though, he didn't say anything. His silence only left me feeling more on edge.

When we got to Jay's Audi, he hit the fob to unlock it and pulled his door open. I stood beside the passenger door for a moment taking deep breaths, psyching myself up for whatever came next.

What did happen could not have shocked me more.

Getting in the car, I dropped my bag on the floor and pulled the seat belt over me. Jay still hadn't said anything, but I could sense his agitation. His broad shoulders were still and hiked up, and his hands gripped the steering wheel with brutal force.

"Cassie—"

I flinched and shrank back into my seat, preparing for his onslaught.

"I'm sorry." I blinked, wondering if I'd heard him right. Was he apologising?

Jay turned in his seat to face me. His eyes looked bleak and watery as he ran a hand through his hair. "I'm so sorry, Cass. Jesus. I am so fucking sorry." He took a shuddering breath and grabbed my hand, pulling it to his lips.

"I'm so, so sorry," he repeated against my knuckles.

Stunned, I froze and stared at Jay, not knowing what to say or do.

"Seeing you with your friends tonight, I realised something." He lifted a finger to my face and trailed it gently down my cheek. I flinched at his touch, and he noticed. Pulling his hand away, he steadied remorseful eyes on me. "I've not been a good boyfriend to you recently. God...."

I watched him in total bewilderment as he stared out of the window over my shoulder. What was going on? Where was this all coming from? Only two minutes before I'd been sure he was going to say something about Adam, or the way Liv, Wes, and Nate had treated him. I didn't know how to process an apology. I didn't even understand what he was apologising for. I sat still, afraid to move as I waited for him to continue.

"I've been stressed because of work. I'm worried about your fight—" I opened my mouth to answer that, but he quickly looked at me and shook his head, silencing me. "No, Cass. I am worried, but not in the way you're thinking. I do believe in you. And it's because I believe in you and care about you that I'm worried. I want the best for you. I want you to win and go the whole way. I want you to win the world title you crave. And I'm sorry if I've seemed anything less than fully supportive. I'm sorry I hurt you." His eyes fluttered closed as he whispered the final words.

"Jay, I...." I gulped. I didn't know what to say, how to react. His speech had completely stripped me bare and left me more confused than ever.

He opened his eyes and offered an apologetic smile. "I know I don't deserve it but can you ever forgive me? Will you let me make it up to you?"

I swallowed hard. "You don't need to do that."

"I do. I've been a fucking bastard, and if you kicked me out of your life right now, I would totally understand. But please, Cass, give me a chance to make amends. Don't think about leaving me. Please."

My head bobbed in stunned acquiescence.

Jay reached over the console and grabbed both of my hands, pulling them to his lips. "Thank you. I'll do better, I promise... I'll be the perfect boyfriend. I was going to surprise you on your birthday, but I want to tell you this now to give you something to look forward to."

"What?" I asked, my tension starting to dissolve.

"I want to take you to Thailand." My eyes widened in surprise. "We'll spend a few days in your mum's village so you can meet your family. Then we'll have ten days at an exclusive coastal resort. It will be just you, me, sun, sea, relaxation... it will be great. We'll have a wonderful time away from the stresses we have here." He smiled, showing his perfect white teeth and dimpled cheeks.

"I don't know what to say."

Jay brushed hair over my shoulder and cupped my cheek. "You don't need to say anything other than you'll come with me."

As we drove back to my place, Jay kept my hand on his lap with our fingers entwined. He happily sang along to his music while I stared out of the window.

Shocked.

Stunned.

Confused.

I couldn't quite get my head around Jay's complete turnabout. Did I believe him? Did I even want to go away with him if he was genuine? I couldn't help but think the damage to our relationship was already beyond repair.

CHAPTER TWELVE

Adam

"WHY THE FUCK DID YOU ever trust that guy, Nate?" Wesley slammed the door closed behind Cassie and Jay, his face a mask of pure venom.

I took a seat on the couch Cassie had been sitting on earlier. Liv and Nathan sat opposite while Wesley decided to pace back and forth behind them. The tension in the air was heavy, thick with concern and hostility.

"What did she say to you?" Liv asked me, her face drawn into a worried frown.

I picked up the bottle of beer from the coffee table and took a swig. It was going to take something much stronger than beer, though, to calm the bitterness spreading through me like a vile disease. My hand gripped the bottle tightly remembering Cassie's fear-filled features as she admitted what I'd been worried about the last few weeks. Being right felt so damn depressing.

"She finally conceded that he's been hurting her." I took a deep breath, swallowing the overpowering need to chase after them and beat the living shit out of the bastard.

"Fuck!" Nathan and Wesley bellowed in unison. Liv sucked in a harsh breath.

Wesley halted his pacing. He dropped his head back, and with his eyes closed and his hands tightly gripping his hair he mumbled and cursed under his breath. Nathan jumped to his feet and stormed toward the front door. He was hard-faced and distant, his hands clenching into fists over and over. Both men appeared to be at the limit of their control and ready for the kill. I knew how they felt. If it hadn't been for Cassie pleading with me to give her time to deal with Jay her way I don't know what I would have been capable of, kick-boxing master or not.

Liv scrambled to her feet and chased after Nathan, pulling on his shirtsleeve. "Nate, stop. Stop! Think about this for a minute. If you go storming in there, you'll make things worse for Cass. We need to be smart if we're going to be able to help her."

He paused midstride and stared down at his wife. "You know I'm right," she murmured.

"Fuck that," Wes said, barrelling across the room. "I'm gonna take that piece of shit out. I knew he was a controlling prick; I didn't realise he was that bad, No one hurts our Cassie. No one."

As he levelled with Liv, she pushed a hand hard against his chest. "Stop it! Will all of you just stop." I could see she was on the verge of tears, her hands shaking. "Adam, tell us what she said exactly."

"She didn't give me any details, just said yes when I outright asked if he'd been hurting her." Nathan and Wesley bristled, still facing the front door. "She told me to give her time to talk to him, to end things with him."

"And you just let her fucking go with him?" Wesley turned abruptly, stepping into my personal space.

Determined not to be intimidated by his size and known fighting abilities, I straightened my spine and stared him down. "It's what she wanted. Believe me; I wanted to go out there"—I pointed toward the balcony—"and throw him over. But she begged me to leave it. Begged me to allow her to deal with it in her way. What, you expect me to betray her wishes?"

"Yes!" he bellowed.

"Stop it!" Liv shouted loud enough that we all stopped and looked at her.

"Adam's right," she said more softly, looking at each of us in turn. "Cassie has confided in Adam. She obviously trusts him. And no, before you start bitching," Liv glared at Wesley, stopping him from saying something. "We have to believe that she will continue trusting in him so that he can help her. If you both disregard her feelings, she will never forgive you. She's vulnerable and hurting at the moment. She needs us all to support her however she needs us. If that is stepping back and letting Adam be the one she relies on, then so be it." She took a deep shuddering breath then offered me a sad smile. "You have to help her, Ad." She looked on the verge of tears.

Wesley didn't like it, his eyes burned furiously, but

he reluctantly agreed with a single, sharp nod of his head, and then he marched off out of the room, slamming the door behind him. Nathan pulled Liv into his arms and kissed her head. He was still tense but the need to fight slowly evaporated. He looked over, his face now a calm mask. "Don't let our girl down, Adam."

I nodded. "I don't intend to."

IT HAD BEEN several days since I'd last seen Cassie and I was going out of my mind with worry. I sent her several text messages, and she always replied with simple, vague responses letting me know that she was okay. On the fourth day, I'd been about ready to break down her door when I saw her emerge from the spa and rush toward the studio. Physically she looked beautiful, despite her baggy clothes, but I could see there was a mental weight dragging her down. Her eyes seemed dark and lifeless, her hair dull and hanging lank down her back.

As she hurried across the lobby, her eyes darted around as though she were searching for something or someone. I'd emerged from the changing room and was partially hidden by a pillar so she couldn't see me. I needed to know what was going on and was no longer prepared to wait for the tiniest of crumbs she fed me. I needed to find out if she'd kicked the bastard to the kerb.

I got my answer when two minutes later I followed her into the studio. Hell, if she didn't want to speak to me then I'd just find the answers out for myself. I'd join in the damn kick-boxing class. I snuck into the back of the room and tried to camouflage myself between a punching bag and lifelike, life-sized mannequin—damn that thing was scary looking. The large room was full of people with varying levels of ability training on several matted sections. I scanned the room and quickly found my target. At the far end, Cassie warmed up with who I assumed were the most advanced students. I bit back a curse when I saw Jay standing close to her talking to another guy. Their body language didn't scream awkwardness or animosity. In fact, Jay seemed almost smug with the rare look he shot her way.

She's still with him?

I needed to find out more and moved further along the wall, trying to blend in. The last thing I wanted was to be spotted by either Cassie or Jay. When Jay's eyes suddenly shot up to look around the room, I turned into the nearest group, showing him my back.

"You alright there?" A young guy asked in amusement, halting his repetitive kicking actions to a pad.

"Just checking things out. I'm thinking of joining," I lied.

"Cool. You should join, Jay's an awesome instructor." I held back my biting response to that statement.

Nodding, I looked over my shoulder, relieved to see Jay's attention now focused on another student. Bianca, I think I'd heard Cassie call her before.

"Yeah, I'll think about it."

I moved away from the group closer to Jay and Cassie. Cassie was punching and kicking a pad held up by another girl. I winced at the brutal force she hit the pad with and vowed never to piss her off too bad.

Settling against the wall within earshot, I bent over and started fiddling with my laces, praying I looked convincing. Cassie wasn't talking, just beating the shit out of the pad. Jay, however, seemed to be a little too friendly and flirty with Bianca. How did Cassie not notice this?

I wasn't getting anywhere with my stealthy undercover cop routine, so I decided to sneak out and wait outside.

I was halfway to the door when something grabbed my elbow and tugged.

"Adam, what are you doing in here?"

Shit! She'd seen me.

"Hi, Cass," I said brightly, hoping she didn't see right through me.

"Are you spying on me now?" she seethed, her voice thick and low. She continued tugging on my elbow, pulling me into a semi-private alcove as she looked over her shoulder.

I pulled out of her grasp and turned. "What do you expect me to do, Cassie? You're barely responding to my messages. I'm freaking the fuck out here thinking about you, scared to fucking death that idiot has done something to you." I was panting harshly as my fears and frustration surfaced.

Cassie crossed her arms over her chest and looked over my shoulder. She wouldn't meet my gaze. "As you can see, I'm fine. I told you in our texts that I was okay. I'm *alright*, Adam. So you can stop *freaking the fuck out.*"

My eyes narrowed at her snarky tone. "There is no need to be like that, Cass. I'm so very sorry that I care so fucking much." *Too much.* I turned to leave.

"No, Adam, wait. I'm sorry," she said, panicked, reaching for me again.

I exhaled a deep, steady breath, letting go of the tension. "We need to have that talk, Cassie."

"I know. But not here." She looked around to make sure we weren't being watched. "Can you meet me in my treatment room in ten minutes?"

I nodded. "I'll be there."

I waited until she'd made her way back over to her group before stepping out of the alcove. Just before I slipped out of the room Jay peered over, his eyes darkening seeing me sneaking away. They narrowed in understanding as he looked from me to Cassie.

Cassie re-joined her training partner on the mats while Jay continued glaring at me with his arms crossed over his chest as I slipped out of the room.

Back in the locker room, I quickly changed back into my work clothes, hoping I hadn't just made things worse for Cassie.

CHAPTER THIRTEEN

Cassie

GRABBING MY WATER BOTTLE AND towel, I prayed I could escape without Jay stopping me.

I felt like that clichéd statement, stuck between a rock and a hard place. I knew Adam would come looking for me if I didn't talk to him. That couldn't happen. I couldn't risk an argument erupting between him and Jay.

After his speech on Friday at Liv and Nate's, Jay had been determined to keep me close. He'd been very possessive, staying with me the whole weekend apart from a couple of times when he'd disappeared for an hour or two. I'd felt smothered. It had been a welcome relief when he'd reluctantly left my house early on Monday morning.

"Going somewhere, Cassie?" I'd only made it a few

steps before Jay's commanding voice halted me mid-stride.

"I've got a headache. I'm going to call it a night."

He approached from the side, his face unreadable. "Why didn't you say so?"

Running a hand down my cheek and around the back of my neck, he gripped tight, making me wince.

"Jay, you're hurting me." My words were harsh through gritted teeth. I didn't want to make a scene in front of everybody.

Shifting behind me, he pulled my body against his. His voice was deep and full of warning when he placed his lips against my ear. "You better go straight home then, baby. I'll be around to check on you later."

A cold sweat broke out across my body at the apparent threat in his tone. I broke away from him and practically ran all the way to my treatment room. I pushed the door open and fell to my knees. The tears of fear, frustration, and sadness that I'd been repressing for weeks finally fell.

The door opened and closed behind me, and then Adam was at my side, dropping to his knees and pulling me into his arms.

He didn't speak for several minutes; he simply let me sob until my body stopped convulsing, the tears had all dried up, and I was a hiccupping mess against his firm chest.

Eventually, when I'd managed to regain some composure, he brushed the hair from my face and kissed my forehead. "I shouldn't have gone in there like that," he whispered. "I'm sorry if I upset you."

"It wasn't you." I sniffled, pulling myself from his chest.

"What's wrong then?"

I sighed. If he wanted me to talk, now was as a good a time as any. "I think it's time I told you the full truth."

Adam held me close while I finally laid myself bare and told him everything. I knew he was struggling to control his emotions. Occasionally, when I mentioned something specific Jay had said or done, Adam would suck in a deep breath through gritted teeth, his whole body tensing beneath mine. He remained quiet, though, allowing me the time and space I needed to tell him everything. He had no idea how much that meant to me, how much I needed that from him.

"Do you have any idea how much I want to go in there right now?" he eventually said when I quieted. We were still on the floor with Adam leaning against the wall holding me tight to his side. My arm was wrapped around his waist as I rested my head against his chest, taking comfort from the steady beat of his heart.

"And what good would that do? He's an egomaniac, Adam. He's strong and fast, and if you confront him, he won't take it well. You won't stand a chance against him if he hits out."

"Someone needs to teach him a fucking lesson," he growled.

I lifted my head to look at him. "Please, I'm begging you, leave it. I don't want you getting hurt."

"And what about you? You think I want you getting hurt?"

I shrugged and rested my head back on his chest, absently drawing circles over his hard muscles.

He hugged me tighter and rested his chin on top of

my head. "Cass, you have got to get away from him. It's killing me seeing you hurting so much."

I sighed but remained silent.

After a quiet minute of listening to the steady thump-thump of Adam's heartbeat, I spoke up. "Jay spoke to me on Friday after we left Liv and Nate's and I'd thought maybe he'd changed...."

Adam scoffed. "Leopards don't change their spots, Cass. It's only a matter of time before he does something there may be no coming back from."

I shuddered at the cold, harsh truth. Now I'd spoken everything out loud, I realised just how manipulative Jay had become. He'd been sneaky in his attacks on me, slowly stealing my self-esteem and knocking away at my confidence. I could even see that what he'd been doing physically—the touching, the gripping, the use of my body for his sexual fulfilment—had been getting worse. Adam was right, one day soon things could become a whole lot worse.

But Jay wouldn't take my decision to break things off without a fight. He was a proud man with a massive ego. There was no way he would let me go that easily.

I swallowed hard against the deep lump that formed in my throat, thinking about the conversation I needed to have with Jay.

"Hey," Adam said, cupping my face in his hands and lifting so I'd look at him. "What's going on in that head of yours?"

"He's not going to let me go. He's not stable, Adam. He's going to argue, and shout, and... Oh God, this is all my fault." I jumped to my feet, the words tumbling out in a rush with the sudden feeling of panic consuming me. The tears I thought had all dried up started falling again.

Adam quickly stood and wrapped his arms tightly around my waist, cooing calming words into my ear.

"I don't know if I can do this," I admitted through a shuddering breath.

"You can. I have faith in you."

"I'm not so sure."

Adam moved his hands to my shoulders, holding me so I would see the sincerity in his calm ocean eyes. "Sometimes you have to be prepared to fall, to hit rock bottom. Only then can you pull yourself up until you're standing strong and proud once again."

My mouth opened to tell him I wasn't so sure he was right, but he hushed me with his fingers on my lips.

"However this goes, Cass, whatever you do, you have people here to support you. But you have to end it with him."

Our gazes met and held, an unspoken connection passing between us. Adam was feeding me strength, showing his confidence in me and giving me something I'd not felt for a while... hope. I hoped I was showing my trust in him.

"Okay," I croaked.

He tugged me back into his embrace, holding me close where I felt warm, protected, and safe. "Good girl. It will all work out, I promise," he murmured against my forehead.

"Isn't this cosy." The sudden opening of the door broke our moment of peace. We stepped apart as a furious-looking Jay stood in the doorway. His eyes were wide and wild, his body tense and ready for battle. "Would you mind getting your fucking hands off my girlfriend," he seethed.

In a protective move, Adam pulled me behind him. "That's rich, coming from you."

"What the fuck is that supposed to mean? Cassie, get over here now."

"Don't move a muscle, Cass," Adam said harshly. His arm continued to hold me back.

"Cassie, I said get over here. Now!"

Fearful that things were going to turn nasty, a strangled scream bubbled up from my throat. I couldn't have these two men fighting over me. More so, I couldn't risk Adam getting hurt.

Taking a deep breath, I stepped aside and shot Adam a wary but appreciative smile before turning to Jay. He grinned smugly as Adam said, "Cassie, what are you doing?"

Keeping my eyes on Jay, I asked Adam to leave. I knew what needed to be done and now was the time to reach in deep for the inner strength Jay had been stealing from me for months.

"I'm not leaving you with him."

"Adam, I'm not asking, I'm *telling* you. I need to talk to him. Alone." I still hadn't taken my eyes from Jay, whose expression flickered between triumph and confusion.

"I don't like this, Cass,"

"I'm not asking you to like it. But I need to do this my way."

Adam grumbled, taking an unsure step toward the door. He paused momentarily and only continued when he met my pleading gaze.

Jay stepped aside to allow Adam to pass, as he did

they glared at each other, clear warnings passing between them.

"I'm giving you five minutes," Adam warned, shooting me a look that warned I wouldn't have a second more. When the door closed behind him, leaving me alone in the room with Jay, I seriously doubted the bravado behind my decision to do this on my own. I had no plan, didn't know what I would say. And from his lethal glower, I seriously feared what Jay might do.

Jay broke the silence first. "Care to explain to me what that was all about?"

I stepped around the massage bench, putting a much-needed barrier between us.

"We need to talk."

"No, *you* need to talk." He sat on my desk chair, crossing his arms over his chest, and stretched his legs out. The relaxed position could not hide the deep rage in his dark steel eyes. "Why was there a guy in here with his hands all over you?"

I wiped my shaking, sweaty hands on my tracksuit bottoms and decided to just be honest. I needed him gone. Out of the room, and out of my life. "I can't do this with you anymore, Jay. I can't see you anymore."

His brows shot up. "Excuse me?"

I swallowed and nervously ran a finger along the leather of the bench. Then, as if he were channelling positive thoughts my way, I thought of Adam and his inspiring words. I knew that no matter what happened in the next few minutes I was going to hit rock bottom. It was inevitable. Somehow, though, I found strength in knowing that by doing this I would then be able to start rebuilding myself into the person I used to be.

Looking Jay in the eye, I purged everything I'd suppressed under his manipulation. "I can't take your crap anymore. You've been treating me like shit for a while now, knocking me down, hurting me—physically and emotionally. You've taken away the one thing that made me who I was—my strength, my fire." With each word my confidence grew. I leant against the bench, putting Jay within touching distance. "I'm done being your punching bag, Jay. I'm done taking your abuse."

"Have you finished?" He moved to the opposite side of the bench, leaning in intimidatingly.

I stood firm, maintaining eye contact even when my hands shook and my pulse raced too fast.

"Yes. We're through, Jay."

A dark, humourless chuckle vibrated from deep within his chest. "Not by a long shot. Are you that fucking stupid?" He slammed a fist down heavily on the bench. I flinched, taking a cautious step back. "I own you, Cassie. Every. Fucking. Inch. Of. You. You are nothing without me! Nothing!"

"No—"

"Yes!" His roared word echoed off the walls.

Suddenly, the door burst open and three men rushed in yelling. I screamed as Adam, Wes, and Nate each lunged for Jay, their faces masks of thunder. The message bench topped over as Adam bumped into it reaching out for Jay. His fists swung lightning quick, catching Jay off guard with jabs to the jaw and a knee to his abdomen. I heard a sickening crunch and a groan, and then Jay was falling to the floor.

"Fuck, that felt good," Adam murmured, shaking

out his hand as he glared down at Jay.

I stood in a daze, barely breathing.

"You okay, Cass?" Nate asked from across the room.

I nodded. "I think so."

Standing at Jay's side, Nate grabbed him by his shirt and pulled him to his feet. "You're finished here, Masters. You hurt one of mine, I hurt you."

Jay spat and fought against Nate's tight grip. "Fuck you, Oakes. What are you going to do? Take me down? Bring it on."

Nate snorted and pushed Jay away. "I'm not going to bring myself down to your level, you piece of shit—believe me, I want to, though. Instead, I'll do the next best thing to hurt your sorry arse."

"Yeah? What's that?"

"You're out. Take your shit and get the hell out of my gym."

"You can't do that. We have a contract."

Getting into Jay's face, Nate replied coldly, "I own the place, I can do what I fucking like. And if you'd read the small print you would have found it means shit anyway. I've always had the power to terminate it at any time."

"This is bullshit!" Jay roared. Then staring straight at me, his voice was icy when he said, "We will never be over. You owe me, Cassie."

Three deep male voices growled in response and my friends took an intimidating step closer. Jay, finally realising he was outnumbered, had the sense to leave but not before levelling me with a glare that promised he would not be going away quietly.

After a minute of staring at the empty doorway

expecting Jay to return any second, I slowly turned and found three pairs of eyes on me.

I exhaled a deep breath. "Well, that went well."

"Why didn't you tell us sooner, Cassie? I would've happily kicked his arse out a long time ago," Nate said.

"What were you thinking, keeping something like that from us?" Wes grouched.

"I still want to knock him out," Nate grumbled.

I blocked them both out. There was only one person I could focus on, and he was staring back, his face a picture of pride and rage.

As the adrenaline rush began to recede, I suddenly felt weak and drained. My arms felt like lead weights, and my legs were slowly losing the ability to hold me upright. White lights dotted my vision, giving Adam an almost ethereal appearance—my guardian angel. I was breathing shallowly through my nose and felt a sudden bone-chilling cold, despite the sweat now covering my clammy skin.

But I kept my grateful gaze on Adam, focusing on his mesmerising beautiful blue eyes. They were eyes you could get lost in, and at that moment, they had me totally transfixed. A small smile tugged at my lips as the white lights burned brighter, more intense. I felt like a summer wildflower swaying freely in a warm breeze....

"Catch her, she's going," were the last words I heard before my legs gave out and the light turned to dark.

WHEN I CAME to, a pair of blue eyes were level with mine, blinking in concern.

Feeling dazed and confused, I had a quick visual scout around. I was still in my treatment room, lying on the padded bench covered by a thick blanket. The harsh ceiling lights were off, the room bathed in a delicate golden glow from the dimmed inset wall lanterns and my retro lava lamp sitting in the corner. The place was silent except for the quiet hum of the air conditioning system and the persistent drip, drip from the tap I'd been meaning to get fixed.

"What happened?" I croaked through a dry throat.

"You fainted."

I what?

"I did?"

I'd never passed out before in my life, well apart from the odd occasion when I'd imbibed far too many Jager bombs and barely made it to my bed before collapsing in a drunken sleepy heap.

Adam chuckled, a warm, hearty sound that instantly soothed my frayed nerves. He gently pushed a lock of hair away from my face, his fingers smoothing it over my shoulder. "Yeah. One minute you looked like you were ready to take on the world, the next you were flat out cold."

"Oh no." My hands flew to my face, hiding my embarrassment and shame.

"Hey, there's no need to hide, sweetheart." His voice took on a soft and reassuring tone as he gently held my hands and eased them from my face, keeping our fingers entwined on the edge of the bench. "It was understandable, given the circumstances."

I frowned meeting his eyes again. "What circumstances?"

"You don't remember?"

My mind hastily replayed the previous hour or so, flicking through fractured images of Adam in the studio, Jay's angry voice spitting venomous words, raised voices, Wesley, Nate, Adam....

"Oh shit!" Through a grimace, I jerked upright, fighting the blanket from my legs as I flung them over the side of the bench. I held back a sudden rush of dizziness, sucking in a deep breath and closing my eyes to calm my tormented body and mind. When the cloud passed, my worried gaze traversed his face, along his toned arms, and finally to his hands—hands that had punched Jay. For me.

I gasped. "Adam, your hand. You hit him. I can't believe you did that!" My voice rose in pitch along with the apprehension crawling its way over my body.

Adam's hands fell into his lap, and I immediately grabbed for them, repeatedly turning them over, inspecting them closely for injury. I couldn't believe he'd hit Jay, especially with the power and accuracy he'd landed the punches. He'd always appeared to be anti-violence, always so calm and rational. Controlled. He was the type of person who would advocate mediation and discussing issues calmly rather than using fists to do the talking. I'd been sure that was one of the reasons I'd not been able to get him into the studio to try out kick-boxing. I'd thought he didn't approve, was against any form of physical combat. Tonight, as he'd rushed into the room like a raging bull, his sole focus had been on hurting Jay. To protect me.

"Cass," he said, slowly retrieving his hands from my close inspection. "They don't hurt; I'm okay."

I was anything but okay. Unease rippled through

me thinking about what happened. Jay's threat to me would now surely extend to Adam, too. He wasn't the type of guy to let things go.

"But—"

With a brusque shake of his head, Adam silenced me. Lines of conflict and deep emotion spread across his handsome face. He appeared to be recalling memories of those few tense minutes. His beautiful blue eyes—now darkened and glazed over—narrowed, his voice hard and bitter when he spoke. "He's damn lucky he's not on ice in the mortuary right now. When I see him hurting you like that…." A curse rushed from his lips, his hands scrubbing furiously down his face. "I wanted to fucking kill him, Cass."

Holy shit.

His words momentarily startled me, his hostility shocking. This was a side of Adam I'd not encountered before, a tough, strong, powerful side. I'd always liked Adam's soft and compassionate personality—his easygoing, caring nature. I realised then, though, that I loved—in a fucked-up sort of way—this new, raw, gritty, and passionate side. It showed he was highly protective—to the point of extreme emotional self-torment—of those he truly cared about.

Does that mean he cares about me?

Still in a semi-haze, I forced myself to focus. "Thank you, Adam… for what you did."

His deep-set scowl softened into an affectionate smile. "No thanks needed. I would've done the same thing for any woman."

The sudden bite of hurt burned through my chest, scalding and scarring. I had no right to feel that way. Had no reason to believe that I'd been anyone of any particular importance to him, yet it stung. It was absolute craziness considering only minutes before I had ended a relationship. But I felt connected to Adam. On some deep, fundamental level I wanted to be important to him.

My mind and body were weary—tired from the day, exhausted from the months of pretending nothing was wrong. Now it was over, I just wanted to curl up in my bed and hide away from the world. I needed time to process the tornado of thoughts twisting through my head.

With tears threatening to spill, I lowered myself from the bench, taking a moment to guarantee my balance before stepping to the side, away from Adam. Without his warmth near me, I felt chilled. I immediately wrapped my arms around myself, my whole body protectively folding in on itself as I stared at the tiled floor. I sensed Adam's eyes on me, watching, assessing my every move.

"I'm tired. I think I'm just going to go home," I said, taking a tentative step toward the door. I still felt a little unsteady, weak from fainting, exhausted from the weight of so many emotions squeezing the life from me.

"You shouldn't be alone tonight, Cass," he said in a concerned whisper. "You've been through too much. Why don't you come home with me?"

I shook my head. "Thank you, but no. I just want to be in my own home."

"Please," he implored. "Just for tonight, come home with me. You can have my bed and I'll sleep on the couch. You need time to process what just happened. You shouldn't be alone."

I sighed and shook my head. "I need to do that on my own, in my own bed. I'll be okay, Adam."

"Well you're not driving. I'll take you. I need to make sure you get home safely," he demanded, the bold determination in his voice suggested arguing would be useless.

Still, I tried.

"There's no need. I'm alright."

Ignoring me, Adam stood, his long legs eating up the distance from bench to doorway in five confident strides. He grabbed my hoodie from the coat rail and held out a hand, beckoning me forward. "Then you won't mind me taking you. Come on, let's go. I won't take no for an answer."

Defeated, I grabbed my bag from under the desk and took the sweatshirt from Adam, following him from the room and locking up behind me. He wrapped a comforting arm around my shoulder and led me out of the spa, through the lobby, and out into the warm summer night air. With each step we took, a nervous energy developed within me. My eyes darted around the building and parking lot, expecting Jay to appear at any second. I was a sweaty, jittery wreck by the time we reached Adam's car. I loathed that Jay wielded that level of power over me, that he'd stripped me of my former pride and confidence.

Adam led me across the lot to a black Insignia parked strategically away from other cars, the deep orange and pink glow of the twilight sky reflecting off the tinted windows and shiny paintwork. I looked at the car, an affectionate grin pulling at my lips. It was so him, modest yet masculine. Most guys I knew drove expensive luxury vehicles or flashy sports cars. Not

Adam. He'd chosen something respectable, something that didn't scream over-the-top or make huge egotistical statements. It was just another of the many facets of Adam Ashworth that I was slowly piecing together.

The lights flashed and the alarm beeped as we approached. Taking my bag, Adam opened the passenger door. I felt the weight of his gaze as I settled into the comfort of the soft black leather seat and he closed the door.

Adam rounded the front, threw our bags into the back and slipped into the driver seat. With his hand poised over the ignition, he froze, staring through the front windscreen. My body stiffened, fearful of what, or who, he was looking at. I followed his gaze out across the parked cars and landscaped borders and found nothing of interest. No crazed ex-boyfriends or axe-wielding maniacs.

Finally, he blinked out of his daze and turned to face me. "Cass, I'm so sorry I didn't protect you more against him. I didn't... you wouldn't... I should've...." Frustrated hands scrubbed along his face and gripped at his nape. "I should have protected you."

Startled, I sank further into the seat. I had no words; the ability to throw a smart comeback or any appreciation had deserted me. I merely blinked.

Stunned.

Without another word Adam put the car in reverse and eased out of the space. During the drive back to my place, other than confirming my address, Adam was quiet, contemplative. I found my attention diverting from looking out the window to studying his handsome face in profile. From the tautness of his jaw, the fraught lines between his eyes, the occasional tiny shake of his head—so slight it was almost imperceptible—I knew he was still stewing over the events of the last hour. His words, the way he'd said them with such conviction and sentiment, had touched me someplace deep. It was a feeling I'd never experienced before; well, not since I was a young girl who had a father I adored, one I believed had hung the moon and scattered stars into the night sky to give me something magical to wish on.

Adam pulled the car into a vacant spot outside my whitewashed Victorian home. All the lights were out; the blinds covering the front windows were closed. Nobody was home. I looked at the bright floral plaque hanging proudly on the wall beside the front door, a warm sign welcoming visitors. A pang of sadness gripped at my chest, thinking of Nana. God, I missed her. My dad... Phillip had been furious when he discovered Nana had left the house to me in her will. At first, he'd contested it, had made it difficult for me to live there. Then we were both handed letters she'd written months before she died. In those letters, she had been clear that to her genetics didn't matter. In her eyes, I was her granddaughter and always would be. She wanted me in her home, bringing life and love into it. The will had been airtight, and Phillip had had no choice but to concede the house to me. It was just one more thing he detested about me. But I loved my home and the memories that came with it. It was untainted, a place of sanctuary.

I swallowed back a tight ball of emotion, thinking I needed Nana right then. I needed for her to be sitting in her favourite armchair by the fireplace, knitting needles clicking together as she so beautifully created another fabulous garment for somebody. Always ready to offer comfort, she would peer up at me over the rims of her dark red spectacles, her knowing green eyes shining with love as she'd place the needles and wool to the side and spread her frail arms wide. I would run over and curl up in her lap, releasing all my troubles in a fit of sobs, as she would run tender hands along my arms and back, comforting me. Nana had the most amazing hugs. So full of love and understanding.

Compassion.

Reassurance.

Stepping out of Adam's car, my eyes remained glued to that welcome sign. Internally I begged for Nana's reassurance and strength.

CHAPTER FOURTEEN

Adam

"ARE YOU COMING IN?"

Cassie's softly spoken words pulled me from the cloud of confusion swirling over my head. From the moment she'd passed out in her treatment room, a new and overpowering emotion had caught me by surprise. It was beyond the levels of concern and care that had already been growing. It went beyond acquaintanceship and friendship; it was an inexplicable need to cherish this woman and protect her from anything ugly in the world.

I didn't know how to deal with those feelings.

Things were so messed up.

I was supposed to be seeing Justine again in a few days, and Cassie had just broken free of an extremely toxic relationship. But at that moment, as I watched her through the open passenger door looking all kinds of beautiful and vulnerable, I wanted her. Not as a quick fuck or a passing fancy. Not as a friend with benefits. I wanted her.

Completely.

Undeniably.

"Please, Adam. I...." She looked over her shoulder toward the dark house. "I don't want to be on my own." Her voice was so sad, leaving a knot of tension on my chest.

Exhaling heavily, I shut off the engine and climbed from the car. "You're not on your own, Cass."

I trailed Cassie along the short pathway to her front door. With trembling hands she dug through her bag for the key. It took a moment of fumbling and shaking before the lock finally gave way, allowing the door to drift open to reveal the darkness within.

She flipped a switch, bathing the hallway in a soft golden glow.

Cassie removed her trainers and kicked them into a corner littered with several other pairs of women's shoes. "I'm just going to run upstairs to get changed. Make yourself at home."

I watched her firm backside jog up the carpeted stairs and disappear at the top. Closing the door, I slowly made my way further into the house, looking at the many frames hung on the pale yellow walls. There were several pictures and paintings of lilies and a few smaller landscape prints, but what caught my eye was the large image placed centrally over the fireplace in the living room. It was a black-and-white wedding painting several decades old. The man wore a formal dark suit, the woman a long white or ivory dress with long lace sleeves. A floor-length veil trailed down her back and had been expertly placed to curl around her feet. She held a simple bouquet of white lilies. I stepped closer, searching the faded canvas for a family resemblance.

"My nana. I never knew my grandpa. He died before I was born." Turning, I found Cassie standing in the doorway resting against the frame. She'd changed out of the frumpy sweatpants and baggy T-shirt into some pale grey pyjama bottoms and a white camisole top that did little to hide the fact she wasn't wearing a bra beneath it. I sucked in a breath and quickly looked back at the painting. It was wrong of me to be checking out any part of her body, let alone her exquisite pair of perfectly formed breasts.

"They looked happy," I said, nodding at the picture.

"They were. They had a simple but overpowering love. She never got over him dying so young." She moved beside me and stared up at the picture of her grandparents.

We continued to stare for a few minutes; Cassie lost in her memories and me mesmerised by the awareness of how close she stood to me. I could feel her heat, smell the sweet scent of her body spray, and hear her gentle breaths... breaths that soon became laboured and choppy.

At her first shuddered sob, I wrapped my arms around Cassie, holding her close.

"God, I feel like such a fool, Adam. Why couldn't I see what he was doing to me? Why did I let it go on for so long?" Her voice broke as she buried her face into my chest, tears soaking through the material of my T-shirt to burn me with a fresh wave of hatred for Jay.

"Shhh," I cooed against her ear. "That doesn't matter. You're free of him now."

"Am I?" Her head shook as she sniffed. "I don't think he'll let me go that easily. Jay's too proud for that."

I bristled at the thought of that prick coming anywhere near her again. There was no fucking way I would let him.

"He's going to be pissed Nate is kicking him out of the studio."

"Cass," I placed two fingers beneath her chin and lifted her face to mine. "It doesn't matter what he thinks or says or does. We've got your back. Over my dead body will I let him get anywhere near you again." My eyes bored into hers, desperate for her to see she was no longer alone. Desperate for her to see how much I cared about her.

Her eyes were sad and red-rimmed, tears still swimming in their depths as she stepped back. She inhaled a deep breath and released it slowly, swiping across her eyes with the back of her hand. "Can we please not talk about him right now? I need a drink. Do you want one?"

I followed her into the kitchen where she grabbed two wine glasses from a cupboard and a bottle of red wine from the wine rack.

"Can I ask you something?" she questioned, fumbling with the corkscrew, her hands still shaking. "How are things with you and Justine going? I haven't seen her around much because of her shifts. She said your date went well. I think she really likes you, Adam.

She needs a good guy in her life. That last piece of scum totally screwed her over, I mean, what kind of arsehole—"

"Cassie...." She was rambling, her words spewing from her mouth like water from a burst pipe. I took the bottle from her hands and swiftly pulled the cork free. Pouring a glass, I handed it over, and she immediately shot half the contents back. "Take a deep breath and calm down, okay? You're not competing for world's fastest bullshit talker."

Her lips quirked up into a semi-grin as she took my advice and sucked in a deep breath through her nose and exhaled it slowly through her mouth.

"Better?"

Her smile spread, leaving the tiniest flicker of lightness in her eyes. My intention was to help bring back her usual vibrant megawatt glow. "Yeah. Seriously, though, how are things with you two? Tell me all."

I followed her back into the living room and took a seat next to her on her chocolate-coloured couch. I sat forward with my elbows on my knees and my hands clasped together.

"There's not much to tell. We text, have the occasional short phone conversation, that's it."

Her left brow rose. "That's it?"

I nodded and tilted my head to the side, hoping she would see the sincerity in my expression. The truth was any communication I had with Justine was pleasant enough and friendly; it just lacked any real emotional response. I didn't get the intense sense of protectiveness and longing I felt whenever I spoke with Cassie, or when we text each other.

I was beginning to realise my feelings for Cassie were so much stronger than I'd ever imagined. I wanted nothing more than to pull her into my arms and make us both forget everything.

But the timing was wrong.

With the fucked-up Jay situation, and the *what-are-we-doing-here* thing I had going on with Justine, it almost felt like some sick bastard was laughing in my face, telling me I wasn't worthy of love.

I grabbed her drink from the coffee table and gulped back a mouthful, regretting not pouring my own.

"Help yourself, why don't you." She chuckled, the sweet sound of it easing some of the pressure sitting on my chest.

We sat in silence for a few minutes. Cassie was staring ahead, lost in her thoughts while I watched her out of the corner of my eye, studying the face that seemed to consume all my waking moments.

I startled when she suddenly sat up and jerked around to face me, her face glowing with enthusiasm. "We should watch a movie. Something funny. I need a good belly laugh."

How could I ignore her pleading puppy-dog eyes?

I shrugged. "Sure, why not. None of that rom-com shit, though."

Pursing her lips trying to stifle a laugh, she turned, throwing a cushion at my head. "Some of that *rom-com shit* just happened to be filmed locally. How could you call it that? *Notting Hill, Love Actually*, they are some of the best films ever!"

I rolled my eyes. "Whatever."

"Seems I have some educating to do, Mr

209

Ashworth."

I was grinning by the time she turned around and bent over a padded box near the TV. My smile disappeared quickly when her pert backside waved at me from across the room.

Jesus Christ, Adam. Get a fucking grip.

"This one." Startled, I dragged my gaze from her arse when she straightened, twisting around with a DVD case in her hands, a broad smile on her face.

I groaned.

"*Dodgeball.* Seriously?"

"Were you just checking out my butt?"

"No, why would I be looking at your butt? Again, *Dodgeball.* Seriously?"

"It's a classic and makes me laugh. Are you sure? It looked like you were totally checking out my butt."

"Can we please stop talking about your lovely backside, it's very distracting." I ignored her brows shooting up to meet her hairline. "If you insist on torturing me, can you please just get on with it?" I gestured toward the DVD case in her hand.

She tutted reproachfully, turning back to the television to load up the movie. I watched her move gracefully around the room turning down lights, refilling her glass—I noticed she poured one for me this time—and grabbing some snacks from the kitchen. When she finally settled on the couch, curling into the back with her legs curled under her, I was flooded with the strangest feeling of contentment. It was screwing with my head. With everything the day had thrown at us, I should have been plotting a murder or beating the shit out of a punching bag to erase some of the anger I felt toward Jay. But, damn, sitting so close to Cass, watching her from the corner of my eye, hearing her light chuckles as the movie progressed, it was doing a number on my head.

I had to stifle a low groan when she shifted in the seat, her foot brushing against my crotch as she dropped her feet in my lap. Grabbing the foot before she realised what was stirring beneath my boxers, I rested it on my thigh and began massaging the underside. Bad idea. Her quiet whimpers and moans of appreciation had me at full mast in the blink of an eye.

Reluctantly, I let go of the foot and rested it back on the cushion. She made a gentle noise of protest but otherwise her focus remained on the movie.

Halfway through, I sensed the shift in her emotions a moment before I heard the deep shuddering sound of a masked sob, and then another, and another.

All inappropriate thoughts were quickly forgotten as the need to comfort her took over. I wrapped my arms around her, hugging her against me. God, it killed me to hear her cry. She came to me easily, snuggling into my side with her arm over my chest, her fingers digging into my skin as though she were clinging on for dear life. She could hold me as fiercely and for as long as she needed because I had absolutely no plans to let her go.

"It's going to get easier, Cass," I whispered, my lips lightly pressing against the crown of her head.

"I can't believe I'm letting him make me feel like this," she replied softly. "He was toxic, I know that, but I can't help this feeling of loss. He's been in my life as a friend for so long. I owe him so much."

I tensed and pulled back so I could see her face. "You owe that piece of shit nothing, Cassie."

She sighed, attempting to ease out of my hold but I held her tighter. She needed to learn I wasn't going to let her run away from her torment any longer. With my support, she would face every damn emotional and physical hit he had given her. Then we'd bury it, and she would move on, back to the Cassie so many people loved.

Resigned, she sagged into my side and absently drew circles against my chest while she stared off into space.

"I blamed myself," she eventually whispered while I ran my fingers through her silky hair. "I thought he didn't like the way I looked, the way I dressed. I figured I wasn't doing enough to please him. That I wasn't worthy of his love."

"No. Don't you ever fucking think that," I stressed, gently pushing her shoulders back and holding them so she would look me in the eye again. "He was manipulating you, Cass. He was dragging you down, moulding you into something to suit his fucked-up ideal. None of this is your fault."

She swallowed, her eyes misting over again. "But—"

"Not. Your. Fault." I placed fingers over her lips, silencing her argument. She needed to hear the truth of how people saw her, how *I* saw her. "He was a fucking fool for mistreating you, Cassie. You're funny, smart, caring. You work hard and are the most dedicated person I've ever met. You're beautiful." Her eyes softened, the hint of a blush staining her cheeks. I moved my hand to cup her face, gently caressing the crimson spot with my thumb. "So beautiful," I repeated on a whisper.

Sucking down a deep breath to stop myself from saying anything else, I removed my hands from her and rested back on the couch. I hoped my words were somehow penetrating the wall of insecurity Jay had built around her. There was nothing else I could give her, nothing else that would help exorcise her irrational thoughts.

She needed time, time to process, time to understand and time to heal. All I could do was hug her a little tighter and allow her my shoulder to cry on until she was eventually out of tears and had fallen asleep curled around me again, her soft breaths gently brushing over my skin.

THE SWEET SOUNDS of early morning bird calls roused me from a broken sleep. At some point during the night, we had ended up lying on the couch with Cassie's back snuggled into my chest. I spent most of the evening fighting off sleep so I could watch her, occasionally stroking my hand along her bare arm or kissing her head and whispering reassurances. I kept telling myself that she shouldn't feel like perfection in my arms. That the tightness across my chest was anything other than the feelings I'd grown for her.

Soft light poked its way through the gaps in the blinds covering the large bay window. It bathed Cassie in a golden glow, highlighting her beautiful face relaxed in sleep. I continued to watch her, wanting so desperately for time to stop. I wanted to remain in that moment, holding Cassie close and loving her in my arms. I wasn't ready for the morning when I'd have to let her go and carry on as if something monumental hadn't shifted in me.

Noise from the front entryway disturbed the peace and tranquillity of the moment. Cassie softly sighed and wiggled further against me when I protectively wrapped my arms around her tighter. My nerves were a highly spun coil waiting to see what or who was in the house. Going into protective mode, my eyes darted around the room looking for the nearest weapon to grab if needed.

Footfalls echoed on the wooden floor in the hall getting closer. My body was tense, ready to jump into a fight to protect Cassie when Justine appeared in the doorway. The minute her eyes landed on me I saw the flash of recognition followed by a frown of confusion, a brief smile, and then finally hurt when she realised whom I was cuddling.

"Justine," I spoke quietly, shifting Cassie, trying not to wake her as I stood.

She silenced me with a finger over her lips and nodded her head toward the kitchen.

"In the kitchen," she mouthed and backed away.

Checking Cassie hadn't awoken, I followed Justine.

Closing the kitchen door behind me, I rested a hip against the counter and silently watched Justine. She stood with her back to me, washing her hands in the sink as she stared out of the window into their small back garden.

"I'm surprised to see you here, Adam. I could have sworn I saw...." She shook her head. "No, It can't have been, not if you were here like that."

"Saw who?"

She seemed a little sad when she turned around. Her shoulders slumped, and the brightness I'd previously seen in her green eyes had faded.

"It doesn't matter. I must have been mistaken."

"Look, Justine, I know what that must have looked like in there," I said, pointing toward the living room. "But I was just comforting Cass. I swear."

She lifted her gaze, her face a confused blend of acceptance and regretful, sad eyes.

"You don't need to explain. It's okay. I understand."

My head shook. "No, you don't. I know we've only been out once, but it was wrong for you to walk in to see that. Not that there was anything to see. Nothing happened."

A small smile pulled at her lips. "I like you, Adam, I do. I think that's obvious. But I can tell your heart is elsewhere and I don't think I'll ever be able to compete for it."

Moving further into the room, I sank onto one of the wooden chairs at the table. "I'm over Olivia, you know I am."

"I'm not talking about Olivia."

I frowned, confused. "Then who?"

"Cassie."

"What? No! I told you, nothing is going on with Cassie and me. I was just comforting her. She broke up with Jay last night and didn't want to be alone."

Her eyes widened in surprise. "She did?"

"Yeah. She was in a bad way."

"Shit." She studied her twisted hands for a moment and then looked up, hitting me with determined hazel eyes.

"It's a good job she's got you then. She's going to need you right now."

I wasn't entirely sure what she meant; there seemed to be a deeper meaning that she was trying to convey.

"She hasn't *got* me. We're just friends," I clarified, although I knew in my heart Cassie meant more to me than just a friend.

Justine pulled out the chair beside mine and sat. She briefly studied the small vase of flowers in the centre of the table and then returned her focus to me. "I won't lie and say I didn't hope something would happen between us because I did. But it's obvious to anyone who cares enough about the two of you that you're in love with her."

My head shook, lost for words. Internalising a few feelings was one thing, but trying to justify them, that was completely different. I didn't know what to say to someone calling me out on it. Was it love or just a strong sense of protectiveness for a good friend? Even as I thought it, I knew the answer. Justine was bang on the money, just as Liv had been. I'd fallen for Cassandra Burton, and I'd fallen hard.

"I know love when I see it," she continued. "It's in your eyes when you look at her, in the way you talk about her with such reverence. And, despite what she had going with that slimeball, I see it from Cassie too whenever you're around. She has never once looked at Jay the way she looks at you."

She stood and walked toward the door. "I'll be here for her, of course, I will, but right now she needs you, Adam. Fight for her. Help her. Bring back the Cassie we all know and love."

"Justine," I called as she opened the door. She peered back over her shoulder. "Thank you. I never meant to hurt you."

She offered a small smile. "I know you didn't. But the heart wants what the heart wants. Just look after my girl, please."

Mind completely blown, I crossed my arms on the table and rested my head on them. How did I go from loving one woman so completely to having the same feelings for another? Then I realised that the feelings I'd harboured for Liv all those years were nothing compared to this new heart-flitting emotion now consuming me. Justine was right, though; Cassie was going to need her friends around her now more than ever. I had no idea what I was going to do with these new feelings. The timing certainly wasn't right to admit my love to Cassie.

Whatever happened, I would be there for her, supporting her, encouraging her... loving her.

CHAPTER FIFTEEN

Cassie

THE NEXT TWO WEEKS FLEW by in a blur. I felt light and free during the day, trying to forget about Jay and concentrating on finding me again. But my nights were plagued by regret and shame.

Adam was there for me through it all.

When I should have been working, I'd get text messages from him checking in. He'd offer little anecdotes that would make me laugh and help brush aside my issues. Then, at seven in the evening, he'd stroll through the doors of Golden Oakes looking all blond bombshell hot in his suit. He'd saunter out of the changing rooms looking sexy as hell in his workout wear, which was mostly a T-shirt that did little to hide the tight, athletic body beneath and shorts that showed off muscular calves and thighs. He was a sight to behold and easily held the attention of every woman in the near vicinity. I'd get this strange surge of pleasure when he grinned at me across the lobby—where it had become a habit to wait for him. Without a second look at the hair flipping, preening women around him, Adam would stride straight over to me and pull me into his arms. It fast became my favourite time of the day and my favourite place to be.

Today was no different.

"Hey. How are you? How's your day been?"

I grinned and playfully swatted at the hand that reached up to tuck loose strands of my ponytail behind my ears.

"No different to the last time you asked when I spoke to you about an hour ago."

He smirked. "Smart arse."

In the days since Adam had forced me to recognise the absolute truth about Jay's and my relationship, I'd come to cherish the texts, the calls, the times we spent together.

In this short span of time he had grown to mean so much to me. Maybe more than Nate or Wes. Some days I wondered if I was just hero-worshipping him for protecting me from Jay. But the truth was these feelings have been here since I met him the very first time at Nate's place in France. Back when he was still pining over Liv. Adam was one of those guys: gorgeous, charismatic, friendly, an all-around great guy. And he seemed to dig our friendship slash relationship as much as me. I say relationship loosely because we were constantly skirting the boundaries of the term. It was as though we both knew there were feelings there, but with everything else going on, neither of us wanted to rock the boat by taking them any further.

"So, what are we doing today? Cardio? Weights? " He started walking towards the locker rooms to change. A small jolt of anticipation raced through me imagining him hot and sweaty, his arms bulging from the exertion of pushing weights. I bit down on my lip trailing my gaze down his muscular back to his firm, pert arse. God, he had a fine backside.

He stopped suddenly and turned causing me to stumble into him. His arms extended quickly to grasp my waist, preventing me from an embarrassing and ungainly arse plant on the floor.

"I've been thinking," he said, his eyes raking over my body. "I might start swimming again to spice up my routine."

Good God. The thought of his already athletic body showcased in Speedos with droplets of water dribbling down his lightly tanned chest had my pulse racing and my tongue begging to reach out for a taste.

It was difficult to decide which visual was better— Adam in swimwear, water droplets trickling down his body as he raked a hand through his wet hair. Adam in workout wear, sweaty with muscles bulging and veins popping, and his sounds of exertion… Oh, God. Or Adam in one of his hotter than sin suits, looking all powerful and dominant.

"Are you okay, Cass? You've gone very red." A large palm pressed against my cheek and forehead. "You feel a bit clammy." The hand moved to my neck, stroking over my sensitive pulse point. "And your pulse is racing."

Suddenly, I was lifted off my feet, engulfed in strong arms as Adam carried me toward the private staff area.

Yanking myself from x-rated visions of Adam's aquatic and other sexy as hell adventures, I shrieked, locking my hands behind his neck.

"What are you doing? I'm fine, you nut. Put me down." I laughed, twisting my fingers into the overlong strands of his honey-blond hair.

"I thought you were ill," he muttered, sliding me down his body, my feet still dangling off the floor. Our faces were now inches apart, intimately close.

His stormy blue eyes met my brown ones, the magnetism between them firm, unyielding. Under my touch his shoulders lifted and fell, his lungs sucking in a deep breath of... what? Anticipation, longing? A large knot of lust lodged itself within the walls of my throat, preventing me from being able to swallow. For the longest moment, we stood mute, our eyes and the deafening silence communicating a multitude of thoughts and questions.

He shifted his arms, the movement jostling my chest against his. A shiver of need misted over my bared flesh. Goosebumps erupted, and my nipples tightened beneath the white cotton of my sports bra.

God, what was I doing? I had to rein these feelings in. He was my friend, a close friend. Someone I'd come to trust and respect.

I untangled myself, my feet hitting the floor, and I took two steps back before I decided to tackle him right there in the GO lobby. "I'm fine," I mumbled, forcing myself to appear unaffected and meet his gaze.

Blinking several times, Adam took a moment to come back from the haze of whatever weird cosmic connection it was we'd just shared. With a brief shake of his head and a swipe of fingers through his hair, he too took a step back, further breaking the invisible threads that had been pulling us together.

It's getting harder and harder to resist him, I thought as he took another step back.

"I'm just going to get changed."

When the door closed, safely containing him inside the locker room, I puffed a long, deep exhalation and leant against the wall. Our shared moment had been intense—more intense than anything we'd experienced before. I'd desperately wanted his lips on mine, grazing them, sucking on them. Those were crazy thoughts. I still had unresolved issues from everything Jay related that I needed to overcome. Contemplating any form of relationship with another guy, whether emotional or physical, was something I should have neither wanted nor needed. However, when I thought about Adam those fears and doubts didn't exist. I just felt at peace.

A guy and a girl came around the corner holding hands. Laughing and mumbling, they playfully nudged each other's shoulders, grinning like a young couple in love. She said something causing him to skip in front of her putting his back to me. Walking backwards, he held on to her hips as he leant in to place an affectionate kiss on the tip of her nose.

They smiled politely at me as they walked past and then kissed before retreating into their respective locker rooms. They seemed to have such an easy and uncomplicated affection for each other. It made me reconsider my love life. My hopes and dreams had always revolved around my career and reaching the very top level as a kickboxer. I'd also been fiercely independent, not wanting to rely on a guy for anything.

Even with Jay I'd never considered anything long term, no happily ever after.

The care and compassion I'd seen from Adam had me second-guessing those beliefs. He had me thinking that maybe someday I'd fall for a great guy—just like Adam—and have the happiness and contentment that Liv and Nate had found.

Wesley yelling my name disrupted my little trip down what-if lane.

"What's up?" I asked, strolling up to the reception desk.

Sitting on the stool with his feet resting on the desk, he screwed his face up in disgust.

"Your mother is on the phone." He waved the handset at me, covering the mouthpiece with his palm. "She's being her usual *lovely* self, dictating how I should run my business and staff. Apparently I'm doing a piss-poor job of running this hugely successful chain of gyms and leisure facilities, and it's all because we still have you working for us. Who knew?" He rolled his eyes with a heavy sigh. "We'll just kick our most highly regarded employee to the kerb because she thinks you need to be sucking up to some bastard in a fancy suit. Pack your stuff, Cass. You're out." His hatred-laced voice was full of malevolence and disdain.

He shoved the phone handset into my hold mouthing *fucking bitch* as he did so. Yeah, my mother was not his favourite person.

Both Wesley and Nate had been on the receiving end of my mother's vicious tongue when it came to my choice to work with the guys. She could never accept my decision to work for a living doing something I enjoyed. And because the guys had taken me under their wing and been like brothers to me since, she despised them. The feelings were very much mutual.

Taking the phone, I slipped into the back room and settled on the edge of the desk before speaking.

"Hello, Mum," I said coolly. After the incident with Phillip at their house, I'd hoped she would call to check on me and make excuses for his behaviour, but my phone had stayed silent. It was just another reminder of how little I meant to her.

And now she was calling when I least wanted to speak to her. I'd deliberately ignored her calls all month, and only replied with vague responses to her text messages. Without too much difficulty, I could guess what her reaction would be when I told her about Jay.

"Cassie, why are you not answering your mobile? That man is so rude. I shouldn't be spoken to like that," she barked into the receiver.

I desperately wanted to call her out on the irony of her remark but refrained, opting instead to try and get her off the phone as quick as possible. I wanted to get back to Adam.

"I'm about to work out, my phone is locked away in my treatment room," I replied, closing my eyes, waiting for her next words.

As expected, I heard the small grunt of her disgust. "Maybe if you married that nice young man you wouldn't feel the need to work in that place any longer. Then I'd be able to speak to you when I needed to."

My teeth sank into the tender flesh on the inside of my cheek while I slowly counted to ten. I knew my next words would not go down well.

"I'm not with Jay anymore, Mum."

"What? What do you mean?"

"I mean I'm not with Jay anymore. We broke up. A month ago."

Her gasp was loud and clear down the line, as was the disappointment in her voice when she spoke again. "Oh, Cassie. What did you do?"

"Me? I didn't do anything. I couldn't take the way he was treating me anymore."

"You foolish girl, can you do nothing right? That man is ideal for you. Strong, upstanding, he has a bright future ahead of him. He already has financial security. You need to swallow your pride and fight to get him back."

He was only ideal if I planned on becoming an inconsequential being that would probably one day end up dead. I didn't say that though, there would be no point, she'd probably tell me to stop being so ridiculous and start treating the man better. And I should have known better than to want her to ask what he had been doing and offer me support.

Needing to wrap the conversation up so I could go back to someone who did seem to care, I asked, "What did you want, Mum? I have things to do."

I heard glass hit marble. No doubt she was already making good progress through her nightly bottle of Shiraz. "I was planning another party, hoping both you and Jayden would attend. Mr Damitriov is in town, and I thought he would be a good contact for that lovely young man of yours. But seeing as you cannot even keep an honest, dependable man interested, I guess I'll just have to introduce them another way."

"What do you mean you'll have to introduce them another way? Mum, I want nothing more to do with him."

Met with nothing but silence, I pulled the phone from my ear and stared at the frozen call timer in disbelief. She'd hung up on me. If I had expected any different, I would have been devastated that she assumed the breakup had all been my fault. However, what did shock me was her clear intent to somehow continue a relationship with Jay. Again my mother proved I was nothing but an inconvenience to her, someone she would use if it benefited her and toss aside when I didn't.

Sucking in a deep breath, I closed my eyes and tried to find my little slice of heaven, a place where scorching blue eyes and full luscious lips smiled at me. I forced myself to stand and marched out of the room, throwing the phone onto the desk when I hit reception.

The hurt and anger heating my blood dispersed rapidly upon seeing Adam casually leaning against the taller side of the desk, deep in conversation with Wes. A blue T-shirt almost an exact match to his eye colour stretched taut across his wide shoulders and back, showcasing the ripples and ridges of his defined muscles. A pair of black track pants sat teasingly low on his hips. My heart did a little happy dance taking him in from head to toe. From the first time I'd met him I'd always known he was handsome, a real head turner. However, getting to know him on a deeper level, experiencing his natural charm and compassion, only intensified the delight that was Adam Ashworth. Simply put, he was beautiful.

"Hey," he said, looking up with a broad smile as I approached. "Everything alright?"

"It is now."

"Are you ready to get sweaty then?"

Cocking a brow, I shot him a teasing look. "With you? Anytime."

He smirked. "Yeah?"

"Absolutely."

"What did you have in mind?"

"Well...." I sauntered over, swaying my hips provocatively. Standing before him, I looked up through my lashes, making sure I had added in a lip bite before I continued speaking. "I was thinking after a quick warm up we could lock ourselves in a room, just the two of us."

The playful grin slipped from his face, replaced with darkening lust-filled eyes, and a look of need. He swallowed hard. A small surge of joy radiated through me, knowing my teasing was having the desired impact. It had been so long since I'd flirted and joked in that way with a guy. Jay had always been so intense and serious. We'd gone from friends and training partners to him sneaking in with his controlling ways. I hadn't even seen it happening, not until it was too late.

These new playful interactions with Adam felt amazing. For the first time in too long, I felt alive, like the old me.

"And what would we be doing in this room?" he asked, his voice deep and gravelly, and laced with a shot of sinful sex.

Keeping my voice low and my movements practised, I stroked a finger along his arm. "I'm sure there would be some sweeping of hands over limbs."

He visibly shivered under the gentle caress. "Maybe we'd end up tumbling to the ground, followed by a little bit of fumbling around. And I'm almost positive at some point legs would end up wrapped around bodies."

He swallowed again. "Cass—"

My lips pulled into a line as I desperately tried to contain a laugh.

"Are you ready for that Adam?"

His eyes closed, his breathing deep as though he were trying to calm a raging desire for something. When he met my gaze again, I knew my teasing had worked. Guys could be so easy to play with sometimes.

"Right then, it's time to do this." With a sharp clap of my hands, I broke the spell, pulling Adam back to the present.

I grabbed his wrist and tugged, urging Adam to follow me. I didn't fail to notice his deep inhalation or the discreet way he adjusted the slight bulge in his track pants. Still grinning like a fool, I stopped and looked over my shoulder toward the desk. "Wes, can we use your room?"

The idiot was chuckling as he looked at Adam and then me, but he eventually reached for a set of keys and threw them to me. I caught them easily with my free hand. "Make sure you wipe everything down after you use it, I have to train in there later. I don't want to be thinking about how hot and heavy you two were getting, " he yelled after us. I turned and blew him a kiss before dragging Adam in the direction of Nate and Wes's private training suite, grabbing a couple of towels as we passed the stack by the door.

"Good luck, man," Wes yelled, his laughter trailing behind us.

We stopped outside the cardio room, and I slipped in front of him. "Warm up first but don't wear yourself out. Meet me back here when you're through, I have plans for you, Mr Ashworth."

He smirked. "What if I already have plans for you, Miss Burton?"

"Then they'll have to wait. My plans are more—" I shrieked when I suddenly found myself airborne and resting over a broad, firm shoulder. What was it with him and his need to fling me about like I weighed nothing? I had to admit; I kind of loved it. "Let me down, you big oaf," I yelled, the words muffled because of my laughter.

I felt his chest vibrate against my thighs with his amusement. "Where to? Bikes or treadmill?"

"Treadmill. Always the treadmill."

Trying to keep hold of two thick towels and a set of keys while upside down and clinging on for your life was surprisingly difficult. I nearly dropped them a couple of times and had to fumble to regain my grip. Each time, I felt Adam's hold around my thighs tighten. I knew we must have looked crazy but for some reason, I couldn't find it in me to care.

We walked in the direction of the long rows of treadmills and found two adjacent to each other. Stopping in front of one, Adam let me down, slowly lowering me along his hard body. "Warm up, Cass, but don't wear yourself out. I have plans for you," he mimicked my earlier words with a smirk, and then jumped onto his machine to start his workout.

Feeling buoyed from our playful interactions, I

stepped onto my machine and set it for my usual thirty-minute run. For the first five minutes, I lost myself in the music channel as my pace steadily increased. By the time I hit full speed, my blood was warming nicely, my lungs offering a gentle protest at the added exertion. I chanced a glance over at Adam and noticed our speeds were set identical, as were our strides hitting the belts. He offered me a grin that very nearly knocked me onto my arse then turned his attention back to the overhead television monitors.

We ran the full programme and then stepped from our machines, wiping sweat from our faces. With our synchronised actions, it felt as though we were a team having done this very same thing with each other for years. Everything with Adam always felt so natural and comfortable.

"So," he said wiping the towel along the perspiration covering his sculpted arms and neck. My eyes trailed the movement with avid interest. "About that wrestling...."

I laughed and nodded to Wes's training room. "Come with me."

We weaved our way through the room and stopped in front of a wooden door, the white plaque indicating the area beyond was private. Nestled between four fitness studios used for body combat and various other classes, Nate and Wes's room was every fighter's fantasy place. More than double the size of the adjacent studios, it was home to several punch bags, speed balls, ropes, pads and all manner of high-tech equipment that helped them train for the top of their game.

Adam's eyes bulged when I unlocked the door and

swung it open. I had to admit the facilities were pretty damn impressive, as was the regulation-size cage that sat proudly in the centre of the room. It always humbled me when I walked into their domain and thought about how far my guys had come. One a world champion several times over, the other hopefully about to realise that dream for himself.

"Wow," Adam said, stepping further into the room as I shut the door behind us. "So this is where the magic happens? I feel like I'm in a museum or something and can't touch."

I laughed and picked up the closest thing to me, a black glove. Throwing it at him, I said, "You can touch. It's only another training room."

"I beg to differ. This room is the training space of the Golden Boy; some people would kill to be where I am right now."

I threw the other glove to him and picked up a set they kept in there for the occasional time I joined them. "You make him sound like a god or something." I pulled on the gloves and started tightening the laces.

"In the eyes of many he is. Nathan is a huge inspiration and role model to a lot of people."

I shrugged. "I guess. To me, he's just Nate, one of my closest friends. He's no different to you or me."

He snorted. "He intimidates me."

"Oh come on. You've got to see how caring and protective he is of Liv, and of me. He's a wonderful, down-to-earth guy who just happens to have the dedication to succeed and a lot of talent. You have more in common with Nate than you think."

"I'm not sure about that. And what the hell do I have these for?" he asked, holding up the gloves.

Gnawing on my bottom lip, I considered Adam for a moment, suddenly doubting my decision to bring him here. I'd tried to encourage him to try out my sport several times in the past but he'd always been resistant. Kick-boxing was something I wanted to share with him, a part of me, my passion. But was I selfish trying to force it upon him?

I sighed and started tugging on the laces of my gloves. "I'm sorry. I shouldn't have brought you in here. We should have stayed outside. I just thought…." I trailed off, not knowing how to finish the sentence honestly. What did I think, that I could get him to love the sport suddenly? That if he did, he'd want to spend more time doing it with me?

"Hey," he cooed, stepping in front of me and lifting my chin so I'd look at him. "What is it you want, Cass? Whatever it is, I'll give it to you."

"Really? Anything?"

He nodded with an encouraging grin.

Returning his smile, I grabbed his gloves and held them up. "I want to train with you."

"You what?" His brows shot up.

"I need to keep training and pushing myself. Without Jay, I no longer have a club, coach, or promoter, but I still want to enter the fights I'd planned to. Nate's going to do what he can to help, but our disciplines are so different. Plus he's busy with Liv and expanding GO. I was just hoping you'd help me out a bit until Nate sorts something out for me."

He was thoughtful for a minute, his blue gaze searching mine. The slight twitch of his lips and the deep, readying breath told me he was coming round to the idea.

"I've not done anything like that before, Cass. I don't know how much help I can be," he said apprehensively.

"You don't need to be an expert. Just follow my instruction and let me kick you a few times and we'll be golden."

He chuckled. "Just keep those kicks away from the boys, please. I'd like to father kids one day."

Now, that was a cute thought. I could just picture him playfully sparring with a few little blonde haired, blue-eyed kids, laughing as he toppled over and they all piled on top of him. I'd be on the sidelines laughing with them as I gently rubbed my swollen stomach.

Whoa! Where the hell did that come from?

I pulled myself back to reality and hit him with my wide-eyed, full toothy grin. "Does that mean you'll train with me?" I squealed hopefully.

His face softened and he narrowed the distance between us. "Against my better judgement, yes, I'll train with you. Just go easy on me, okay."

Before I could stop I'd launched myself at him, wrapping my arms around his shoulders and laying kiss after kiss on his cheek. He laughed, circling his arms around me.

"Thank you, thank you, thank you! You have no idea how much this means to me. How much you mean to me. God, I love you."

His eyes widened and his breath hitched as I realised what I'd said.

CHAPTER SIXTEEN

Adam

"I MEAN... UM... WELL, OF course, I love you... as a friend. You're one of my best friends now," Cassie stuttered, backpedalling. An adorable dusky pink hue decorated her cheeks as she turned away to march further into the room. Following, I chuckled quietly, finding her discomfort endearing.

And pleasing.

So very pleasing.

I knew what she meant; after all, she meant the world to me, too. And as much as I'd like to think she loved me in the way I knew I loved her, I understood her feelings were purely platonic.

"So, what does a Cassie Burton kick-boxing session consist of?" I sidled up next to her as she leant over a cabinet in the corner of the room fiddling with a stereo system.

She shot me a quick look and then returned her attention to the iPod in her hands. A heavy bass line with thumping drumbeat and a screaming vocalist suddenly belted out through hidden speakers. The music was angry and frenzied, no doubt setting the pace for a tough workout to help Cassie battle her inner demons.

"Usually, I'd be sparring, beating the crap out of someone."

I reached over and adjusted the volume to something less ear-splitting. "How about we start off with something that won't result in me needing surgery?"

Finally, the smile returned to her face as she laughed. "Don't tell me you're going to take the fun out of this for me? C'mon, Ad, don't you want the full experience?"

Keeping a straight face, I stroked a gentle trail over her jaw, along the exposed flesh of her shoulder. "Yes please," I murmured, my voice seductively dropping an octave.

Secretly elated by the way she seemed to lean unconsciously into my touch, I traced my fingers along her face again. She felt warm, her skin silky soft and inviting.

I suddenly wanted more, needed to know if her skin felt that smooth all over. Stepping closer, I swallowed deeply and trailed my fingertips down her neck and along her collarbone.

A heavy exhalation had me snapping my attention to Cassie's face. She'd closed her eyes, her head tilted in a way that indicated pleasure. Did she feel what I felt?

Taking a tentative step, I edged closer until there was barely any space between our bodies. I could feel her warmth through my clothing, further tantalising my need to give more, and to take more. My body ignited into a furnace of lust and desire, heated from Cassie's presence and the need to touch her.

Running the risk that I was stepping into creeper territory and could end up with a kick to the groin, I wrapped my free arm around her waist and tugged gently, pulling her against my chest. We'd been in this position before, several times, but this time it felt different; this time I held her because I was sure I'd stop breathing if I didn't. Touching her didn't seem like enough; I wanted to bury my face in her glossy hair and inhale the scent of her fruity shampoo. I needed to slide my lips across hers and taste what I knew would be her sweetness.

Slowly, I lowered my head and brushed my lips over hers. They were just as I'd imagined, soft, plump, and warm.

Sweet.

Tantalising.

I needed more.

Pulling her in closer, I pressed my lips against hers with more force, demanding they feel the intensity of my sudden desire to claim them.

I felt her gently shudder and with a breathy gasp, she whispered, "Adam... what are you doing?"

What was I doing?

Panting, I dropped my hands and took a couple of steps back, putting an infuriating amount of space between us for Cassie's sake. Not mine. The pounding of my heart and almost unquenchable desire to grab her again were sure signs that if I'd been unsure of my feelings for her before, there could be no denying it now.

"I'm sorry," I mumbled, raking my fingers through my hair. "I shouldn't have done that. Do you want me to leave?"

Please say no. Please say I haven't just fucked things up with us.

She still seemed to be in a daze, as her head slowly shook no. Then, after several tense moments, she appeared to come to her senses, her eyes refocusing and blinking away clouds of disorientation.

"No."

"Are you sure? I stepped over the line right then."

With the receding tides of lust came the realisation of what I'd done. I'd taken Cassie's trust and dumped it straight into the deepest, darkest well of disrespect. She was never going to forgive me.

Looking me straight in the eye, she studied me for a tense moment, her eyes sparkling with an unknown emotion. Then, shocking the hell out of me, she gripped my T-shirt into her fist and pulled me to her, our lips colliding, teeth clashing. My arms banded around her waist, steadying us from toppling to the mats beneath our feet. I held her tight, not prepared to let her go until I'd had my fill, or until she came to her senses and pushed me away, whichever came first. I suspected it would be the latter.

Licking her soft, plump lips, I could barely believe it when she opened up, granting me the access to dip inside. My eyes closed as I fought the urge to take things too far, to take everything. I needed Cassie to take the driving seat, to lead us into whatever she felt comfortable with.

She was tentative at first, easing into the kiss with light flicks of her tongue against mine. God, she tasted divine. The subtle flavours of mint and orange drove me mad. Hungry for more I slid a hand around her nape, holding her in place. Our tongues tangled, twirling and moving against each other in a perfectly choreographed dance.

It was beautiful.

It was intoxicating.

I was breathless, wanting more, but scared to push too far.

"Cass," I murmured against her lips, my voice hoarse with desire.

"Ssh, no words."

Her hands moved into my hair, tangling with the strands and encouraging me to deepen the kiss. My pulse raced so fast I feared an imminent cardiac arrest, but that only fuelled the desperation, the overwhelming need brewing between us.

We needed to stop, take a breather, but fuck if I could pull myself away. She was making it near impossible with the way she tugged on my hair and made these little whimpering sounds that immediately sent all my blood rushing south.

We remained in our lip-locked embrace as I urged Cassie to walk backwards until her back bumped into the wall. Her whimper became a moan as I pulled her hands from my hair and pinned them against the wall. My knees nudged hers apart giving me the room to settle between them.

"Fuck, you are amazing," I groaned. Pulling away

from her lips, I continued to kiss my way along her jaw. Her pulse beat proudly under my lips as I sucked on the sensitive flesh on her neck just beneath her ear.

God, she needed to tell me to stop before I crossed over lines that could never be uncrossed.

"Ahem. As enjoyable as the show is, I'm going to need to call cut on this porno in the making," Wesley's amused voice shouted over the sounds of the music and our panted breaths.

I jerked away, dragging my lips from her silky flesh, and dropped her hands.

"What do you want, Wesley?" she grumbled.

I heard him step further into the room and close the door, but I kept my eyes on Cassie's, searching for the moment she realised what we'd just done and she'd tell me to get the fuck out of her life.

"I don't know what you said to your mum, but she's downstairs demanding to see you. I tried to get rid of her, but her screeching is pissing off the punters. She's bad for business, Cass," Wesley said, sounding apologetic.

Cassie's eyes drifted closed in distress. "Shit. Why can't she just leave things alone?"

I wasn't sure what was going on between Cassie and her mum, but if her shaking head and pinched brow were anything to go by, a meeting between the two was not going to be a happy reunion.

Grabbing her hands, I squeezed them reassuringly. "Do you want me to come with you?" I whispered.

Her pain-filled eyes met mine. "No, I wouldn't put anyone else through one of my mother's tirades."

"You wouldn't be putting me through anything. I want to be there for you."

A small, grateful smile graced her lips. "I know you would. You have no idea how much that means to me. But this is something I need to do on my own, Ad. She's pissed off that I broke things off with Jay."

What the fuck?

"She's annoyed you dumped the abusive, lying, cheating bastard?" I spat incredulously.

"My mother, she's... not your typical parent. I better go hear her out."

As she tried to step away, I gripped her hand, stopping her. "I'll be waiting here for you."

She nodded. "Thank you."

Preventing her from moving away again, I pulled on her hand. She turned her beautiful brown eyes to mine. "Cass, are we okay? I didn't just screw things up between us did I?"

A genuine smile lit up her face, immediately easing my fears. "No, you didn't screw things up. We're okay. Better than okay."

Exhaling deeply, I released her hand and watched her stroll across the room and exit through the door. I had to talk myself mentally down from chasing after her, to stand by her side to tackle whatever argument she was about to have with her mother.

Wesley sauntered over, hoisting himself onto a nearby table. He eyed me curiously as if measuring me up.

"You and I don't know each other very well," he eventually said. "But you seem like a good guy. If you hurt her, though, man, then we will have issues. Do you understand? She's like a sister to Nate and me, and we will do anything to protect her."

I had to hold in the urge to point out that he hadn't

protected her from Jay.

"She was good at hiding what Jay was doing to her," he continued. "And when we found out, God I wanted to kill the bastard. Still do. I'm thankful to you, Adam, for what you did for her. But you have to know that I'm a very protective guy. Cassie's safety and happiness mean the world to me and I will do what I have to do to make sure she is always okay."

Instead of feeling threatened or pissed off by his words, I felt reassured that Cassie had so many people watching out for her.

"Look, Wesley—"

"Call me Wes, all my other friends do."

I nodded. "Okay, Wes. Look, I don't know what is going on between Cassie and me. What you walked in on, that's never happened before. It just happened. I know she's still hurting from the whole Jay thing, and I want to be here for her. I want to protect her just as much as you do. Believe me; I have no intentions of hurting her. Ever. I care too fucking much about her."

We studied each other for several seconds until eventually Wes nodded. "I'm happy she has you. You'll be good for her."

He jumped off the table and clapped me on the shoulder as he walked past. "Now, I think we should get downstairs and rescue Dorothy from the Wicked Witch."

"What's going on there?" I asked, following him out of the room.

As Wesley quickly explained the basic dynamics of Cassie's family, I realised there was so much more to her than I'd imagined. It only made me want to hug her even closer, to help protect her and cherish her.

To love her.

CASSIE'S MUM WAS a piece of work. Wes and I stood outside the open office door trying not to eavesdrop. They were speaking in harsh whispers, but the occasional condescending grunt from her mum or frustrated sigh from Cass was enough of an indication that they weren't having a warm heart-to-heart.

My tense body inched further forward, needing to be closer to Cassie but having the respect to keep a reasonable distance. As the two ladies continued their heated discussion—which appeared to be about Jay—I quietly studied Cassie's mum. In many ways, Cassie was the image of her mother. They were of similar height and build, had the same long, almost black hair, small heart-shaped faces, and dark chocolate eyes. But, where Cassie's features were soft and friendly, her mother's were hard and aloof. It was evident from the tight lines etched into the skin between her eyes that this woman spent a lot of time scowling.

"She's a piece of work, huh?" Wes said, leaning against the chest-height section of the reception desk.

"Is she always like this?" I asked, keeping my eyes trained on Cassie, who seemed oblivious to our presence.

"Yes, has been for as long as I've known Cass."

"And how long is that?" I turned to face him, eager to learn anything new about the woman who'd captured my heart.

"Ah, now, let me see." He tapped on the countertop, deep in thought. "It was in the early days of Nate's career, so around eight years I guess. She was lost and young, just like me. We were in Bernie's gym one day, and she rushed through the doors to escape a freak summer storm." He seemed to get lost in his memories for a moment and laughed. "She looked like a tiny drowned rat. Her wet hair was plastered to her face, her clothes dripping wet causing a puddle on the floor. She looked so out of place in a room full of burly guys lifting weights heavier than she was. Yet she put each and every one of us in our place when she shouted, 'What the fuck are you all looking at. Haven't you ever seen a wet chick before?' Nate, being the gentleman that he is, approached her with a towel so she could dry off. They got talking, and she became a permanent fixture in our lives after that."

"So how come she ended up doing kick-boxing with Jay and not MMA with you guys instead?" Just saying his name sent a violent power surge through my body. And going by the dark shadow that crossed Wes's face, he felt the same.

"Guy's always been a slick bastard. She met him at one of Nate's early fights. They started talking, and he convinced her to join him at his club. Despite us trying to convince her to stick with Bernie and us, she wanted to try something different. She's always loved what she does, so we respected her wishes and supported her dream. Cass had always got on with Jay, so when they got together earlier in the year, we didn't bat an eyelid. Didn't realise the prick was a fucking loose cannon. Jesus." He stood taller and dragged his hands through his hair, clasping them together at the back of his head. "We should never have let him get away with hurting her."

I looked over my shoulder and saw Cassie slumped

in a chair listening to her mother's rant. "I tried. I fucking tried to get her to see what he was doing, but she wouldn't listen."

Wesley eased around the counter and placed a hand on my shoulder. "You did more than Nate or I. That makes me feel like I totally fucking let her down. I'm glad she trusts you, Adam. With a mother like that"— he jerked his head in her mum's direction—"she doesn't trust easily."

I felt the weight of his words, understood the burden of their implications. For whatever reason, Cassie believed in me, and I needed to make sure I did nothing to break that trust.

I was about to tell him I would not let her down when her mother appeared in the doorway, glaring at me.

"Is this him?" she questioned, pointing a red-painted nail in my direction. "Is he the reason you left Jayden?"

"Leave Adam out of this, Mum. He has nothing to do with why I broke up with Jay," Cassie said from inside the room, her voice barely containing her anger.

"I don't know you anymore, Cassandra," her mum huffed, still glaring at me. "You are a foolish girl for letting such a fine young man go. And for what? What can *he* offer you?"

"Hey now. Don't you—"

"Time for you to go, Mrs Burton," Wesley snapped, rescuing me before I shouted something I might regret. "You're not welcome here if you're going to abuse my staff and clientele."

After a short argument between them, Cassie's mum eventually left, telling Wes he was no better than me, that she brought her daughter up better than to be mixing with the likes of us. It was quite clear the woman was delusional.

After watching until Mrs Burton was through the front doors, I swiftly moved into the room and pulled Cassie into my arms.

"Are you alright?" I asked, burying my nose into her hair.

An incredulous, muffled scream escaped her throat. "You know, I thought Jay would be the one to cause me grief after everything that happened. It would appear my mother is actually more upset about the break-up than he is."

"She'll come round."

"No, she won't. She has this insane idea that he was Mr Fucking Perfect, who could do no wrong. She doesn't give a shit that he was a complete arsehole." Her whole body swayed with the shake of her head.

"Does it matter what she thinks?" I asked.

She sighed. "No, not really. As much as I'd like to believe that maybe one day my mother will actually give a shit about what happens to me or what I want, I know it's never going to happen. Well, not unless I marry some wealthy dude and rub shoulders with the upper-class snobs at the country club."

I hugged her tighter, knowing exactly how it felt to have your dreams squashed by your parents. To never be good enough.

"You've had a rough day. Do you want me to take you home?" I asked, stroking my hands up and down her back in a soothing gesture.

"Yeah, that would be great."

CHAPTER SEVENTEEN

Adam

WE ENDED UP GOING TO my apartment. Cassie decided after all the drama of recent days she didn't want to go to her place and be alone. Who was I to argue? If she needed some peace and quiet and a place to gather her thoughts, I was more than happy to give that to her. Besides, I wanted to be there for her. I wanted to be able to hold her and be the shoulder she could cry on. The overwhelming need to be her crutch was huge.

Pulling into my allocated parking space, a rush of nerves shot through me. If I took her into my space, my home, we would be entirely alone. I couldn't help but wonder if what transpired at the gym would happen again. God, I wanted it to.

She had felt amazing in my arms, with her lips

against mine, my cock growing painfully hard and begging for an introduction to the wonders of Cassie's exquisite body. But I knew it was too soon. She'd been through months of hell with a controlling bastard and was only now beginning to find herself again. And even then, I had no idea if she held even the tiniest of feelings for me as I did her.

Ultimately the need to rescue her from her recent darkness pushed the spectres of doubt and fear away. I knew, no matter what, I would do anything for her.

Switching off the engine, I pulled the key from the ignition and turned to face Cassie. She had swivelled in her seat to face me with a hint of amusement shining in her chocolate eyes.

"What are you worried about?" she asked, her grin growing wider. "If I go in there with you am I going to have to wade through several months' worth of dirty clothes? Do you need a few minutes to clear away the porn stash? Is there mould-encrusted crockery on your kitchen counters?"

I shot her an unimpressed look while quickly trying to recall the general state of the apartment. Being a single guy who spent most of my time working, training, or partying, I had to admit I could be somewhat of a slob at times. Housekeeping was not on my list of priorities.

Until then.

Very few people ever visited my home; therefore, I didn't feel the need to ensure I'd dropped yesterday's boxers in the hamper, or picked the towel up off the bedroom floor. And I didn't see it as a problem if I left the dishes in the sink for a day or two. After all, I had enough crockery to see me through several days.

"I'll have you know my place is immaculate," I replied, inwardly grimacing and praying my fairy housekeeper had been over.

"We'll see." She smiled wryly and tucked her arm through mine, resting her head on my shoulder as we walked into the building.

In the lobby, I caught our reflection in the mirror and grinned. We looked as we had done in Liv's wedding photos—perfect together. Cassie was smiling gently, looking comfortable and content on my arm. My smile was just as warm. Stepping into the stairwell, I tugged her closer and placed a kiss on her head. I couldn't resist.

A minute later we were outside my apartment. As I slipped the key into the lock and pushed open the door, I breathed a sigh of relief that for once I had actually cleaned up after myself.

"Nice place," Cassie said, following me inside and dropping her gym bag by the door.

My home was a typical bachelor pad, with charcoal-coloured carpeting throughout, plain walls painted in various shades of grey or white, and very few accessories other than my prized fifty-inch television, sound system and games console. There was no doubt that a young male resided in the place.

I led Cassie through the central living space and into the kitchen, separated from the lounge by the large island. I pulled out one of the stools and motioned for her to take a seat while I checked the refrigerator for something to drink.

"I have beer or wine," I said, poking my head around the door. "What would you like?"

Pulling herself onto one of the chrome-and-black

leather stools, she leant back against the granite counter and smirked. "Are you trying to get me drunk? I need to eat before I have anything alcoholic."

"You want to eat?"

She looked at the clock on the oven. "Considering it is nearly nine, and I haven't eaten since lunch, I'd say it's probably a good idea. I'd hate to scare you off with my growling stomach."

You could never scare me off, Cass.

"Okay, what would you like?" I buried my head in the fridge again, this time looking for food.

"You're going to cook?" she asked incredulously. The high-pitched shock in her voice was actually quite insulting.

"Yes."

With nothing more than alcohol, a bottle of ketchup, a tub of butter, and a shrivelled-up carrot in the fridge, I closed the door and tried the freezer instead.

"Seriously? You're really going to cook?"

"Don't sound so shocked, Cass. It's insulting. I'll have you know I am actually an excellent cook," I said, peering over the door. "In fact, I make a mean lasagne." She burst into laughter when I produced a frozen lasagne with a flourish.

"Let me guess, your garlic bread is the bees knees," she spoke through her titters.

Her joy was infectious, and I found myself laughing with her. "Now that you mention it...." I dipped inside the freezer again and pulled out a package of frozen garlic bread slices.

After the heaviness of recent weeks, Cassie's laughter was like music to my ears, an addicting sound that cloaked me in warmth and had me wanting to do anything to keep the smile on her face and the happiness in her voice.

"Wow, you are really going to spoil me with your culinary expertise, Mr Ashworth," she joked, swiping tears of laughter from her eyes.

"You really want me to spoil you with my expertise, Miss Burton?" I fired back. "I'm sure that can be arranged."

A smug smile formed on my lips as I turned from Cassie's stunned face and placed the lasagne in the oven. She'd caught the double meaning behind my words.

AFTER OUR MEAL, I opened the bottle of Sauvignon Blanc that had been sitting in my fridge for months. I poured two glasses and then joined Cassie in the living room. She was snuggled into the corner of my black leather couch with her legs curled under her and her head resting against the back. The strangest sensation flushed through me as I discreetly watched her from the corner of my eye. She'd kicked off her shoes and socks—a habit I'd always had—and settled into my place as if she belonged there.

She does belong here... with me.

Playing with the charm around her neck, Cassie appeared contemplative as she stared at nothing. I hated the change in her demeanour; I wanted the happy, fun-loving girl of only minutes before back.

Shifting closer, I placed my glass on the coffee table and took her hand, giving it a reassuring squeeze.

"You've had a tough month," I said

compassionately.

She scoffed pulling the lip of the glass I'd handed her to her mouth. "I've had a rough couple of years."

"Want to talk about it?"

"I wouldn't want to bore you with all the gory details."

Wesley had vaguely mentioned she'd had family troubles that culminated in a massive blow-up a couple of years ago. Knowing how interfering families had the ability to drag you into a dark bog of self-doubt and depression, I wanted Cassie to trust me enough to open up to me.

"Cassie, nothing you say would bore me. I want to know everything there is about you."

Her eyes met mine over the top of her glass, what appeared to be hope hidden in their depths.

I squeezed her hand again and then reached for my glass. Settling myself back on the couch, I angled my body so I could give her my full attention, close enough so that I'd be able to touch her if needed, far enough away that she wouldn't feel I was piling on any unwanted pressure.

"I found out a couple of years ago that the man I'd idolised my whole life, whom I'd proudly called my dad, was nothing but a happy childhood fantasy.

"One day he'd been sorting through some paperwork and came across some of my birth documents. He went through them, reminiscing; that was, until he found the little card that detailed my blood group. He knew immediately." She drained the rest of her glass and handed it to me for a refill.

"He knew my mother's blood group thanks to complications during my birth that resulted in her needing a blood transfusion. He also knew they shared the same A blood type. What he hadn't known until that little card fell into his hands is that I'm blood type B. Phillip's not stupid, he immediately understood what that meant. He was not my father."

Placing the refilled glass back in her hand, I retook my seat on the couch, only this time I did sit closer. I sat tight to her side and extended my arm over her shoulders. As she continued, I gently rubbed along her arm, offering my silent support and encouragement.

"He confronted her straight away and with the evidence being waved in her face, she was unable to deny it. They argued, and she eventually told him the truth: that my biological father was some high flying mega-financier visiting from America. They'd had a brief affair when Philip was expanding his company and had regularly been away on business."

A bubble of humourless laughter escaped her lips and she shook her head. "It was your classic case of a guy not wanting anything more to do with the woman when she discovered she was pregnant. He went back to the States, refusing to claim paternity. She had no further contact with him after he left.

"Rather than admit at the time that she'd been unfaithful and risk her comfortable life, she let Philip believe he was my father."

Wow. I was stunned. Completely and utterly speechless. My family issues paled into insignificance when compared to what Cassie had been through.

When I finally managed to find my voice I asked, "So why are they still together? Surely he couldn't forgive what your mum did to him."

She snorted, but there was no humour in the

depths of the sound. "He's a proud man, Ad. He didn't want his private life being gossiped about and didn't want to give her the satisfaction of leaving a marriage with half of his net worth. Instead, he allows her to live in his house and keep up the pretence that they have the perfect marriage. Their marriage is nothing but smoke and mirrors."

"So what about you?"

"What about me? I'm just the unfortunate offspring of a greedy socialite who couldn't keep her legs closed for a random American guy. After he found out the truth, all Philip saw in me was my mother's betrayal. He wanted nothing more to do with me. Saw me as the devil's spawn. In the blink of an eye I lost my father and might as well have lost her too. Without the sperm donor around to blame, it all got loaded on me." Her hands trembled as she placed her glass back on the table. "Unfortunately, despite the fucked up situation, she still expects me to fit the perfect mould she's always had for me."

As silent tears began filling her eyes, the overwhelming need to hold her close and protect her from every evil thing in the goddamn world was like a tangible thing settling over me. She had dealt with more pain and heartache than any person should ever have to encounter, yet she still always tried to remain strong and pretend nothing could affect her.

"God, you're incredible," I growled, tugging her into my arms as emotion began to claw its way through me. The moment she was straddling my thighs my mouth crashed over hers for a hard, demanding kiss. The taste I'd had earlier at the gym, the flirting, it hadn't been enough. I wanted her.

Needed her. I became desperate to make her mine.

"Cassie," I whispered, pulling back and framing her face with my hands.

The brutal honesty of my feelings must have been apparent in my eyes because before I had a chance to plead with her to give me an opportunity to be what she needed, she weaved her fingers into my hair and pulled me back onto her lips.

CHAPTER EIGHTEEN

Cassie

DELIRIOUS. THAT WAS HOW I felt caught in Adam's
web. From the moment he'd caressed my face at the
gym earlier, I'd banished all thoughts of my mother,
Jay... everything to the back of my mind. All that
mattered as his lips had first skimmed across mine was
how right it felt being in his arms. He'd been firm yet
soothing, demanding yet compassionate. We could
have been anywhere at that moment, but it didn't
matter. All that mattered was how I'd been totally lost
in him.

And as I straddled his lap and sought that same
feeling again, I knew that despite my past and recent
break-up with Jay I was a better, stronger person. And
much of that was because of Adam.

His hands moved from his sides to cup my face, his

fingertips nestling into my hair. Demanding thumbs tilted my head to allow his ravenous tongue deeper penetration into my greedy mouth.

I was breathless from the intensity of the kiss and had to pull away. With his deep breaths matching my own and his heart pounding strong under my hand, Adam appeared to be as affected by our connection as I was.

Our foreheads touched, eyes locking on each other as our panted breaths meshed between us. His intense stare caused a static that charged every inch of my exposed flesh, making me hyper-aware of his presence. I was sure the desire in his darkened deep blue irises mirrored my own. It was near on impossible to hide that level of passion. Not that I wanted to.

"Cass, we need to stop," he muttered on a pained whisper across my lips.

Tugging on his hair, I tried to draw him closer still. "I don't want to."

It wasn't that I didn't *want* to stop; I couldn't. The need, the desperation to feel him, all of him, had me going out of my mind. Things had never been like this with any other man; I'd never wanted them to consume me the way I wanted Adam to right at that moment.

Adam fell back against the couch, his eyes slamming closed on a hiss when I shifted on his lap, my heated core rubbing against the thick, hard evidence of his arousal.

"Please, Adam," I whined desperately, sliding my hands over his solid chest then sneaking them under the hem of his T-shirt. A triumphant smirk pulled at my lips at the sound of the pained hiss that escaped through his clenched teeth. He was caving. He wanted this, too.

"Cass, if we do this…."

"Yes?" I moved in again to bite gently down on and then suck his lips into my mouth. The resulting groan was enough to ignite my tight Lycra shorts and set them on fire.

"Fuck. If we do this, things will change."

"And this is a problem because?" I couldn't seem to control my inner wanton hussy that came out to play. She was demanding everything Adam had to give and would not give up until she was lying—fully sated—in his arms. I shifted on his lap once again, deliberately stroking myself over the stiff cock straining to break free of his clothing. The moan that escaped my lips when he hit the perfect spot was a sound so carnal it surely couldn't have come from me.

"There's no problem, babe," he replied, his voice thick with lust. His strong fingers held my hips, rocking me against him just where he wanted me.

"So what are we waiting for?"

Before I had a chance to beg or plead any further, Adam was on his feet, effortlessly lifting me into his arms. I wrapped around his body, locking my arms and legs behind his back as he strode across the living room and kicked open a door off the main hallway. The room was dim but the instant my back hit the softness of a mattress, I knew we were in his bedroom.

The last of the day's light had long since faded, and the bright white moonlight shone through the window, casting his handsome face in a gentle glow. It took my eyes a moment to adjust to the dim lighting, Adam's dark silhouette slowly coming into muted multicoloured focus. My breath hitched at the sight of this man standing at the end of the bed watching me watching him. There was a moment where time stood still and everything ceased to exist beyond those four walls. All that mattered right then was the burning emotion swimming in Adam's eyes. I initially thought it was probably coming from his primal need to mate, but as I stared into those huge pools of deepest darkest blue flecked with silver, I felt the intensity that only came from genuine emotions. He felt it, too.

I struggled to swallow past the lump that formed in my throat and used my elbows to shift back on his bed until my head hit the pillows.

"Fuck, Cass," he growled, crawling slowly across the king-sized surface until he straddled my body, my thighs pinned between his knees. "You have no idea what you do to me."

I shivered, goosebumps formed along the path his mouth took as he kissed his way along my body.

"Are you sure you want this?"

His words, although spoken with conviction, held a level of uncertainty I'd never heard from Adam before.

Nodding gently, I lifted my hand to his face and caressed the light stubble framing his jaw.

"I've never been more sure of anything in my life. Please, kiss me, Adam. Kiss me and make love to me. Show me what it can be like. Show me how to fall."

His nostrils flared and eyes swam with so many emotions as he studied my face before he finally dropped his mouth back to mine. The kiss started out tentative, gentle, far from the passion of minutes earlier. He lowered his body over mine; blanketing me with his strength and warmth as his hands began to roam.

The kiss grew in intensity, our need for each other eclipsing any uncertainty. Pushing my hands into his soft golden locks, I pulled him closer, needing our mouths fused together so there was no doubt in Adam's mind I wanted him. He responded instantly, flicking his tongue against my lips demanding entrance. I opened for him and moaned as our tongues met, coiling around and stroking each other.

"Fucking beautiful," he breathed, moving a hand from my hip and curling it around my back. He leant back onto his knees, pulling me with him, our kiss never breaking. In a stealthy move, he unhooked my bra with a quick flick of his wrist and had my T-shirt lifted above my breasts in no time. Our lips parted only long enough for him to yank off the top and bra and then he crushed his mouth back against mine.

Locking my arms around his nape, I eased back onto the mattress, pulling Adam so he was once again on top. We both moaned when he landed with the steely length of his erection positioned perfectly between my parted thighs. He rocked gently, hitting me in the perfect spot to make me gasp and tug on his hair. God, he was driving me crazy.

My pulse raced with the need for more. I pulled my mouth from Adam's with an audible gasp, my head rolling back as I sucked in a deep breath of air. He used the move to his advantage, immediately pressing his mouth to my neck and sucking gently on my fevered skin.

I squirmed and whimpered as his lips trailed down my body, taking the time to kiss and suck on my heavy breasts that wanted to scream when he abruptly pulled away to continue his descent.

"God, Adam—" My desperate words cut off into a whimper when his warm mouth sucked on the sensitive flesh of my hips. His hands slowly dragged my shorts and underwear along my legs until they slipped over my feet. He tossed them to the floor along with the shirt that he effortlessly yanked over his head.

Keeping his gaze locked on mine, he climbed from the bed and pulled on the tie of his track pants, pushing them over his narrow hips until they dropped to the floor, leaving him in nothing but a sexy pair of dark boxer briefs that strained to contain what I knew was an impressive cock.

With no shame, I licked my lips and waited for the moment he dropped his boxer briefs to give me the full impact of his magnificent naked body.

We'd been in this position before in France, only then feelings hadn't been involved. We'd been two people simply enjoying an unexpected sexual experience. Granted, there had been an attraction between us, an underlying connection that until recently I hadn't understood or appreciated. But I knew then that Adam's heart was elsewhere, and that the sex was just that... sex. Now, though, something felt different. The passion was the same, the hungry looks were the same, but underneath it all was a new longing that I wasn't convinced came purely from the urge to fuck.

Standing naked in front of me, Adam hit every hot button I had, and then some. His lean lightly tanned body glistened in the moonlight with a fine sheen of sweat and the longer strands of his hair fell in an acutely sexy way over his forehead. His thigh and stomach muscles clenched and rippled with each calculated movement he made toward the bed.

As I slowly studied this stunningly sexy man from head to toe, I bit down on my lip, needing the slight sting to remind me to stay still. The urge was strong to tackle him to the ground so I could taste him all over as he had done me. I closed my eyes to block off the sight.

"Look at me, Cass," he whispered, his voice sounding close. "Open those beautiful eyes, babe, and really look at me."

My eyes flew open and immediately met his.

"You've been through a lot recently. I need to make sure we're on the same page here. If we do this, there will be no regrets this time. We're in this together... you and me. I'll be yours and you'll be mine because I won't be able to quit. Not this time."

I nodded and swallowed hard.

No regrets.

Absolutely no regrets.

"God, you are so beautiful, Cassie. I can't wait to feel you again."

Pulling open the drawer of his bedside table, he grabbed a condom and then eased his way back onto the bed, covering my body with his. His head dipped to tease me with a deep but all too brief kiss before his lips teased my body again. Goosebumps tickled my fevered skin, and I fought the urge to groan loudly when his tongue skimmed over an ultra-sensitive spot on my ribs.

By the time his lips were in touching distance of where I desperately needed him, I was ready to offer my soul to Satan for just a tiny touch. When it came, a light flick of his tongue over my clit, I mewled, my back arching in pleasure.

"You like that?" he whispered, blowing a cold stream of air over my heated sex.

"Y-yes."

"You want more?"

"God, yes!"

I was all ready to beg when his tongue flicked out and drew a long line through my sex and then circled relentlessly around my clit. I didn't know what to do with myself as he ruthlessly took what he wanted while giving me pleasure well beyond anything I'd ever experienced before. Jay had always been such a selfish lover. My pleasure had not been his concern; he'd simply taken what he wanted. Now, under Adam's expert lips and tongue, I realised what I'd been missing out on, what Jay had deprived me of.

"Oh. My. God!" I cried out, a sudden rush of exhilaration racing through my body when he added a finger and then a second to his delicious torment.

My skin felt tight, fevered. Pressure low in my belly started as a dull ache and increased in intensity until my whole body felt alight.

"I'm not going to last, Adam. That feels too fucking good." I felt the smile on his lips as he sucked hard on my clit and curved his fingers deliciously inside me.

"Adam…." His name was loud and drawn out like a prayer as my body convulsed under the power of an orgasm unlike anything I'd ever felt before.

It was heaven. It was hell. I wanted it to stop. I never wanted it to end.

Through my scattered thoughts and panted breaths,

I watched through hooded eyes as Adam ripped open the condom wrapper with his teeth. He carefully rolled the sheath over his thick length. Seeing his own hand stroking over his dick was one of the most erotic things I'd ever seen and only added to my arousal and the desperate need to feel him inside me. Then he was between my legs, lowering his body over mine positioning himself at my entrance.

"I was a fucking fool, Cassie. All this time I was looking at the wrong girl." He stared down into my eyes, the silver flecks shining brightly in the ray of moonlight. "It should have been you. It is just you." Then with his lips on mine, one arm holding his weight, he took himself in hand and gently pressed his cock against my entrance.

The cry that left my lips as he pushed in deep was a plea for more, for everything.

He rested his forearms on the mattress and tangled his fingers into my hair, gazing into my eyes as he slowly and deliciously drove his cock into me, rotating his hips with each forward stroke.

"I'm in heaven right now, babe. You feel incredible," he whispered, dropping his head for a kiss that totally consumed every fibre of my being.

Kissing me deeply, and with his body so intimately connected with mine, there was no doubt in my mind that this was more than sex. This was making love.

He pulled back, inhaling sharply. "I'm not going to last, Cass. I need you to... Christ." His eyes rolled, and his movements grew faster, more erratic... so fucking sexy.

My pulse raced and I dug my fingers into his biceps, trying to ground myself for what I knew was going to be an orgasm that sent me shooting for the stars, or falling over the edge.

"Cass—" He cried out at the same moment every muscle in my body tensed and released as I moaned a garbled version of his name.

It was beautiful.

It was astounding.

It was a moment in time I would never forget.

CHAPTER NINTEEN

Cassie

ADAM LOOKED MAGNIFICENT WHEN HE re-entered the bedroom, having disposed of the condom and cleaned up. With the room now bathed in a gentle glow from the light pouring through the partially open bedroom door, I could clearly see every sexy, tanned inch of his naked body as my eyes trailed his movements across the floor. Clutching the duvet to my chest, I waited for the moment he realised what we'd just shared was a huge mistake and ran out on me.

Instead, he climbed into bed and pulled me tight against his body with a kiss to the top of my head—something I realised he liked doing, a lot. I immediately hooked one leg over his, turning so my chest pressed against his and my hand rested over his heart, drawing random patterns through the light smattering of dark blond hair there.

With Adam's hands stroking along my back offering a small amount of reassurance, I became lost in thoughts of our day. I was still in shock that things had progressed as they had with us. And he'd said that things would change, that I would be his. I didn't know what he meant exactly, but I found myself holding on to a little bit of hope that maybe he saw a future for us. Then I began panicking, wondering what the hell I was thinking. It hadn't been that long since I'd broken up with Jay; there was no way I should have been considering a new relationship with someone else. Surely it was too soon?

"Are you doing that overthinking thing again?" Adam asked with his lips once again pressed to my hair.

"What happens now, Adam?" I whispered into his chest. "Do we chalk this up as another fantastic experience and get back on with our lives?"

The growl that brewed deep inside his chest vibrated against my ear.

"Fuck, no! Did you not hear me before?" He moved a hand to cup my cheek and tilted my face to look up at him. "I meant every word, Cass. And in case there is any doubt, let me repeat; we're in this together... you and me. For as long as you want."

We're in this together... you and me.

We're in this together... you and me.

I repeated the words over and over in my head, trying them out for size. Surprisingly they seemed to fit really well, maybe a little snug around the heart but I was sure, given time, they would stretch until they formed the perfect protective shell around my entire being.

"Hey, babe, look at me." He shifted beneath me until we were lying face to face, his palm cupping my cheek while his eyes searched mine. "I wanted to give you time to process things, but I guess we need to have this discussion now. I appreciate that things must be confusing for you at the moment with Jay and everything that happened. But, the thing is, I've been falling for you since the wedding, maybe even since France. At that time, I couldn't see it, I was too caught up in what I thought was love for Liv. It seems I've been confusing my feelings all along, though. I realise now that what I felt for Liv was a profound protectiveness, and yes love for my best friend. But I wasn't *in love* with her, Cass. I know that now because of how I feel about you. You changed everything."

His eyes remained locked on mine. Unguarded and expressive, they held me captive with their sincerity.

"Getting to know you better, my understanding of loving someone and being in love with someone has completely changed. I'm ready to be in love, Cass."

My eyes filled with tears and one stray droplet escaped, slowly gliding down my cheek. Adam's thumb moved to catch it before another one fell.

"I don't want to rush things because I know you need time to find yourself again. And then, when you're ready to let go of the past, I'll be right here waiting for you with outstretched arms. Just so you know, though, tonight proves there is something between us and I won't let it go. I won't push, but I also won't let you get away from me. That's not an option."

I sniffed and nodded against his chest, while Adam pushed a hand into my hair and wrapped the other around my back to hold me close. As our breathing slowed to a synchronised pattern, my eyes grew heavy and then eventually closed. I fell asleep not thinking of my past, but of a bright future.

THERE WAS SOMETHING utterly delicious about waking up cocooned in strong masculine arms. The tantalising sensation of warm lips peppering light kisses along my bared body had me grinning. Adam's intoxicating male scent of musk and spices surrounded me, providing a sensory overload.

"I'm sorry," he whispered, pressing a kiss to the erogenous zone just under my ear. "I know I said I'd give you time, but, fuck, Cass, having your hot little body rubbing against me is driving me insane."

I felt just how crazed he was when his erection poked me from behind, setting off a swarm of butterflies in my stomach.

"Good morning to you, too," I murmured, stifling a yawn.

"God, you even sound sexy in the morning," he growled, licking the outer edge of my ear.

"You don't sound so bad yourself."

I stretched my arms above my head and groaned in pleasure at the delightful pull on my stiff muscles.

"Carry on making noises like that, see what happens, Cass."

When I deliberately straightened my legs and groaned, I quickly found myself on my back with my hands pinned above my head. Adam's strained yet stern face hovered over mine, his eyes burning with a sensual warning.

"I'm warning you, babe. I'm just about holding on to the last thread of control here. I've had your naked body rubbing up against me all night, and your sexy little murmurs in my ear. Have you any idea what that does to me?"

He shifted his hips, brushing his rock-hard cock against my inner thigh, so close to the throbbing that was building in intensity.

"Show me," I whispered. "Show me what it does to you."

His eyes flashed, and moments later, his lips were against mine, bruising them with a passion that stole my breath.

"Did that show you?" he asked, coming up for air. His morning voice was husky and laced with seduction.

He began kissing a trail of heat along my neck and chest, stopping only to nuzzle into the valley between my breasts. Slowly, the sheet around me started to slip from my body as his lips continued their journey. He took his time sucking and nipping at the soft flesh of my stomach and lower. I moaned at the sensation, my eyes closing again as I soaked in the pleasurable tease.

He released my hands, and I immediately pushed them into his hair, gripping the silky strands. My legs were nudged apart, and he peered up my body. "It's time for your wake-up call, babe." Then, without warning, he dropped his mouth to my sex. By the time I'd screamed his name several times, I was well and truly awake.

"LISTEN TO ME, young lady. You have responsibilities at this establishment. I will not tolerate you throwing a *sickie*."

"Whatever, idiot."

Adam was in his kitchen making breakfast while I phoned Wes to beg for the day off. Adam had said he felt rebellious too and wanted to play hooky. He wanted us to do something fun together. I wasn't going to argue. I needed a day off.

Wes chuckled. "Don't worry about all those poor people who are going to suffer without your hands on them today. We might just have to subject some of them to Dane." I could picture his eyes going wide in pretend shock. Dane was our male therapist. He was well known around the gym for his crazy bedside manner. Our clients either loved or hated him.

I pulled myself further up the bed to rest against the headboard when Adam appeared in the doorway carrying a tray. I grinned widely and trailed his sexy body as he paced across the room. "I'm sure the place can survive without me for one day, Wes."

His voice softened. "You're right, we can. We'll miss you, though, kiddo." I heard shuffling and then a door slamming.

"Is this a bad time?" I asked.

"No, I'm just about to go for my morning run. You're not the only one training for a big fight now," he replied, his tone suggesting a secret.

"What does that mean?"

"It means you are talking to a UFC title contender."

"What? No way!" I bolted upright, startling Adam, who then nearly dropped the tray full of food and coffee. "How? When? Where?"

Wes laughed at my excitement, and I heard his footfalls as he ran down the stairs in his apartment building. "I got the call last night. It's not set in stone yet. You know how it is; my guys talk to their guys and hash it all out. But if everyone can get their shit together, it looks like I'll be fighting Paul Maynard at some point."

"Oh my God, Wes, that is amazing. You've worked so hard for this."

"Thanks, Cass. Listen. Don't worry about the gym today. I'll get Colin to clear your appointments. You deserve a day off. Just... take it slow with Adam, okay? I hate that you were hurt by that other piece of shit; I don't want to see you hurting anymore."

I looked up at Adam and smiled, feeling content. "I know, Wes, and I'm grateful for your concern, but I'll be okay. He's a good guy."

Adam placed the tray on the bedside table and gently stroked his fingers along my cheek with a reverent smile on his lips.

"I know he is," Wes replied. "Just don't rush things, okay?"

I sighed. "Okay, Dad."

He laughed again, breaking the serious vibe.

"Good. Can I go for my run now? Some of us have to work later."

I chuckled. "Sure. I'll still be in tonight for my workout."

"Are you sure you won't get enough of a workout throughout the day?"

"Wesley Oakes!" I shouted in feigned outrage.

The sounds of cars and children shouting came through the phone along with the barest hint of panting, and I knew Wes had started running. "What? It's just a question. Look, Cass, if you're around tonight can you do me a favour and close up? Nate's made plans with Liv, and I'm hoping to meet up with a cute little redhead. I hate to ask, especially with recent events, but I've been after this chick for months."

"It's no problem. Go get your redhead," I replied, smiling up at Adam. "I'm sure Adam will be with me to make sure everything's okay."

"Thanks, Cass. You're an angel."

I ended the call with a grin on my face and lightness in my body that had been missing for a long time. Even after everything, I felt surrounded by love from people who genuinely cared about me, and I about them.

"Good news?" Adam asked, settling on the bed beside me.

I grinned. "Yep. Wes got a title chance. I'm so proud of him."

He reached for the tray and pulled over a plate piled high with eggs, bacon, and toast. He grabbed a slice of toast and lifted it to my lips. "That's fantastic! Bite."

I took a bite and Adam continued watching my mouth as I chewed. "Will you still fight, now that... well, you know?" he asked.

I nodded as I swallowed. "I hope so. I'm just waiting to hear if Nate has found a new coach for me."

"And if he doesn't?" He picked up a slice of bacon and held it just out of reach of my lips until I answered.

"I don't think that will happen. With all his connections I bet he has someone lined up by the end of the week. If he doesn't, well I guess I have to say goodbye to my big fight dreams." I shrugged.

"You should never give up on your dreams, Cass."

As we sat and ate breakfast, Adam alternating between feeding me and then him, I told him how much the fight meant to me, and he promised that no matter what, I would get that chance.

"What about your dreams, Ad? You must have some too," I said, cuddling against his side.

"I don't have any."

"Bullshit. Everyone has dreams, or at least something they are striving for."

When he exhaled deeply, I moved in his arms, almost lying on top of him. I crossed my arms over his chest and rested my chin on them. I stared up at his unsure face and waited.

"I do have one," he mumbled.

"What is it?"

"To not be working with my old man anymore."

I blinked in shock.

"I'm living *his* dream at the moment," he continued. "Well, his and my grandfather's. I became an architect and joined the company because I promised my pops I would. I realise now, though, that he wouldn't want me doing something I'm not happy with. Dad, on the other hand, doesn't give a shit about my happiness. All that matters to him are appearances and money. He wants me working for him because it makes the company look like a wholesome family-run unit. Reputations mean business, and Ashworth Moore has always had a stellar reputation, thanks to my grandfather and dad."

My chest tightened with sorrow and empathy. I

understood more than anyone what it was like to have parents with unrealistic expectations.

I wrapped my arms around his body and held him tight. "You can't live for other people, Adam. You need to follow your dreams. Life is too damn short for regrets."

CHAPTER TWENTY

Adam

I HELD CASSIE IN MY arms for the longest time not
wanting to let her go. Running my fingers through her
hair or along the subtle curve of her spine, I tried to
catalogue her every last detail; the silkiness of her
warm skin, the fruity smell of her body wash that
seemed stronger mixed with the scent of sex. Every
now and then she'd make a soft purring sound that
had my dick twitching with interest, and my thoughts
straying to dirty places.

I shifted onto my side, pulling Cassie with me so we
faced each other. My hand stroked along the curve of
her waist, and I marvelled at how perfectly she fit me.

Staring into the light gold flecks of her brown eyes,
I realised I had only one dream—a future with her. It
was so clear in my mind, a vivid vision of us several

years on, married with happy kids that looked just like their beautiful mother.

Before I let myself get too caught up in thoughts of *what if that could be a real possibility*, I needed to concentrate on here and now. And right now I had plans to spoil Cassie. I wanted to wine and dine her and enjoy every second I had with her.

I moved onto an elbow, forcing Cassie onto her back and exposing her gloriously nude body. As my eyes feasted on every delectable inch of her shoulders and chest, a dusky blush coloured her flesh. I fought off a chuckle when her teeth gnawed at her lip, and she dragged the sheet up tight to cover her breasts. Funny how she hadn't been so bashful about her nakedness only a few minutes earlier.

"Don't do that," I growled, splaying my fingers across the soft cotton of the sheet and yanking it from her body. "Don't hide from me, Cass."

"Adam—"

I moved again in a rush, this time straddling her hips. With one hand I interlaced my fingers with hers, and with the other, my fingers combed through her hair. The soft dark silk spread out and contrasted perfectly against the brilliant white of the pillow her head rested on.

"You're beautiful."

She screwed up her nose and shook her head. "I think you need to go to the opticians."

I stared her down in disbelief, wondering where the fuck these insecurities were coming from. She had always been so outgoing and full of life. I so desperately wanted to get that Cassie back, to banish the damage Jay had done to her psyche. I wanted her happy, vibrant, and taking ownership of her place in the world.

My nose ran along her jaw, and I whispered in her ear, "You. Are. Beautiful."

She sucked in a sharp breath, her hand floating up to trace the path my nose had just taken.

"But right now," I said, sitting back on my heels and grinned down at her wide, startled eyes, "I want to take you out somewhere."

I planted a quick kiss to the tip of her nose and then jumped from the bed, eager to get our day started.

As I gathered up the breakfast dishes, she closed her eyes with a sigh, a look of contentment on her face.

"Don't fall asleep on me," I joked, leaning in for another kiss.

"I won't. Where are we going anyway?" she said, opening her eyes and stretching out.

"It's a surprise. Somewhere nice."

She wiggled to the edge of the bed and scraped fingernails along my side, grinning wickedly. I nearly dropped the tray when she traced over the front of my boxers.

"Um, Cass?"

"Mm-hmm?"

"Cass, you need to st—" Her wandering hands halted at the sound of my phone belting out an obnoxious default ring tone.

Leaving the tray, I reached for the phone with the tinkle of Cassie's laughter in the background. I met her amused gaze as I hit the green telephone icon and pulled the phone to my ear. "Hello?" I said into the phone as Cassie chirped, "You really need to change that godawful sound."

"Good morning, little brother."

Ah, shit. Now was not the best time to be humouring my brother's juvenile tendencies.

"Now's not a good time, Cal."

He snorted. "So I hear."

"Huh?"

"I'm sure that was a female voice I heard in the background. Am I right?" I opened my mouth to fire back a witty response, but he continued before a word had passed my lips. "And before you try and fool me with some bullshit line, I called the office. Trish said you called in sick. Seeing as you never call in sick, I figured you were either dying—it's not good to scare your big brother like that, by the way—or there was a woman involved. I placed a grand on the latter."

I rolled my eyes and shook my head.

"Not that it is any of your fucking business, but I'm not dying."

"I knew it! If only that bet had been real. So, tell me, Romeo, is it that cute little brunette we met at the bar? What was her name again?"

I smiled down at the *cute little brunette* lying on the bed next to me. "Cassie. And yes, it's her."

He whooped immaturely. "Way to go, bro. So, I guess she'll be joining us for lunch then."

I jerked back, and Cassie's eyes widened in alarm. "Excuse me?"

"Lunch. You, me, and the brunette pixie."

"Cassie," I growled.

"Oh, testy much? It sounds like someone has it bad." He wasn't wrong. "I'll meet you at Charlie's at one. See you later." And then he was gone, leaving me with nothing but silence and a pounding head.

"Caleb?" Cassie asked, her voice light with humour.

I nodded. "Yeah. It looks like we're going to Charlie's for lunch." My brows pinched together in bemusement. How had my brother managed to hijack my day off with Cassie?

"Sounds like fun. He seems like a fun guy."

"There is nothing fun about him wanting to spend time with my woman," I grunted, lowering my head for another kiss.

She pushed me away, laughing, and jumped from the bed, dragging the sheet with her. "I better take a shower if we're going out."

As she sashayed her way into the bathroom, I groaned and flopped back onto the mattress. The thought of Cassie naked in my shower had my dick iron hard in an instant. I was so tempted to follow and make her dirty before she cleaned up. But she'd seemed excited about our lunch date, and I doubted we'd be going anywhere if I got my hands on her again anytime soon.

With a muttered curse, I adjusted myself in my boxers and grabbed my jeans. Alone time with Cass would have to wait. I had a surprise to plan.

CHARLIE'S WAS THE place we lovingly referred to as the snob's greasy spoon. It was a vibrant café bar that overlooked Covent Garden's famous cobbled piazza that we loved coming to, thanks to its welcoming vibe and mouth-watering meals.

Shortly before one, with my fingers firmly

interlaced with Cassie's, we walked into the busy restaurant. The place was full with a delightful mix of tourists, construction workers, students, and business people on working lunches. It was places like Charlie's that helped me appreciate London as such a great place to live. You could be a mega-billionaire or a piss-poor student, a teenager or a pensioner; everyone mingled and got on with their business knowing they belonged.

Through some feat of luck, we managed to snag a table by a window on the first floor that looked over the busy market below. While we waited for Caleb to arrive, we ordered drinks and chatted about our backgrounds. I was fishing for ideas and hoping for some secret guidance on my afternoon plans.

"You have got to be kidding me," I mumbled under my breath when I peered up and saw Caleb walking towards us with my smiling mother by his side.

Cassie followed my gaze and smiled when she spotted Cal. The smile soon fell away, replaced with intrigue, when she saw his striking blonde company. At nearly fifty years old, my mother was still beautiful. When it came to Mum, I lucked out in the gene lottery. I'd inherited her golden hair colour and almond-shaped blue eyes. Our personalities were also very similar. I couldn't say I'd taken any noteworthy attributes from the old man.

"Mum, I wasn't expecting you." I stood to kiss her cheek when they reached our table.

Caressing my cheek, she smiled; a loving look that instantly made me feel guilty for not contacting her recently. "Maybe if you called me once in a while, I wouldn't have to gatecrash lunch with your brother," she said without malice, taking a seat on the chair Caleb pulled out for her on my left.

"Hello," Mum said, smiling across at Cassie.

Cassie's face paled, her natural smile replaced with a nervous frown. Under the table I grabbed her hand, giving it a reassuring squeeze as I introduced the two women.

"Mum, this is my girlfriend, Cassie." I was surprised how easily the words had flowed from my lips. Even more surprised by the depth of happiness I felt at saying them. "Cassie, this is my mum, Lillianne." I briefly caught the spark of amusement in Cassie's eyes before she shut it down. I could only hope that she liked my mum as much as she seemed to like the flower.

"It's nice to meet you, Mrs Ashworth," Cassie said.

"Please, call me Lilly."

The conversation paused for a moment while we gave the waitress our order. Mum then continued reeling off question after question about how Cassie and I knew each other.

"I must admit," she said, taking a sip from her glass of water. "I was intrigued when Cal said he was meeting Adam and his new lady for lunch. I jumped at the chance to come and see for myself who had finally managed to steal my son's affection away from Olivia. I just wish he'd told me about you himself. But seeing as he never bothers to contact me anymore, I know so little about what is going on in his life." Her head tilted as she shot me a disgruntled glare. This time, it was Cassie's turn to squeeze my hand when my whole body tensed.

"I'm sorry. I have no excuse for my behaviour. I know I should call more often, but I'm either trying to avoid Dad at the office, or by not calling home. It's wrong, I know. I promise I'll be better."

"Oh, darling," she said, her eyes full of sorrow. "I know your father can be a little overbearing"—Caleb snorted in the seat opposite me, earning him *the* look from Mum—"but he only wants the best for you. We both do."

"You know that's not true," Caleb said, sitting back in his chair. He made an imposing figure with his thick arms crossed over his broad chest. "I had the balls Adam hasn't quite discovered yet and got out. Dad only sees a puppet version of himself in Adam, not the brilliant young man he is. He plays on the promise made to Gramps by an innocent and naïve child. Adam is good at his job, bloody good, but he's not happy at Ashworth Moore. He needs something more than that place can give him."

I met and held Cal's gaze across the table. My brother might be the biggest pain in the arse most of the time, but he always had my back. I dipped my head, silently telling him thanks.

"Is that true, sweetheart?" Mum asked.

"I guess." It was the first time I'd ever admitted to Mum how I honestly felt about the family business. Of course, Dad knew, and I was surprised he'd never said anything to her. It was probably because he never took my feelings seriously and therefore didn't want to concern my mother.

Mum's hand reached over to rest on top of mine. "Why haven't you said anything? All those years of studying and it's not what you want to do?" I shook my head slowly. "Oh, Adam."

My heart broke a little to see the pain I'd caused in her eyes. "I don't want to disappoint anyone," I said weakly. "You, Dad, Gramps, you always made such a huge deal out of us boys eventually running the company, being the greatest architects London has to offer. There was a lot of pressure to do as you all wanted."

"My sweet, silly boy. All we've ever wanted was for you to be successful in whatever you chose to do. We encouraged you into the business because we honestly thought that was what you wanted. Don't you remember? As a young boy, you were always doodling designs and playing those games on the computer." When her eyes filled with tears and her lower lip trembled, Cal shifted his chair and wrapped an arm around her shoulders. "You have to be happy, Adam. If you no longer want to work for Ashworth Moore, then you need to leave. You need to find what it is you enjoy."

"But what about Dad?"

She dabbed at her eyes with a napkin. "Don't worry about your father. He's a stubborn man who thinks he knows best. He forgets how powerful a mother's protective nature is, though. Leave him to me."

"Now all the mushy stuff is out of the way, can we eat please?" We all laughed at Caleb's easy way of dissolving tension.

Throughout the meal Mum's words sat heavily at the back of my mind. I realised I had a tough decision to make. Did I stick with what I'd trained for so long to do? Or did I follow my heart to do something fulfilling? I couldn't make that decision overnight, but

I vowed to make it soon.

"It was lovely meeting you, Cassie. You have no idea how delighted I am to finally see my baby boy happy with someone." Cassie's cheeks turned a vibrant shade of red when Mum hugged her outside Charlie's.

The two ladies had gotten along well, sharing stories that both embarrassed and humbled me. It warmed my heart that Cassie found it easy to talk with Mum. With her own mother not giving two shits about her, it was nice to know that Cassie would have a motherly figure to go to if our relationship grew as I hoped it would.

"It was lovely meeting you, too, Lilly."

Mum's smile was radiant when she pulled her arms from Cassie and tucked them around my waist. "And you, my boy," she whispered quietly. "Take care of that girl. She's special, Adam."

"I promise I will."

She stepped back and pressed her warm palm against my cheek. "I love you, Adam. Never forget that. Don't be a stranger. Give you mother a call once in a while." She gave me a pointed look.

I chuckled. "I will. I love you, too."

We watched Caleb and Mum walk toward his car. When they were out of sight, I took Cassie's hand in mine and kissed her palm. "Sorry to put you through that. I honestly had no idea she was coming."

"I must admit meeting the parents wasn't how I saw today going, but I'm glad I did. She's lovely, Adam. You're lucky to have her."

After the afternoon's revelations and honest talking, I could finally see that I was lucky. I had two amazing women in my life.

I smiled. "Yeah, I am."

"THERE IS NO way I'm getting in one of those things. No fucking way, Adam. You must think I'm crazy. How high does this thing go anyway?"

Cassie's neck craned upward as she spoke about the giant steel and glass capsules of the London Eye. While she'd been in the shower earlier, I'd distracted myself from thinking about her naked body by going online to see if I could get tickets. I'd lucked out with a late booking site and managed to snag tickets for a VIP capsule, complete with a bottle of champagne and a box of luxury truffles. It had cost me a small fortune, but I knew it would be worth every penny.

"Come on, Cass, the view from up there is amazing. You'll love it, I promise."

I knew with absolute certainty that it would be. And I wasn't talking about the London skyline. I couldn't tell you what possessed me to want to take her on the attraction; I just knew I wanted to hold her and feel like we were in our own little bubble while we watched life moving on below us.

I finally coaxed Cassie into our private capsule and when she realised how spacious it was she softened toward the idea slightly. By the time we were halfway to the top, she was plastered to the glass wall looking out and had nibbled on two truffles and sipped on half a glass of champagne. It was safe to say her initial fears had faded, she was now positively in love.

"Oh, Adam, it is so beautiful up here," she gushed when the capsule reached the highest peak.

From my spot near the middle, I took a moment to

soak her in. With the late afternoon sun shining through the glass, she looked so vibrant and full of life. Her hair glistened, and her cheeks were rosy with excitement. She had never looked more beautiful.

My eyes met those of our accompanying host and he acknowledged me with a short nod of his head. He knew the drill. People who hired the private "cupid" capsules weren't doing it because they wanted a running commentary on London scenery. They wanted privacy with their loved one, time to experience the grandeur of our great city as though they were the only two people in the world sharing the view. He turned to look the other way, effectively giving us as much privacy as the confined space would allow.

Stepping behind Cassie, I nuzzled into her neck, studying her profile in the glass reflection. "I agree, it's the most spectacular view I've ever seen," I whispered into her ear before nipping on her lobe.

"But you're not looking out," she fired back as my arms tightened around her waist and I hauled her against my body. She was warm and smelled of vanilla and exotic fruit, a scent that was pure Cassie. I began rubbing slow, seductive circles over her flat stomach, causing mild tremors to run through her body. She sighed, leaning further into me.

"I don't need to."

"How can you know if you don't look?" Her voice was hoarse; loaded with a sexual longing I was quickly becoming addicted to.

Her head fell back against my chest, our eyes remaining connected through our reflections. "Because for some reason you're all I seem to be able to see right now. You've blinded me to everything and everyone else."

I felt the heavy rise and fall of her chest as her breathing quickened. Her hands came to rest on mine.

She sighed. "Thank you, Adam."

I turned her in my arms and tiled her face up so I could look deep into her eyes. "For what?"

"For believing in me. For not giving up on me. For being you. So many things," she replied softly.

"You don't get it do you?" I ran a finger down her soft cheek still holding her gaze. "I'm the one who needs to be thanking you."

I pressed my lips to hers and as we made the slow descent back to ground level, I kissed and held her and made a silent vow to never let her go again.

CHAPTER TWENTY-ONE

Cassie

As WE DISEMBARKED THE GIANT glass capsule back to the safety of solid ground, Adam grasped my hand and held it tight. I'd never liked heights. I couldn't even step out on to the balcony at Nate and Liv's place without losing my shit. There was a reason the law of physics wanted our feet planted firmly on the ground, and I had no intention of fucking up some cosmic mojo by defying those rules. However, after my heart had stopped its attempted jailbreak from my chest, I actually started appreciating the view from the capsule—inside and out. Adam had this calming aura surrounding him that drew me in and immediately eased any fears or tension. When he'd shared his innermost thoughts, laying bare his heart and soul, I'd forgotten all about floating in a glass pod, and fell a little deeper for him.

It seemed crazy to me that not so long ago, I'd been caught in Jay's dark magic spell. I was struggling with how quickly Adam had reeled me in, albeit completely voluntarily. I mean, who in their right mind would move on from an abusive partner so quick? That would be me apparently. But despite my concerns about timing, I never once questioned what Adam was doing. I trusted him implicitly.

We walked along the bank of the river Thames in comfortable silence for a while, taking in the sights and sounds around us. Everything was so natural between us, like we'd been doing this for years, not a matter of hours.

My phone vibrated in the back pocket of my jeans, and I had to reluctantly drop Adam's hand to grab it. Swiping my finger across the screen, I was greeted with a text from Nate.

Got you sorted. Former European champ Mitch Bardsley will be at GO at 7. Don't be late. Use our room.

I grinned at Nate's text. Always Mr-to-the-point. Despite his typical lack of manners, I knew he'd gone out of his way to arrange this new trainer for me. Both he and Wes had offered to help me train for my fight, but I knew I couldn't work with two overbearing gorillas constantly nit-picking. I needed practical advice and technical expertise. As much as I loved the guys, kick-boxing simply wasn't their thing, and they knew it.

I shot Nate a quick reply saying I would be there and buried the phone back in my pocket.

"Everything okay?" Adam asked, leaning against

the back of an iron bench patiently waiting for me.

My grin widened. "Everything's wonderful. Nate's managed to find a new trainer for me, a former European champ. He's coming to the gym tonight."

Adam curled his fingers around the top of the bench and pushed himself to stand. Grabbing me by the hips, he tugged me against his body.

"You'll have to let me watch. I bet you're a little spitfire on those mats. Damn, the thought of you in those tight shorts and barely there sports bra kicking some dude's arse, it's enough to have me salivating, Cass."

Pushing up onto tiptoes, I moved my lips to his ear. "Would you rather it was your arse I was kicking?"

The growl that rose from his chest had me damn near whooping with joy. I absolutely loved playing with him like this.

"Kicking my arse, no, but I can sure as hell think of some other moves I could help you with on those mats."

Swatting his hands away from my arse cheeks, I laughed, taking a few steps back.

"Pervert."

He grinned. "You know it."

CHAPTER TWENTY-TWO

Cassie

IT HAD BEEN A MONTH since Adam had taken me on that magical ride on the London Eye. A month of him continuing to confess his feelings and encouraging me to do the same. I still had down days when I thought about Jay and how he'd treated me. How he'd played me and manipulated me until I was nothing but a shell of my former self. But I was so much better. Whenever I found myself withdrawing into my head, Adam would appear at my side, offering reassurance and comfort.

When I first told Jay we were through, I'd expected him to put up a huge fight. I wasn't arrogant enough to think he couldn't live without me, but he was a proud man and wasn't the type to take being dumped easily. For the first several weeks after the split, I'd expected him to call or visit, making demands on me. But as time moved on and all I'd received was a couple of early text messages that I deleted without reading, I began to hope that maybe I was worrying unnecessarily and that he'd let me go.

That was until he managed to sneak a call past the receptionist at GO one afternoon.

I'd just finished with a client and was preparing for the next when the phone in my treatment room rang. I was happily singing along to Kelly Clarkson while I searched through a drawer for my jar of Tiger Balm. My cheeks had flushed lava hot when I moved on to wipe down the bench and recalled what Adam and I had been doing on it the previous evening. Who knew that a massage could be so much fun?

The loud ringing of the phone broke into Kelly singing about being stronger.

I dropped the cleaning cloth on the bench and danced over to my desk. "Y'ello?"

"Cassie."

That one word sent my good mood plummeting to somewhere in the region of the South Pole. All memories of the previous evening vanished in an instant.

"What do you want, Jay?"

"We need to talk." The sound of his deep, throaty voice had me falling onto my desk chair.

"We have nothing to talk about."

"That's not true."

I sighed. "Jay, I said everything that needed to be said that night. I don't want to talk to you."

"Yeah, I figured as much when you didn't reply to my text messages."

"What did you expect? That I'd welcome you back with open arms? That's never going to happen."

"Don't be so sure about that."

A frustrated scream fought to break free. "I've moved on, Jay. You need to, too."

"Ah, yes. How is the new boyfriend? What's his name again? That's right, Adam. The two of you seem very... cosy."

The cold, calculating way he said those words sent a tremor of unease through me. How did he know anything about Adam and me? I protectively wrapped my free arm around myself.

"That has nothing to do with you," I whispered.

"I beg to differ. He's taken what I needed. Therefore, I'd say it has everything to do with me because I have every intention of taking it back."

"What do you mean?" The words scratched as they left my dry mouth.

"You owe me, Cassie. And one way or another, you will repay me. I'll see you around."

I sat for the longest time after he hung up with the phone receiver shaking in my hand. I had no idea what he thought I owed him, but it was clear I needed to be vigilant when it came to Jay.

A WEEK HAD passed, and there had been no further contact from Jay. I hadn't told the guys about the phone call; I knew they would only freak out and seek some form of macho revenge. Instead, I screened all my calls and texts and became extra observant when we were out.

Eventually, I started to put Jay behind me, and a

new sense of determination for victory took hold. I needed to prove that Jay had not counted me out and called time on my fighting dreams. I was not going to allow one stupid phone call to drag me under.

My new trainer, Mitch, turned out to be an absolute godsend. He was patient but firm and in the few short weeks we'd trained together, I'd learnt so much from him. I was fitter, leaner, and faster. For the first time in a long time, I could focus solely on my form and technique without the fear of negative criticism or insults.

Using their contacts, Mitch and Nate confirmed my space at a European Championship in Manchester in February. They also guaranteed that I would fight against a top-seeded opponent. If I won, I'd be able to book my flight to Hamburg for a shot at the World Championship.

It was a dream I'd held for so long, it almost seemed unreal that it was actually happening.

And with Adam by my side through it all, I felt alive. I was full of hope and wishes for a bright future.

"Can't you just stop here for a minute? I'll run in, grab my things, and be right back out."

I'd been spending so much time either working or training that Adam had surprised me with an afternoon off. He picked me up at lunchtime and whisked me off to Hyde Park. We spent a few hours sitting under a large oak tree by the Serpentine enjoying a relaxing picnic and each other's company. All thoughts of Jay and his veiled threats had disappeared as Adam sneaked his hands under my shirt and stroked my back while his tongue stroked mine. My smile didn't falter the whole time.

Eventually, though, I'd had to get back for my training session with Mitch and needed to close up for Nate and Wes. Adam hadn't grumbled, he'd packed up our stuff and held my hand as we walked back to his car.

Besides, he would be at the gym anyway.

Adam seemed to spend as much time at Golden Oakes as I did. Much to my delight, he'd built a solid friendship with Wes and Nate. I would often see the three of them huddled together in conversation or playfully throwing punches at each other. It lifted my heart to see everyone who meant the world to me getting along so well.

Adam slowly inched his Insignia along my road, searching for somewhere to park. It had gone past six in the evening, and my neighbours were mostly home, leaving no vacant parking spaces on our busy street.

"I'll come in with you," Adam said, casting me a glance from the corner of his eye.

"Seriously," I replied, already pulling on the door handle. "There's no point. Just double park here and I'll be out in a minute."

Before he could argue, I stepped out of the car and walked briskly toward my house a few doors down. It had been a lovely sunny day, and the air had that warm late summer evening laziness to it. So I couldn't understand why I suddenly felt chilled to my bones. An ominous feeling settled over me, leaving me jittery and on alert.

At the garden gate, while rifling through my bag for my house keys, I had the odd sensation that I was being watched. My head shot up as I quickly scanned the area. Nothing seemed untoward, until I spotted him; or at least I thought it was him. Walking away from me on the opposite side of the road was a guy that looked remarkably like Jay. He had the same height and build, and I'd recognise his arrogant swagger anywhere. Even the maroon sweatshirt he wore with the hood up, I vaguely remembered.

I stood rooted to the spot, scared to move or even breathe. Yet I couldn't seem to look away.

My face must have shown my fear because in the next minute Adam was at my side gently cupping my shoulders as he searched my face. A car drove past, the driver hitting their horn, clearly annoyed at having to squeeze past Adam's abandoned vehicle.

"What's wrong?" His voice was filled with concern as he continued to study my panicked expression.

When I remained mute, he moved to stand partially in front of me but not blocking my view down the street. I couldn't meet his gaze. Mine was still focused on the retreating male who'd pulled what I assumed was a phone out of his pocket and lifted it to his ear.

"Cass, please. Talk to me. What's going on?"

My mouth opened to answer, but what came out was a frightened yelp when the hooded man looked back just as he reached the street corner. His wicked smirk and the sharp shake of his head told me all I needed to know. I'd become too complacent.

Jay had no intentions of letting me go.

CHAPTER TWENTY-THREE

Adam

CASSIE WAS SCARING THE CRAP out of me with her stiff posture and wide, scared eyes.

"Cass, please. Talk to me. What's going on?"

I was damn near going out of my mind with her silence. I couldn't decide whether to shake her out of her daze or pull her into my arms and get her as far away from whatever had her freaked out as possible.

When her lips parted with a terrified cry and her eyes grew as wide as saucers, I immediately shot around, following her trail of sight. My heart beat frantically in my chest, but as I looked around, nothing seemed untoward. An elderly lady was out walking her poodle, a couple of girls were playing hopscotch on the pathway, and a guy wearing a hoodie walked briskly around the corner out of sight.

I turned back to Cassie. Holding her by the shoulders, I dipped to meet her scared eyes.

"Cass, babe, you've got to tell me what's freaked you out."

Slowly, her eyes shifted, moving to meet mine. Blinking, the cloud of unease evaporated until she blessed me with her dark chocolate irises once again. My body relaxed as Cassie's did the same. A hint of a smile tugged at her lips, but her hands shaking as she pushed strands of hair away from her face told me how rattled she was.

"I'm being silly," she muttered. "I thought... I thought I saw Jay."

"What?" I dropped my arms and spun around, my eyes quickly scanning every visible inch of the south end of Cassie's street. "Are you sure? What the fuck was he doing here? What did he do?"

Rage burned deep inside me at the thought of Jay being anywhere near Cassie. She hadn't mentioned him since the night I'd hit him, and I'd hoped he'd had the good sense to stay away. But with the way she was shaking and her face void of any colour, I had to wonder if he'd only been biding his time? What if he still wanted her and was coming back to claim her?

No. I shook my head and stretched out my balled fists in an attempt to drive away those thoughts. She wouldn't go back to him, no matter what he said or did.

She'd been totally honest with me over the past several weeks, telling me how he'd made her feel and how settled and at home she felt being with me. I felt the same. Almost in the blink of an eye, I'd gone from liking her as a friend to loving her as my everything.

And that was why, when Jay threatened her new happiness, I felt like the protective caveman she'd turned me into.

Cassie's features softened, the tightness around her eyes disappearing. She lifted a hand and gently rubbed along the lines I knew creased my forehead. "It might not have been him. I... it just looked like him, okay? No need for the big alpha bear to make an appearance."

Despite her casual words and attempt at humour, I knew her well enough now to notice the tremor in her voice, that little quiver betraying her lies. It was Jay, she knew it. I knew it.

Releasing my hold on her arms, I eased my hands around her back, splaying them across the gentle arc above her backside, and held her close.

"Don't lie to me, Cass. I need to know if that bastard is hanging around. Is this the first time you've seen him?"

She sighed and rested a hand against my pounding heart. "Seen him, yes."

"What do you mean?"

Her fingernails became fascinating objects. She chose to study them rather than look into my eyes. "I spoke to him a couple of weeks ago," she rushed the words, as though I wouldn't understand the implication if she said them quickly enough. Fortunately, I was adept at hearing women's babble.

"What? When? Why didn't you tell me?"

Resting my chin on her head, my eyes wandered to the end of the street again as I processed her reply. I couldn't believe that piece of shit had the audacity to contact her. If I caught him around her again, I'd give him more than a couple of quick punches next time. "I don't like it, Cass," I said, trying to calm myself. "If he's harassing you, I think you should come and stay with me."

"What? No!" She pushed against my chest, and I took a step back. "I won't let him drive me out of my own home, Adam."

"I don't look at it that way. We've been spending a lot of time at each other's places anyway, this would just be an extension of that. I would feel better if you weren't alone when we're not together."

"I won't be alone. Justine will be here. Besides, Jay might be a dick, but I don't think he'd be stupid enough to try something."

She cut off my argument with a *don't-you-fucking-go-there* glare.

She exhaled slowly. "Look, I appreciate your concern, I really do. But I need my independence, Ad. He controlled me for far too long. I still need my own space to be me. Please understand that."

"Jesus, Cass, I don't want to control you. I'm not saying that…. Fuck, I just want to hold you and make sure you're safe."

"And I love you for it. Just, give me time."

My heart that was only just returning to a steady beat swelled in joy. We had yet to say those three words to each other and for a moment, I thought that she was declaring her love. I then realised it was just an expression. I knew the strength of my feelings for her, but I didn't think she reciprocated. Not yet.

I swallowed and nodded. "Okay. When I'm not with you, though, you need to make sure you lock yourself in, and if he shows up, you need to call the guys or me straight away. We'll be here in an instant."

"I promise."

She pressed her lips against mine, her hands sneaking under my T-shirt, and all thoughts of Jay soon disappeared. When she pulled away far too quickly with a smirk on her face, I was ready to drag her up to her bedroom.

"You are a wicked, wicked woman, Cassandra Burton," I rasped and slapped her tight, firm arse as she skipped to her front door.

"Only for you, Mr Ashworth." She unlocked the door and rushed inside to grab her training stuff. I grumbled under my breath and waited at the gate for her.

WHILE I WAITED for Cassie to finish her session with Mitch, I decided to take a swim. I needed to push aside all the thoughts and concerns racing around in my head while driving my body to exhaustion. There was nothing like pushing my body through the water, focusing on correct breathing and stroke to banish stress and tension.

The pool had emptied out, cleared by the lifeguards and trainers. Colin hadn't been too happy about me staying but reluctantly agreed because I was waiting to assist Cassie with closing up.

Something was freeing in having the entire pool to myself. The overhead lighting had been dimmed and beyond the two glass walls the world was black, twilight having morphed into nighttime. I stopped for a moment, crossing my arms on the edge as I stared out into the darkness. All I could see was the reflection of the pool and its surroundings. The whole scene was so calm and peaceful.

Pushing away from the edge, I glided into the water, extending my arms ahead to execute the perfect front crawl. I focused on keeping my body flat, my elbows slightly bent as they proceeded through each stroke. Within twenty-five meters, my form was fluid again, a breath after every third stroke, my arms and legs moving me through the water with ease.

I was nearing the twenty-five-meter mark on length number forty when movement off to the side distracted me, faltering my stroke pattern. Continuing to swim, I turned my head to peer over at the entrance. A spark of desire shot through me seeing Cassie leaning against the wall. She looked sexy as hell in her tight fighting shorts and cropped training top. The garments were like a second skin on her, doing little to hide what I knew was underneath. Her hair had been pulled back into a ponytail that hung down her back. From her sweat-glistening skin and damp tendrils of hair plastered against her face, I knew she'd just come from her training session. Stealing a breath, I licked my lips and continued swimming, although now with much less determination. Or focus, because that was solely zeroed in on Cassie.

Smirking, she unfolded her arms—arms that had been resting beneath her breasts, pushing them up and together in a way that begged for my lips and fingers to be on them—and ambled towards me. At the edge of the pool, she kicked off her shoes and socks and sat down to paddle her feet in the water. I swam over, holding the rounded concrete edge of the pool on either side of her thighs.

"Hi," I greeted, my voice thick and husky from exertion.

Her smile was warm and wide, and all I wanted to do was pull her face to mine and maul her perfect ruby lips.

"Hi. Are you nearly done here?"

"Nearly. Why, did you need me for something?"

My body inched closer to hers, an inexplicable draw that had me needing to be as close to her as possible whenever we were in the same room together. Even when we were apart, I mourned her loss and longed to be near her.

She kicked her legs in the water, causing gentle waves and splashes to lap against my body.

"Don't I always?"

"Do you want to be more specific?"

She laughed, but it abruptly cut off when my cold, wet hands landed on her thighs, inching upwards, massaging and stroking. Teasing.

"Adam," she gasped, "what are you doing?"

My fingers made their way to her hips, and I held tight, staring up into her wide, sparkling eyes.

"What do you need, Cass?"

"I—"

Tucking my hands under her arse, I pulled her off the edge. She splashed into the water with a gasp and locked her hands around my neck.

"Adam, what the hell—"

I didn't give her time to hurl a tirade of verbal abuse. Instead, I ran a hand along her back, the other holding her pert backside as I leant in to catch her plump bottom lip between my teeth, tugging it softly.

"Adam," she whispered.

Her words drifted away, her body becoming lax, submitting to my need to devour her.

She shivered, her skin beading into goosebumps under my touch.

Soft kisses soon turned desperate. I took advantage of her soft moans and pleas, letting my tongue slip between her lips to caress and explore. Her tongue was wet and warm against mine. Desperate. Demanding.

She curved her body closer to mine, crushing her breasts against my chest, her pelvis grinding against mine. Needing no further encouragement, I hiked her further up my body, curling her legs around me. She wove her fingers into my hair, tugging at the stands with a force that had my scalp singing in pain. The sharp sting, mixed with the knowledge she was coming undone, had me groaning against her lips. Things were quickly turning frantic.

Pulling my mouth away for a much-needed breath, I licked a trail along her jaw and neck, savouring the gentle taste of chlorine and a whole lot of Cassie. Sweet and addicting. I retraced the path with an unpredictable pattern of licks, kisses, and soft nibbles. I began walking backwards, wading deeper into the pool. Cassie's head fell back, her ponytail fanning out on the surface of the water. God, she looked so beautiful, her darker olive-hued skin flushed with desire and glistening in contrast against my paler complexion.

I stopped walking just before the water reached chin level and supported Cassie with one arm banded around her waist; the other stroked her chest, tracing every inch. My fingertips brushed over her perfect breasts. Her nipples hardened beneath the wet cotton of her sports top, encouraging my fingers to stroke and pinch them. Her whimper was all the encouragement I needed. Using the hand supporting her, I pulled her against my pelvis and pushed my rock-hard dick against her core. My need became as desperate as hers appeared to be. As we moved against each other, our moans echoed around the room above the sounds of lapping water and filter systems.

Just as it had been since the first time we'd reconnected physically, my need to be inside her, to feel her heat, was overwhelming. Grasping her hips, I held her so with every step I took toward the shallower end of the pool, she brushed over my dick, causing us both to moan in pleasure. Cassie pushed herself up using my shoulders and crushed her lips onto mine for a brief but intense kiss.

"Adam—"

Scraping my lips and teeth along her jaw, I whispered in her ear, "I need to be inside you, Cass. You're driving me insane. I feel like a fifteen-year-old boy right now." Her laugh was short, cutting off when I deliberately thrust my dick against her most sensitive area.

In the shallow end, I slowly laid Cassie onto the sloping floor, the water gently lapping at her feet. I climbed over her, my knees pinned against her thighs, my hands resting on each side of her head. We stared at each other, our eyes having a silent conversation. I needed Cassie more than I could have ever imagined and it seemed the feeling was mutual.

Resting my forehead against hers, I exhaled a slow breath. My emotions were in overdrive. I needed her. Physically. Emotionally. For now. For tomorrow.

Forever.

I closed my eyes briefly, and when I opened them again, Cassie was smiling.

"I love you, Cass," I whispered, threading my fingers through her hair, holding her head in my palms.

Her smile faltered, and I feared I'd misjudged my decision to lay bare my feelings. It was too soon. She was still trying to rebuild her life after Jay. I wanted to slap myself for being such a fucking idiot.

Then her smile returned, only this time it was more radiant than ever. Breathtaking.

She reached up, wrapping a slender hand around my neck to pull me down.

"I love you, too." Her words were little more than a breath whispered across my lips.

"Cass, God," I murmured, desperation consuming me when her nails scraped along my shoulders and she pressed her body into mine.

My lips grazed over the fullness of hers, hands caressing every inch of her skin leaving a trail of quivers. The kiss turned frantic. Need consumed us. We couldn't get enough.

When I ran my fingertips underneath the waist of her shorts, she pulled back, gasping for breath. "Adam, we need to stop. We can't do this here."

"Why not? There's no one around." I nipped at her bottom lip and nibbled along her jaw.

"Because... Oh, God... That feels so... We're putting on one hell of an x-rated movie right now."

That grabbed my attention, and I pushed up on my hands, looking down into Cassie's amused eyes.

"What do you mean?"

"This part of the pool is monitored by CCTV. I doubt Nate will appreciate an unscripted porno being recorded by his state of the art surveillance equipment."

I cursed under my breath and looked up. Sure enough, there hidden in the rafters were three small domes with blinking red lights.

I wasn't going to let something like a few security cameras take this moment from us. "You know everything about this place," I said, returning my attention to Cassie. "Are there any blind spots in here?"

The amusement in her eyes faded away, replaced with desire and longing. She swallowed and pointed at the far end of the room where the walls fanned out into a large hexagonal conservatory filled with sun loungers.

"In there. You can't see into the sun lounge when all the lights are off."

Before she'd finished speaking, I was on my feet and lifting her into my arms. I walked over to the light switches and hit them, blanketing the area in darkness save for the blue glow of the pool. Then I made a hasty retreat to the sun room. Cassie snuggled against my chest, kissing and biting at the skin on my neck and shoulder. Her lips were a sensual caress and only fueled my desire to be with her.

Grabbing a couple of towels from a pile by the doorway, I spread one out on a sun lounger in the furthest corner and lowered Cassie onto it. Staring down at the woman who owned my heart, I took a moment to catalogue her beauty. Her dark hair splayed out on the white towel, her chocolate eyes glittering in the moonlight streaming through the glass roof, the way droplets of water clung to her silky skin begging to be licked off.

Cassie watched intently as I slowly and deliberately removed my dripping shorts, dropping them to the floor beside the lounger. Next, I pulled off her shorts and underwear. When I reached for her top, she surprised me by climbing onto her knees and tugged it over her head. She kept our gazes locked, her arms remaining stretched above her head as the top slipped from her fingers.

We were completely naked, surrounded by glass but there was no sense of fear that we might be seen. We were in a bubble of love, where nothing but each other mattered or even existed.

Cassie ran cold fingertips along my chest and across my stomach. My breath caught, and my muscles tightened in anticipation of where her touch would go next. Her fingers wrapped firmly around my cock with a gentle tug that I felt all the way through to my balls. I sighed in pleasure and closed my eyes, concentrating on her heavenly movements. My hips began to move involuntarily, thrusting into her small fist, meeting her slow and steady rhythm.

Lost in the pleasure, I choked on a startled groan when the heat of her tongue caressed the length of my cock from tip to root and back again. My eyes flew open and stared down in wonder. Cassie stared right back through long lashes, her dark eyes shining with love. Keeping our gazes locked, I tangled my fingers into her hair and let the feeling of her lips moving over my flesh consume me.

My heart pounded faster. My balls tightened and

begged for release. I reluctantly tugged gently on her hair. I needed to regain my composure before I erupted too early. There was no way I was going to come without being inside Cassie's heavenly warmth.

"I need to be inside you," I whispered into her ear.

Cassie's eyes flashed with a hint of regret. I loved that she was prepared to put aside her own pleasure to concentrate on mine. But that wasn't me. I was all about equality and ensuring she was fully satisfied before I was anywhere near exploding.

Encouraging her to lay back, my dick fell free of her lips with a satisfying pop. I traced the fullness of her breasts, waist, hips, and thighs, marvelling at how luscious her body was. How smooth her skin was.

She was amazing. Breathtaking.

When my gentle touch had her whimpering and begging for more, I stroked a finger along her sex, fucking delighted to find she was already hot and wet, ready for me.

So perfect.

Still locked in each other's gazes, I repeated my earlier question.

"What do you need, Cass?"

"You, Adam," she choked as I slipped a finger inside, curling it in a way that I knew drove her crazy. "Just you. Always you. Please, please, Ad. God, I need you."

Fuck me. Her desperate cries were nearly my undoing. Never before had I been brought to my knees simply by a woman's lusty sounds of need. Cassie had me locked in her intricate web and I never wanted to be rescued.

Removing my finger, I aligned our pelvises and

stroked my rock hard dick through her heat, before pushing just the tip inside. Our chorus of pleasured moans echoed around the room heightening the sensuality of the moment.

I needed to be inside her. To be be one with her.

"Ah, fuck," I groaned, dropping my forehead to her shoulder with a frustrated sigh as I pulled out and held my pelvis away from hers.

"Adam?" Cassie's fingers wove into my hair and tugged gently. "What's wrong?"

I silently counted to ten, trying to calm my racing heart and furious dick. When I looked up it was with regret, regret that I'd been so fucking irresponsible.

"Sorry, Cass. You get me so worked up I forgot I don't have a condom."

I held my breath and waited for her to push me away, yelling about being so careless.

Instead, she stroked wet hair away from my face. "Is this the time we have the birth control, risk of infection chat," she asked trying to contain a grin.

My breath escaped in a rush and I chuckled. "Yeah, I guess. Or we can just—"

"Adam."

"Honestly, Cass. It's fine. I should never have—" I shifted to stand but she planted her hands on my shoulders holding me in place.

"I'm covered," she said softly searching my eyes. "I got check out after I left... you know. I had to know I was okay."

Hope bloomed inside me. Was she okay with this?

"I'm good too, I promise. I've not been with anyone else in months, and even then I made sure I was covered."

She smiled. "I believe you."

"You're really okay with this?"

She nodded. "I'm really okay with this. I want you, Adam. I want to feel you, all of you."

God, could this woman be any more perfect?

Before she could change her mind, I pressed my lips to hers and kissed her deeply. I slid deep inside her heat, filling her completely as heaven's blessings rained over us from a canopy of bright stars above. Her back arched off the lounger, grinding onto my dick with a moan. I moved with her, taking my cues from her, hoping to prolong the moment for as long as possible.

I pulled back slowly and thrust into her again and again, harder and deeper. She shuddered and dug her fingernails into my shoulders. Her cheeks flushed with a magnificent pink hue and she was panting hard, her eyes wide and gazing into mine in awe. With her face lit by the bright ray of moonlight, she had never looked so fucking beautiful. She wrapped her thighs around my hips, gripping tightly as though she were afraid I would disappear. That was never going to happen. Not if I could help it.

She tightened around me the deeper I pushed, and I feared I'd not be able to last long. She felt too good. Too perfect. She was my undoing.

"Please, Adam, faster. I need you to go faster. I'm... I'm... Oh shit." With one press of my thumb against her clit, she clamped onto my dick so hard I nearly followed her into bliss. But I wanted more. I slowed to shallow thrusts, allowing her time to regain her breath. When she was once again coherent, I pulled her against me and flipped us over so she straddled me.

"Take me, Cass. You have all of me now. I'm yours. Take what you want."

A single tear escaped the corner of her eye, leaving a silvery track along her cheek. I reached up and brushed it away, sucking the salty evidence of her love from my thumb.

She began to move, throwing her head back and thrusting her chest forward as pleasure once again consumed her. My fingers moulded to her breasts, rolling and pinching her nipples.

When she screamed my name again, orgasming with such intensity I felt the pressure of it all the way to my heart, I followed her over. I groaned long and loud, my own release seemed never-ending, the pleasure intensified from being bare and having the knowledge that a part of me would remain within her.

With Cassie slumped over my chest, our bodies still connected in the most intimate of ways, we fought to catch our breath.

"Did you get what you need?" I asked several minutes later.

She laughed, the vibration of it shaking against my chest. "I got more than I needed. So much more."

I closed my eyes and rested my head back on the lounger.

"Me too."

SEVERAL MINUTES LATER, we were cleaned up and changed. Cassie was double-checking everything was put away and turned off before she closed up for the night. I followed her into the office, immediately looking at the bank of monitors lined up along one wall. I focused on the image of the pool, intermittently scrolling through the three different camera angles.

"Are you sure we're not going to appear on some seedy Internet sex site?" I asked, peering closer at the screen as it moved on to the camera closest to the conservatory. "I've got no plans of ever becoming a porn star."

Laughing, Cassie wrapped her arms around me and peered around my side. "No. See." She pointed to the screen. "You can only see the entrance. We would have been completely out of sight."

I exhaled a deep breath of relief. Although I feared others seeing what took place in that room for Cassie's sake, my main concern was the possibility that anyone else might share in those moments. They were sacred to me. I hadn't just enjoyed a brief moment of unexpected sex with my girlfriend; those moments had been so much deeper, had held so much love and reverence.

"Are you ready to get out of here? I'll drop you home." I turned away from the screens, already missing her. We'd been spending so much time together, either staying at her place or mine. Tonight, though, I'd reluctantly agreed to one night apart. Cassie had told me earlier that she wanted to spend some time with Justine before she started another long stint of night shifts. It ruined the plans I'd made, but who was I to keep her from her best friend. Besides, I had some last-minute work to do on the Brightmann plans before I met with their representatives tomorrow. I would just enjoy my surprise with her when I next saw her.

With a final glance around the room, she flipped

off the lights and locked the office door. "Yeah, let's go."

CHAPTER TWENTY-FOUR

Cassie

I COULDN'T REMEMBER THE LAST time I'd felt so happy. Things with Adam were great. Better than great, they were amazing. He was such a fun-loving, generous, and kind-hearted guy, the complete opposite of what Jay had been. They were night and day. Whereas Jay had been dark, ominous, and often scary, Adam was bright, welcoming, and he wore his heart on his sleeve. He hid nothing from me. I knew exactly where I stood with him.

Walking along the pathway toward my house, I looked over my shoulder and smiled. Adam's car sat idling beside a Toyota Aris, once again double-parked because there were no parking spaces within a three-block radius. He watched me expectantly through the windshield, waiting until I was safely ensconced in my home before driving away. He was forever my protector, another thing I adored about him.

I felt a small stab of disappointment and regret as I dipped a hand into my bag for my keys. I'd been the one to ask for a night away from him when he'd obviously been so keen to spend the night with me. But I'd been serious when I'd said I still needed my independence and having control of my own life. Plus I needed to catch up with Justine. I loved being with Adam and couldn't seem to get enough of him, but I felt my relationship with my best friend was suffering. She had taken the news of my relationship with Adam well—much better than I had expected, but I often wondered if she'd been blowing smoke up my arse just to keep me happy. I needed a night alone with her to make sure she was doing okay and not working herself into an early grave. Didn't mean I wouldn't miss him like crazy, though.

And after our declarations of love that evening, I needed to speak with my best friend more than ever. I hoped she would be able to offer some reassurance that I wasn't jumping into something so serious too quickly. It all felt so sudden, even though the chemistry between us had been there for a while. I needed to know that I wasn't using Adam as the rebound guy.

So with the knowledge that I would be with him again in less than twenty-four hours, I blew Adam a kiss from my position at my gate, just as an angry motorist beeped him for blocking the road. I laughed along with him when he dramatically pretended to catch the kiss and then blow one straight back. Then he shot me a regretful pout and took off down the street. I watched him until his taillights disappeared around the corner. He might have been out of sight, but he was definitely not out of mind. I was already giddy with the prospect of what our *cosy* evening tomorrow would involve.

The first hint that my evening was about to turn to shit came when I glanced across the street and noticed a familiar black Audi TT parked between old man Anderson's vintage Morris Minor and Estelle's canary-yellow VW Beetle. My heart momentarily pounded in my chest until I reasoned that there was probably hundreds of black Audi TT's on the streets of London. After my fright earlier, I was just being paranoid.

Holding my keys in my hand, my head was downcast as I walked along my path thinking about Adam. That was why I didn't hear the car door open or acknowledge the female figure stepping up behind me.

"Hello, Cassie. I've been waiting for you."

Startled, I swung around, the keys fell from my hands, and I gasped, slapping a hand over my racing heart. "Jesus, you scared the shit out of me, Bianca. What are you doing here?"

She moved out from the shadows and under the glow of a nearby streetlight, I could see the deep frown lines marring her usually immaculately made-up face. She looked tired and concerned.

"I need to talk to you."

"About what?"

I had nothing I wanted to say to her. After the way she'd lusted over Jay under my nose when I was with him, she was the last person I wanted any contact with. Well, apart from Jay, that was.

"Can I come in?"

"No. If you want to talk to me do it here, and then you can be on your merry way."

She sighed, nodding as though she'd expected this response from me.

"That's your call. It would be better if we did this inside, or at least go somewhere more private."

"Not happing. Just spit it out, Bianca, I've got things to do this evening."

She studied me for a moment, steeling herself for whatever she had to tell me.

"When was the last time you saw Jay?" she asked, her expression stoic.

I wanted to laugh. Was she serious? Did she think I still had a thing for that controlling jerk?

I scoffed. "Oh, what's the matter? Is lover boy cheating on you now, too? Tell me, Bianca." I took a step closer, needing to see her expression clearly in the dim lighting. "Did you enjoy shagging him behind my back? Did it feel good?"

Her eyes widened, her mouth dropped open, words frozen on her tongue.

"Well you have him now, and I'm so fucking grateful. That man is a piece of work. You deserve each other actually."

"Cassie, you've got it all wrong. I was never with Jay."

I barked a humourless laugh. "Don't give me that shit. You were all over him. It was kind of pathetic really."

I watched, confused, as she seemed to rally her defences. A calmer, collected presence replaced her perplexed, wary stance.

"I promise, there was absolutely nothing going on with me and that man. He's a nasty piece of work, not even worthy of a place stuck on the bottom of my shoe."

I frowned. "But—"

She lifted a hand to halt me. "Like I said, I need to talk to you about something. Are we going in or doing it out here?"

"You're not coming in my home. Say what you need to and then get the hell away from me."

She might have appeared to detest Jay as much as I did, that didn't mean I had to like the woman.

"Let me ask again, when did you last see Jay?"

"I spoke to him a couple of weeks ago. Why?"

"But have you seen him around? Has he tried to approach you? Think, Cassie, this is important."

The earnest tone of her voice sent my pulse racing, this time from apprehension rather than anger.

"Yes, I've seen him. Or at least I'm sure it was him. There was a guy that looked just like him here earlier today. He was walking away, but when he got to the corner"—I pointed in the direction I'd seen Jay earlier—"he turned, and I saw his face. I thought it was just my mind playing tricks on me."

"Was he alone?"

I didn't like her questions. There was something in the way she spoke and how her big round, green gaze burned into mine. I knew that whatever she was about to tell me, I wasn't going to like it.

"Yes," I murmured. I looked down and crossed my arms over my chest. Either the temperature had just plummeted to sub-zero, or my body was preparing itself for one hell of a shock.

She remained quiet for a moment, her black boot tapping restlessly on the concrete paving.

"Have you ever seen him with any… unsavoury characters?"

My eyes shot up to meet hers. "What do you mean? What is this, Bianca?"

She sighed, her shoulders slumping in resignation. "Okay. No more bullshit. My name isn't Bianca. It's DCI Susan Monroe. I'm a detective with the Metropolitan Police. We've been investigating Jayden for quite a while now."

My legs suddenly felt like spaghetti. "For what?" I squeaked.

"We believe he is involved with a large group connected with several serious drug and arms offences. So far, we've been unable to trace these crimes back to their ringleader so we've been following several suspects hoping they will lead us to the person or people we really need."

Holy shit. Was Jay actually involved in that sort of thing? I couldn't believe it.

My brain quickly scanned over our last interactions. He hadn't been the same man I'd classed as a friend in the months leading to our break-up. He'd once been a calm and welcoming person who would sit with me for hours listening to my worries. I'd never seen any signs of drug use or other illegal activities.

"Are you sure?" I whispered.

Her features softened. "I'm afraid so. Listen, Cassie, I shouldn't be telling you any of this. I could be risking our entire investigation if any of this was to get back to those involved. However, I'm concerned you might be in danger and need to warn you."

"I'm what?" My shaky hand drifted to my mouth.

"Before I tell you what I know, can I ask if Jay was ever alone in your house?"

"No, he didn't have a ke—" Memories of Jay mysteriously appearing in my home with no explanation of how he entered filled my mind.

I swallowed. "Yes, several times."

She nodded with a frown as though my answer had been expected. "And have you ever noticed him leaving anything here or acting suspiciously when he's around?"

"I… I don't know." It was all too much, I couldn't think straight.

"Has he been…." She continued firing off question after question in rapid succession. I barely answered, too stunned from what I was hearing.

"Do you know if he'd planned on taking a trip abroad?"

I blinked into the darkness and then a thought hit me like a bolt of lightning—our conversation about Thailand. "Yes, he wanted to take me to Thailand. We were going to spend a week in my mother's village and then have a week at a resort in Phuket."

She nodded, her expression saying she assumed as much. "Cassie, I think that trip was a just a ruse. I believe it was Jay's intention to use you as a mule."

"A what?" I choked.

"He was going to plant drugs on you to smuggle through customs."

The colour drained from my face as the implications of her words registered.

"He what? Oh my God!"

My body shook, overcome with fear, anger and

sadness that I'd ever allowed that man any part of me.

"Cassie, sit down. You've gone really pale." What did she expect? It wasn't every day I received news like that.

She helped me ease down onto the step and the crouched to watch me carefully. I must have looked dreadful because she looked panicked and ready to call for help.

"I don't understand," I said, wetting my dry lips. "I never saw anything, never heard anything."

"He's a master manipulator, an expert at covering his tracks. He had too much to lose if you discovered the truth."

I buried my head between my knees and took a few deep, calming breaths.

"But surely I would have seen or heard something. Christ, I was with the guy for over six months. We were friends a lot longer than that. I should have seen what was going on. I should have known. I could have stopped him, done something."

She placed a hand on my shoulder trying to calm me from the full-blown panic attack I was racing into.

"Cassie"—she spoke as if I were a skittish animal ready to bolt—"if you'd found out the truth and confronted him, I doubt you'd be here to have been able to do anything about it."

I felt sick. "What do you mean?"

"These men are dangerous, Cassie. The circles Jay moves in are evil men who don't think twice about maiming or killing those who get in their way or cross them. I hate to be blunt, but you need to know the full facts so you can protect yourself."

The dark evening sky was caving in on me, slowly

suffocating and choking. I couldn't breathe and any second I was going to lose the contents of my stomach. My head fell to my knees again.

"What are the full facts?" I murmured, wanting to know yet fearing the very worst.

"Are you sure you want to do this out here? Maybe we should go inside so you can sit down."

My head shook. "No. Please, just tell me so you can get out of here. I don't want my home tainted by this stuff."

"But it already is, Cassie," she said regretfully.

"What?" My head shot up, the speed of the motion causing another wave of nausea. "Why do you think that?"

Bianca—Susan, whatever her name was, exhaled deeply and motioned to the doorstep. "Can I join you?"

I shuffled over, allowing her space to take a seat next to me.

"Okay, here's what we know, or believe." I turned my head, ready to listen to her every word. She stretched her legs out and stared ahead. "About a year ago, Jay became involved with a group smuggling and selling drugs and weapons out of South London. He started off small, occasionally buying cocaine from one of their sellers—Eddie Jameson. Have you heard of him?" I nodded. I'd overheard a couple of Jay's hushed phone conversations and remembered hearing the name mentioned.

"Well, Eddie turned informant after he got arrested for dealing. He has filled in a lot of blanks but still hasn't been able to give us what we need—the head honchos. He tuned us in to Jay after he started bypassing Eddie to get his drugs elsewhere. The details of why or how are not known, but he got caught up with the group. Maybe he owed them, or maybe he saw an easy way to earn a lot of money. Whatever it is, we don't know and at this point, it doesn't matter. When he lost his job five months ago—"

"He what?" I sat up straight, shaking my head. That couldn't be right. "Jay works. He has a job at a big financial investment company in the City."

"He did have," she said, matter of fact.

She was wrong. I'd seen him go off to work myself. Heard all about the regular conferences and work trips he'd taken in the last few months. "You're wrong. He went to a big conference just before we split up. He was gone all week."

She sighed as if I were stupid. "He wasn't at a conference, Cassie. He met up with some guys at a warehouse in Streatham. We lost their trail when they left and when we raided the warehouse we didn't find what we'd hoped for. We did find evidence of drugs having been there and a wooden crate later tested by forensics showed traces of gunpowder. We didn't see Jay for four days after that. You do the math."

No, no, no, this wasn't happening. This man I thought I knew, who at one point had meant the world to me, was nothing but a lying, cheating crook. Scum of the earth.

"There's more. As I said, I've been trailing him for a while now, that's the reason I joined your kick-boxing club."

"You're not really a kick-boxer? But you're so good at it."

It was a pointless statement but in my addled mind,

it was something I could easily focus on.

She smirked. "I kick-box. I've been a regional champion for the last two years actually. It's a shame it all went to shit at Golden Oakes really, I think we could have been great training partners."

My head bobbed. I had nothing else to say.

"Anyway, I followed him several times and noticed him coming here when you weren't around. He'd let himself in, stay for around thirty minutes or so, and then leave."

"No. That can't have happened. He didn't have a key."

She shot me an exasperated look. "He did, Cassie. Each time the house was empty. He would knock first—presumably to check your housemate wasn't home—and then he'd let himself in. We've not been able to determine what exactly he was doing in there, but it's possible he might have been using your place to hide drugs and weapons."

My eyes widened in disbelief a second before my fragile tummy decided it couldn't take any more sickening news. I jumped to my feet and barely made it to the small flower bed in my front garden before I was throwing up, wishing it was all just a bad dream.

In an instant, Susan was behind me, holding my hair back as she expressed her regrets and apologies.

Suddenly it all made sense. The abrupt changes in personality, his recent bedraggled appearance, the hushed phone conversations and last-minute work conferences. Christ, I had been so bloody naïve.

"What happens now?" I asked, my voice barely above a whisper.

She stepped back as I stood wiping my mouth with

the back of my hand.

"Now, you be extra vigilant. Jay has been quiet the past two days and before that he was spotted in this area. If he has been using your house, then he won't want to lose that. He's volatile, Cassie. If you see him, you need to get to a safe place and call me immediately. Don't try and confront him and definitely don't do anything silly. He is only a small pawn in a much larger game of chess, and with your support, we hope to take each of them down and claim checkmate. But we need you to do your part." She reached into her pocket and pulled out a small white card, handing it to me. "Here's my card. If you see or hear anything suspicious, you call me immediately, no matter the time of day or night. We'll have someone with you in minutes."

She paused a moment, staring over her shoulder at the door. "I think it would be wise for both you and your housemate to stay elsewhere for the time being. Until we know for sure where he is and what he's doing, and can be certain you're not in any danger, I think it would be for the best."

Being chased from my own home was not something I wanted to think about. However, with everything Susan spoke of, I didn't have much choice. I only hoped Adam was up for playing house for a while.

"Take care of yourself, Cassie."

I watched her walk along the path and climb into the passenger side of a black BMW. The car took off into the night, taking my sense of safety with it.

So much for my quiet girlie night in with Justine.

Now, I'd have to explain why we couldn't stay in

our own home and hope she had somewhere she could stay while the whole mess was sorted out.

THE SECOND HINT that I should have run away as far and as fast as I could was when my door pushed open far too easily when I turned the key in the lock. But as fragments of my conversation with Bianca—Susan— drifted through my mind, thoughts of imminent danger were buried deep in my psyche, leaving me dazed and confused. Those thoughts should have been front and centre, screaming at me to run.

"He'd let himself in."

"We suspect he has been using your place to hide drugs and weapons."

Holy shit! Bile rose in my throat imagining what he'd been doing and what could be hidden in dark corners of the one place I'd always felt safe. What exactly had Jay pulled me into?

With my thoughts and emotions all over the place, it was a stupid move on my part to enter the house despite a niggling little voice telling me to get the hell out of there.

The house was dark when I stepped inside. All the lights were off except for the one that I always left on at the far end of the narrow hallway. Through the slightly ajar living room door, I could see the gentle glow of the lamp that was also always left on. Breathing a sigh of relief, and silently chastising myself for letting Susan's words affect me, I forced the front door closed, making sure the locking mechanism clicked into place.

"Juss, you home? We need to talk." I shouted up

the stairs, hearing Eminem and Rhianna blasting out from her room. I shook my head, imagining she'd fallen asleep on her bed. Like me, she detested any form of hip-hop and would quickly change music channels or playlist whenever a track came on she didn't like.

Unzipping my jacket, I hung it on a hook just inside the doorway and made my way into the kitchen to plug my phone in. The uneasy feeling that had gripped me like a vice from Susan's visit wouldn't let up, although all evidence indicated everything was okay.

Thinking about the look on Adam's face as he drove away, I dropped my bag onto the kitchen counter and connected the phone to the charging cable. I left it to do its thing and wandered upstairs. I needed to pack an overnight bag and break the news to Justine. I just hoped she understood.

Opening my bedroom door, I nearly tripped over my own feet at the sight before me.

While I'd been out, the room had been transformed into a warm, romantic haven. Soft light illuminated the room from dozens of candles and tea lights that flickered and danced on every flat surface. A large bouquet of white roses and calla lilies sat elegantly in the centre of my dressing table. Next to the flowers a bottle of champagne sat chilling in a silver bucket with two glass flutes beside it and a small navy velvet box.

I felt rather than saw someone move in behind me and smiled. Tears stung the backs of my eyes as I took it all in.

"You're a sneaky bitch, Juss. Did he get you to do this? He wanted to surprise me? He's coming back isn't he?" I asked softly, grinning as I lifted my hand to my chest. Adam had been with me all night so he must have had help. Justine. It made me love them both even more that they had gone to so much effort to surprise me.

"Do you like it?"

I froze. The blood running through my veins suddenly ran icy. The person standing close behind me, his breath singeing my neck, wasn't Justine, or even Adam.

"I thought I'd surprise you, Cass. Do you like it?"

I choked on a sharp breath as bile rose and fought to escape my constricted throat.

"Jay," I whispered, terrified. "How did you get in here?"

"You really need to get that door of yours looked at, babe. Anybody could easily force his or her way in." Oh God, how had I been so blind? Everything now made sense. No matter the number of times someone came to fix the door, it always seemed to play up again shortly after.

"He'd let himself in."

Of course, he didn't need a key; he'd been tampering with the door so he could have easy access whenever he needed it, leaving both Justine and me in danger in an unsecured property.

Keep calm, Cass. Keep him talking until you can call for help.

"What… what are you doing here?" I flinched when I felt him step closer, his hands moving to my shoulders and squeezing gently.

"I missed you. You've made your point, Cassandra, but now it's time to grow up and come back to me where you belong."

His words, along with the unwelcome sensation of his nose grazing along my neck, snapped into my senses, turning me from fearful to enraged. I'd spent far too long being manipulated and bullied by this man, and I wasn't going to stand here allowing him that power again. Our relationship had been a sham from the very beginning. He hadn't wanted me, he'd wanted a verbal punching bag; someone he could use to stroke his ego by taking his macho bullshit. Someone he could use to help him hide his illegal activities. I needed to get him out once and for all.

Tugging free of his hold, I moved away and twisted to meet his gaze. It was then I noticed the blank, glassed-over look in his eyes, a clear sign he'd been drinking and probably taking something, too. Eminem and Rhianna continued to sing about loving the way you lie, and I realised it was coming from my sound system.

Justine. If the music wasn't coming from her room, where was she? I immediately began to panic, fearing he'd hurt her.

"Justine!" I yelled, barging past him towards her room.

He grabbed my hand in a painful clasp, yanking me back.

"She's not here," he said, his words slurred and laced with anger.

"Where is she?" I struggled against his hold, but he just tightened his fingers around mine, squeezing until I winced in pain. "What have you done to her?"

Tears stung my eyes as I thought about her being hurt somewhere.

"How the fuck should I know? I'm not her

330

keeper."

A relieved sob shook my chest, knowing he hadn't hurt her. Then the panic returned, thinking she could come home any minute. We'd been planning this evening for days, there was no way she would let me down, not without letting me know if something had come up.

I needed to get away from him. I had to call Susan and Justine. And I desperately wanted Adam's comforting arms wrapped around me.

"Sit." Yanking my arm, almost dislocating my shoulder, he pushed me onto the bed. I landed with a thud and gasped in pain when my head hit the solid oak headboard.

"So," he continued, as though he hadn't just nearly knocked me out, "I don't like repeating myself, but I guess I'll have to. When are you going to stop having this fucking ridiculous hissy fit and grow up? I need you back, Cassie."

"You need me back?" I choked, shaking off the dull pain in my head. "Are you having a laugh? Do me a favour and take a long walk off a short pier, preferably into shark-infested water." His eyes darkened dangerously, burning into mine, but I didn't heed the warning. I continued my rant, too worked up to consider the consequences. "You think the way you act with me is right, Jay? You think manipulating me is okay? Why would I accept that? I'm better than that."

I flinched back when he took a step closer, his hand balling into a fist by his side.

"I've never manipulated you," he sniffed.

"Bullshit. You treated me like crap for months. I was just too blind to see it."

Ignoring my outburst, he stepped over to the dressing table. He grabbed the bottle of champagne from the bucket and poured a glass, holding it out to me. I ignored it, crossing my arms over my chest.

"You'll come back to me." He casually lifted the glass to his lips and sipped on the cool liquid, his menacing eyes never leaving mine. His eerie calmness was beginning to terrify me.

My head shook. "You need to go, Jay. It's over between us."

"I'm not going anywhere."

"But we're over, Jay. You hurt me too many times. I can't take you back, not after that."

His fingers tightened around the glass and neck of the bottle. "We will *never* be over, Cassie. You don't get to just decide we're through. You're mine. Always have been and always will be," he sneered.

My eyes widened in horror. He was delusional.

I jumped to my feet, my anger resurfacing. "Yes. We. Are. I hate you!"

"You love me!"

Tears of resentment and frustration dripped down my cheeks as my words came out in a strangled howl. "No, I don't! How could I when you're such a controlling bastard? Get out, Jay. Get the fuck out of my house and out of my life."

"This is because of him, isn't it!" Jay bellowed, hurling the bottle and glass across the room. They hit the wooden table beside me and shattered in an ear-piercing crash on the wooden floor.

His eyes were feral, almost demonic when he looked up. "I apologised for the bullshit you accused me of before. I even forgave you for your sluttish ways, for cheating on me and fucking *him*. But it ends tonight, Cassie. You've had your fucking fun. Now you're coming back with me. If I have to drag you out of here, don't think I won't do it."

"You're a fucking psycho!"

My heart pounded hard in my chest, but fear drove me on. I had to get away from Jay and I needed Adam. Powered by pure adrenaline, I ran from the room and down the stairs to the kitchen. I grabbed my phone, and with a shaky hand, I unlocked the screen pulling up Adam's contact while I hurried toward the back door. Just as I heard Adam answer, Jay was in front of me, his features maniacal.

"I don't think so," he thundered, knocking the phone from my hand. It hit the stone tiled floor and shattered at my feet.

"Don't you *ever* fucking run from me again."

It's said senses are heightened, and you see things in slow motion when you're in danger. The moment Jay's hand lifted toward my face, everything slowed. I noticed every millimetre of space his hand sliced through, the deep inhale of his breath, the snarl on his lips and the blackness of his eyes when he shouted the word "bitch." The back of his hand connected harshly with my cheek. The sharp pain was immediate but only registered when my head cracked against the corner of a cupboard, and my body slumped to the floor. In shock, I blinked up through hazy vision at the man I'd once thought cared for me.

Thoughts of escape ran through my muddled mind, but my body felt too weak, unresponsive. Despite my will begging my limbs to move, I couldn't.

Jay's expression turned gleeful as he stared down at

me for a brief moment. A small, almost indiscernible whimper escaped me when he stepped closer, only to reach for a glass tumbler and the bottle of Scotch that had been sitting on the kitchen counter. And then he turned and walked away.

My vision turned from hazy to cloudy, and the fight in me drained away.

The kitchen door slammed closed behind Jay's retreating form.

As everything changed from murky to black, I had only one thought: *Adam, I love you. I'm so sorry.*

CHAPTER TWENTY-FIVE

Adam

I WAS STILL SMILING WHEN I pulled my car into the underground parking lot of my apartment building. The sexy look on Cassie's face when she blew me that kiss would stay with me for a long time.

She had burrowed herself so far under my skin she was now a fundamental part of me; the life in my soul, and the beat of my heart. Declaring our honest feelings for each other had shifted something between us, a new mutual respect that went way beyond physical desire.

It had been torture forcing myself to drive away and not leave the car parked in the middle of the road. What I'd really wanted to do was follow her into the house and ravage her sexy body. And I would have if I hadn't needed to be up at the arse crack of dawn for a meeting. I would have been lip locked with Cassie with her luscious body spread out beneath me.

I would just have to make up for lost time tomorrow.

My phone chirped a happy tune as I made my way to the staircase. Pulling it from my pocket, I grinned seeing Cassie's name on the screen.

"Hey, beautiful. You missing me already?"

The sound of a deep, growling voice that most definitely wasn't Cassie's made my blood run cold. Then, when the line went silent, I froze with the phone to my ear.

"Cass! Cassie, you there?"

Nothing but silence.

"Cass?"

As fear started to claw at me, I finally snapped to my senses, needing answers. The line had disconnected so I frantically redialled, only to get voicemail. Over and over I tried her number with no response until I couldn't take it anymore. There was something very wrong; I felt it in my gut. Taking off across the parking lot, I jumped in the car and peeled out onto the street, not caring what traffic laws I violated.

My mind was spinning, fearing every worst-case scenario. Either Cassie was with another guy, or she was in danger. I didn't know which I would prefer to find when I got to her house. Neither was acceptable.

On the way over, I called Wesley and Justine, holding on to hope that either had been in contact with her. When they confirmed they hadn't spoken to her, the ominous feeling in me grew. Justine was supposed to have been spending the evening with her, but she'd been called in to cover a night shift at the hospital and hadn't had a chance to let Cassie know. By the time I screeched to a halt in front of Cassie's house—thanking the stars for a parking spot right outside—my heart was pounding way too hard and way too fast. My knuckles ached from gripping the steering wheel so tight. I flung the door open and sprinted up the pathway, yelling her name as I went.

"Cassie! Open the fucking door!"

I hammered my fists against the wood over and over, but it remained closed. Stepping back I looked over the front of the house. There were no lights on anywhere, just an orange glow that shone through her living room and bedroom windows. I stepped closer to the front window, hoping for any indication of what was going on. A grey haze billowed out into the cool evening air through gaps and cracks in the old wooden frames. Looking back at the front door, I noticed the same haze drifting lazily out from underneath.

Smoke.

Shit!

"Cassie!" I hammered my fists on the door again and again to no avail. Suddenly a strange hissing sound came from inside, followed by an almighty crash as the front windows blew out, sending flames licking up the front of the house and glass shards flying through the air.

"What's going on?" A voice shouted from the street.

"Fire! Call the fucking emergency services," I yelled, already ramming my shoulder into the door over and over.

"Don't go in there. You'll get hurt," the voice shouted.

"My girlfriend's in there," I roared over the hiss and pop of the flames as they intensified. The smoke was getting thicker by the second, choking me as I jarred my shoulder against the wood again.

"You'll kill yourself if you go in there."

"Just get the fucking fire brigade and an ambulance here, now!"

Finally, the door gave way and swung inwards. The scene in front of me was one of absolute carnage. Flames licked at the walls, and thick smoke filled the narrow hallway. For a moment I just stood there, lost in the destruction. Fear and panic robbed me of motor function; all I could do was stare.

Then I heard a faint coughing sound and snapped back to reality. Cassie was trapped inside somewhere, and I needed to get to her.

"Cassie! Cassie!"

"Here, put this over your nose and mouth if you're going in." A cloth was thrust into my hand from behind as I stepped over the threshold. "You're crazy, kid. You're going to kill yourself."

"I have to get to her," I shouted through the cloth as I stepped cautiously into the hallway. "Just get the damn firefighters here."

"They're already on their way."

With the cloth covering my nose and mouth I moved faster down the hallway, fighting off the instinctual want to retreat from the intense heat of the flames that now crept across the floor and caught on the wooden stair rail. I stood for a moment, faced with the choice of checking the kitchen or living room, or risking the stairs to see if Cassie was in her bedroom.

"Cassie!" I cried, feeling desperate. Where was she?

I made the calculated decision that Cassie was most likely in her bedroom. Just as I reached the bottom step to go for her, a loud popping sound echoed around me as something crashed down from above. I jumped back, coughing into my cloth as flames engulfed my only way to the first floor.

"Fuck! Cassie, baby, please, where are you?" My yells were desperate, punctuated by racking coughs as the smoke grew thicker by the second. Time was running out. There were flames everywhere, and the smoke was so thick I could barely see a foot in front of me.

"Cassie!"

"Adam?" The sound was so quiet that I barely heard it.

"Cassie?"

This time, the response I heard was a cough, but it was enough to let me know it was coming from the kitchen. I looked around desperately for a way through. A pile of burning debris that had fallen from the ceiling above blocked off my only way into the kitchen. I felt panic bubbling up within me. I had never felt so helpless, so desperate to do the right thing but unable to.

"Son, you need to get out, *now!*" I heard from the elderly neighbour outside just as heat scorched my back and a loud crash echoed in the area behind me. The ceiling above the front door had caved in, exposing the bedroom above. I was trapped. I had two choices: give in and let the flames and smoke take me, or fight my way in to Cassie and pray that I could get us both out to safety.

Hearing her cough in the kitchen was enough to

steady my resolve. If I could help it, there was no way were going to die in that fire. Without any further thought, I ran as fast as I could through the flames towards the kitchen.

The thick wood of the fire door wouldn't open at first, and the metal handle was too hot to touch. Eventually, with a guttural grunt and as much power as I could put behind it, I managed to kick open the door. As soon as it swung open smoke billowed into the room, which had been temporarily protected. It was so thick that I couldn't see a thing and flames were gaining on me by the second. I pushed the door closed, hoping it would continue to give us a moment's reprieve from the destruction currently engulfing the rest of the house.

Squinting into the smoky darkness, I fell to my knees, my lungs protesting the lack of clean oxygen. Staying low, I crawled across the floor, feeling my way toward the sink. I knew if I had any hope of staying conscious long enough to save Cassie, we needed clean damp cloths to filter the air we were breathing. When I got to the sink, I sent up a silent prayer of thanks that the drawer of dishcloths had yet to be swallowed up by the fire. Quickly saturating two dishtowels, I discarded the cloth I'd been using and replaced it with the new wet ones and then set about finding Cassie.

I turned around, and that's when I saw her, a dark shadow barely visible through the thickening smoke. Cassie's body was lifeless, sprawled out across the tiled floor. A dark pool of something surrounded her head.

"Cassie?" I shouted desperately, running toward her. The hallway would now be completely impassable. Our only way out was through the back door.

The hiss and crackle of the fire was getting louder as it encroached on us. A loud crash followed by a bang could be heard over the ferocious sounds of the fire and I knew we'd run out of time I had to get her out, alive; the alternative was not something I would allow myself even a second to consider.

I sprinted to the door and with one hard kick, the wood splintered around the handle, which broke off and fell to the floor. Grabbing the jagged edges of the wood, I yanked the door open, immediately hearing the hiss and pop of the hungry flames as they sucked on their new energy source and rose from the ground as fiery warriors. Needing both hands free, I sucked in a deep breath through the damp cloth and held it. I dropped the makeshift mask over Cassie's face and crouched low, snaking one hand under her back and the other under her knees. With my lungs screaming, I grunted, pushing up onto unsteady feet, holding Cassie's limp body close to mine. I momentarily lost my balance as I straightened and we crashed against the table now being devoured by greedy flames. I cried out in pain, feeling the skin on my back burning through the cotton of my jacket. Knowing it was now or never, I stumbled across the floor and out through the door into the cool night air.

When we were far enough away from the burning building, my steps faltered, and I dropped to my knees still holding Cassie. My back was burning, and I could barely suck in a cleansing breath through protesting lungs. My eyes screamed from all the smoke. Through the cracking, wheezing, and popping of the fire I could hear the faint sound of sirens approaching the front of the building.

We were safe.

Laying Cassie down, I immediately fell onto my back on the evening damp grass and closed my eyes. Now we just had to wait for the paramedics to find us.

"PLEASE, MR ASHWORTH, you need to rest."

"What I *need* is for you to listen when I say I'm okay. You've patched me up, now I just want to check on my girlfriend."

The young nurse, whose name was Emily, I think, shrank away from my poor bedside manner. I didn't give a shit. Poor thing. She was obviously newly qualified and hadn't had much experience with pissed-off men needing to get to their women to see with their own eyes that they were okay.

"But you've—"

"Look"—I glanced at her name badge—"Emily. I appreciate your concern, but I'm going out of my head in here. I need to know that Cassie is okay. I'm sure you can understand that. Now, are you going to let me go or not?"

"I—"

"You might as well let him go. He'll either keep hounding you until you crack under the pressure, or he'll just walk anyway."

Redirecting my glare from my nervous nurse, I found Caleb in my cubicle holding the ugly blue curtain back. His smirk told me he'd been enjoying our verbal sparring.

"I wouldn't suggest going anywhere without these, though. You don't want to get picked up by hospital security for indecent exposure." He threw a bag onto

342

the end of the bed, a T-shirt and socks spilling out onto the white sheet.

"How did you know I was here?" I grabbed the bag and started pulling out the remaining items.

"Apart from the million calls I had from Mum, I also heard from the lads at the station. Chris was driving one of the trucks that were deployed to Cassie's place. He was out front when they got you guys out of the garden and brought you round to the ambulances. He recognised you from the few times you'd been to the station and called me. I'd just got back from a hoax shout. Our Watch Manager told me to get out of there so here I am."

Nurse Emily watched the two of us for a moment then wisely left when I started yanking at the ties on my ugly hospital gown. Caleb sauntered over to the plastic chair in the corner and dropped onto it.

"Some privacy would be nice," I mused, lifting a brow just as I was about to drop the gown.

He smirked. "Nothing I haven't seen before, little bro."

"Yeah, but the last time I dropped my clothes in front of you, I was probably five."

If he wasn't uncomfortable with me being naked, there was no way I was going to be. I had more important things to be concerned about, such as getting to Cassie as soon as possible.

I dropped the gown and immediately heard Caleb's sharp intake of air. "Fuck me," he muttered. As I pulled on a pair of boxer briefs, I peered over my shoulder to find Cal staring at my back. "I deal with that shit every day, see things no human eye should ever have to witness. When it's someone you love, though…."

"It's nothing, Cal, just a little burn."

"Just a little burn? A finger accidentally catching the iron is a little burn. Getting a little too close to the steam from the kettle is a little burn. That"—he gestured toward my back covered in gauze and bandages—"is not a little burn. Fuck! Adam, what were you thinking? You could have been killed!"

I pulled on a pair of jeans, and as I straightened, a hacking cough had me leaning on the bed for support while I fought to catch my breath.

When I could finally speak, my voice was croaky, thick with the smoke still sitting in my lungs. "The only thing I was thinking was that Cassie was in danger. I had to get to her."

"You really love her, huh?"

I pulled the zipper up on a hoodie and lifted my eyes to his. "Yes."

He nodded, his face softening in understanding. He knew damn well that if our roles had been reversed he would have done exactly the same thing. If it had been Rachael or the kids lying unconscious in a burning building, he too would have rushed in with no thought of the consequences.

"Well okay then. I guess you should go get your woman."

Five minutes later, I stood at Cassie's bedside fighting the urge to pull her into my arms and never let go. She looked so weak and vulnerable.

I traced a finger along her arm, careful not to touch her IV line. Various dressings covered her other arm, head, and part of her leg. I wanted to remove the oxygen mask covering her beautiful face, but it was helping her breathe clean air.

Eventually, after watching over her for many long minutes, I dropped onto the chair beside her bed. I winced in pain as my T-shirt pulled taut across the burns on my back. Despite the discomfort, I welcomed the pain. It served as a reminder of what had happened, of what could have been if I hadn't found Cassie when I did. I would happily wear any number of scars if it meant she was safe, and I'd still be able to hold her in my arms.

Cassie groaned and fidgeted, and I was straight back on my feet, looming over her, waiting for the moment she opened her beautiful brown eyes to let me know she was okay.

"Come on, Cass. Open your eyes for me, beautiful. Let me know you're alright." She didn't. Another tiny whimper and her body settled again.

"I'm so glad she has finally found someone who loves her like she deserves. God knows I've done a bad job of it lately."

My eyes met those of an older gentleman standing in the doorway of Cassie's room. With dark hair streaked with grey and lines etched around his silver eyes, he appeared to be around my father's age. I spent a moment trying to place him, but he was unfamiliar.

He stepped further into the room, extending his hand.

"Forgive me. I'm Phillip Burton, Cassie's…." He trailed off, seeming unsure how to finish his introduction. I didn't know much about the guy other than what Cassie had told me. From what she'd said, he'd turned against her when he found out he wasn't her biological father.

Reluctantly I shook his hand and introduced myself, although he seemed to already know who I was. Apparently he'd been in the waiting room with our closest friends, having rushed across London to get there as quickly as possible. He had been with Cassie's mother when she'd received the call from the hospital informing her of Cassie's trauma. It was a telling sign that Phillip was there and her mother wasn't.

He gestured to the two plastic chairs beside Cassie's bed. "Shall we take a seat?"

"I know you probably don't think much of me, Adam," he said after a few minutes of silence.

"I don't know enough about you to make that call," I replied, stroking my thumb over Cassie's hand in mine.

"I'm sure she's told you about our wonderful family dynamic."

"She's mentioned things are difficult, yes."

He scoffed and then surprised me when he reached over to caress Cassie's cheek. It was such a warm, heartfelt gesture, combined with the way his lips turned up into a semblance of a smile while his eyes somehow seemed to convey both worry and love at the same time.

"When I discovered she wasn't mine, not biologically, I didn't know how to react. I didn't know how to deal with my feelings and emotions. I'd never felt so much hatred for another person in my life. That hatred was never aimed at Cassie, though. I hated her mother for her years of deceit. I hated myself for having not seen what had been under my nose all that time. I hated the bastard who deserved the right to call

346

her his daughter but had never once shown an interest in knowing her—yes, I later discovered that he was aware of Dee's pregnancy and wanted nothing more to do with her or the baby. I never once hated Cass; I just didn't know how to act around her anymore. I mean, how do you look the person in the eye that has always meant the world to you and not see lies and deceit staring back at you? I never stopped loving her, though."

I was stunned. How did you respond to something like that?

"I'm not proud of the way I treated her, Adam." He whipped his hand away as though he didn't deserve to be touching her. "God, I said some awful things the last time I saw her." His voice cracked, and I looked over to see a single tear escape his eye.

"I didn't mean it. Any of it. I was just projecting my frustrations for Dee's charade onto Cass. I was drunk and an idiot. I didn't mean it, Cassie; God, I didn't mean it, sweetheart."

When it became apparent his emotions were getting the better of him, I decided maybe he needed some time alone with Cassie to privately express his regrets.

"I'm going to grab a coffee," I said, standing. "I'll give you some time alone with her."

He just nodded and mumbled his thanks.

As I left the room, I hoped Cassie could hear his words. She needed to understand she was loved.

347

CHAPTER TWENTY-SIX

Cassie

DARK AND DANGEROUS EYES FULL of menace stared down at me. They were the eyes of the devil himself. With fire flickering in their depths, I soon realised he'd dragged me into his hell.

He moved, lifting an arm ready for attack. I screamed. The sound of my pleas for escape from the cell he'd locked us in were lost amid the angry crackle, hiss, and pop of the flames surrounding us.

Please, Jay, let me go.

There was no point begging, he wouldn't listen. Those fiery eyes of his remained glued to mine, his silence saying more than words ever could.

He had no intention of letting me go.

His hand shifted again, and I flinched, groaning in pain as heat from our blazing prison scorched the side of my body.

Please, Jay, let me go. Let me go!

I repeated it over and over, the rush of words a broken record of appeal spinning in my head.

A new pain registered in my head and I cautiously lifted a hand to touch the throbbing spot. It was a different kind of pain to that of my body, a pain that whitewashed my fiery landscape when touched.

"Careful, Cassie. Don't try to move, sweetheart."

I recognised the deep voice, only it sounded sad. It reminded me of my childhood when I'd tried climbing the old oak tree at the bottom of the garden and Dad would warn me to be careful. And then he came to help, smiling up at me as I beamed down at him from my perch on the lowest branch.

I carefully blinked my eyes open, flinching at the bright light trying to invade the darkness. I hissed and slammed them closed again.

"I'll call the doctor."

There was that voice again, reassuring and calming, encouraging me from the darkness.

Slowly, I tried again, blinking my eyes once, twice, three times. My surroundings gradually came into focus. Stark white walls and ceiling, strip lighting bathing the room in more light than was absolutely necessary with my pounding headache. I looked out of the corner of my eye and saw a metal stand with a clear plastic bag hanging from it. A sideboard was stacked with small boxes. Then my eyes drifted over to the man sitting beside me.

"Dad?"

I noticed his eyes water as the sound of my voice grated on my throat. I coughed, and something pinched over my face. A mask? My hand lifted to remove it, but warm fingers closed over mine.

"You need that on, Cassie."

"Where am I?" My voice didn't sound like my own. It was raspy and thick. Each word felt like a grater rubbing over my throat.

"You're in the hospital. Do you remember what happened?"

Memories of those fiery eyes came rushing back. The heat. His cruel words. Smoke. Flames. Banging my head. Adam. The last thing I remembered was Adam's panicked voice before everything turned black.

Sudden panic gripped me by the throat.

"Adam." I tried to move, but everything felt like it was on fire and hurt like hell. "Where's Adam?"

Oh God. He'd come for me, but what if he'd been hurt? Or worse.

"Adam's fine. He's just popped out for a few minutes."

A rush of relieved, smoke-infused air left my lungs setting off another coughing fit that had me gasping for breath.

"I'm going to call the doctor."

By the time the doctor arrived—a middle-aged Asian guy who introduced himself as Dr Vanshi—my breathing had settled down, and the coughing had ceased. Still, I felt weak, and every breath had my lungs screaming.

"You've been through a nasty ordeal, Miss Burton." Dr Vanshi seemed like a nice enough bloke, but his formal interactions did nothing to ease my frayed nerves.

And I still didn't know where Adam was.

"You suffered a nasty blow to your head, and you

have partial thickness burns on your left arm and leg. Our main concerns at the moment are a concussion and smoke inhalation. The burns, although nasty looking, should heal in time. They have been dressed for now, and those dressings will need to be replaced every couple of days to prevent infection." He wrote a few things in a folder and then dropped it in a holder hanging on the end of the bed. "We'll keep you on fluids and oxygen overnight and re-evaluate things tomorrow. Unless you have any questions, we'll leave you alone."

I was sure I'd have plenty of questions later, but right then I was still in shock.

The nurse standing with Dr Vanshi smiled warmly and said she'd be back to check on me later, and then they left.

We sat in silence for a few minutes, both lost in our thoughts. Then, belatedly, it occurred to me that Phillip was sitting at my bedside looking worried. I pulled off the oxygen mask, ignoring his stern look of disapproval.

"Why are you here, Phillip?"

I hadn't meant to sound harsh, but the last time I'd seen him, he'd been so cruel. His words had cut deep.

He leant forward, resting his elbows on his knees. His face was full of dejection and remorse as he stared at his clasped hands.

"I'm here because you're my daughter, and you're hurt. Where else would I be?"

"But—"

He looked up, glossy eyes meeting mine. "I'm so sorry, Cassie. Nothing I say will ever excuse the way I've treated you. When your mother received the call to say you were here, I felt my carefully reconstructed world fall apart again. I won't go into the whys and hows because we both know the depth of your mother's deceit. Dredging that up right now won't help either of us. But, when she said you'd been hurt and were in the hospital, I didn't think twice. I was in my car and on my way here as soon as I could. I couldn't bear the thought of my little girl being here scared and alone."

"And Mum?" I had to ask, but her absence in the room was pretty telling.

His gaze dropped, and his head shook.

"I see."

"She will never change, Cass. I was blinded by her beauty and elegance when we first met and couldn't wait to have her on my arm. When her true self began to show through I should have done the sensible thing and left her. But I was—still am—a proud man. I didn't want to be the one with a failed marriage, to be seen as the guy who couldn't hold his wife's attention. It was easy to fake appearances and then live our separate lives in private. But that was wrong. You and I both are innocent in her lies. It should have been her I pushed away, not you. Never you."

When he reached for my hand, I didn't recoil. I soaked in his warmth and relished the comfort he'd always been able to give me.

"I love you, Cassie. Don't ever forget that. You have no idea the guilt I'm carrying for the things I've done. It took me nearly losing you in that fire to understand that blood isn't always thicker than water. You are my daughter, despite what genetics say. You are my baby girl and always will be."

We spent several minutes in an embrace hampered by the lines and equipment connected to me. By the time Adam stepped through the door a while later, we were both crying and promising each other that everything would be okay.

Pulling away, Philip wiped his eyes and stood. "I'm going to give you some space. I think it's time to go home and do what I should have done a long time ago. I'm going to ask your mother for a divorce and move on with my life. Wherever that takes me, you will always be a part of it. Although it seems you have your own exciting journey ahead of you." He quickly peered over his shoulder at Adam. "He seems like a great guy, Cass. I am so happy about that." Then he placed a quick kiss on my forehead and left, giving Adam a pat on the shoulder as he passed.

Adam stood in the doorway, his body stiff with tension and his dark blue eyes filled with worry. Under his intense scrutiny, I felt my own anxiety dissolve. It was as if his mere presence alone could banish the spectres of despair. All the worries in the world disappeared. Nothing else mattered when he was near.

"I should have been here when you woke up," he eventually said, his voice much deeper and thicker than usual.

I licked my dry lips. "You're here now."

"I should always be there when you wake up."

I felt my pulse push up a gear with the clear intent behind his words.

Swallowing down the huge ball of emotion in my sore throat, I attempted a warm smile, but it felt fake. Not because I didn't want that with Adam, but because the weight of the previous hours sat heavily on my mind. I was confused and needed answers.

"Is that so?"

He stepped up to the bed and ran a fingertip along my cheek. "That's so. How are you feeling?"

"Like I was hit over the head with a meat mallet and got mistaken for a burger patty on the barbeque." My attempt at humour earned me a hard, unimpressed look.

"Nothing about what happened tonight is funny, Cassie. Fuck, I thought I'd lost you. I thought…." He sucked in a ragged breath, his body shuddering from fear and what ifs. "I didn't know where you were. I didn't know where to look. The whole place was on fire, but all I could think of was getting to you."

I gasped. "You saved me?"

"Yeah. When you called, I knew something was wrong. I drove straight over. When I saw the smoke I couldn't think of anything other than getting to you."

"Thank you." I had no other words. Nothing seemed good enough, powerful enough to convey my level of love and gratitude for this man. He was my real life night in shining armour, my superhero.

He took my face gently between his palms. "I would do anything for you. I'd go to the ends of the earth and drop into the pits of hell if it meant you were safe. I love you, Cassie. God, I love you." His eyes closed in remembered pain as his forehead rested against mine.

"I love you, too. So much," I whispered feeling a tear trickle down my cheek until Adam's touch blocked it.

I needed him close, needed to feel his warmth and comfort like a security blanket. After several minutes of pleading my case, he reluctantly kicked off his shoes and carefully climbed onto the bed beside me. It was awkward with my IV line and trying not to hurt each other's injuries, but eventually, we settled facing each other on our sides with my bandaged arm and leg resting over his body. The steady beat of his heart and the gentle touch of his hand stroking my hair soothed away the lasting remnants of fear. As I succumbed to sleep, all I could think about was how right being with Adam felt.

CHAPTER TWENTY-SEVEN

Cassie

"WHITE OR RED," I ASKED Justine, holding up a bottle of Merlot and a bottle of Pinot.

She had finally been able to take some time off from her exhausting nursing schedule and had come round to Adam's apartment—well technically my apartment now too, seeing as I was living there with him.

"You know me, if it's wet, has an alcohol content but isn't whiskey, then I'm easy," she teased, chuckling.

I discarded the red into its slot in the wine rack and grabbed two glasses. We'd been planning this evening for two weeks, ever since Justine burst into my hospital room the first night I was there. At the time, we'd been emotional wrecks, having just discovered there was very little left of our home and belongings after the fire had destroyed it all. I felt so guilty that she had lost so much because of me. Justine felt guilty because she hadn't been home to warn me about Jay. It took Adam's voice of reason to help us see neither of us could be blamed for Jay's psycho ways.

"I don't need to know about your promiscuous sex life thanks," I joked, handing her a large glass of wine before curling into the far end of the sofa with my own glass.

Justine settled back, mirroring my pose on the opposite end of the couch. "What sex life? I work too bloody hard for one of those. In fact, I'm pretty sure I've forgotten what sex is."

I chuckled, rolling my eyes. She could plead all the innocence she wanted, but I didn't believe her for one minute. I knew from the grin tipping the corners of her mouth that there was a story to be told.

I took a sip of my wine, enjoying the cool liquid soothing my throat. "So there is no dishy doctor, hot as hell nurse, romantic radiographer, sexy—"

"Alright already! Christ, what's with the adjective explosion?"

Unable to hold it back, I snorted in a most unladylike fashion. "So, there are none of those on the scene?"

Her cheeks flushed a wild shade of cranberry. "I wouldn't say that."

"So there is! Tell me more." I leant in closer, eager to hear my friend's news. I had been worried when Adam and I first recognised our true feelings for each other. Knowing Justine liked him had been hard to overlook. I didn't want to hurt her; she had been a good friend for most of my life. However, when the heart decided on someone there was very little you could do to convince it otherwise. Now, she was just happy that Adam and I were together, that our relationship was growing stronger by the day.

"There isn't much to tell you yet."

"Don't give me that," I fired back, putting my glass on the coffee table and scooting closer to her. "I need a name, age, location, job title, family background, inside leg measurement and political views. Does he want to get married, have children—"

"Oh, God, stop!" Laughing, she threw a cushion, missing my head by a mile.

"You've got a lousy shot."

"And you've got a big mouth."

I shrugged. "Just showing an active interest in my best friend's love life."

"Okay. His name is Andrew. He's a physiotherapist at the hospital. Thirty-one. I don't know much about his family or political views. He's tall, so I guess a thirty-three inch inside leg. He's been there and done it with the marriage thing, and I don't know about children. There. Happy now?"

I grabbed my glass and scooted back into my corner of the couch. "Wow."

"Yeah."

"So you like him, huh?"

She sighed, a dreamy look settling across her face. "It's early days, but yeah, I really like him."

I was so happy for her and hoped it all worked out. She'd been screwed over by some real losers in the past and deserved a good guy who would cherish her.

"Enough about me. Tell me how things are going

with your own Mr Wonderful."

I bit down on my lip feeling my pulse race at the mere mention of Adam.

"He's... wonderful."

"You've got to give me more than that. How are his injuries?"

"Healing." Adam liked to downplay his injuries, but when I'd caught sight of him wincing a few days after the fire, I knew they were more serious than he let on. When he'd eventually removed his shirt, revealing more than half his back covered in dressings, I'd broken down. It was at times like those that I realised how close we both came to dying in that fire. Our wounds would eventually heal into scars, some would even fade until they were barely noticeable, but the emotional wounds would be much harder to recover from.

Justine took a sip of her drink and placed the glass beside her on the end table. "Did you hear any more from the fire investigators?"

I cringed, not wanting to think about it. The memories of that night were still so fresh. I had nightmares about Jay, what he'd said, how he'd behaved, what he'd done. The worst part of all was thinking about all the memories that were lost due to him. When I'd been allowed into the house to see what could be salvaged—there wasn't much—I'd been sick to my stomach seeing all of my gran's pictures as little more than ash on the ground.

I hadn't even been able to get up to what was left of my bedroom because the staircase had been utterly destroyed. I was told there would have been nothing worthy of recovery up there anyway.

The fire investigation team determined that the fire started in my room. When Jay had thrown the bottle of champagne at me, and it crashed into the bedside table, it must have toppled over a candle. Instead of the liquid snuffing out the flame, they concluded the candle caught some paperwork I'd left there. Eventually, other items ignited, and with the fire going undetected it wasn't long before the whole room was alight. At that point, it would have become unmanageable without the fire brigade.

"It has been ruled as misadventure. Hopefully, now I can continue with the insurance claim."

"It's a fucking good job that bastard died that night because I'm telling you right now if he hadn't I'd be doing it instead."

I sucked in a harsh breath. No matter what happened that night, I still found it hard to believe Jay was gone. The firefighters had discovered his dead body while dousing the flames. I hadn't asked for all the gory details, but it was assumed he was high on something and had fallen asleep. He hadn't even realised he was going to die from an event of his own making.

"Right or wrong, he didn't deserve to die."

"That's a matter of opinion," she muttered.

"At one time, he was a great guy. He supported me through a lot. He just lost his way, that's all."

"Are you listening to yourself? Cassie, he was a monster. If it weren't for Adam, you'd be a pile of ashes, too."

"Can we please change the subject?" I snapped. In all honesty, I wanted to put the whole ordeal behind me. Reliving it over and over wouldn't change the outcome.

Chagrined, she picked up her glass and pulled it to her lips. "I'm sorry. I didn't mean to upset you."

"No, I'm sorry. I didn't mean to snap. It has just been a lot to take in, you know?" She bobbed her head in agreement. "Anyway, enough of the morbid; tell me more about physio guy." She laughed, and just like that we moved out of unsafe territory.

We spent the next hour finishing off the bottle of wine and enjoying our friendship like old times. I had missed having that time with her to just chat and laugh.

"So, when's the wedding?"

I spluttered on a mouthful of wine, spraying Adam's expensive couch.

"Classy," Justine joked as I thumped my chest.

"It's a bit early to be thinking about that, don't you think?"

"Says who? First comes love, then comes marriage—"

"Annnd you can stop that right there," I cut into her singsong statement.

"What? Are you telling me you don't want to marry him?"

"Who's marrying who?" We both startled at the sound of Adam's happy voice.

He walked further into the room, dropping his phone and keys on the side table and loosening his tie.

When our eyes met, my heart stopped and restarted wildly. It was always the same. Whether we'd been apart a couple of hours or the whole day, seeing him again was like reuniting after we'd been apart for months. I couldn't get enough.

Justine muttered a brief greeting that I didn't listen to, my focus on the handsome man who had completely stolen my heart. Adam laughed, and I found myself grinning along with him.

"One day soon," he said to Justine, but his gaze remained on me, his eyes sparkling with love and affection. He opened his arms, inviting me into an embrace that I was only too happy to take. In a hurry, I scrambled off the couch and rushed to his side. He looked so hot with the top button of his shirt undone, tie loose and sleeves rolled up showing off his muscular arms.

I wrapped my arms around him and held on tight. "How did it go today?" I asked, leaning back so I could watch his face when he answered.

He stole a quick kiss and beamed down at me. "He didn't take it too well, thinks I'm making a huge mistake, but it felt great to finally stand up for myself."

"So it's definitely happening?"

He nodded, drawing one fingertip along my shoulder. "Yes. I spoke to my mum, your dad, and Nate today. Everything's coming together, we just need to tighten up a few clauses and sign the contract. This is really happening, Cass."

It was an amazing feeling, seeing the man I loved so passionate about his new venture. And I was positive he would make a huge success of it.

"We should celebrate." My voice took on a seductive purr as I lifted onto my tiptoes and whispered in his ear.

At his quiet growl, I smiled and nuzzled into his neck.

"We definitely should," he growled, tugging me

tight against his body.

"Okay, if you two are going to get all mushy and shit, I'm out of here."

Adam spun me in his arms, wrapping his arms around my chest as Justine gathered her stuff together. "Are you still staying with your friend? You know you're welcome to my spare room right?" he asked her.

"Thanks, Adam, but you two need your privacy; you know, for all that celebrating." They both laughed, and I felt my cheeks heat.

"The offer's there if you need it."

While Adam walked Justine out, I went into the kitchen to place our dirty glasses in the sink. Resting against the counter, I couldn't contain the smile on my face thinking about the future ahead of us. We'd had a rocky start, but there was no disputing where we were now. I loved him more than I ever thought possible.

His arms crept around my waist and pulled me back against his firm chest. "Did you hear back about your fight?"

My head fell back to rest against his shoulder, and I let out a frustrated sigh. "Mitch pulled me out. He said I could go for it again when I'm healed. But what if by then I've lost my edge because I can't train properly?"

"Then you'll train when you can until you are as sharp as ever. And you will be, Cass. I believe in you. You fought too hard to fall at this hurdle." And that was one of many reasons why I loved him. All it took were a few reassuring words and an encouraging smile to have me swooning at his feet.

I turned in his arms, flashing a seductive grin. "You're absolutely right. Now, about that celebration...."

He lifted a mischievous eyebrow, and I narrowed my eyes.

"Adam, don't you fucking dare—" I shrieked when he swooped me over his shoulder and began walking toward our bedroom.

"Congratulations to me."

EPILOGUE

Adam

Six months later...

"SHE DOESN'T LIKE HEIGHTS. SHE won't do it."

"She's a fighter, of course she will."

"In personality and strength of character, yes. In the ring, absolutely. Up there"—Liv pointed up into the trees—"she's at the mercy of rope and metal. I'm telling you, she won't do it."

Nate laughed and pulled his wife against his side, planting an affectionate kiss to her head. "I think you're projecting your own fears onto her, my little Jelly Bean."

"No, I'm not. I just know how she feels," Liv

huffed, her arms crossing over her chest in a cute display of outrage.

As they continued their playful bickering about whether Cassie would jump off the wooden platform or not, the woman I loved checked that her helmet and carabiner were secured and stepped toward the edge. She looked down, a huge grin lighting up her face. My chest squeezed with pride seeing her so happy, so confident. Nothing was going to stop her from doing this.

That was my girl.

Beautiful.

Smart.

Courageous.

A fighter in more ways than one.

After the fire incident, Cassie threw herself headfirst back into life. Fears and insecurities became things of her past. As far as we were both concerned, life was too short to not take it by the balls and demand everything we could possibly experience.

And that was why she couldn't wait to try the newly installed aerial assault course and zip lines at the Golden Oakes outdoor pursuits adventure centre.

Unable to look away, I watched as she spoke over her shoulder with Wes and our new employee, Theo. I presumed they were discussing final safety instructions and tips. It was only fitting that Cassie was one of the first to test drive the new attraction; after all, she had been instrumental in helping me realise my dream.

With one final look and a blown kiss in my direction, she stepped off the platform. Despite knowing she was safe, my heart skipped a beat as she hurtled down the wire towards me shouting and screaming her joy, travelling at speeds of over 40mph.

When she reached the end and jerked to a stop, my broad smile matched hers.

"Oh. My. God. Adam, that was the biggest rush," she cried, flinging her arms around me while I fought to disconnect her equipment.

"So you approve then?" I asked, crouching to help her out of the harness.

"Are you serious? This is the best thing ever." She stepped out of the straps, and I stood again. "I'm so proud of you, Ad. This place is going to be a huge success, I know it is."

"And I've got you to thank for it."

Taking her hand, we wandered back to where Liv and Nate stood with my mum and Cassie's dad, watching Wes prepare for his descent on the line.

Holding her close, I realised how lucky I was. It was thanks to these people that I'd been able to leave a job I didn't enjoy, giving me the chance to partner with people who believed in me to open the centre. With savings and financial backing from my mum, Phillip, and Nate, I'd been able to realise my dream of working outdoors, doing something I actually enjoyed.

After his run on the wire, Wes joined our little group.

"So, when are you going, Liv?" he asked.

She planted her hands on her hips and shook her head. "That would be never."

"Aw, come on. You're not going to let a little thing like fear get in your way of the adrenaline rush, are you? And you call yourself a fighter's wife." He shook his head, faking disgust.

"I'm not afraid. I just don't feel the need to fly like

you guys do."

We all watched in amusement as they continued throwing insults back and forth.

"Let's face it, you're just scared," Wes fired back. He could barely contain his huge grin seeing Liv getting riled up.

"I'm not scared. I CAN'T, okay?"

Silence descended on us, everyone shocked by Liv's outburst. Finally, Nate broke the tension. Rubbing his hands along her sweatshirt-covered arms, he said, "Come on, JB. It's safe, I promise. It's not like you to shy away from a challenge."

They stared into each other's eyes for a moment. Liv seemed to be silently telling him to leave it. But Nathan Oakes was never one to do anything he didn't want to. He asked her again why she wouldn't do it; what was she afraid of?

"Ah hell," she said, throwing her hands in the air. "I was going to tell you this later." Then on tiptoes, she whispered something into his ear. Nate's eyes grew wide, and he pulled back to gaze at his wife. Liv was biting her lip, looking unsure. I didn't know what was going on between them, but I felt my old need to protect her surface. Sensing my concern, Cassie squeezed my hand, letting me know we needed to give them their space.

When Nate spoke, his voice was soft and laced with wonderment. "Really?"

Liv bobbed her head.

"For sure?"

She laughed, her eyes brightening.

"Really? Are you serious? I'm going to be a dad?" A collective gasp could be heard among us as Liv once again nodded and smiled.

"Holy shit!" Nate yelled into the trees before scooping his giggling wife off her feet and twirling her around. Setting her back on her feet, he turned to face us. His eyes were glossy and his hands trembled as he placed a protective shield over Liv's belly. His voice choked with emotion when he announced, "Everyone, can you believe it, I'm going to be a dad!"

As everyone around us broke out into loud cheers and congratulations, I took a moment to look around me. These people were my family, some by blood, others by friendship and love.

When I first introduced Liv to the gym so many months ago, I could never have imagined my life would take such a dramatic turn. However with their support and encouragement, I'd taken the risk to follow my heart.

As I watched Cassie hug and congratulate our friends, a new and unexpected longing slugged me in the gut.

"Wow, I can't believe the gentle giant is actually going to be a father. That's unreal," Cassie said, snuggling into my side.

I wrapped my arms around her and looked over at Liv, who was already glowing with motherly pride. "Yeah, and I can't quite believe Liv's going to be a mum."

"Are you still sad it's not with you?" She said the words casually, as if she was asking a simple question, but I heard the underlining insecurity in the tremor of her voice.

How could she even think that? Cassie was everything to me, and I wanted to give her everything back in return.

I rested my chin on her head and breathed in the familiar scent of her shampoo. "Not anymore. I was just thinking I don't envy having to put up with her moody, hormonal arse for the next several months."

Cassie's laughter vibrated against my chest, and I took a moment to just hold her close and imagine what our future would look like.

"They are going to make wonderful parents," she mused.

"You know, one day soon that will be us, right?" I said, holding my breath, waiting for her rebuttal. We'd spoken about marriage and kids in an abstract, always skirting around it happening with us kind of way. But I knew what I wanted: a life with Cassie, and a home full of our children's laughter.

When she looked up into my face, her eyes were bright and full of hope. "You want kids with me?" she asked, her tone soft and loving.

"With you, Cassie, I want it all. Forever."

PLAYLIST

Best Friend
Jason Mraz

Bad Romance
Thirty Seconds To Mars

Let It Go
James Bay

Marionette
Flyleaf

Daylight
Maroon 5

Shake It Out – Acoustic
Florence And The Machine

Blow Me (One Last Kiss)
Pink

Hurricane
Thirty Seconds To Mars

I Need A Hero
Sarah Buxton

Everybody Hurts
R.E.M

Kiss Me
Ed Sheeran

Stronger (What Doesn't Kill You)
Kelly Clarkson

Love the Way You Lie
Eminem, Rhianna

If you would like to listen to the playlist in full and
you're on Spotify, follow the link:
http://bit.ly/PreparedToFallPlaylist

ABOUT THE AUTHOR

E.J. Shortall is a homebred resident of London, England. During her youth, she enjoyed getting lost in the worlds of fictional characters and writing their tales. But then life got in the way and making up stories was forgotten. Following a moment of inspiration, a new fire for literature was reignited, and she decided to put pen to paper not expecting anything to come from the few words she had. Soon those few words turned into her first novel. With the encouragement of friends and family, Silver Lining was first published in February 2014. Now, several books later, she feels it is safe to say she loves 'this writing business.'

She writes captivating contemporary romantic fiction that will draw you in and leave you wanting more.

"I'm on one amazing roller coaster ride at the moment and loving every minute of it. I have met so many new and wonderful people, discovered new music gems to integrate into my stories, and learned so many new skills. I cannot wait to see where this journey takes me."

If you would like to join E.J. on her journey, please follow or contact her. She would love to hear from you!

Social Links

Website:
www.ejshortallauthor.com

Facebook Page:
http://www.facebook.com/AuthorE.J.Shortall

Facebook Reader Group:
https://www.facebook.com/groups/fansofE.J.Shortall/

Twitter:
@EJShortall

Newsletter:
http://bit.ly/EJShortallNews

Google+:
https://plus.google.com/+EJShortallbooks

Instagram
https://instagram.com/ejshortall/

Email:
author@ejshortallauthor.com

ALSO BY E.J. SHORTALL

Prepared To Fight (Golden Oakes #1)

Live each day as if it were your last. Worry only about yourself. Work hard and never, ever fall in love. That's Olivia Buchanan's motto and she stands by it every day.

Feisty, headstrong and confident, recent graduate Liv is fighting to succeed in the male dominated field she has chosen as her career. As an architect for her best friend's father's respected London based company, her chance to shine and become recognised comes when she lands the prestigious account for GO Sports and Leisure.

Armed with her plans and determination, Liv is ready to deliver the presentation of her life. That is, until *he* walks in. The mysterious personal trainer from the gym. The only man to have ever made her heart flutter. But he isn't all he seems.

When MMA fighter, Nathan Oakes offers Liv a business proposition to join him in Southern France, she's left questioning his motives and wonders if she should refuse. She's also equally intrigued by the prospect of what the trip could do for her career.

Liv has no time for a relationship. Nate doesn't want one. When forced to live side by side, feelings are stretched and emotions are battled. Can they keep their professional and personal lives separate, preventing them from falling into something they both need to avoid?

http://myBook.to/PreparedToFight

Silver Lining (Silver series book one)

Amber Merchant had it all. Living with and engaged to her teenage sweetheart, a nice house and the job of her dreams. Not anymore!

Following a devastating revelation from her Fiancé, Amber finds herself single once again and moving on. To protect herself she vows to stay away from men and guard her wounded heart.

During an evening out to celebrate her newly single

life, a chance encounter with a tall, dark and handsome stranger leaves Amber's head reeling. Intrigued by her draw to him but scared for her heart she flees.

Craig Silver, twenty nine year old CEO, is the last person Amber needs in her life. Battling his own demons, Craig is content on a life of meaningless affairs, one night stands and no commitments.

At first it seems their attraction is mutual... until she runs.

When fate intervenes and their paths cross again, Craig refuses to take no for an answer. Encouraging Amber to take a chance on a single date he sets them on a path of love, lust, truth and deception.

http://mybook.to/SilverLining

Silver Dove (Silver series book two)

Full of romance, intrigue, emotion and passion, Silver Dove is the concluding part to Craig and Amber's story that began in Silver Lining.

After the chaos of their early relationship and with

their history of broken pasts behind them, Craig and Amber prepare to say 'I Do' on their Happy Ever After.

Life rarely runs to plan though.

Amber has fought long and hard to bury her fears and become a stronger person, but when old feelings resurface and tragedy strikes, it takes an intervention from Craig to prove her doubts are unfounded and to believe in love and hope.

Just when they think they are at a point where they can be happy and move forward together, the pair find themselves fighting obstacles and difficulties that will truly test the strength of their bond.

Can Amber gather the strength to fight against the forces trying to destroy her? Will Craig keep his promises of remaining truthful? As a couple are they tough enough to battle through these turbulent times and emerge stronger than ever?

http://mybook.to/SilverDove

My Perfect Gift: A Christmas novella

Christmas isn't the same anymore for Lara Hollywell,

not since she lost her greatest gift of all, her fiancé. Now, she spends her holidays with family remembering Christmases past and contemplating a life without love, a life where only dreams and fantasies keep her company.

Blake Snowden is tired of being seen as nothing more than the man with deep pockets and a handsome face. He wants romantic walks, snuggling by the fireplace and kisses under the mistletoe. And he wants it all with his beautiful Head of Marketing, Lara.

When Blake rigs the company's annual secret Santa draw to get Lara's name, will they both discover more than the perfect gift in their stockings on Christmas morning?

http://myBook.to/MyPerfectGift